Ride, Cowboy, Ride!

ALSO BY BAXTER BLACK

The Cowboy and His Dog
A Rider, a Roper and a Heck'uva Windmill Man
On the Edge of Common Sense, the Best So Far
Doc, While Yer Here
Buckaroo History
Coyote Cowboy Poetry
Croutons on a Cow Pie
The Buckskin Mare
Cowboy Standard Time
Croutons on a Cow Pie, Vol. 2
Hey, Cowboy, Wanna Get Lucky?
Dunny and the Duck
Cow Attack
Cactus Tracks and Cowboy Philosophy
A Cowful of Cowboy Poetry
Horseshoes, Cowsocks, and Duckfeet
AgMan; the Comic Book
Hey, Cowgirl, Need a Ride?
Blazin' Bloats and Cows on Fire!
The World According to Baxter Black; Quips, Quirks and Quotes
The Back Page
Lessons from a Desperado Poet
Rudolph's Night Off

RIDE, COWBOY, RIDE!

8 Seconds Ain't That Long

A rodeo novel

BAXTER BLACK

TWODOT®

GUILFORD, CONNECTICUT
HELENA, MONTANA
AN IMPRINT OF GLOBE PEQUOT PRESS

A · **TWODOT**® · **BOOK**

Project editor: Meredith Dias
Layout: Sue Murray

Library of Congress Cataloging-in-Publication Data
Black, Baxter, 1945-
  Ride, cowboy, ride! : 8 seconds ain't that long : a rodeo novel /
Baxter Black.
    p. cm.
  Summary: "This hilarious new novel by America's best-selling cowboy
poet, Baxter Black, offers a funny, fast-paced inside look at the lives
of rodeo cowboys and the women they love—or that they want to love"—
Provided by publisher.
  ISBN 978-0-7627-8046-4 (hardback)
  1. Cowboys—Fiction. 2. Rodeos—Fiction. I. Title.
  PS3552.L288R53 2012
  813'.54—dc23
                              2012012854

Printed in the United States of America

10 9 8 7 6 5 4 3 2 1

This novel is dedicated to all those people who work behind the scenes in rodeo to make it run smoother, look better, and stay on course. In particular, stand-outs like Sonny Linger, Darrell Barron, Sunni Deb Backstrom, and Linda Santos

The Hell Creek Bar

In the Hell Creek Bar by the light of a star, you'll find yourself where the cowboys are all talkin' 'bout horses they've rode. The buckers they've known, the times they've been thrown, and the stories they tell might cut to the bone . . . long as the whiskey flowed.

And amongst this crew who'd forked a few, they could rally on and bally hoo and make you buy a round or two just to hear one more. They'd crack a smile like a crocodile then try to put the truth on trial and all the while their lies would pile like beernut bags on the barroom floor.

They were kinda loud for a Hi-Line crowd, Jordan tough—Dakota proud, where drawin' out just ain't allowed and you better back your claim. They might concede Texans succeed but the bulk, they'd say, of the saddle bronc breed comes from the land of the Sioux and the Swede and proudly carries the flame.

And I learned right quick in their bailiwick it didn't even count a lick if you were a bareback man. "That's child's play," they'd sneer and say, "The only game there is to play is saddle broncs, 'cause that's the way it is in ol' Montan."

To slap yer hide on a bareback snide ain't nothin' but a dishrag ride. A good cowboy just can't abide floppin' around that way. Ridin' broncs is an eagle's wing, a prehistoric reckoning, a panther's pulse about to spring, a buckin' horse ballet.

Like skippin' rocks or tickin' clocks, an army tank with Mustang shocks, a magnum load with the hammer cocked, a moment caught in time. Suspended there, this purist pair, with Casey-Necktie *savoir-faire*, two poets in an easy chair makin' ridin' rhyme.

And I'll make a stand that a good one can ride through a storm in ol' Cheyenne, a Champagne glass in the hack rein hand and never spill a drop. 'Cause he's a strain of the old time chain who'd ear'em down, grab a hank of mane then swing aboard the hurricane and fan 'im 'til he stopped.

"So, how 'bout you? You forked a few?" He meant to let me *parlez-vous* and prove for true I'd been there, too, whenever the flankman pulls. I said, "Oh, well, I rode a spell," but more than that I didn't tell this hardcore Hell Creek clientele 'cause, hell, I used to ride bulls!

The Present
March 3, Lafayette, Louisiana
Cooney Looks Back

A RUGGED, KINDA GOOD-LOOKIN' COWBOY WAS STANDING AT THE COUNTER OF A pawnshop in Lafayette, Louisiana. He was staring at a poster on the wall.

"I know her," he said.

The dark-haired man behind the cash box looked up at the poster, then back at the cowboy.

"Sure," he said and went back to counting his money.

Cooney Bedlam let his eyes linger on the poster.

It was her, all right—the former Miss Pica D'TroiT, with a long Eye and capital Tease.

She was standing in an aerie on a rock cliff, her fiery reddish-blonde hair fanning out behind her like flames on Batman's cape. Black leather bandoliers crossed her white tank top while a falcon perched on her gloved right hand. In the other she brandished a black and silver Model P2 .44-caliber automatic pistol.

POWDER RIVER PROJECTILES, MAKER OF FINE FIREARMS was emblazoned across the bottom of the poster.

But it was her cocky smile that held him. Alluring certainly, but hinting of a slightly hazardous, slippery-when-wet sort of danger. A predator's smile, one that should be labeled WATCH YOUR STEP.

Cooney remembered the first time he'd seen it, the smile, that is: in Tucson, at La Fiesta de los Vaqueros Rodeo in February, a little over a year earlier. Gosh, it seemed like it had been ten years. He had won the saddle bronc riding that afternoon, which qualified him to compete in a match bronc riding with the reigning Pro Rodeo Cowboys Association (PRCA) world champion saddle bronc rider.

At the party afterward, Cleon List had offered a toast to two of the best saddle bronc riders in the world today. But there weren't just two at the party. There was another full-fledged, all-natural, bronc-forkin', rough stock rider in the crowd . . . with painted toenails. It was none other than Pica D'TroiT, distaff cowboy and part-time Powder River pistol-packin' pawnshop pinup girl.

Looking up at the poster in the pawnshop, Cooney realized he was holding his breath. He took a deep one and let it out.

ACT I

CHAPTER I

February, One Year Earlier
The Tucson Fiesta de los Vaqueros

THE MATCHED COMPETITION WAS A POST-RODEO EVENT THAT HAD BECOME a local feature at the Tucson Fiesta de los Vaqueros Rodeo. Not officially sanctioned by the PRCA, a rodeo committee member, Cleon List, exuberant fan and high roller, had devised it as a way to have one more party, putting up $5,000 for the winner, $2,500 for the loser. If they both bucked off, two more horses were drawn, and they tried again, ad infinitum. In the past ten years they had never gone past round 1.

Cooney's competition was Lionel Trane, the current world title holder. He was the man to beat. Lionel epitomized the traditional saddle bronc rider—aristocratic, seamless, elegant, graceful, made of steel that bent like an epee. He was purpose, poise, and power, poetry in pursuit of perfection.

Unlike Lionel, Cooney was a wild-rag, rough-cut bronc rider from the land of the Sioux and the sage, where the buffalo is tough and the sheep are precious. He also rode bulls, which in purist bronc riding circles marked him as someone who might actually win a gold buckle but also never change his jeans, wear the same socks for two weeks, and pack his good shirt wadded up in a dop kit. Cooney fit the profile. He was, as they say, "purty ranchy."

Cooney was out first and had drawn a good horse. He'd ridden him twice in the last two years and won money both times. But as he was dropping down into the saddle, positioning his feet and fitting the hack rein in his hand, he happened to glance up. Her face was floating amidst the cowboys worrying over his horse's head. It startled him, broke his concentration. Under normal circumstances women were not behind the chutes.

Her mouth seemed too big for her face: voluptuous lips, bee-stung beauties, lush as orchid petals, creamy red, full, expectant, beckoning, "*Bésame lips.*"

In that tick of time, that frozen moment, she held him in her power. Those insistent lips slid into that same posed poster picture-perfect insurrectionist grin. The tip of her tongue touched her front teeth, and she crossed her eyes! Crossed her eyes!

It was so goofy and unexpected that he jerked back, almost laughed, and then the big horse moved underneath him. His left hand lifted on the hack rein automatically, he set back, and the gate swung open.

In the photo taken by rodeo photographer Horatio Fuji, Cooney's traveling buddy, Straight Line, had just released the horse's halter. The man pulling the flank strap tight was leaned back like a water skier, his eyes closed and his jaws clenched with the effort.

The focal point for Horatio's artistry was Pillsbury Snakeskin in midair with Cooney Bedlam on his back. Snakeskin, a thirteen-hundred-pound, shaggy black and tan gelding, was still gaining altitude. His front feet were folded back like a steeplechaser, his back hooves were two feet off the ground. Snakeskin's flaring nostrils were just tipping over into the dive.

The braided hack rein was in Cooney's left hand. It coursed up along the neck, went between the little and ring fingers, through the palm, and flew out over his shoulder like a cheetah's tail. In the photograph you could see the bottom of Cooney's left boot, oxbow stirrup snugged against the heel, spur tight against the massive neck. The left leg of his fringed chaps flew like a sheet in the wind. He was perpendicular to the horse, who was at a forty-five-degree angle.

And everything, including the long mane that stood up like the sail on a marlin, directed the eye of the beholder to the furious face of Cooney Bedlam, bronc rider. It was all captured in the moment, frozen for posterity, the outcome of the next seven seconds unknown. The Earth stopped in its rotation by Horatio Fuji, like a cave painting on a wall.

It was Cooney's mother's favorite photo. She made it into placemats for her family and friends.

After the match, which Cooney lost by a point, picking up $2,500 as his second-place consolation fee, he saw her again. She was on Lionel's arm at the annual post-ride party thrown by Cleon.

Lionel was five feet ten inches, according to his stats. Pica came up to his shoulder. Built more like a dirt bike than a Harley, she had a feline muscularity, lithe but powerful.

When Lionel introduced her to Cooney, she kicked on the high beams and dazzled him with her smile. Then her eyes reached up and touched him.

It was as physical as a handshake! The look was so piercing, so intimate that it could have been uncomfortable, but it tickled Cooney. He laughed! They never actually spoke a word. Someone tapped her on the shoulder; she turned and was gone.

He forgot to breathe for a full thirty seconds.

That evening after Cleon List's post-rodeo party, Cooney and his traveling partner, Straight Line, had retired to their motel room.

Cooney had stripped and thrown his clothes onto the floor. Straight folded his shirt and packed it in his war bag. Then he went into the bathroom to floss his teeth and preen.

Straight was as fastidious as Cooney was slack. He pressed his own jeans and shirt daily, even carried an iron. Shined his boots often, brushed his hat, and was conscious of the latest cowboy fashion. He modeled himself off of Lionel Trane, who was five years and two world championships ahead of him. He was always on the lookout for an opportunity to audition to become a spokesman for Dodge or Wrangler or Copenhagen, Air Canada, shoot, even Dunkin' Donuts, he didn't care. He did a few runs up the musical scale and "Peter Piper pickeds." Straight was also a very good saddle bronc rider. It was his only event. He had qualified five times for the National Finals and won the world championship three years before, but he saw a future career in broadcasting.

"I've been thinking," Straight said after he'd put on his pajama top, lain down, and said his prayers, "I could become a cowboy poet. I been keepin' track of some of those cowboy poets, and they get a lot of publicity! That's what I need to expand my bronc riding image, make me a sort of Renaissance man, like Michelangelo or Longbrake."

"I didn't know Bud wrote poetry," said Cooney.

"Sure he did!" said Straight. "I had to write a story about him in English."

"Could you mean Longfellow?" asked Cooney.

"Yes! Maybe I could. I wonder if he rode broncs like Bud?" mused Straight. "Here's the thing: There's a famous cowboy poet that lives down in Benson, Lick Davis. You remember him; he rode Kamikaze. I've got his CDs, well, you've heard them. I had his book once 'til somebody stole it. Anyway, I'm thinking we don't have to be in Valley City 'til Thursday, so we could go down to Benson. It's on the way, right on Interstate 10, stop in and see him, get some poetry tips.

"What do you think?" asked Straight.

"Whatever bobs yer cork suits me," said Cooney, still relaxed under the sheets. "Say, do you know that girl that was with Lionel at the party?"

"I think she's kin to the D'TroiT brothers from Pincher Creek," answered Straight. "Why?"

"Oh, I feel like I talked to her last night," said Cooney, ". . . but I never said anything."

"That doesn't make sense," said Straight.

CHAPTER 2

February 28, Monday
A Visit to Benson

THE NEXT MORNING STRAIGHT AND COONEY TOOK EXIT 303 OFF INTERSTATE 10 and drove into the small town of Benson, Arizona, whose city seal for years had boasted a cow, a locomotive, and a box of dynamite. It had recently been supplanted by the less rustic and more touristy "Home of Karchner Caverns!" At the corner of Safeway and Stoplight they pulled into Hank's Restaurant to ask directions.

"What'll ya have, boys?" asked the waitress as they sat down at the counter.

"Oh, coffee, I guess," said Straight. "Do you have any of those flavored creamers like Irish Cream or Hazelnut, French Vanilla?"

"Sorry, all we have is milk, or this here powdered stuff," she said.

"Okay, that'll do. Two coffees then. Oh, make mine decaf," said Straight.

As she was pouring their order Straight asked if she knew where Lick Davis lived.

"Up there on Highway 90, not too far," she told them.

"Do you know him?" asked Straight.

"Sure," she said. "He comes in here all the time."

"You reckon he'd mind if we went up and met him?" asked Straight.

"Probably not. You could call and warn him you're coming, make sure he's there," she suggested. "His number's in the phone book."

They finished their coffee, thanked the waitress, and looked up Lick's number. Straight punched it into his cell phone. "Posthole Poetry Company, may I help you?" a pleasant voice said.

Fifteen minutes later Straight and Cooney were being directed around back of a nice adobe ranch house that overlooked a mesquite-filled canyon half a mile wide. A tall, slim figure in a cowboy hat stood poised on the edge of the rim, apparently taking in the view.

6

"Look," said Straight quietly. "He's meditating. I been thinking about doing yoga myself. He's probably seeking inspiration, experiencing Zen. Gosh, we might be seeing a moment of poetic insight, a release of creative energy . . ."

Cooney laid his hand on his partner's arm and stopped him. "Give him a minute, Straight. He's takin' a leak."

"Howdy, boys," said Lick, welcoming his two visitors. "I'm glad y'all came by!"

Lick Davis, former bull rider, NFR (National Finals Rodeo) qualifier, ranch hand, day work cowboy, pen rider, feed salesman, horseshoer, vet assistant, brand inspector, cattle hauler, and now best-selling cowboy poet in the universe, offered his hand. He was about five foot eight in his stocking feet and looked pretty solid considering it had been twenty years since he had rodeoed. He wore a big mustache, and it was hard to tell how old he was. There was gray in his "stash" and hair, but his face was unlined. The men shook hands and introduced themselves.

"What can I do for ya?" he asked with a smile.

"Well, to get to the point," said Straight, "I'm considering becoming a cowboy poet, and I thought if I talked to you, you could give me some pointers."

"Are you planning on making money at this poetry?" asked Lick with a straight face.

"No, not necessarily," said Straight, "more to enhance my present career of bronc riding. A way to make myself a more valuable, a more attractive candidate for endorsements. Present a well-rounded appearance, able to be a better spokesman for someone."

"Gosh," said Lick. "I'm impressed! You've really got a plan." He looked over at Cooney, who seemed to be quite comfortable staring out over the canyon, listening to the bull manure pile up around him.

Just then Lick's secretary stepped through the door and told Lick he had a phone call.

"Tell 'em I'll call back," instructed Lick.

"It's Jake," she said.

"Okay," Lick said and went into the house.

He returned to the backyard in less than five minutes.

"We've got a cow loose," he reported. "Have you boys got time to help?"

"Sure, I guess," they replied.

"Well, come with me," said Lick.

It took nearly thirty minutes to get three horses saddled and the sixteen-foot gooseneck trailer hooked up. "You got chaps?" Lick asked.

"We've got our rodeo chaps," said Straight.

"They might be a little delicate for this kind of work," suggested Lick. "I've got some old leggin's in the tack room. Come on."

The chaps he unhooked from the wall looked more like rusted fenders off an old Chevy pickup. They were stiff enough to stand up by themselves. Straight borrowed a pair, but Cooney opted to wear his own purple and silver bucking horse chaps with pink fringe and his initials on the side.

"Here's a rope for you each, and maybe you better grab your own spurs," said Lick.

Twenty minutes later they pulled up to the EG Corrals. Jake was already unloading his horse.

According to Jake, who was the cowboy taking care of the cows on the twenty-five sections of a Tucson developer's dream, at least one pair, maybe more, had been spotted in the fenced-off portion where the planned housing development had begun. At least thirty of the houses had been completed and were occupied, an equal number were under construction, and the remainder of the lots were marked but vacant. The area was crisscrossed with curbs, fire hydrants and streets, some paved and some gravel.

The whole development was surrounded by native untamed flora: deep sandy arroyos covered with thick mesquite, cat claw, white thorn, barrel cactus, sotol, yucca, mescal, cholla, prickly pear, ocotillo, snake weed, desert broom, guajia, hackberry, discarded plastic milk cartons, backpacks, jackets, trash bags, shoes, blankets, and all manner of clothing and bathroom artifacts, the latter compliments of the "exchange students" who crossed the border from Mexico daily on their way to the Denver Hilton, the South Point in Las Vegas, and Tyson's meat-packing house in Dakota City.

Jake explained the situation, "One of the ladies in the built part of the subdivision said there was some cows and calves in her neighbor's yard. She said she scared 'em away."

Lick took Straight and went to the far side of the arroyo that ran along the north side of the development. Jake and Cooney took the sandy bottom and the south side. In less than ten minutes they found the tracks and soon spotted four cows and one calf.

"There's a trail up ahead that cuts south of the houses to a gate," said Jake to Cooney. "We'll stay behind and hope for the best."

Lick and Straight spread out from the other side and tried to keep up. The cows were movin' at a high trot.

Riding through twenty-foot-high brush and mesquite thickets was a new experience for both Straight and Cooney. The horses they were riding seemed perfectly at home pushing through the limbs and branches and thorns, but the cat claw and mesquite tore at their clothes. There were lots of cow tunnels through the mesquite, which the horses could also squeeze through. Unfortunately, the only thing sticking out on the horse was the cowboy!

Suddenly a small-horned red cow that looked like a picnic table with the head of an anteater broke from the bunch! Her calf, a red white-face about the size of a greyhound, raced after her. Lick, who had kept his rope handy all through the drive, dug in the spurs and fell in hot pursuit! "Come on, boys," he shouted.

Both Straight and Cooney spurred up and joined the chase. *Roja con Cuernos,* as the cow was called, was flying through the brush like a porpoise in front of a sloop, her calf right behind her. They were headed for the houses. Straight was trying to get a loop in his rope while crashing through the branches that slashed his face and arms and legs. Big puffs of white feathers flew off his down jacket as the thorns ripped the fabric.

Cooney was no better off. He actually was bent over like a jockey, hanging on to the horn, weaving his head right and left, back and forth, up and down, as his horse swerved constantly, ducking and diving, jumping little arroyos, plunging into tunnels, and leaping unseen chasms! Cooney lost his hat, peeled the initials off the left side of his chaps, shredded the sleeves on his NFR contestant jacket, popped the left lens out of his $12 truck stop sunglasses, and took a solid slap across the ear by a bullwhip mesquite bough.

After what seemed like days, they broke into a clearing. Lick, who was trying to get his rope untangled, was still tight behind the cow. By now she had decelerated to a trot. Lick pulled back on the reins, taking the pressure off the cow. She slowed and finally stopped, breathing heavily.

Lick eased up to her, and she turned away. He threw a long loop and caught her head and a front foot. He took his dally and set his horse.

"Get another loop on her head!" he hollered at Straight. Straight dropped one over the horns.

They settled the cow a minute and watched as Cooney finally came up out of the mesquite. His face was covered with red spots like spattered paint. The one lens left in the sunglasses gave him a pirate-like asymmetry. Twigs festooned his flyaway hair. There was a three-foot piece of broken mesquite sticking out of his collar. His pretty rodeo chaps were covered with scratches and deep gashes. Ribbons of tattered cloth feathered his sleeves like fringe. He looked like he'd been in a sword fight!

"Looks like you forgot to duck," observed Lick. "I'm gonna go take a look for the calf. Straight, you hang on to the cow."

Lick pitched his slack to the ground and trotted over toward the houses with Cooney riding behind him picking sticks and stickers out of his hair and off his clothes. They swung up Chango Circle, where three occupied houses sat side by side along the otherwise vacant street. Momentarily they heard a scream coming from the middle house—the only one on the block with green grass, newly laid sod around it. A chain link fence was under construction and now surrounded all but the front of the driveway.

Lick stopped just short of the new sod.

"It's out back," a lady was screaming from an open window. "I'm afraid it will tear up my new grass. You've got to stop it. Catch it! What should I do?!"

"Just stay in the house, ma'am," said Lick calmly. "Can you rope, Cooney?"

"Yessir," he replied.

"Okay, you stay here and watch the gap. If he comes racin' around and you can get a loop on him, do it. If you can't, just guide him over to where his mama is. I'm gonna sneak around on foot and push him out to ya. Got it?"

"Whatever jerks your slack suits me," said Cooney.

Lick stepped off his horse and quickly hobbled him. As Lick started around the back of the house the horse hopped over to the new sod and started grazing.

The two-month-old, 220-pound, red brockle-face bull calf saw a slippery figure come into view around the corner. He studied it a moment, decided it wasn't friendly, and trotted away, out of sight. Lick followed. Soon they were loping around the house, making boot-heel and calf-track divots in the sod. The lady of the house watched them pass by . . . three times. Then nothing.

She stepped to the front door and peered out the little window.

Lick saw her face in the glass, and, just as he shouted, "Don't open the door!" she opened the door.

The calf, which Lick had finally trapped on the little redwood deck front porch, shot through the open door, between the lady's legs, and into the living room. The calf leaped over the beige sofa and cornered into the kitchen, where his hooves hit the slick linoleum, and he slid sideways under the small breakfast table, scattering chairs, napkin holders, a copy of the *San Pedro News Sun*, and a fruit bowl into the atmosphere!

Lick, who was right behind, dived under the table after him.

At that moment Cooney came into the kitchen from the dining room entrance. The calf burst out of the now-trashed breakfast nook right into

Cooney's arms and knocked him flat on his back. Cooney managed to grab a hold of one foot and hung on. Down the calf went through the tiled hallway, dragging Cooney like a prolapsed uterus. Lick leaped over the scooting Cooney and grabbed the calf in a headlock. "Get me a rope, a piggin' string!" hollered Lick to anyone who would listen. As if on cue, an ironing board fell from the wall, delivering a man's terrycloth robe complete with matching belt.

In two shakes of a cow's tail Lick and Cooney had the calf hogtied.

The calf relaxed and quit fighting. Lick and Cooney flopped back against the wall, breathing like two asthmatics climbing Pikes Peak. The screaming had stopped, and they could hear the lady dialing three numbers: 9-1-1. Lick ran into the kitchen and took the phone from her hand.

She drew back in horror. "Don't hurt me!" she cried.

"Sit down, ma'am." He uprighted a kitchen chair and set it between them. "We'll have this calf out of here in just a moment. Can I get you a glass of water?"

She continued to stare at him. He filled a coffee cup with water and handed it to her.

"Are you familiar with the open range laws of the state of Arizona?" he asked.

She didn't respond.

"They say that it is the responsibility of a landowner to fence any livestock out of their property. Thus, according to the letter of the law, you would be liable for any damage done to the calf once he entered your premises. I know it is a technicality, but it is certainly worth remembering before we . . ."

She leaped out of the chair and grabbed Lick in a chokehold! They went down into the landfill that was once the breakfast nook. She was banging his head against a plastic cat food bowl. Fish and bird-shaped kitten biscuits flew around his head!

Cooney ran to the ruckus and, seeing Lick in danger, grasped the woman's hind leg and pulled her away from Lick. He tripped and lost his balance, slipping in the green stuff on the kitchen floor just as she threw a roundhouse right, catching him below the left ear, which sent him crashing into the cabinet below the sink!

"Don't move, or I'll shoot!" said Lick. The woman turned on him, and suddenly the air went out of her. Her shoulders sagged, and she collapsed into the chair. Then she started laughing. Lick started laughing. He dropped the banana that he had been pointing at her. Soon they were all laughing uncontrollably. Cooney was still on the floor, leaned back against the kitchen cabinet. He started laughing, too.

11

"Surely we can let bygones be bygones," said Lick.

"We'll see what Moose thinks," she said. "My husband. He's the new city attorney in Benson."

Then she started laughing again as Lick and Cooney gathered up their captured beast and slid out through the stained carpets, broken pottery, trampled landscaping, and newly planted sod that now looked like the moon with a bad haircut.

Forty-five minutes later Lick, Cooney, and Straight were parking the old pickup and trailer across the street from the Horseshoe Cafe complete with saddled horses in the trailer and dogs in the back. Inside they sat near the bar, and Straight and Cooney each ordered a cheeseburger and a beer. Lick had a piece of coconut cream pie and a tequila and tomato juice with a jalapeno in it. "Sort of a Mexican bloody Mary," he explained.

He ordered another, so Straight decided to join him. Cooney stuck to beer. Two hours later Lick was expounding on the relevance of cowboy poetry in the Third World, and Straight was staring at him starry-eyed.

"Yessir, Son, if you know cowboy poetry you can walk into any bar from Barcelona to Bartlesville and never buy a drink. Think of Robert Service, Rudyard Kipling, Banjo Paterson, Curly Fletcher, Harold Pushkin . . . They traveled the world over and never paid a tab! All because they could recite, incite, delight, and ignite all manner of barroom brawls, lover's quarrels, exploratory surgeries, and stays of execution!

"It will be your window into the world of the literary, learn-ed, loquacious, and libidinous . . . because, my young friend, the girls love it!"

"Bar maiden!" Lick gestured grandly, "bring us the damages, and we shall depart your fine hospitality." Then, turning to his two companions he said sotto voce, "I shall cover the tab if you will leave the tip. A generous one, if I may suggest, so that you will be well spoken of in years to come. A tip that will make their eyes smile. Remember it is the waiter and not the chef that makes sure your food is hot and your glass is full."

They left a $20 bill with Lick's approval. Then they walked down the block to Paige's Palace, where Lick introduced them to their professional rodeo predecessors hanging on the wall. "Yessir, boys," Lick expanded with a fresh beverage in his hand, "all the greats stood at this bar, spit in that spittoon, used that same leaky toilet. Casey Tibbs stood in that doorway, Hawkeye Henson sat at that table, Jack Roddy beat Harley May arm wrestlin' on this bar, and Larry Mahan invented the fuzzy cowboy hat by staring at that scraggly javelina head mounted on the wall!"

After Paige's they worked their way to the Arena Bar at one end of town and the Riverside Bar at the other. During their foray Lick had the opportunity to evaluate some of Straight's poetry attempts. They were sophomoric, lacked meter, didn't rhyme, and were uninspired, but he noted to Straight that, although his writing lacked something, his delivery had potential. Lick's suggestion was that Straight memorize poetry from the dead guys. He could still be a hit. It would show his ability to recite lines and make him look Hollywood cool.

This honest but kind assessment removed a huge burden from Straight's shoulders. He immediately relaxed and passed out.

Cooney and Lick loaded him into the back of the pickup with the dogs, covered him with a tarp, and swung by the Chute Out for a nightcap.

They chose a small, tall, round table and sat on stools. Lick ordered one more tequila with tomato juice and a jalapeno, while Cooney had his eighth beer of the day.

"So, how'd you and Straight get hooked up?" asked Lick.

"I'm from up around Buffalo, South Dakota, and he's from Buffalo, Alberta."

"I've been to both Buffaloes," Lick offered. "Stayed in the Tipperary Motel in one and went to a cow sale in the other. I'd say they're both off the beaten path."

"We met rodeoing, at Lethbridge, I think. He's a couple years older. He was on a college team. I had a rodeo scholarship, actually went for a semester but had trouble with the classes. The advisor said I had a learning disability. I just figgered I was stupid. Math, chemistry, man, I never did grasp it. Flunked 'em both. I made an A in English, but that wuddn't enough. So I just went back home, worked on the ranch, and started rodeoing between gathers and calvin' and brandings.

"I was winning a little, then Straight and I teamed up three years ago, and we've been doing it full-time. He won it the first year we teamed up. He's qualified for the finals five times in a row, and I finally qualified last year.

"He's hard to scrutinize sometimes, but he analyzes my every ride and has sure helped me." Cooney paused to sip his beer. The seven o'clock news was playing on the television above the bar.

Suddenly Cooney heard his name, and they both looked up. The screen showed a group of fancy western-dressed folks all watching Cooney and Lionel Trane being feted last night at Cleon List's party.

The camera closed in on the two of them; Pica D'TroiT stayed in the frame.

"Whew! That little girl's a looker," said Lick.

"Sure is," sighed Cooney as he let out a breath.

"Say," said Lick, "about Straight's poetry . . ."

"You don't have to say nothin'," said Cooney. "I know how it sounds. You gave him good advice."

There ensued a long silence, then Cooney spoke. "In the name of cowboy, I ride for the brand. I watch for the tracks on the face of the sand. I glory the work all the Lord will allow. My calling is simple, I follow the cow."

Lick Davis, who was not clear-eyed, turned his head squarely to Cooney. "Where did that come from?" he asked.

"Me," said Cooney. "I made it up."

"I think that might be the beginnin' of some fine poetry," said Lick sincerely. "Is there more?"

"Just bits and pieces," said Cooney. "Some of it doesn't hang together that well."

Lick stared at the young man with a new respect. He let it set a minute, then said, "I believe, Son, that your water runs deep. Let's go to the house. Miss Lou will fix us somethin' to eat."

"Don't you reckon you better call her and see if it's okay?" asked Cooney, realizing she might want some warning.

"Oh, no," said Lick. "I drag people like you home all the time; she treats everybody like a Trevor Brazile! By the way, leave a tip that will inspire this kind barmaid to nominate you to the Gratuity Hall of Fame."

They walked out into the clear, cool evening to the truck and trailer parked in the alley across the street. Being too tight to drive but too tired to walk, they woke Straight, locked the truck, unloaded the horses, called the dogs, mounted up, and rode the three miles cross country to Lick's house.

After Miss Lou's supper of reheated chicken enchiladas and chile cheese souffle, they retired to the living room. Straight quickly fell asleep in his chair.

"Where you boys headed next?" asked Lick.

"Houston's the big one, but we're goin' to Valley City first," said Cooney.

"Valley City, by gosh, home of the North Dakota Winter Show! I did a program for them. In the dead of the winter, as I recall," said Lick, who had been everywhere. "It's a long haul up there, ain't it? And out of the way. There's bound to be rodeos down south that are closer to here and Houston."

"We'll pick up Austin and Houston, then Laughlin after that, but we go to Valley City every year. Make a point to. Us northern boys gotta take care of North Dakota," explained Cooney.

"There's sure a bunch of you bronc riders come from up that way, on the Hi Line, and Canada, too. Never figgered out exactly why but . . ." Lick paused. "I think that's pretty decent of y'all to not forsake your homeland. It would be easy to move to Texas. Lots of 'em do."

Silence reigned. Cooney fidgeted.

"Somethin' on yer mind?" asked Lick.

"Oh, nuthin'," said Cooney, shaking his head. "I's just thinkin' about that girl. The one that you saw on the TV. The one that was with Lionel. Did you ever have a woman talk to you with her eyes, or her face? I mean, never sayin' a word, but still you knew she was talkin' to you?"

"Every day, cowboy," said Lick.

"Well, how do you know what they want? Or what they're tryin' to say?"

"It's too complicated to worry about, Son," spoke the wise man to the youth, "It's been my experience that the best way to deal with the female mind is to just live up to their expectations . . . which are pretty low. You don't have to play dumb, 'cause the truth is you really *don't* have a clue."

Ah, yes. Men discussing women. It's like cavemen discussing the internal combustion engine.

Men are grounded in the barter technique. They understand flowers for a kiss, candlelight for a hug, fraternity pin for a peek, and engagement ring for what's behind door number 1.

The rules governing men's behavior are as simple as the card game of war—high card wins.

The rules women play by cover reams of single-spaced, small-font computer printouts in which exceptions abide, words are made up, as in "change on your dresser" is called "loose change," and clarification of "what she really means" is as comprehensible as Mongolian throat singing.

"We have *one* thing going for us," said Lick. "They need us to continue the species."

Not for long, noted Cooney to himself. *They're cloning sheep now.*

CHAPTER 3

March 1 and 2, Tuesday and Wednesday

Valley City, North Dakota

COONEY AND STRAIGHT BID LICK GOODBYE THE NEXT MORNING, TUESDAY, and hit the road. On Wednesday they flew the United Express flight from Denver to Fargo and landed at 2:45 p.m.

In Fargo, Cooney's cousin, Sherba Norski, met them at the airport. She still lived with her mother, Cooney's aunt, Trinka Tweeten. Trinka's house was in Valley City, and she always expected him to stay with them during the Winter Show and Rodeo. Sherba was a full-fledged, card-carrying, lutefisk-eating North Dakota Norwegian. She was tall, large boned, full figured, pink cheeked, big handed, and had the requisite crown of light blonde hair and bubbly personality.

The boys tossed their war bags and saddles into the back of her little quarter-ton pickup.

"Man, Cooney," she said, "you must've got in a fight with a wildcat! That's a wicked cut on your ear. Did you put anything on it? No, of course, you didn't. A couple of those scratches are looking red and swollen. I'll doctor you up when we get home." Sherba was a paramedic and had a nursing degree from Valley City State University.

He smiled, and it hurt a little. "Whatever you say, Shur . . ." It felt good to be around her again. She would baby him a little.

Comfortable catching up occurred between cousins as the snow-covered North Dakota plain rolled by under their wheels. The scenery was so bright that Cooney found himself squinting in spite of his new sunglasses.

Straight had fallen asleep in the back seat compartment.

After supper Sherba took Cooney for a drive down by the Sheyenne River that flowed through town. They parked in one of the deserted camping areas. The waning half-moon reflecting off the snow was almost bright enough to read by. It was clear, 8:00 p.m., and minus-2 degrees.

Sitting there in the warm cab watching the moonlight dancing on the frozen river, Cooney listened to Sherba talk about her hopes and dreams.

Finally he said, "Let's take a stroll."

Out onto the ice-covered river they walked, then trotted, and slid like crazy kids.

It was a Norman Rockwell moment. They lost their balance, pirouetted, fell, got up, and laughed. They were breathing heavily as they skated and shuffled back toward her pickup.

Without warning Cooney felt the ice crack, and seconds later he was waist deep in a hole in the ice!

Sherba quickly lay on her stomach and crawled over to him. His parka was bunched up around his waist, which prevented him from descending deeper, but he was soaked to the skin.

She reached his arm and after several moments of struggling was able to pull him out onto the ice.

Sherba pulled and pushed him over to the shore and up the bank. He was already shaking badly.

When they finally made it to the pickup she leaned him against the bed and dropped the tailgate. Ice was forming on his jeans and on the moon boots he had borrowed from Aunt Trinka.

"Let's get those pants off quick," she said, assuming her practical paramedical proficiency. She lifted and leaned him onto the tailgate.

"Lie back," she instructed.

He did, and his feet stuck straight out.

She pulled off the moon boots and his wet socks. Pushing up his parka, she unbuckled his new Fiesta de los Vaqueros championship buckle and unfastened the brass button. The zipper was frozen, but she managed to get it down partway. Ice cracked as she tugged off the Wranglers, now stiff as cardboard. With a mighty jerk they came free, the wet underwear with them.

His legs were blue.

"Sit up!" she said, pulling on his arms. "Let's get you into the truck!"

When she pulled him forward he screamed! She stopped pulling.

"What's wrong!" she asked. "Is your arm broken? Your hip? What is it?"

The parka hood had fallen back from his head. In the moonlight he looked like he was wearing black lipstick. "S-s-s-s-sss—tuck!" he shivered.

"No," she assured him, "we're not stuck. This is a four-wheel drive."

"N-n-n-n-n-n-no-I-I-I—um-s-s-s-tuck!"

"You're not stuck," she said sternly, thinking he was delusional and imagining he was still in the water. Then it hit her like a shot of schnapps right out of the freezer! Stuck to the tailgate!

She raised the hem of his parka and pressed his white flank where it touched the metal tailgate. She pulled up on the skin. He cried out. The skin stretched but stayed fast to the metal.

Thinking fast, she pulled off her moon boots and slid them over his bare feet. Then she followed up by peeling off her parka and putting it over his legs. She couldn't lift him up to tuck it under him, so she tied the sleeves around his waist.

"Now you just hold on, Baby." She gave him a peck on the cheek. "The hospital is less than ten minutes away!"

Across town at the Eagles Club, the North Dakota Winter Show Queen Committee was holding its celebratory banquet. Dinner had been served, and the new queen and her court had been greeted, seated, feted, and treated like the royalty they were.

Following a grand introduction by Uncle Oley, the popular KVOC radio broadcaster, newly crowned queen Salinka Mortonmortonson strode to the microphone. The nineteen-year-old Valley State freshman was as picture perfect a rodeo queen as one could imagine. Long blonde hair, black western hat complete with tiara, handmade jewel-encrusted jacket and pants, tight tangerine boots that matched her blouse, and a smile you could mine coal by!

She was known to her friends as Salinky or just Slinky. It was a nickname that fit like the stretch polyester pants on her slender figure. It fit. For months she had practiced her toastmistress gestures, which included full smiles, head tossing, and what appeared to be a referee indicating a holding penalty. At the moment she was giving her acceptance speech.

It was nervousness, she decided later, and maybe the fact that she had never practiced with a microphone, that led to the overlap of an arm sweep and a roll to the right, instigating the ensuing tangle of microphone cord and tangerine boot.

Down she went! She pitched forward off of the two-foot-high dais and reached out. Her momentum carried her outstretched arm over the end of the banquet table in the first row. It came down hard on the edge and broke her wrist. She lost her hat in the storm!

Pandemonium joined the royal family and reigned! Slinky was quickly surrounded by her equally coiffed, decked out, and poised rodeo princesses, all the mothers in the room, Uncle Oley, and an unfortunate waiter who had been picking up the desserts of butterscotch mousse with canned pineapple topping and a sprig of pine bough, none of which had been eaten.

The crowd surged toward the stricken queen like lemmings to a fire exit! The waiter was swept along with them, balancing his tray above the masses. Alas, it shot out of his hand and surfed across the bobbing heads into the whirlpool that circled the queen.

Slinky was screaming, mothers were screaming, princesses were scream ing, albeit poised screaming, and Uncle Oley was screaming, but only because one of the big-footed aunts was standing on his hand.

Slinky's plaintive wail sailed over the crowd like a siren. "Is it my waving hand!? Is it my waving hand!? Is—it—my—way—ving—hand . . .?!"

Within minutes the anguished Slinky, with her mother, was in the back seat of the Suburban of one of the directors. They wheeled out into the street headed toward the Mercy Hospital emergency room, followed by the reporter/photographer for the *Valley City Times Record* and twenty vehicles carrying the remaining mothers, the royal court, and Uncle Oley, who was doing a running commentary into his pocket recorder. He could replay it during his commodity report tomorrow on the air. He felt Geraldo Riveraish.

Back at the Eagles Club, the disheveled waiter sat at one of the tables savoring a butterscotch mousse.

———

As luck would have it—and it sometimes has its way—the anguished rodeo queen and her entourage arrived first. Her mother and the director helped her out of the Suburban in front of the emergency room door. She had adopted a stoic expression. She would bear the suffering necessary to maintain the decorum expected of royalty.

The reporter had parked in the street and raced to the hospital entrance to photograph the brave queen as she exited her coach. He was snapping away. Salinka looked very together. In the back seat of the Suburban on the way to the hospital, her mother had fixed her hair, straightened her hat, wiped the butterscotch off of her face and clothing, and reapplied her makeup.

Salinka was in pain, but she waved at the camera, with her nonwaving hand, and gave a wan smile. She was beautiful.

As Salinka was whisked through the automatic doors, members of the crowd who followed her began to debouch from their vehicles parked on the street and make their way to the emergency room.

It was at that moment that Sherba Norski's little four-wheel-drive quarter-ton rig slid past the entrance, parting the crowd! She didn't mean to hit the brakes that hard, but the sudden stop rendered Cooney horizontal again, banging the back of his head. He screeched!

The sixty or so people who had been so concerned about the queen were stopped in their tracks. They went silent.

Sherba pulled Cooney back into a sitting position. "Wait here," she said, unnecessarily, and raced through the automatic doors.

Cooney looked like Yoda sitting on his nest. His facial muscles were stiff and unmovable. The hood had fallen back from his head. One of the moon boots had slipped off his foot. His hands were in the pockets of his parka. He expression was immutable, a result of frozen cheeks, a double entendre if there ever was one.

"Isn't that Cooney Bedlam?" somebody asked.

"Ya know, I was just thinking the same thing," another observer agreed.

A high school-aged boy, brother to the second runner-up to the queen, said enthusiastically, "Yes! It is. I have his picture on my mirror. I tore it out of the *Sports News* when he won in Bismarck!"

The young man approached Cooney, digging a program from the queen's banquet out of his jacket pocket. He stuck it under Cooney's chin. "Can you sign this?" he asked. "You're my favorite. I've seen you on ESPN! Man, I never thought I'd actually get to talk to you. I wanna ride bulls, too, but my mother said she wasn't sure . . ."

About that time Sherba came rushing out to the truck, followed by all the emergency room staff, night duty security, the doctor on call, and the maintenance man.

"Back up, Kid," instructed Sherba.

"See," she said to the crowd, "he's frozen to the tailgate just like he stuck his tongue on a pump handle." She raised the parka covering his knees. "Solid."

"Let me just get some information before we admit him," said the emergency room clerk. She was talking to Cooney's head, which appeared waxen. "Name?" she asked.

"Cooney Bedlam," answered Sherba.

"Age?"

"Twenty-five," Sherba again.

"Weight?"

"One sixty or seventy, I'd guess," Sherba once more.

"Height?"

"Five ten, maybe," Sherba herself.

"Occupation?"

"Rodeo rider," Sherba for sure.

"Insurance?"

"Not sure," she said. "Write 'Blue Cross.' We'll find out later."

Cooney had barely moved a muscle during the interrogation.

"So, how did this happen?" asked the doctor.

The crowd surged forward.

"He fell through the ice and froze to the tailgate," said Sherba. "Now let's get him unpeeled."

A faint cry for help came from the emergency room. The doctor in charge looked around to see the entire emergency room staff surrounding her.

"Is there nobody in there with the patient?" she asked.

Embarrassed, two of the nurses returned to the injured queen, who had been left on the table staring up at the surgical light.

"All right, team," instructed the doctor, "take his temperature. Get his blood pressure. He's a little shocky, maybe hypothermic. Jensen, start a saline drip. Get some heat lamps out here. Start warming up the tailgate. Yorgie, bring some heating pads."

Then she spoke to the patient: "Mr.—what was his name?"

"Cooney."

"Mr. Cooney, can you hear me?" she asked.

He didn't answer.

She peered into his eyes with her ophthalmoscope and saw no untoward dilation of the pupils. They shrank in response to the light: a good sign.

"Mr. Cooney, I know you can hear me. You're just a little logey; your mind is in the refrigerator. I'm Doctor Shin-Guard. That's right, just like the . . ." Then, realizing he probably missed the humor in her hyphenated name, she continued, "You're at the hospital, and you've had an accident. We're going to take you inside as soon as we can . . . as soon as you can . . ."

She turned as the hospital crew came swarming back. Soon the maintenance crew had two racks of halogen bulbs shining on the bottom side of the tailgate, creating a grotesque shadow on the ceiling above. Heating pads were laid up against Cooney's legs underneath the parka.

Drops of moisture began to coalesce on the tailgate and drip from beneath. The staff members attempted to lift him up, pulling him forward slightly. He came part way and then cried out!

Dr. Shin-Guard lifted up the parka covering his knees. Cooney's skin was coming loose at the edges, but he was still not free. "Teri, run in and bring me a pitcher of warm water, pronto. I think he's still attached by a dangling participle." Teri raced to the automatic doors; the electronic eye winked; Teri whizzed through.

Cooney was beginning to gain a more conscious state. His legs were tingling. He could feel warm water being poured into his lap. As he became more aware, the bright lights blinded him from below. Over the glare he saw a wall of people. All manner of people: Children, adults, old people, all dressed up, stood around him in a semicircle staring. He had a brief thought that he was at his own funeral, then realized the men were still wearing their hats, which relieved him.

Several someones were slowly prying him from the tailgate of . . . of what? He couldn't think.

Suddenly he felt a gust of air, a frigid blast on the front of his legs. The back of his legs felt like they were on fire. He began to tune in to the voices around him.

"Pick up that parka, Jensen!"

"Never mind, the top one came down."

"Not far enough"

". . . in the building."

"A gurney?"

"No, let's just . . ."

"He's too heavy!"

"Look out!"

The next day an entire page of the *Valley City Times Record* was dedicated to "Busy Night at Hospital!" The bottom right-hand corner contained a photo of Salinka Mortonmortonson, newly crowned rodeo queen, wincing at the camera and holding her arm as she climbed out of the Suburban.

The rest of the page, eight photos in all, was dedicated to the arrival, dislodging, and admission of Cooney Bedlam to the hospital for an "unnatural attachment." The best photo was one in which Cooney had fallen face down. Teri, Jensen, and Dr. Shin-Guard had grasped him by the arms and were dragging him forward. This caused the parka to pull up above his waist. Some artful airbrushing was used to make the photograph acceptable for a family newspaper, although the uncensored version was racing across the Internet like a virus.

Despite Sherba's protestations, not everyone believed the "falling through the ice" story.

"At least," Aunt Trinka had reminded them the next day, "no charges were filed."

For two days Cooney submitted to Sherba's healing touch, repeatedly lying on his belly as she carefully administered antibiotics, pain pills, and topical anesthetic balm to the afflicted areas. If one were to apply the Rorshach analogy to a description of scorched epithelium, it would call up a giant butterfly with a bone in his teeth!

He was able to stand but was forced to wear a loose hospital gown, split up the back. It was humiliating. He stayed inside Aunt Trinka's house all day Thursday. The incarceration had been without incident until Friday morning. Sherba had applied her medicants to Cooney before she and Trinka went to work and admonished him to stay off his ... back.

An hour after they left, Cooney decided that a breath of fresh air would push back the cabin fever and do him good. He put on his socks, boots, and hat, then pulled on an old down jacket over his hospital gown like a cape. Then he grabbed a piece of toast and walked out onto the back porch.

Stepping carefully onto the concrete sidewalk that led to the driveway, he walked toward the corner of the house. A weak sun was shining on that side, and its reflection off the snow made everything seem brighter. Two tire paths on the far side of the driveway were the only part that wasn't covered with ice. At the bottom of the drive, pushed to one side, was a berm of dirty snow piled four feet high.

In the distance he could see the huge leafless cottonwoods that ran along the banks of the Sheyenne River. The town across the way was bustling with activity. Tonight was Rodeo Night!

Cooney drew in a deep breath, then let it out, allowing his shoulders to sag. A slight gust of wind blew up his skirt and lifted against his hat. Cooney reached to set it back on tight. His left hand accidentally hit the piece of toast he was holding and knocked it from his right.

"Oh, foot!" he said, still holding his hat and bending over to pick up the toast.

23

Booger, a tough cinder block of a red-merle blue heeler, had been watching Cooney from across the driveway. His masters, the Bjornsens, had driven to the optometrist's office that morning to get Brian's eyes checked. They left Booger in charge.

Cooney had not noticed the stealthy dog in the neighbor's yard. When the triangular piece of toast spread with butter and Concord grape jelly hit the ground, Booger sprang from his hiding place and closed the ten-yard distance in three giant leaps!

DEAR READER,

KNOWING WHAT YOU KNOW NOW, IT IS POSSIBLE THAT SOME OF YOU ARE PICTURING A HIDEOUS COLLISION WITH COUNTLESS RAMIFICATIONS. BUT YOU MAY NOT BE AWARE THAT CERTAIN DOGS AND CANINE BREEDS ARE REVERED FOR THEIR AGILITY: GREYHOUNDS CAPABLE OF TURNING ON A DIME AT FULL SPEED, RETRIEVERS THAT CAN PINPOINT A DOWNED HUMMINGBIRD IN FORTY ACRES OF CANADIAN THISTLE, AND POODLES ABLE TO PLUCK THE EYEBROWS OFF A MIGRATING FRUIT FLY!

UNFORTUNATELY, BLUE HEELERS ARE NOT ONE OF THEM. SO, THE COLLISION IS INEVITABLE. BUT CAN YOU FORESEE COONEY'S APPEARANCE TEN MINUTES LATER AT QUEEN SALINKA MORTON-MORTONSON'S FIRST FORMAL CEREMONIAL FUNCTION? HUM? THE UNVEILING OF THE TWO-TIMES LIFE-SIZE STATUE OF KNUTE KNORSKY (NO RELATION) ASTRIDE THAT FAMOUS NORTH DAKOTA BUCKING HORSE NAMED YA, YOU BETCHYA?

WELL, HOLD ON TO YER HORSES. IT CAN GET WORSE.

The angle was perfect. The hospital-furnished curtain rose and parted as Booger careened through the hairy pillars, banging off both sides as he dived for the toast!

Cooney pitched forward, jacket flying. His palms hit the ice-covered cement, stuck just long enough for his center of gravity to tip. In a defensive maneuver he tucked his head and rolled.

He landed in a single luge position with enough forward momentum to sail down the drive like a hubcap off Teddy Roosevelt's nose at Mount Rushmore! It took less than five seconds for his boot heels to reach the pile of frozen snow. It lent no traction. Cooney rocketed up the side and shot into space like an Olympic ski jumper!

Meanwhile, on his way to deliver a generator to the rodeo grounds, Torsen Ebertson had just turned onto 5th Avenue and was up to 15 mph when he passed Aunt Trinka's house. The generator was loaded toward the front of Torsen's double-axle sixteen-foot flat-bed implement trailer.

Cooney had the good sense not to flail in flight, which allowed him to clear the near-side foot-high side rail on Torsen's trailer. He didn't skip like a flat rock when his tail assembly touched down. Rather, he slid just far enough for his boots to wedge underneath the opposite side rail.

Torsen was lucky in hitting the green light just right and blithely glided through a stop sign. Along the way many people waved at him. He was hard of hearing but observed that it was such a nice morning and it certainly was a friendly community.

He slowed to 25 mph as he turned onto the rutted, snow-packed road leading up to the rodeo grounds. A crowd was gathered in front of the Winter Show entrance. Torsen pulled to a stop behind the gathering to see what was going on.

Salinka Mortonmortonson, queen of the North Dakota Winter Show, was just stepping up to the podium. She was prepared. She had researched the historical significance of Knute Knorsky and had practiced her presentation until she had it down perfectly. Her mother had tastefully beribboned the cast on her right wrist so that it would not be a distraction.

"Testing, testing," she began. "Can you hear me in the back?"

Several heads turned to determine if they were, or were not, the back. They gasped in unison!

Cooney Bedlam, already a name on the lips of local gossips, sat on the flat-bed trailer in a white gown. His knees were tucked up, his arms wrapped around them. His boots still protruded through the side, and the brim of his black hat was bent up in front like Gabby Hayes. The skin on his face, arms, and knees was the color of an Albertson's meat counter special: bright red.

Uncle Oley, the newspaper photographer who had been at the hospital two nights ago, was already thinking *Pulitzer!* The picture that made the front page of the next day's *Times Record* reminded readers of a statue of a pilloried pink Rodin or possibly a scene from *One Flew over the Cuckoo's Nest*.

The fallout, beyond the requisite humiliation (squared) and the additional excoriation, was a complaint filed with the general manager of the North Dakota Winter Show *and* the commissioner of the PRCA on behalf of one Salinka Mortonmortonson, her mother, and other injured parties against the plaintiff, one Cooney Bedlam, for obstruction of royal duties.

That night at the rodeo Cooney and Sherba watched as the loading gates rolled open and the saddle broncs were loaded. They came in single file. As soon as the first one reached the final chute, the gate closed behind him. The gates clanged behind his followers.

Straight Line was over chute 4. Normally Cooney would have been beside his traveling pardner to help him get down on his horse, but not tonight.

Straight had arrived at the giant Quonset that served as the Winter Show building two hours before the rodeo. In the contestant warm-up area he had laid out his bronc saddle and given it a thorough check. Specially made for his event, the saddle's cantle was medium high, the pommel and swells were prominent, and there was no saddle horn.

The leather back cinch straps looked like ones on a regular saddle. The under-the-belly, leather back cinch buckled on both ends to the cinch straps. It was designed, as was the front cinch, to be easily put on and adjusted from either side.

Latigo straps two inches wide were attached to the front rigging rings on both sides of the saddle. Each ran down and through rings on the wide cotton cinch. The latigos were then looped back through the cinch rings and secured with a full duke of Windsor.

Shooting off the front like wings on a penguin were the fenders. When one saw a bronc saddle stretched out on the ground the stirrups seemed to be reaching out, trying to hug somebody. The association tree and the front binds kept them in that position.

The stock contractor furnished each bronc a big leather halter. The bronc rider attached his thick, soft, plaited rein through a ring on the halter slipknot style. Often Straight would place the back strap of the halter where he wanted it, then secure it by braiding a few strands of mane around it. Finally he would tuck or tie his rein so it didn't drag the ground while the horse was waiting.

Next he placed his saddle onto the horse's back, high up on the withers, loosely pulled up the front cinch, then buckled the back one. Chute help would put on the wool-lined flank strap behind the saddle, and the horse would be ready to push on up into the bucking chutes.

As Straight's draw, Witch Hazel, made his way to chute 4, Straight was snugging his chaps, squeeging around, making sure there were no folds in his Wranglers under the chaps.

Straight was a handsome man. He had a fashion sense. His jeans were pressed, and he wore the popular, glitzy, silver concho belt that looked vaguely Navajo. Tonight he was wearing the Montana Silversmith Championship buckle he'd won at Cheyenne Frontier Days last July. His spurs were chrome, the rowels loose and blunt, and his riding boots were scuffed and comfortable. The spurs never came off the boots. The spurred boots came off at the end of the ride and went directly into his war bag.

Clean shaven, he had trimmed black hair and a serious look in his eye. His chaps were beautiful, flashy red and white with sparkling gold trim. In a patriotic gesture he had a small maple leaf sewn on next to his brand, which some would describe as an S Bar but which he called a straight line. The gold fringe reflected bright light and flashed as he spurred. Tonight he was wearing a starched light yellow cotton shirt under his black protective vest with BROOKS BULLETIN monogrammed on the sleeve. His Uncle Jamie was the publisher of the little Alberta newspaper and sent him $300 a month Canadian for gas.

Although Straight was tuning out the extraneous noise during his pre-ride warm-up and concentration, he could feel the excitement when the announcer proclaimed, "Now, ladies and gentlemen, rodeo fans, we come to that classic pro rodeo event, the saddle bronc riding! Skill and precision, grace and beauty, power and . . ."

Straight leaped onto the catwalk behind the chutes. It was crowded up there. For each saddle bronc rider there were two spectators, two helpers, a cameraman, and somebody's new girlfriend. Conspicuously absent was anybody who made a living with a rope.

He stood over Witch Hazel and mentally reviewed his "book": powerful out of the box but unpredictable, then weakens after the second or third jump. Trick was to not "miss him out," that is, to have your spurs in position over the point of his shoulders when his front feet hit the ground.

Witch Hazel stood quietly in the chute. On the catwalk Straight did a little cowboy ballet. He had his rowels touching each other, his boot toes at 180 degrees, and was doing squats. Flexibility, the ability to snap your feet forward, lock in the spur, and rake—that was the key.

They started at chute 8 and worked their way down. After the first two, the chute help moved the horses up. Each had been saddled loosely in the riggin' chute and the flank strap installed. Straight moved with Witch Hazel. He was now two away. He reached down, caught the near side latigo, and pulled it tight. Then he tied it off. One more tug on the back cinch. He unwrapped his rein and automatically measured his handhold against the back of the pommel.

The cowboy in front of him was down on his horse, waiting for the previous bucker to clear the arena. In the back of his mind Straight heard the gate next to him swing back and the crowd roar!

Straight climbed down into the chute and sat against the cantle in the saddle seat. He dropped his legs down over Witch Hazel, slipped his feet into the stirrups, and let his boots rest by the front cinch. He pulled his hat down until his ears were flat and took hold of the rein with his left hand. He ran the soft rein between his third and little fingers, thumb up. A minor adjustment here, a scootch there.

Looking down from the announcer's stand over the top of chute 6, a watcher would see a legless cowboy reared back, crown pushed out of his hat, his left hand holding the rein that came up from the left side of the horse's neck. On the inside, away from the arena, his right arm gripped the top rail of the back of the chute.

One of the gate men in the arena had a short cotton rope looped around the horse's neck near the head, holding it against the gate. A cowboy on the catwalk had a grip on the leather tail of the flank strap. The chute boss held a taut cotton rope that would swing the gate open wide instantly. Another one of the chute help held tight to a small rope double looped around the front of the gate to prevent any accidental opening.

Two judges in zebra vests stood in the arena on opposite sides of the chute. The stock contractor prompted the next rider to "get to it!"

"Anytime!" shouted the chute boss.

Straight leaned back, pulled hard, and lifted up on the rein. The muscles in his cocked arm would have pinged like steel pipe if you'd touched them. His body tensed, his eyes sighted down the top of the swells, he gritted his teeth and nodded his head.

From the stands Cooney and Sherba watched the gate swing back, exposing the entire contents of the bucking chute in an instant as if somebody had pulled a curtain. The gate opened from the rear end of the horse, causing him to swing toward the opening. He pushed off his front legs, pivoted on his hinds, and appeared to go straight up into the air!

Cooney, watching from a professional perspective, saw Straight snap his legs forward and lock his spurs in the neck at the point of the horse's shoulder. From Sherba's perspective she saw an explosion!

Witch Hazel reached his apogee and then, instead of coming down in an arc, dropped like a twelve-hundred-pound anvil landing on all fours! The crowd could feel the jolt that shot through Straight from tailbone to skull.

Straight held his rowels in position somehow. The horse then catapulted forward and landed on his front feet. Straight raked back with his spurs as Witch Hazel kicked his hind legs straight out behind him. He made another classic buck and then, unable to unseat his rider, gave up. He made a few half-hearted attempts and finished unspectacularly.

The automated scoreboard read "67."

CHAPTER 4

March 16, 12:01 a.m.

On the Road from Houston to Austin

THE GREEN GLOW OF THE DASHBOARD REFLECTED OFF STRAIGHT'S GLASSES. A long string of headlights shone like a fluorescent snake in his side mirror. The radio clock read 12:01 a.m.

The big Cummins diesel under the hood of his 2500 Dodge pickup roared along like a purring Tyrannosaurus rex. A light south Texas fog slid damply over the pickup's nose, forehead, and Capri camper, leaving turbulence in its wake.

Straight was pumped! He had qualified to ride in the final go in the saddle bronc riding at Houston Livestock Show and Rodeo. He would make his ride in Austin, then return to Houston for a shot at the "big money"!

He'd been talking steadily since he and Cooney had left Reliant Stadium, "Yessir, Cooney, this is just what I need to make my breakthrough. I did four interviews! I think that girl with OVER THE TOP ATHLETIC COSMETICS did the best. She asked about my karma, if I did chants, believed in reflexology, and how I achieved Zen.

"I told her everything . . . she even wanted to know if I used lip balm. If I'd considered endorsing lip balm. Turns out her company has invented a lip balm that absorbs into your lips like DMSO . . . makes them fuller, larger, and still protects against chapping!

"She went blitzo when I mentioned I liked doing poetry. She said I was so Renaissance, so Rhodes scholar, so sensitive . . ."

Cooney was laid back on the passenger side but still listening. "Reflexology?" he asked.

"Yeah," said Straight, "-ology, the study of reflexes. Action by the horse, an equal and opposite reaction by the cowboy. Reaction, reflex . . ."

"Do you know what a podiatrist is?" asked Cooney.

"Not sure," said Straight, "but a doctor of some kind. *Po* for *potion*, making potions? I don't know."

"My second cousin is a podiatrist in Minneapolis," said Cooney. "A foot doctor."

"Maybe I could make a poem about a foot," said Straight. "That would impress her. 'Foot,' 'foot' . . . what rhymes with 'foot'? I love rodeo, all the dust and soot, and when I'm riding saddle broncs, nothing's more important than my foot."

Cooney mused a few seconds, then said, "A poem about a bronc rider who finished second because he failed to mark his last horse on one side. It goes, 'Upon the cowboy's tombstone they decided they should put, He aimed for world champion and missed it by a foot."

"Naw" said Straight, not getting the bad pun, "I'm thinking more serious, more Renaissance. Rodeo Renaissance. A traveling poem like, 'My pal and I had done our ride and were driving back to Houston . . .'"

Straight stopped, stumped. "Well, it doesn't have to be Houston, maybe Pocatello. No, that would be harder to rhyme. How 'bout Dallas? . . . I got a callous in Dallas . . .'"

"Give it a rest, Straight. You made a great bronc ride tonight. You may not be a poet, but you can sure ride a horse."

The truck slid through the night carrying our two heroes from Houston to Austin. At 3:00 a.m. Straight woke up Cooney, and they changed drivers.

The sky was light when Straight woke up. They were twelve miles southeast of Austin on Highway 71.

"Are you ready?" asked Cooney.

"To ride, you mean, or eat?" said Straight groggily.

"No. To hear the start of your traveling rodeo poem."

"Sure!" said Straight, all ears.

"The title is 'A Conversation at the Mortuary between the Sheriff and the Reporter.' 'Which 'un was the one they hung, that fateful day in Houston? It's obvious, the sheriff said, the one they hung's the noosed 'un!'"

Straight laughed. "Now that's pure Renaissance if I ever heard it!"

"Actually," said Cooney, "try this, 'We left the city limits while the chickens all were roostin', our pockets full of money from the rodeo in Houston.'"

Straight sat up straight. "That's it!" he cried, "How does the rest go?"

"That's as far as I got," said Cooney.

"Wow. Austin," Straight said, already working on the next line, "Austin . . . what rhymes with 'Austin'? 'Boston,' 'Crosston,' 'Dosstin' . . ."

"If we wore our rubber noses we'd be rhino-osser-austin!"

COONEY WAS TOO GOOD FOR HIS OWN GOOD. IT WOULD GET HIM INTO
TROUBLE SOMEDAY. POETRY IN THE WRONG HANDS CAN BE DANGEROUS.

What Cooney admired most about Straight was his ability to focus.
Whether it was riding broncs, driving down the road, constantly calculating
about taking advantage of his rodeo celebrity, or even playing games, he was
able to concentrate all his energy on what he was doing.

Straight was left-brained, which meant he went by the rules, colored
inside the lines, and would practice 'til he got it right. School had not been
easy for him. College required that he study more than most, and that's what
he did. So, although he did not graduate on the dean's list he had a respectable high-C average. This allowed him to rodeo for Kansas State and qualify
for the scholarships he'd been awarded.

His upbringing had been fairly typical of ranch kids. His folks were
cattle people and worked hard on a ranch northwest of Buffalo, Alberta, 216
kilometers east of Calgary and 80 kilometers north of Medicine Hat. They
disciplined their children and loved them. Because the ranch depended on
the kids to help, extracurricular activities were at a minimum.

Straight had been a responsible older brother and was driving himself
and his younger brother and two younger sisters to school, thirty-two kilometers one way, by the time he was thirteen. His brother, Border, was very
smart and was skipped forward two grades. Thus he and Straight were in the
same class.

Straight was the more athletic of the two, but Border's intelligence was
intimidating. It spawned an inferiority complex in Straight, who, despite
Herculean study sessions, could never do as well academically as his younger
brother. They didn't have many fistfights, but there was always a feeling of
tension between them.

This self-induced competition, a psychologist would deduce, was the
cause of Straight's prodigious determination.

After three years of traveling together Straight and Cooney had formed
a nice bond. Each man had his private doubts and secrets, but neither was
prying by nature. Cooney was usually quiet, let others do the talking, whereas
Straight was always talking, planning, suggesting, pushing.

Cooney questioned, Straight plotted. They were business partners; neither had yet to cry for the other.

31

CHAPTER 5

March 16, Wednesday
Pincher Creek, Alberta

PICA D'TROIT SAT UP AGAINST THE HEADBOARD OF HER OWN BED. THE morning sun reflected off the snow-packed hillsides and pushed its way through the second-story window and its lacy curtains into her bedroom. She loved winter. She loved Alberta. She even loved winter in Alberta! But she wasn't sure she loved Lionel Trane.

They had met at the National Finals Rodeo in Las Vegas in December, just four months ago. Subsequently, they had arranged a weekend in Denver in January during the National Western Stock Show Rodeo and spent three days together in separate bedrooms—her choice. Following the Tucson rodeo two weeks earlier he'd gone on to Houston, and she had flown home.

Lionel was too busy being Lionel Trane to have much time for her. He was ten years older than Pica's twenty-four and at the top of his game. He had children from a previous marriage. His time was not free.

Pica, too, was a bronc rider, and her three older brothers were saddle bronc riders. One had retired from rodeo, but two were still on the circuit. The boys had so many championship buckles among them that they could have triple-handedly ballasted an offshore drilling rig in the North Sea!

Perrier, the youngest of her three brothers, had said she was as good as they were. Alas, there was little opportunity for her to prove it. Although most rodeo fans thought female contestants were prohibited by the Canadian and American Professional Rodeo Associations, officially they were not. They just were not encouraged. However, her father, Juneau, had rodeoed a little and encouraged them all.

Juneau and his brother, Uncle Firmston, ran a hunting and fishing guide business in the national and provincial parks in the Rocky Mountains that furnished their western horizon. Pica had worked for them all her life, and when she had graduated from high school five years ago she had signed on full time. Like her father and uncle, she was a skilled tracker, marksman, and photographer. She also did most of the camp cooking.

Pica took her laptop from the bedside table and opened it to check her e-mail. Nothing from Lionel, but that didn't hurt her feelings any. Cooney Bedlam slid into her mind. She didn't know him, had never talked to him, but she had teased him at Tucson— "flirted," some would say. She remembered he'd laughed when she made a funny face at him. There might be more to him than meets the eye, she thought. It occurred to her that she could e-mail him . . . just for fun. But how proper would it be for her to contact him out of the blue?

THIS IS A DILEMMA, DEAR READER, THAT IS NOT AN ISSUE FOR MOST WOMEN BORN AFTER THE FALL OF THE BERLIN WALL. AFTER ALL, THEY ARE SERVING ON THE FRONT LINES IN THE WAR ON TERRORISM, GETTING FIRED AS CEOS, GOING TO JAIL FOR ILLEGAL STOCK TRADING, RUNNING FOR PRESIDENT, AND, IN SOME CASES, PAYING CHILD SUPPORT!

SO, TO PICA, THE ISSUE IS NOT SHOULD A WOMAN INITIATE A FRIENDLY CONTACT WITH A MAN BUT RATHER WOULD SHE DO IT WITH ANY PERSON REGARDLESS OF SEX THAT SHE DID NOT KNOW WELL? AND THE ANSWER, TO THIS SWEET-HEARTED, GREGARI-OUS, GOOD-LOOKIN', BRONC-RIDIN' BEAR HUNTER WAS . . . WELL, OF COURSE, I SHOULD!

SHE DIDN'T ASK HER MOTHER.

It took Pica less than fifteen minutes of Internet searching and texting her brothers to find Cooney's e-mail address.

"Dear ICE MAN," she began. "I see you are entered up in Austin. Brave of you due to your injuries. Butt I saw you ride in Tucson (see photo). I hope you draw up good. I'll be cheering for you.

"A FAN"

She attached a photo of Cooney from the *Valley City Times Record*. She punched "send."

CHAPTER 6

March 16
Rodeo in Austin

OUR TWO HEROES HAD PULLED INTO THE HUGE PARKING LOT AT THE TRAVIS County Expo Center in Austin at 9:00 a.m. and parked. While Straight went visiting, Cooney climbed into the back of the camper to take a nap. He woke at noon and took out his smartphone to check his e-mail. He scanned the trash, then spotted "Pica.dt@NK.CA." "CA" for "California"? No, Canada. It was from her, the girl with Lionel Trane. Had to be. Who else would Pica be? He opened it. "Dear ICE MAN," it began. Of course, everybody in the rodeo world had heard about his ice skating adventure in Valley City, and she had seen him ride in Tucson. If she followed rodeo she might have seen him before that. Straight had said she was the sister of the D'TroiT brothers. They were Canadian.

"Butt I saw you ride"? Sounds like her sense of humor. But how would she know he was entered up in Austin? Simple enough: just call PRO COM or ask her brothers to check.

Cooney then brought up the attachment. It was a close-up photograph of himself, above the waist, sitting on a bronc in the chute, hat pulled down, rein in hand. She, or somebody else, must have taken it the moment she had crossed her eyes behind the chutes during the match ride in Tucson because Cooney appeared to be laughing out loud!

She had gone to a little trouble to find his e-mail. But just why was she writing? To be friendly? To wish him luck? To show him the photograph? To get better acquainted? No matter, it suited him fine.

He tried to picture her in his mind. That first flash behind the chute had turned into a giant smile in his memory. Red lips, white teeth. He tried to recall their second and last meeting at the party after the match ride. That memory was all backside: big hair and hip pockets.

Her physical memory was not as strong as the emotional imprint: that same feeling that she had reached out and touched him without laying a finger on his skin. It felt good.

Cooney's chest tightened. He considered sending a reply, but he couldn't just dash off a "Wish you were here" postcard. He would need to give his reply serious thought.

Austin is not a town that minds its own business. It thinks of itself as inclusive, encouraging diversity, a melting pot. But true to its uptight underbelly, it was, and remains, squeakily politically correct.

A small contingent of animal rights activists was condemning the Austin rodeo in the local paper. Columnists floated the word *cruelty* editorially.

Waiting to pounce after the rodeo ended were twelve activists standing inside a thirty-by-twelve-foot rectangle marked by a chalk line on the sidewalk outside the Travis County Expo Center, where the rodeo had been held. They were chanting vitriolic slogans and carrying signs that displayed cows in bondage, dairy calves in small crates, and a stuffed toy horse hanging by his head from a gallows, puppet-like.

The majority of the departing crowd ignored the protesters, although three television news teams were there to film them. As the crowd trickled to a thin line the protesters increased their verbal attack. The cameras kept looking over their shoulders toward the dwindling line in search of a reaction.

A gaggle of teens posed for the cameras with victory signs, "We're number one," "Hi, Mom," and giggles. They walked on laughing. The two city policemen assigned to the protesters called it a night and followed the teenagers.

"I guess that's it?" said one of the television crew. He addressed Ernst, the leader of the protesters, a dark-haired, bearded thirty-something. Ernst was wearing a white sheet with barbed wire and blood painted across his chest and a Lone Ranger mask.

"How do you think you did?" the reporter asked. "Was it effective? Do you wish the crowd would have been more . . . oh, more combative?"

"We were prepared," answered Ernst with a grin. He fished a key chain out from under his sheet, "Pepper spray!" he said, holding it up to the camera.

"Look!" said Nara Visa, television news reporter. Coming down the wide concrete walkway toward the parking lot were eight cowboys.

The other reporters, cameramen, and protesters followed her arching finger. Each reporter stole a glance at his or her watch: 9:12 p.m., still time for the ten o'clock news!

"What's goin' on?" asked Belvidire Deer, bareback rider.

"Protesters," said Straight.

"Animal right lunatics," elaborated Izzy Bosun, bull rider.

"Whattya say we walk on by, just go have a beer?" suggested Purple Hays, a second bull rider.

"We can try," said Big Bill Brown, smiling, but Cooney detected a trace of playfulness in his voice.

The television crews placed themselves so that the cowboys would be forced to walk between them and the protesters. To do otherwise, the cowboys would have to cut through the grass and climb a two-foot wall.

The protesters behind their lines broke into full cry: "Rodeo is cruel! Cowboys suck! Dirt bags! Animal abusers! Cowboys are full of bull! Cowboys think 8 seconds is great! Free the slaves! Blackie, your ancestors were slaves. How can you enslave animals?" That last jeer was aimed at Izzy Bosun, who was black. It stopped him.

Izzy Bosun was five foot three, weighed 136 pounds, and looked like he was twelve years old. He turned and looked into the line of white sheets, black masks, bloody banners, and tennis shoes. Silence fell like a guillotine blade.

"Who said that?" asked Izzy into the quietude.

He stepped forward and crossed the chalk line. Five seconds passed until one of the news reporters whispered to the protesters, "Do something. We're running out of time."

"You can't cross that line!" said Ernst, recovering his voice.

Izzy started for Ernst, who stood at six foot three. Purple Hays stepped up quickly and took Izzy by the crook of the elbow.

"Leave it alone," Purple said. "He's not worth it. This is how he makes a living, getting his name in the papers. Let's go have a beer."

"Yeah, you better take the little munchkin home," said Ernst with a sneer. "Beer might stunt his growth."

Ernst never knew what hit him! He fell like a giant oak tree. Purple was trying to pull Izzy off the top of Ernst. It was like trying to tear a wolf off a newborn calf!

Big Bill stepped between the tussle on the ground and four converging protesters. The convergers stopped in their tracks. Three others of their party had dropped their banners, shed their costumes, and were racing for the parking lot. Three cowboys joined Big Bill in the face-off while Cooney slipped over to two women protesters still dressed in their sheets, hanging back from the melee. Together they watched the ruckus. Purple was still trying to contain Izzy. Big Bill was trying to start a fight, and Ernst was out like a light.

"We've only got three more minutes, Big Guy, to make the ten o'clock news!" shouted a reporter. "If you're going to do something, do it quick!"

"We've got enough, Francois. Let's go!" shouted another newsy.

"Can't you stop them!" cried one of the women. "This is a peaceful protest!"

A siren wailed in the background.

"C'mon, girls," said Cooney. "Let's get out of here."

He took them by the elbows and turned them, and they ran for the parking lot. When they were clear of the scene they stopped. It took a minute to catch their collective breaths.

"Better get outta those sheets," suggested Cooney. They did. "Where's your car?" he asked.

"We came with Ernst. We all met at the Armadillo Plague. It's a microbrewery. Our cars are there."

"Okay. We'll take a cab," said Cooney.

<hr>

Thirty minutes later, at 10:15, they walked into the Armadillo Plague and found a seat at one of the tall, round tables set away from the bar, where patrons were watching the television screen that hung over the tap handles on the wall. The local news anchor was saying, "And next, cowboys and animal rights activists collide outside County Expo auditorium! Stay tuned right after this message."

During the cab ride Cooney had gotten better acquainted with Ruta and Melda Martha. Ruta had dark, curly hair, a pretty face, olive complexion, and dark brown eyes. Cooney would have guessed that she was Italian, but her grandparents were Romanian Jews.

Melda Martha was a Houston suburban-raised yuppie. She was a brunette with hazel eyes, a thin girl. She had a sharp tongue and soon recovered it.

Cooney put money onto the table for the beers they ordered.

"Did you make that riding bulls?" Melda Martha challenged him.

"No, ma'am," answered Cooney. To himself he thought, *Riding broncs, yes, but not bulls.* At least *this* $20 bill he justified in his mind.

"Give it a rest, Melda Martha," said Ruta testily.

All eyes were on the television. The watchers cheered when the line of shouting protesters appeared on the screen. Then the camera cut to the image of Ernst displaying his pepper spray.

The next cut showed cowboys walking into the scene. There followed many quick cuts, all narrated by Nara Visa.

They included Izzy standing in front of the protesters in an aggressive stance. Then his attack, Ernst falling, Purple Hays pulling on Izzy, the clash of Big Bill, the cowboys, and the protesters. Police came rushing into the scene, followed by medics hauling Ernst away on a stretcher, and a pullback to Nara Visa.

She concluded, "And so the battle rages on for the heart of Austin. Is rodeo really a sport or just another example of man's inhumanity to animals to be eliminated from our no-longer-cowboy culture like bullfighting and kosher ritual slaughter?

"This is Nara Visa from the Travis County Expo Center."

"Kosher ritual slaughter?" said Ruta. "What's kosher ritual slaughter got to do with it?"

Melda Martha said, "Well, you know, VACUM (Voices Against Consuming Ungulate Meat) says that the way the Jew butchers do it . . ."

"Rabbis," corrected Ruta.

"Yes. The way the rabbis kill the sacrificial lamb is barbaric," stated Melda Martha rather professorially.

Cooney sipped his beer and listened to the exchange. Apparently Ruta was a new convert to the protest business.

Suddenly three of the now-unmasked protesters strode into the bar, followed by a limping Ernst. His head was bandaged, one eye was swollen shut, and someone had bathed his beard in Betadyne or French dressing. It was the color of an oil-on-water puddle at the auto repair shop.

He was welcomed like a king! Cheers and shouts, drinks all around! Cooney had another beer. Finally everyone settled down, and Ernst took the floor. His speech was slurred by a split lip and loose tooth, but orating was his game, and he could play hurt.

"A great victory . . . our mighty cause . . . savage beasts . . . prehistoric mentality . . . someday a world . . . all animals roam free . . . attacked by twenty or thirty . . . stood our ground . . . fought back . . . a Goliath . . ." he paused to take a drink from his beer mug.

"Did he mean Izzy was Goliath?" asked Cooney. He didn't think he was speaking loudly, but in the hallowed atmosphere of Ernst's victory speech,

Cooney's words rang like an expletive dropping during a moment of respectful silence at a funeral.

All eyes turned to Cooney's table. Malevolent glares bore down on him. Now he knew how it felt to be microwaved. Cooney looked around the room. No one looked away. "Well," he said pleasantly, "did you mean Izzy was Goliath? He's shorter than this stool. Probably weighs 140 pounds. Maybe he's like Mighty Mouse or the Tasmanian devil. Or maybe you meant he was David and you were Goliath?

"If you hadn't called him 'Blackie' or talked about slavery . . . he's funny about that racial stuff. He won't ride on Martin Luther King Day or Juneteenth. Nobody kids him about it. He's tough, and he's got a short fuse. We could have warned you, but I never thought about it, anyway . . ."

"Shut up, you stain upon America! You heathen animal torturer!" roared Ernst. "Hang him from the yardarm!"

Cooney was not a person who cared much about clothes. Muddy boots, crushed hats, dirty jeans, frayed collars, or holey socks were not taken into consideration when he entered a fray. He did not glance down to see what shirt he was wearing before he threw his beer bottle at the closest attacker!

The butt of his Possum Finesse Lager bottle bonked a feisty-looking redheaded boy square on the nose. Carried by his momentum, Red crashed into Melda Martha, spraying the whole table with blood! She screamed as the two of them went down over her stool!

Cooney scrambled back just to find himself in a corner. The menacing crowd was advancing. He reached back over his shoulder in search of a weapon and laid his hand on a flyswatter. He brandished it. "Stay back!" he yelled, "and no one will get hurt!"

Someone from the back said, "He's armed!"

A gasp erupted from those who couldn't see the action. The crowd fell back like the tide expecting to hear gunshots.

"What?" yelled a handsome, fine-featured young man named Simon. He was face to face with Cooney less than four feet away. He looked around. "Who's armed?" he yelled in a panic.

The pressing crowd rapidly shrank to six people, including Red, Melba Martha, Ruta, Simon, Cooney, and a Goth-looking woman wearing black lipstick, black dress, and facial piercings that made one want to ask if she had fallen into her grandpa's tackle box.

Cooney took the initiative. He grabbed Ruta by the arm and pulled her to him. "Anybody move," he growled, "and I'll swat her!"

Simon started to smile.

"You think this is funny?" snarled Cooney. "You think I'm joking!"

Simon was confused. All he could see was a flyswatter. But he was a *Star Wars* baby and was unable to easily distinguish "virtual" from reality. Could it really be a weapon? Would it turn into a cobra in his hand? Did it fire lightning bolts?

Cooney pushed Ruta toward the door, holding the flyswatter threateningly. No one approached them. Once outside Cooney dropped the weapon and ran after Ruta to her car. As they pulled out of the parking lot they looked back to see Simon standing on the sidewalk. He was holding the flyswatter like a light saber. He looked puzzled.

Ruta was round in all the right places.

They lay on the sofa in the living room of her apartment she shared with two roommates who were already in bed.

Cooney and Ruta were both breathing heavily. The pungent odor of sweat, excitement, fear, and feral instinct enveloped them like a steam bath. She had taken off his shirt and undershirt. They were sticky with beer and blood. He had untucked her shirttail.

The exposed portions of their skin were drawn together according to the Bernoulli law of hormonal physics, which says, in essence, one does not have to be underwater to feel the current. Her skin was soft and bumpy, his was rough and hard. They rolled, rubbed, and roused, slipped, slid, and skimmed, ummed, oohed, and aahed, touched, tingled, and tasted, curled, caressed, and kissed, writhed and sighed, rose and fell, pitched and hit, saw the stars, shot the moon, and never once mentioned rodeo or saving the whales.

Chapter 7

March 17
Cooney Awakens in Ruta's Apartment and Rides in Austin

Cooney woke the next morning to the sound of women getting ready for work. They were wolfing yogurt, gnawing Pop-Tarts, and sucking coffee.

Ruta appeared, bringing him coffee in sofa. He sat up, his feet still covered by a blanket. He beard was scratchy. The hair on his chest was sticky, and his buttocks chafed.

She was dressed in a jungle-print smock with lots of beads and a bracelet. Her freshly washed long, dark hair curled and sproinged around her head.

"I work at a health food store," she explained, gesturing toward the colorful smock. "Vitamins, echinacea, chamomile tea, garlic, Chinese herbs, you know." She paused a moment and watched her roommates depart.

"I'm not sure what to say about last night. The whole thing, the protest, then we wind up here . . . It's, I just, uh . . ."

He stared at her over his coffee. "You want to come to the rodeo tonight?" he asked.

"Are you gonna ride a bull?" she asked.

"Yup. And a saddle bronc."

"Is that how you got that scar?" she asked, pointing at a healed surgical incision on his right shoulder. "And that one?" She pointed at his left elbow.

He nodded.

Her big brown eyes softened for a moment as she looked into his. She nibbled her lower lip, then looked away, averting his gaze. "I don't think so," she said, more to herself. "I think you were a once in a lifetime."

Cooney shrugged.

"You can clean up, shower if you like. Call a cab. I've got to go to work," she said.

"Thanks," he said.

She opened the door to leave, then turned. "Bye. It's been . . ." she hesitated, unable to find the words.

"A rubbing of cultural tectonic plates," he finished.

"Yes," she said, smiling. "That's good." She closed the door on another ship that had passed her in the night.

I HAVE COME TO BELIEVE, NOT IN FATE, BUT IN FORKS IN THE ROAD. WE HUMANS HAVE THE ABILITY TO MAKE CHOICES. WE CHOOSE TO GO LEFT OR GO RIGHT. YOU STEP OFF THE CURB THIS WAY, AND YOU GET HIT BY A CAR. YOU STEP OFF THE SAME CURB THE OTHER DIRECTION, AND YOU MEET SOMEONE WHO CHANGES YOUR LIFE.

YOU DO HAVE A CHOICE, BUT THERE IS NO WAY TO CONTROL ALL THE RIPPLES ONCE THE ROCK HAS BEEN TOSSED. NOTHING IS INEVITABLE.

COONEY AND RUTA MAY NEVER SEE EACH OTHER AGAIN, BUT IT IS QUITE LIKELY THEY WILL REMEMBER EACH OTHER A VERY LONG TIME. HE WILL ALWAYS THINK OF HER AS "THE JEWISH GIRL," AND HE WILL COME TO HER MIND EVERYTIME "RODEO" COMES UP. AN UNUSUAL LEGACY FOR TWO PEOPLE WHO DON'T EVEN KNOW EACH OTHER'S LAST NAME.

That night at the Travis County Expo Center, Cooney stood on the catwalk behind the bucking chutes, watching the saddle broncs file in. He paid no attention to the team roping action that was proceeding at the other end of the arena.

Ten minutes earlier in the riggin' chute Cooney had saddled Crooked Nose and attached the plaited rein to his halter. Crooked Nose was a stout, tan and white paint off the Fort Belknap reservation in Montana with shaggy hair, a long mane, and four white feet. The horse's name came not from a physical deformity but from the Northern Shoshoni who sold the horse to the stock contractor. The book on Crooked Nose was "out straight, bucks hard, and likes to bite."

Cooney splayed his boot toes 180 degrees 'til the rowels on his spurs touched. He did several deep knee bends, holding on to the inside board of the bucking chute. He stretched his back and neck.

He was aware that the first saddle bronc rider had burst into the arena.

"Yer in the hole!" said the chute boss as he passed in front of Cooney.

Cooney untucked the tail of his rein from the halter and mechanically brought it past the swells, measuring: X plus 2; fist, thumb, and two fingers. Not too long, not too short.

Straight, who had ridden the night before, steadied Crooked Nose's head as Cooney swung over the chute and dropped down into the seat. They fitted his feet into the fiberglass oxbow stirrups. Cooney kept his knees bent so his legs did not fall between the horse's ribs and the sides of the chute. He folded his chaps back at the knees.

With his free right hand he pulled his black felt hat down until the tops of his ears were flat. He remembered something he'd read about five-time world champion bareback rider Bruce Ford. The writer had said he liked a cowboy "whose hat didn't blow off in a storm!"

"Yer up!" said the chute boss.

One of the arena helpers ran a small rope through the boards, around the horse's neck, and pulled its head snug against the gate. This steadied him and helped assure that they would break out of the chute in the right direction.

A second helper ran a piece of cotton rope around the post and the chute gate to keep it from opening while they pulled the latch back. When Cooney called for his horse, both helpers would jerk their ropes free, and a third man would swing the gate wide open.

At that split second it was theoretically possible to see horse and rider posed against the backdrop, framed by the wide-open chute.

"Ready?" asked Straight.

Crooked Nose was beginning to squat and push against the right side of the chute, mashing Cooney's boot.

"Pull my foot up!" said Cooney. Straight did.

Cooney furiously nodded his head.

RIDING A SADDLE BRONC IS LIKE LAUNCHING A ROCKET INTO OUTER SPACE. SO MANY THINGS HAVE TO GO RIGHT: THE LENGTH OF THE REIN, THE SET OF THE BIND, THE SWING OF THE STIRRUPS, THE COORDINATION OF THE SPURRING WITH THE RHYTHM OF THE BUCKING, THE BALANCE, THE GRIP, THE TIMING, THE LEVERAGE, AND THE LIFT.

WHEN EVERYTHING COMES TOGETHER AS PLANNED, NO MATTER HOW HARD THEY BUCK, IT LOOKS SMOOTH AND EASY. MOST BRONC RIDERS WOULD AGREE, CERTAINLY WHEN COMPARED WITH BODY-PUNISHING EVENTS LIKE BULL RIDING OR BAREBACK.

COMPARING SADDLE BRONC WITH BAREBACK IS THE EQUIVA-
LENT OF COMPARING PUTTING A MANNED SHUTTLE INTO ORBIT
AROUND THE EARTH VERSUS FIRING A MONKEY OUT OF A CANNON!

The chute gate blew open like a starved caveman stumbling onto a refrigerator in the wilderness! As Crooked Nose pivoted on his hind legs he pushed his rump against the back of the chute for leverage. Cooney lifted on the rein, straight-armed, and snapped his legs forward. The blunt rowels of his spurs pressed into the straining neck muscles of the big paint.

Cooney pushed his feet into the bottom of the stirrups. The pressure straightened his legs and pushed him an inch above the saddle seat. His hip pockets pressed high upon the cantle.

Horse and rider rose like a boat climbing a wave, crested, then tipped over into the swell. Crooked Nose's front feet drove into the soft arena dirt as his hind legs kicked straight out behind him.

Cooney pushed his right arm straight out over Crooked Nose's neck and lifted like he was holding up a fish. His rowels swept a long arc from the point of the horse's shoulders, down past the cinch, and across the ribs and belly that protected the abdomen. At the posterior point of the arc Cooney was forward in the seat, his thighs pressed against the swells.

Simultaneously, Crooked Nose reached underneath himself, planting his hind feet as his front hooves came out of the dirt. The massive muscles of his rear end pistoned, pushing his body forward and up to begin the second jump.

As Crooked Nose began to climb again, Cooney's legs retraced the arc, flank to neck, like cocking a revolver.

At the confluence of coordinated synapses, commonly called "perfect timing," Cooney's rowels were planted in the horse's neck just as the big white hooves hit the ground. The ensuing concussion reverberated through the centaur bones from coffin to cranium.

This bronco ballet, this rock-and-fire rough stock rumba, this tumultuous, tender two-step in 8-second time is as complicated as the combustion engine in Dale Junior's sprint car. Intake, ignition, explosion, exhaust; rockers rocking, valves hissing, oxygen sucking, plugs firing, and gas igniting. Lifting off, ejecting boosters, clearing the surly bonds of Earth, achieving trajectory, mission accomplished! . . . Unless a sunfish, side step, slipped stirrup, or shifting seat intervenes, and we then have, "Houston, this is Apollo 13 . . . we have a problem."

But not tonight. Cooney Bedlam, sore butt and all, rode Crooked Nose like pinstripes on a Yankee. They scored an 84 and top money in the second go. It paid $2,023.

CHAPTER 8

March 27, Easter Morning
Somewhere on the Road

AFTER COONEY'S RIDE ON CROOKED NOSE AND HIS BULL RIDE LATER IN THE performance, for the weekend they drove back to Houston, where Straight had qualified for the final round.

The next week they stayed in Texas and hit rodeos in Nacogdoches and Huntsville. And this morning they were driving down Interstate 10 West, headed for the Laughlin River Stampede in Nevada. They were somewhere between San Antonio and Fort Stockton when Cooney finally decided to respond to pica.dt@nk.ca. It hadn't been easy. He'd actually gotten chest palpitations trying to think of something to say, which scared him a little. Something was happening to him.

Cooney always had a soft heart. Regarding girls, he was shy. He was not a smooth talker, even though he did well in English composition class. But girls found him attractive, so any girlfriends or dates he had were usually the result of his being in the right place at the right time or were initiated by the girls themselves. They taught him what little he knew about women. His knowledge was superficial. He knew how to put gas in the tank and check the oil but very little about female maintenance, air pressure, and warning lights!

Thus, this attack of infatuation for Pica D'TroiT was a new feeling for him—disorienting. He hardly knew her. He had spent less than thirty seconds in her company, and that was accumulated over two occasions! It was like obsessing over a poster or a picture in a magazine.

Now she was e-mailing him. He had delayed almost two weeks in responding. He was unsure, self-conscious, and experiencing the same jitters of anticipation that had plagued him in speech class.

He got out his smartphone.

"Dear Pica," he began. Then deleted it. "Pica," no, "Miss D'TroiT." *No!* What would Shakespeare say? The words flowed out of him:

To my Alberta rose . . . I know it's too soon to speak of marriage and children, but you linger in my memory like a footprint seared into the tar of La Brea, a handprint painted on a cave wall in France, like a lip print pressed on a hotel mirror at South Point in Las Vegas!

Oh, that I could once more drink in your ravishness, even through a frosted window pane, my feet freezing, my tongue frozen to the glass, merely stealing a glimpse as you pass by from salon to ballroom, my life should be compleat!

No more shall I say, lest I be construed forward,
Signed your humble . . .

Humble what? Servant? Horseman? Lecher? Ghoul? Salacious cad?

Cooney read it over and was stunned by what he had written. He felt his face turn red. He reached for the "delete" button to erase it all.

━◆━

Straight had been absentmindedly listening to a preacher on the radio. Because it was Easter morning, the sermon centered on the resurrection of Christ. The cruise control was locked on 79 mph. West Texas was rolling by.

Out from the road streaked a scraggly coyote still shedding his winter coat. Startled from his comfortable cocoon, Straight swung to the left and hit the brake!

The coyote corrected course. The pickup swerved, the dash trash slid to starboard, and Cooney's smartphone shot out of his hand. He grabbed for it, and his fingers touched the device in intimate places as it flew beneath his hand.

In seconds all was well, as if nothing had ever happened. Except for the pile of sunglasses, receipts, pens, Skoal can lids, and expense book that now lay like a snowdrift on the right side of the dashboard. Oh, and the phone displaying "sent" on its innocent screen display.

"Oh, no!" moaned Cooney.

"What's wrong?" asked Straight.

"I just sent a horrible e-mail to . . ." He stopped.

"Who?"

"Uh, nobody," muttered Cooney.

"Come on, man, who? You've never sent a horrible e-mail to anybody! I've never heard you say a bad word about anyone! You're Mister Nice Guy."

"Well, it wasn't horrible, just inappropriate."

"Hey," said Straight, "I'm yer partner. It couldn't be that bad. Who was it to?"

"Pica," said Cooney.

"D'TroiT? Lionel Trane's girl? Wow. What did you say?" asked Straight.

"I don't want to talk about it. I just sorta was fooling around and said I liked her, I guess," explained Cooney.

"Well, that's not so bad. If ya like her you're allowed to tell her. Of course, Lionel might not think it's that cool."

"I'm not worried about Lionel. It's that she might get the wrong impression," said Cooney.

"What? That you'd like to dip her in Miracle Whip and nibble pitted olives off the tips of her toes! That's not the wrong impression; that's the right impression! You like her . . . don't you?"

"A lot, but I . . . hardly know her," said Cooney.

"Then just think of your e-mail as a lure in the water. A woolly maggot-fly floating on quiet pool. Maybe you'll get a bite," offered Straight.

More like a tire jack thrown in a six-foot stock tank! thought Cooney. *Oh, my, what did I do?*

CHAPTER 9

May 2, Morning
In a Motel in Leduc, Alberta

In the weeks since Houston and Austin, our heroes made rodeos in Laughlin, Nevada; Logandale, Nevada; Oakdale, California; Red Bluff, California; and Clovis, California, and then drove to the Denver airport, where they flew to Edmonton, Alberta, to work Canadian rodeos in Stavely and Leduc.

Straight was on a hot streak. He had added $15,000 to his total, which put him in fifth place in the national standings in saddle bronc. Cooney held his own and was twelfth in the saddle bronc and thirteenth in the bull riding.

This brisk, still-wintry morning they had plans to fly back to Denver, then take a leisurely drive to Oklahoma for the Guymon Pioneer Days Rodeo, where they'd be up Friday, May 6.

"Cooney! You'll never guess!" Straight was saying as he shook his partner awake.

"You're getting married?" guessed Cooney, coming out of a restless sleep. "You've been given an honorary degree in sconeology from BYU? You've been asked to join the next space shuttle as the primate representative?" Cooney could be quick with the wit even if a bit disoriented when caught unawares.

"No, no! I just got an e-mail from Nova Skosha, the girl from OVER THE TOP sports stuff! They want to endorse me!" Straight was beside himself.

"Son of a gun, Cooney, it's what I've been working toward. I set my goal, and it's coming true. Today OVER THE TOP, tomorrow Wrangler, Justin, Copenhagen . . ."

"NASA, *Good Housekeeping,* the Catholic diocese," injected Cooney.

". . . Dodge, Southwest Airlines . . . oh, man, I better get planning. I don't want to blow it."

"Have you finished the Houston-to-Austin goin'-down-the-road poem? It would be cool to do that at my acceptance speech."

Cooney was sitting up by now. His clothes were strewn over the floor and the end of his bed. Straight was wearing his Rope and Ride pajamas—the ones Cooney said looked like a bedspread he had when he was in grade school.

"So," said Cooney, rubbing his eye, "when will the festivities occur?"

"My first public appearance will be at the buckin' horse sale."

"In Miles City?" asked Cooney.

"Exactly. They want to do the weekend. They'll introduce me as their spokesman. I'll hang out, do media. They've already talked to the committee. OVER THE TOP will be a major sponsor. I'll present the awards and introduce the new product, do TV, you know, let's see . . ." Straight paused, "I'll need some new jeans, Wrangler, of course, but the regular or Twenty X? Twenty X, I think. They are gonna custom make me some shirts with their logo . . . I'll have to order new chaps . . ." Straight planned on.

These two men were not necessarily affectionate with one another. They were business partners, but their mutual respect was strong. Straight had taken Cooney as a traveling buddy and was in part responsible for his improvement.

Straight was the more experienced, having made the finals five times and having won the world championship in bronc riding two years ago. As a young man, he had stuck it out and finished college. Most would agree that he was also the more handsome and photogenic of the two.

But both knew that Cooney was a natural rider, fearless, and, despite his ranchy habits and demeanor, smarter.

Cooney was touched by Straight's childlike joy. He swallowed back a wisecrack as his friend stood there in his goofy, uncool pajamas and fleece-lined bed slippers literally squirming with excitement.

Cooney reached out and shook Straight's hand. Their eyes met. Straight had become a puppy beseeching a "good dog."

"I'm proud of ya, Straight. You're the best. Nobody deserves this more than you . . . I mean it."

Cooney squeezed his handshake a little firmer. It was as close as these two nonhuggers from nonhugging male families had ever come to a hug.

They parted grips, and Cooney lay back on the bed and asked, "So, what are you endorsing?"

"It's for chapped lips. She said they are calling it LIP LASTER!"

"Whatever tickles you squeegees my windshield," said Cooney, smiling.

Cooney had another reason to be happy that cool Canadian morning. Yesterday he had built up enough nerve to e-mail to Pica D'TroiT. He'd let a month go by, hoping . . . well, he didn't know what he was hoping, maybe that she'd forgot about his last bizarre communication. Her original reply had mortified him. She had written:

> O-o-o-o-o-o-o-o-ooooo! You are something else! But hold that thought!
> Pica

Although Cooney had no way of knowing, Pica had been caught completely off guard. His response to her e-mail was so flowery, naked with emotion, seductive, domineering, nothing like she'd expected. She had him pegged for a man of few words, a bumbling, "Aw, shucks," kind of cowboy. His boldness made her back off a step and think about it. Proceed with caution, her nerves told her. Like those times she had been on the trail of a wild beast, confident of her skill and her quarry, guiding a hunter deeper into the forest when suddenly . . . the track disappeared!

Wary, she did not answer his response.

For his part, Cooney had been too embarrassed to reply. Weeks went by, but finally yesterday his yearning, cerebral lust, hormonal urges, and that inexplicable siren's song that lures field mice into snakeholes led him once more to attempt communication:

> Pica,
> How are you? I am fine. Straight, my partner, has got an endorsement by OVER THE TOP sports and will be the parade marshal in Miles City for the bucking horse sale May 17.
> I'll probably go up with him and hang out.
> Sincerely, Cooney Bedlam

He was not proud of the letter, but if Straight could troll tirelessly to catch his dreams, Cooney could at least put a lure in the water.

She had responded last night:

> Cooney,
> Miles City, hey? Not that far!
> Pica

After Leduc and Stavely our heroes headed south to Texas for two weeks: Stephenville, Beaumont, Jasper, and Mineral Wells. On Friday, May 13, Straight dropped Cooney off at the Dallas/Fort Worth International Airport and drove down to ride in Crockett. Cooney took a plane to Birmingham, Alabama, for a Bullnanza, where bull riding was the only event. Straight was to drive to Denver after he finished in Crockett to meet up with OVER THE TOP people, and they would take a private plane to Miles City. Cooney would fly from Birmingham to Denver, pick up the truck, and drive it up to Miles City and meet Straight over the weekend.

Following the bucking horse sale, they planned to drive up to the rodeos in Taber, Alberta, and Maple Creek, Saskatchewan.

CHAPTER 10

May 10, Monday

OVER THE TOP ATHLETIC COSMETICS Offices, Denver Tech Center

TURK MANNIQUIN, PRESIDENT AND FOUNDER OF OVER THE TOP ATH-LETIC COSMETICS, was, according to *Business Weekly,* "the great black shark in the field of specialty makeup."

Or, as *Sports Illustrated* put it, "the Don King of pancake and hairspray."

Once a point guard for the Denver Nuggets, Turk had invested his considerable NBA earnings and star power into his dream of capturing the market for esthetic products that could be worn while sweating.

He began with the Ladies Professional Golf Association and women's tennis but soon realized that with the metrosexualization of young men, another huge market beckoned. Thus was born in his mind LIP LASTER, a lip gloss for men! That it was also a lip balm, protective as well as decorative, made it even more salable.

It had taken a year to develop and another six months to plan a market strategy. It was at this point that a search had begun for the perfect spokesperson. Turk could not afford to hire the usual football, baseball, or basketball star. He opted instead to choose his endorsable athlete based on looks. He'd pay him less but promote him more.

On this fine morning on the tenth floor of one of the twenty-story buildings in the Tech Center on the south end of Denver, Turk sat at the head of his twelve-foot-long conference table and listened to his marketing team.

Seated around the table were Nova Skosha, celebrity recruiting agent, File Blitzer, road manager, a secretary taking notes, and Turk's financial officer. Nova was reporting that she had contacted Straight Line and that his response had been positive.

"So, what's he like?" asked Turk.

"Well, studly, for one thing," she said.

Turk nodded. He knew this was an academic observation by Nova, not a lascivious or romantic one. She was almost asexual, with her practical haircut, hip but simple clothes, and big glasses. She was one of those professional women who are drawn to political, newsroom, musical, or theatrical pursuits, always working backstage, behind the scenes, out of the spotlight but always serious about their work.

"I watched the clips you sent of him riding, performing. He looks like he knows what he's doing. I put the DVD on slow mo, and he reminded me of a bird flying," said Turk.

"I've been following through the *Sports News*, the rodeo paper. He is doing well and this last week has risen to number five in the world standings in the saddle bronc," she said.

"Out of what?" asked File.

"The top fifteen qualify to compete in the national finals in Las Vegas this December. He has qualified, finished in the top fifteen for the last five years and the world championship once. It would be a real bonus for us if he were to win the world championship again this year!"

Nova then laid out her plan to introduce Straight at the annual bucking horse sale in Miles City, Montana, on the third weekend in May. "Like I said, I've already talked to him, and he is excited."

"He's plenty macho," offered File Blitzer. "Got the cred. If he can pull this LIP LASTER off, it will be the greatest unisex campaign since Joe Namath put on pantyhose!"

"Then," he continued, "we find the perfect girl, a counterpart for Straight, put 'em together . . . who knows what magic will happen? We'll make stars out of them! And . . . I might have just the right girl!"

From a folder, File withdrew three promo photos and passed them to Turk.

One picture showed a shapely redhead in a cheerleading pose. The second one, a blonde wearing a bikini, and the third, a striking brunette astride a chestnut Standardbred hunter-jumper, in equestrian English riding gear. She brandished a quirt coquettishly.

"Are these all of the same woman?" asked Turk.

"Yes. She's done lots of modeling, acting. You can see she's a looker, and she can play any part!" said File.

"You are right about that. She's hot!" said Turk.

"Her name is Oui Oui Reese. She auditioned for the Denver Broncos cheerleaders and was selected as an alternate," explained File.

"Okay," said Turk. "Let's see how Miles City goes, then we'll look at the ladies."

The meeting ended.

~ ~

Back in his office File put in a call on his cell phone. "Oui Oui," he spoke, "I brought you up in the meeting . . . Turk says you're hot!"

"Oh, File!" Oui Oui exclaimed, "I love you, I love you, I love you! Can we have dinner, even lunch? You can tell me all about it?"

"Your apartment tonight?" he asked.

"Oh, this is so momentous, splendiculous. I'm so deserving. Filely, you know how I hate to cook. How 'bout we go to Morton's, no, the Longhorn, some place fancy we can celebrate!" she said.

"Well, remember, this is not a sure thing yet, but at least we got a foot in the door."

"But you can make it happen, my little Filefeifer. I know you can, and it will mean so much to me and my career and our relationship. That's why I love you, love you, love you! Oh, and Sweetiefiles, could you pick me up a package of those scrumptious Russian cigarettes I love, love, love. It won't be far out of your way, and I'll be ready at seven. No! Six-thirty. No! Seven. No! Seven-thirty. No! Seven. No! Seven-thirty. There's a Princess Di bio on A&E that I must, simply must, see! So, seven-thirty, on the dot. You know how I hate waiting. Love, love, love, love and kisses! Bye, bye, my ferocious Filomatic!"

File hung up with the palpable memory of her elusive pulchritude.

CHAPTER 11

May 19, Thursday
Straight Hooks Up with OTT and Goes to Miles City

STRAIGHT PULLED HIS DODGE 2500 DIESEL PICKUP INTO THE PARKING LOT in front of Boyle's Aviation at the Centennial Airport in Arapahoe County just south of Denver. He parked the rig, unloaded his clothes bag, and locked the vehicle. Cooney planned to arrive at Denver International Airport later that day on a 5:00 p.m. flight, catch a cab to Centennial, pick up the Dodge, and make a leisurely two-day drive to Miles City.

Straight walked through the glass doors into the waiting area at Boyle's Aviation at Centennial Airport, south of Denver. Nova Skosha rose, a vision in black pants and black, long-sleeved pullover, from a black leather couch and walked right to him smiling. She was sleek, with her short, straight, black hair, a boyish figure, wire-rim glasses, and pale makeup. She was twenty-nine years old but could pass for older or younger. She had an ageless quality about her.

"Straight!" she greeted him. "So good to see you again! We are so pleased you've agreed to be the spokesman for OVER THE TOP, or OTT, as we call it."

They had not seen each other since they had met in Houston two months ago. In the last three weeks since then, they had spoken by phone and e-mailed several times, working on the contract and planning the Miles City trip.

"This is File Blitzer. He's our road manager. He makes sure the booth gets set up, you get to your appointments, handles all the arrangements. He's a detail man."

File extended his hand. "Glad to meet you, Straight. Nova has told us all about you, and we are pumped!"

File had a smooth, baritone, radio broadcaster voice. He was fortyish, with his thinning, dark hair in a ponytail, a stubble mustache and goatee. He, too, was wearing a black turtleneck and black slacks.

To Straight they looked like chess pieces. Pawns or bishops, he couldn't remember. He hated chess. He could never beat his brother.

"Turk expressed his regrets he couldn't be here to meet you. He's in Miami trying to sign Shaq O'Neal for a new product called Pate Shine and Shield. But he looks forward to meeting you soon," said Nova.

"I will fill you in on the itinerary when we get on the plane," explained Nova. "And show you the new logo shirts. If you don't mind, we'll give you some tips, some coaching for doing interviews, product placement, that sort of thing. Our publicity department has arranged media, several public appearances, autograph signings. We will be working with Steve Holip, who does local radio . . ."

"Steve Holip?" interrupted Straight. "Real estate? Horse trainer? The Saturday morning swap meet on KTAL radio in Miles City?"

"Party animal, eccentric art collector, Slippery Steve," Straight didn't say.

"I don't know?" admitted Nova. "We got his name from an ad agency in San Francisco when we were looking for an advance man in Miles City. I've spoken to him several times setting up this trip. He even arranged for you to be the parade marshal Saturday morning!"

"Sure sounds good to me. And any help you can give me, I'm sure obliged," said Straight.

"Good. The airplane is waiting," she said and ushered him toward the door.

Within thirty minutes the Bombardier Learjet 85 leased to OTT ATHLETIC COSMETICS was at twenty-nine thousand feet and taking Straight Line on a direct course into the metaphorical Disney World of show business.

Friday at noon found Straight underneath the bleachers in the corner of a long barroom, signing promo photos, Copenhagen cans, hats, bare arms, T-shirts, boot tops, and programs and posing for an unending stream of photographs. File Blitzer was passing out free samples of LIP LASTER. Both stood in a booth underneath a banner proclaiming OVER THE TOP, STRAIGHT LINE LIP LASTER X FOR EXTREME CONDITIONS!

Steve Holip's friend Darnell was chronicling it all on videotape. It was all very heady for Straight.

The Miles City Bucking Horse Sale is not a PRCA-sanctioned rodeo; it is a livestock auction. For more than fifty years, horsemen, ranchers, and traders have brought in bucking bulls and broncs that they wished to sell as rodeo stock. After each animal bucked out of the chute in full regalia with a man aboard, the auctioneer would immediately offer the beast for sale.

The rodeo stock contractors were the buyers. They were sitting in a special grandstand next to the chutes so they could get a good view of the animal in action. As many as 250 head would be sold over the weekend.

Cowboys would come from miles around to ride the beasts. They would compete for a pot and might get on three or four head each per day. Usually none of the riders was a card-carrying PRCA member, which required that they had earned at least $1,000 in rodeo competition.

Members of this band of eighteen- to twenty-two-year-old testosterone machines fueled each other's machismo and kept throwing themselves in harm's way until their bones ached and their hats crumpled.

So, for a nationally ranked PRCA bronc rider to be on location, even if he wasn't riding, was a sign of respect and validation of the whole weekend and the efforts of the young rough stock riders. Straight was a celebrity here.

While he was on duty, with File helping, Nova took Darnell to videograph some of the action. They worked their way across the racetrack and around behind the bucking chutes.

Nova was telling Darnell what to shoot. They climbed onto the catwalk behind the chutes where the riders stood waiting to mount their rides.

"My gosh! Is that a woman?" asked Nova, pointing to a cloud of reddish-blonde curls boiling out from beneath a big black hat. The rider was over the chute getting down onto the horse's back. Her head was bent forward concentrating on her grip on the rein.

"Shoot her! Shoot her!" commanded Nova just as Pica D'TroiT leaned back in the saddle, took the slack, and nodded her head.

As the gate swung open Nova caught a glimpse of the rider's face: eyes squinted, jaw tight, white teeth clenched, and lips like the bell on a slide trombone! Rolling Stone lips! Mick Jagger lips! Julia Roberts lips! Queen Latifah lips! Angelina Jolie lips! Refrigerator Perry lips! OVER THE TOP outrageous, orchidacious, labile, lovely, luminescent, lascivious, ATHLETIC COSMETICS lips!

Nova watched in awe as the petite bronc rider reached and raked, rocked and fired, rolled and reloaded. Pica completed the 8-second ride, then got off balance and was converted unceremoniously into a lawn dart. She belly flopped into a well-trampled mud puddle and twirled slightly like a leaf pirouetting on the surface of a lazy stream.

"Who is that?" asked Nova to the cowboys on the catwalk beside her.

"Pika Detroit," said two in unison, not knowing the correct spelling of her name.

"My gosh," said Nova, "I think I've discovered the next Michael Jordan!"

She grabbed Darnell, and they headed around to where the riders congregated between rides. Pica was talking to another bronc rider. She had unbuckled the chaps from her thighs so they hung loosely from her waist like an untied apron.

"Do a little filming here please, Darnell," Nova instructed. "Film her in her surroundings without being conspicuous."

Nova took in the crowd that milled in the competitors area. There was a generous mix of older cowboys with big bellies; Indians in T-shirts, sunglasses, and cowboy hats; young men in their late teens and early twenties wearing chaps, boots, and spurs, shirts with numbered placards pinned to their backs, hats in all stages of crumpled and muddy, and a beer in hand.

Pica was listening to a rider not much taller than she. Another rider looked on, sipping his beer. "I think you got a seventy-one," he was saying.

Nova studied Pica the way a horse trainer looks at a two-year-old filly, a taxidermist looks at a mountain goat, and a plastic surgeon looks at asymmetry: "Five foot two or three, well-proportioned," she surmised, "even in a western shirt. Bountiful hair the color of the skin of a peach: reddish, yellowish, strawberry blonde, a lightly freckled complexion, blue eyes, and audaciously brazen lips!"

At that moment there was a streak of mud across Pica's right cheek that extended to the brim of her black hat. Nova waited until the cowboys drifted off and then approached her.

"Pretty good ride," said Nova.

Pica turned to the woman's voice. Nova was at least three inches taller than she was, but who wasn't, with highlighted black hair and the black-on-black uniform of the New York theater.

"I'm Nova Skosha, OVER THE TOP ATHLETIC COSMETICS, and *you* are somethin' else!"

"I'm not sure what you mean," said Pica suspiciously.

"I'm not sure either," said Nova, "but you are either a PR person's dream or an albino tiger beyond exploitation."

Pica just stared.

"Forgive me," said Nova. "I just saw you ride. I'm looking at your lovely . . . fashionable . . ." she searched for better words, "marketably unique look. I work for OVER THE TOP, like I said, and I'm wondering if you have any interest in talking about modeling, using your image . . ."

"Modeling?" said Pica, with a hint of distaste.

"Maybe not modeling, per se, but doing a photo shoot, for instance," explained Nova.

"Modeling, like, what?" asked Pica.

"How 'bout lip balm?" said Nova.

"I don't know," said Pica, "but right now I've got another horse to ride."

"Can I take you to dinner tonight?" asked Nova.

"Talk to me after," Pica replied and turned back toward the bucking chutes.

That night Pica went to supper at Steve Holip's house north of Miles City, where Nova, File, and Straight were all staying.

Pica had driven from Pincher Creek in her own pickup with a camper shell. She parked it in Holip's driveway, where they allowed she could park her rig and spend the night. She had no time for a serious makeover before supper, but she had a natural radiance that negated her hat hair and lack of makeup.

She agreed to ride in the back of Straight's parade marshal's wagon tomorrow morning as a guest and to come by the OVER THE TOP booth for a few minutes to see Straight in action.

Nova was excited; Straight was just a little uncomfortable, knowing of Cooney's crush on Pica; and File was not the least bit happy entertaining possible competition for his lovebird, Oui Oui Reese.

As for Pica, she had broncs to ride Saturday afternoon and a call to make tonight. She excused herself from the crowd at the table and went to her camper. She crawled into the bedroll and opened her phone. "Dad," she said after he answered, "sorry to wake you."

"It's okay," he said thickly, "haven't been asleep long. Are you all right, PC?"

"Fine. I'm fine, Dad. I rode two outta three this afternoon. Up three times tomorrow."

"Good. I'm proud of you, ya know."

"I know, Dad. I wish you were here."

"Me, too, but I had work to do," he said.

"Dad, I need to run something by you."

"Sure, Baby, what is it?"

She explained OVER THE TOP's proposal.

"Well," he said with an auditory smile, "ya know, Straight, he always seemed like a good boy. From Buffalo, I think. Don't know his folks too well. Ranchers. If he's in it, that's to their credit."

"I'm not sure if I'd, ya know, like posing for pictures, signing autographs, and all that. I don't know too many outfitters who do modeling!"

"Lemme tell ya, Darlin', if somebody paid me to model Bermuda shorts, I don't know if I'd do it either, but you're a pretty woman, even if you are strong. But trust your intuition. If you don't have to compromise your principles . . . and you're always putting on Blistik. If their lip balm works as good, then you might get a lifetime supply free, and you'd still be telling the truth."

"I want to ride broncs, Dad," she said.

"I know, Love, but life doesn't always go our way." After a pause he asked, "What's Straight Line like?"

"Nice enough. He's sure named right. Stands up straight, does everything, ya know, by the book. I think I make him nervous."

"Darlin', you make a lot of people nervous, including your mother!"

"I guess so," she laughed.

"Hear those folks out, Love," he said. "It's another window into your future. Who knows, it might actually be a door!"

"Love you, Dad."

"Love you, too, PC."

"Adieu."

"Adieu, too."

CHAPTER 12

May 20, Saturday
Cooney Arrives at Miles City

IT HAS BEEN SAID BY SCRIBES MORE PROFOUND THAN THIS POOR
AUTHOR THAT "NO GOOD DEED GOES UNPUNISHED!" EVEN AS JESUS
BUTTERED THE BREAD OF JUDAS, HE KNEW OF WHAT HE SPOKE.

IN THE CASE OF COONEY BEDLAM, HE WAS IN THAT LONG
LINE OF WELL-MEANING SAMARITANS WHO CANNOT LEAVE WELL
ENOUGH ALONE.

COONEY HAD FLOWN TO DENVER FROM BIRMINGHAM, ALABAMA, WHERE
he had won big money at the Bullnanza, which counted toward his National
PRCA rankings.

The flight had arrived the previous Monday. He had recovered the
pickup at the Centennial Airport as arranged. He stayed in Denver
through Thursday with a friend, then headed north to meet Straight in
Miles City. Car trouble in Sheridan, Wyoming, added one long night. He
also contracted a bit of the stomach flu, which increased the frequency of
his stops.

He arrived in Miles City Saturday at 2:30 in the afternoon. He located a
shady parking spot along the river by the city park. The parade was over, and
most of the crowd was at the fairgrounds watching the bucking horse sale.

He lay down in the camper for a short nap. He slept past 6:00 p.m.
Upon waking he put on his cleanest dirty shirt and walked down Main
Street. He went unrecognized into the Bison Bar and was soon involved
in a $2 limit Texas hold 'em poker game at a table in an alcove by the front
window. By 8:00 p.m. the bucking horse sale had concluded, the street
dance had begun, and the Bison Bar was standing room only.

Cooney was at the end of the table with his back to the crowd. To his left was a sore loser who was getting drunker by the minute. His language continued to increase in profanity as the dealer politely cautioned him about his cursing.

A pretty bleached blonde displaying Caribbean tanned breasts and a turquoise necklace stood beside him lending solace, trying to calm him down.

"Now, Monty, take it easy, Baby. It'll get better," she cooed.

"You @#$%^&*!" Monty called her some very descriptive yet lewd names indicating her canine heritage and manipulative skills.

"He's been drinking," she offered helplessly to the other card players. Then to him, "Maybe we should go, Honey."

Monty, who was a good-sized man, pushed her back so hard that she fell against the crowd.

"Go get me another whiskey and water, you @#$%^^!, and then go wait in the car! I'll deal with you later."

"Sir, I'm going to have to ask you to leave, " said the dealer.

"Deal the #@$%@^&! cards! I'm gonna play!" Monty stormed under thundercloud eyebrows.

"Ya know," said Cooney, "if I was as big a buzzard cloaca as you are, I think I would learn some more inventive phrases."

Monty squinted his eyebrows quizzically at Cooney, who continued, "Obviously you were not born, merely deposited by a bat and recovered by guano miners. You epitomize those irritants that stick to the bottom of a shoe; to be washed off, depilated, or vaccinated against.

"While it is true that once upon a time a mother could have loved you, you have now become the sebum that is secreted from the anal glands of a carpet-scooting Pekinese and not fit to stain the Kleenex that you inhabit.

"As God said to Adam, 'Cover yourself, grab your hoe, and vacate the garden!'"

THE FIGHT WAS ON!

Cards flew as Monty pushed off the table toward Cooney! Cooney was stone cold sober and queasy, but he leaned back, grabbed Monty's arm, and pulled him by, slamming his head into the wall!

Monty had a thick skull and came back strong. Blood streamed from a cut on his forehead as he charged Cooney! Cans and bottles flew sideways as onlookers gave way!

At one point Cooney was sitting on Monty's back, banging his head on the floor. With superhuman strength Monty rose, lifting Cooney with him.

The big man started running for the door with Cooney on his back. He stumbled and fell through the passageway, just as Monty's sweetheart attacked Cooney from behind!

For a brief moment it looked like a conga line gone terribly wrong! Three crash test dummies going through a windshield! A gang tackle! Three frogs mating on the front lawn!

The trio slid ten feet out onto the sidewalk, peeling an inch-wide strip down Monty's forehead and the bridge of his nose.

Cooney was trying to push himself up, but Monty's motherly protector was bashing him on the head and shoulders, all the while screaming "#@#$%@&!"

He managed to roll to one side. She fell over onto Monty, clutching him lovingly. She turned to Cooney, who now lay flat on his back. "You, you #$%&*!" she mouthed, comparing him with a misshapen, indiscriminate vital organ. "If you hurt Monty we are going to sue you!" Then turning her attention to the still-prone Monty, she said, "Here, Baby, let Snookums help you."

For a moment Cooney lay on the sidewalk looking up at the bar sign and street lights. The crowd formed a solid wall on both sides, creating a human fence from the sidewalk to the bar's entrance. His shirt was torn almost off his back. One sleeve was gone. Front and back he was soaked with spilt beer and blood that he had mopped up during the melee. His hat was gone and his dark hair askew. His right eye was swelling. He felt dizzy and nauseous. Miraculously his vision began to clear.

Meanwhile Pica was leading Nova through the crush of boots and hats at the street dance celebrating the bucking horse sale earlier in the day. Pica had qualified to ride in the final go-round that afternoon and had bested five men in the competition. She was in high spirits, but simmering beneath her winner's smile was the resentment that no matter how good she was, they would never take her seriously. She gritted her teeth every time some rodeo chauvinist congratulated her with a "pretty good for a girl."

The two women each bore beer in a plastic cup as they made their way down the three blocks of Main Street that were barricaded for the festivities where four bands were playing on separate stages.

Many businesses were open into the street, including bars, souvenir vendors, and eating places. The mood was festive, crowded, and loud.

The two women strolled through the throng, stopping to visit at shout level with friendly passersby. Eventually they found their way into a less-crowded restaurant just off Main. After being seated Nova began: "The next step would be for you to meet Mr. Manniquin. As I have said, if this endorsement program with Straight works, OVER THE TOP may be looking for a female endorser as well. It would involve flying you to Denver for an interview, maybe a photo shoot."

"What is the job?" asked Pica.

"Traveling, going to rodeos, events, doing photo opportunities, public relations. I'm assuming you're not married?"

"No," said Pica.

"Any current love interests, plans, et cetera?" asked Nova.

"None at present," Pica answered. A vision of Lionel Trane flashed and disappeared like lightning leaves the sky. It was followed by a welling up of Cooney's face as if rising from underwater. It caught her off guard. "Not really," she added.

Following supper, for which Nova paid, they stepped out onto the sidewalk relaxed, full, and feeling good. As they approached the Bison Bar they heard screaming, even over the pounding of four bands and the roar of the party! The crowd in front of them stopped suddenly, throwing up their hands!

Nova and Pica were in the second row and saw it all.

A large man came running out the door in a low crouch! A second man was clinging to his back, his arms around the big man's neck. As they watched wide-eyed, a woman—a Santa Fe-Sedona / Missoula-Monterrey rebuilt—leaped, hair flying, through the air and mounted the second man like Roy Rogers mounting Trigger!

When they hit the slick sidewalk there was a clunk, whomp, and whoosh! The threesome tobogganed to the curb as onlookers scattered!

The man in the middle rolled out from under the flailing fashionista. She dismounted him and rushed to the aid of her felled companion. She cursed the middle man.

Cooney's stomach roiled. He tried to sit up, looked up at the crowd, and in a single moment that would remain seared in his brain, he saw Pica D'TroiT, brilliant, back lit, and beautiful, contort her face into a mask of revulsion. Her lips mouthed the word *COONEY!* . . . Or was it *OOOKEEE*? He couldn't tell. Then he lost his lunch.

Activity resumed like a breaking dam retaking the low ground! Nova and Pica were pushed back with the crowd. They could hear the no-nonsense commands of Sheriff High Pockets to "break it up!"

The wail of Monty's histrionic princess carried like a tornado siren into the cool night air: "He attacked my Mon-Te-e-e-e-e-e . . . He had a *gun-n-n-n-n-n-n-n!*"

CHAPTER 13

May 21, Sunday
Miles City, Morning After

By 8:45 on Sunday morning Julie Holip had set the breakfast table with a baked biscuit, egg, and cheese casserole. The whole house smelled like home cookin'. Steve Holip, Straight, Nora, File, and Pica sat around the table. Grace was said, and conversation ensued.

"I'd expected a call from Cooney by now," said Straight.

Pica looked up.

"Someone saw him last night," said Steve. "He was playing cards at the Bison."

"Who?" asked File.

"Cooney Bedlam," answered Steve. "Straight's travelin' partner."

"Yeah," said Straight, "we're meeting up here in Miles City. He drove our rig up from Denver. We go from here to Taber and Maple Creek. I've got family in the area, so we'll go by Dad's ranch. They'll probably come to both rodeos. Cooney and I are entered up. Cooney won the Bullnanza in Birmingham last weekend."

He glanced at Pica for any reaction. She kept her head down, concentrating on eating.

As if on cue the phone rang. Steve rose and went into the kitchen to pick it up.

"Holip's," answered Steve. "Oh, hi, Sheriff! Yeah, it was a great weekend . . . Sure, I'll tell him. They must've passed out enough lip balm to chapproof the interstate! Yes . . . They're flying out this morning. Their pilots are going to pick them up here at the airport around 10:30.

"Um, uh. He's right here . . . You have? . . . Where is he? . . . When will you let him out? Sure, you can talk to him. Just a sec."

Steve turned to Straight, holding out the receiver. "It's about Cooney."

Straight rose and walked into the kitchen, taking the phone. Steve sat back down at the table. "Seems Cooney had a good time last night!" he joked.

Pica let a moment pass, put on a smile, and said, "Well, I'd best be going. Thank you, Julie and Steve, for the place to park, your shower, and this great breakfast. Nova, you've given me a lot to think about. You've got my e-mail address if something comes up. Even if it doesn't, it's been an experience! Please pass along how much I enjoyed getting to know Straight." She shook hands around, even with File, who hadn't been very friendly to her. Without bothering Straight, who had his back to them, concentrating, she went outside.

It was a brilliant, still, verdant summer morning. The sky was as big as . . . as big as Montana! She climbed into the cab of the four-year-old, three-quarter-ton pickup her dad had helped her buy. She would pass through Lewistown, Great Falls, and Shelby before she crossed the Canadian border at Sweetgrass.

Unfortunately, she could not shake the picture of Cooney Bedlam, in disarray, throwing up on the sidewalk. There was a tiny twinge of pity for him, then she quickly tried to conjure up how someone could get himself into the position of being thrown out of a bar, totally trashed, and then arrested.

He's either more—or less—than what I thought he was, she mused.

It's funny what causes one person to endear himself to another person. So much depends on the receptors with which each is equipped. For instance, if one of the persons has an unnatural affinity for biker dudes, mud wrestling, taking your temperature with your finger, or a sharp skinning knife, it is possible to imagine that same person could feel compassion for a perp caught in the act of a violent, disgusting display of the complete loss of all self-control. To Cooney's everlasting good fortune, Pica had always liked a sharp skinning knife.

Somewhere between Jordan and Grassrange, Cooney banged on the camper. Straight pulled over. Cooney took the wheel, and Straight stretched out on the passenger side.

"Feeling any better?" he asked Cooney.

"Man, I feel like somebody put me in a duffle bag full of walleye and beat me with a steel post."

66

Cooney had good reasons to be having a sinking spell: the physical pounding, the injustice of spending a night in jail, the look of repugnance on Pica D'TroiT's face, and the humiliation of being saved by Straight, again.

The two were traveling partners, all right, Cooney was a year younger, but Straight's advanced rodeo skills and record lent a mentor-student flavor to their relationship. To Cooney, Straight was more dignified, popular, handsome, worldly, wise, serious, and "grown-up."

Like many pairings in which one is perceived to be superior to the other, the lesser's respect is often salted with crystals of resentment. They rise, these ulcerous crystals, unwanted but unstoppable like acid bubbles after a delicious meal of homemade venison sausage with Cajun seasoning.

Then the ultimate blow: to be told that Straight had spent the weekend with Pica, that she might get an OVER THE TOP endorsement as well and to hear that she had left Miles City that morning knowing that Straight was picking him up at the jail.

The unfairness of it all. Out of nowhere, his partner, Straight, was spending time with his obsession. Envy was trickling into Cooney's veins like an IV drip and turning him green.

"Anything I can do?" asked Straight.

Cooney kept both hands on the wheel and stared down the highway. Like a terminal cancer patient taking a deep pull on a Camel filter, he said, "Tell me about Pica."

Straight, true to his workaholic personality, hadn't really paid much attention to her. He had been concentrating on saying the right thing to fans, impressing his sponsors, tirelessly being polite, and signing autographs. Pica had mostly stood in the background and smiled.

"She can smile," he said, sounding as foolish as a customer complimenting a chef on the flavor of his salt: "You sure have good salt here."

"Maybe she has an extra amount of teeth," he added, "and, of course, she's built like a brick lighthouse!"

"Did you go out and eat and . . . you know, talk?" asked Cooney.

"Not really. We all had supper at that guy's house on Friday night. Everybody talked. Mostly the agents, PR, marketing people, all talking about how to promote lip balm."

"So, would you and her like . . . tour together, ya know?" asked Cooney.

"They haven't signed her up yet, hey. They are just sort of . . . considering her for a female counterpart spokesman for lip balm. But Nova, the public relations girl, sounded like she was trying to recruit Pica, feel her out."

"Did she say anything about me?" Cooney asked, inhaling another lungful of virtual carcinogen.

"We kinda kept an eye out for you on Saturday. I'd told everyone you were coming. But you never showed. Then she left this morning while I was talking to you on the phone. I came back to the table, and she'd gone. I didn't get to see her again."

Cooney thought about telling Straight about his brief encounter with Pica on the sidewalk in front of the Bison Bar, but he couldn't. "I wrote a short one last night . . . in the cell," said Cooney. He recited from memory:

Comin' out of the chute on a Pegasus bronc
Your mind is a falcon's, you think you can conquer
The world as you leave it and rise to the sky,
When you ride on the edge, you think you can fly.

A shiver went down Straight's spine.

"I don't know how you do it," he said with a sincerity Cooney had never heard before. "The way you write. It's what I'm feeling like when I'm on a horse. You put it into words."

Straight sighed, paused, and continued. "If I had a wish, it would be to have your way with words. Even for an hour, just to know how it felt to be able to capture what's swelling up in my chest. I feel so inadequate, 'specially around those reporters. I sound like those football players interviewed after a game. I feel like I'm so boring. I'd give one of my NFR buckles to be you for a day. You have such a gift."

Cooney was speechless.

They spent the night in a cheap motel, and the next morning our heroes went north, crossing the Canadian border at Wild Horse, then up through Medicine Hat. Buffalo, Alberta, the closest town to the Chalk Line Ranch, was approximately 100 kilometers north of Medicine Hat, as the Canada goose flies.

It was Monday, May 30, at four in the afternoon when Straight steered the pickup over the two-and-a-half-kilometer dirt road that led to the ranch house. The country looked good this spring. The tanks were full, and the cows were scattered. It looked like all was right with the world, everything was in its place.

Straight was glad to be coming home. His only concern was the fact that his brother, Border, was going to be home from college, too, and they always seemed to get into a disagreement about something. To Straight, college had turned Border into an insufferable twit. It seemed that no matter what

Straight said, Border had to disagree or elaborate or criticize or comment. It was a continuing barrage of one-upsmanship. Because Border had Straight outbrained and outverbiaged most of the time, for Border it was like dueling with an unarmed man.

Maybe it would be easier with Cooney here, thought Straight.

They drove up to the house, and two good-looking young women came running out to the pickup. Straight's sisters, Tyra, twenty-two, a tall brunette with a long ponytail, and Myra, twenty, not as tall but with her dark hair cut short, both had Straight's slender face and hazel eyes. They were screaming his name and laughing as they pulled open the driver's side door and literally pulled him out of the truck.

They were hugging and kissing on him, giving him a grand welcome. Then they attacked Cooney, who had debouched the vehicle and had started around. It was like being mauled by puppies.

Chalk, fifty-two, and Fiona, forty-eight, Straight's parents, stepped off the porch and headed out to meet their bronc-riding son. Fiona gave Straight a formal hug, no kiss. Chalk shook his hand and patted his shoulder. How the daughters became so outgoing was a mystery to all, but they lent gaiety and mischief to an otherwise often humorless household.

Cooney had assumed that Straight's parents had named him Straight Line as sort of a joke. But after meeting Chalk and Fiona, it didn't seem their way. He had broached the subject with Chalk once and learned that it was purely practical. It made a person's name easier to remember, he explained. Cooney thought but didn't say, *Well, why didn't you name him Crooked or Bunt or Side or Maginot?*

Chalk himself had brothers named Timber and County and a sister named Rachael. Chalk explained without the slightest hint of a smile that girls didn't need to worry about memorable first names because when they married they changed their name anyway.

The first time Cooney saw their cowdogs he remarked to Chalk that he assumed they would have a Chow Chow. Chalk looked at him quizzically. Cooney said, "Chow Line. Get it?" Chalk didn't get it. The next two days were leisurely. Cooney, Straight, and Chalk took a couple of rides in the pickup to check water tanks and one long horseback circle to check cattle. The sisters were big on playing games: checkers, chess, rats, tiles, pinochle, cribbage. They had boxes of them.

Straight was a miserable failure at Scrabble or Boggle, anything that involved spelling, but he was a good sport about it because he was unbeatable in checkers or Chinese checkers one-on-one. He had the savant's ability to see things spatially. In fact, the only math course he even understood in school was geometry.

Border, the second son, would be home in time for supper.

Straight grew more agitated by the hour as Thursday tick-tocked by.

Cooney walked with him out to feed the horses. "Something buggin' you?"

"Nothing bad, I guess. It's just that Border will be here soon and . . . well, him and I don't always get along."

"What do you mean?" asked Cooney.

"Oh, we never have got along. It strains the family. I hate to put them through it another time. I had hoped when we got older we'd get more, uh, more understanding of each other."

"It takes two to tango . . . and two to tangle," said Cooney with the simplistic wisdom of an Old Testament believer.

"I know that," he admitted, "but he sucks me into his trap, and I say stupid things, which he then points out, and I wind up getting frustrated and stomp off. I'm just no match for his smart mouth."

"Aw, it'll be all right. Just don't get cornered, and if you do, tell yourself, 'So what?' What difference does it make to you what he says? It won't affect your bronc ridin' or your life.

"Besides, it couldn't be all that bad."

It was all that bad.

Border returned to the same glad homecoming that Straight had enjoyed. The sisters were vivacious, the folks were proud but tight lipped. Straight smiled, shook hands, and welcomed Border home.

Cooney was pleasant, staying in the background and watching the reactions and body positions of the family members as they circulated among themselves. Border was a big man. Twenty-four years old, six foot two, and at least 215 pounds. He had dark hair, a big chin, thick eyebrows, sported a well-groomed beard, and wore little wire-rimmed glasses. He was not necessarily fat, just burly, although it would be easy to guess as he aged he would have a weight problem. If he was trying to look professorial, he succeeded, in an imperious sort of way.

Fiona had prepared tough roast beef from an old cow that had broken her leg and they had home-butchered, plus mashed potatoes, canned green beans, and watery gravy, but the atmosphere was one of bonhomie. Until, five minutes into the meal, Border turned the conversation to Straight: "So, how's the buckaroo, bucking, rodeo-odeo business?"

"I'm still doing okay," said Straight neutrally.

70

"I'm glad. I don't know how some of you and your rodeo buddies do it," he commented as if he were really concerned. "I mean, bashing your heads in for pennies. I tell you, those stock contractors and advertisers and middlemen are making millions of dollars off your naive sense of . . . what would you call it: macho, death wish, pseudo-camaraderie? Competing against each other, always hoping the competition does poorly but having to act like you really want him to win.

"What an effort in futility. You might even win a buckle, but what does that amount to? It wouldn't even buy your gas to the next podunk town. Pretty sorry return on your investment. Just stupid, if you ask me," Border concluded, shoveling a loader bucket of mashed potatoes onto his plate.

The family was glaring at Border. A thunderhead was building behind Straight's eyes.

"I do it for the girls," Cooney said cheerfully.

Myra blew a sticky wad of mashed potatoes out of her mouth. The starchy lava vaporized and clung to the salt shaker in the center of the table. It was so sudden, so out of order, so funny, that even Fiona changed expression and said, "God save the Queen!"

By the time everyone at the table had quit guffawing and giggling, Border had leveled his gaze on Cooney. He wiped his mouth with a paper napkin and cleared his throat, but Cooney spoke first: "So, what do you do to get girls?"

"The opposite sex is not a priority in my life right now," answered Border. "I am engaged in the acquisition of a degree in higher education, and that takes all of my concentration."

"What are you studying?" asked Cooney politely.

"The title of my master's thesis is 'The Misapplication of the Harrod Domar Growth Equation to the Economic Planning of an Underdeveloped Country.'"

"Which one?" asked Cooney.

"Which one what?" asked Border.

"Which country? Or does it mean an area within a country, like say, Nunavut within Canada or Eritrea within Ethiopia or Cohagen within Montana?"

"My model," Border began, as if he were lecturing, "or at least the one I think I will choose is . . . I'm considering a small community in Labrador. Thirty-eight percent unemployment, average income . . . $9,000 a year, an economy built on a dwindling fishing industry . . . or maybe Barwidgee, Western Australia. It could be fascinating and very valuable, an isolated village, or possibly Togo, another impoverished African country.

"You see, Cooney—it *is* 'Cooney,' isn't it? It's important that I choose a country, a place that has significant importance in the world economy, and yet will stand alone as a study unit that can be applied to other models and the data then extrapolated, thus having the far-reaching impact that I expect my work will stimulate. I want to make a significant contribution. It's more than the money, you know,"

"How much do you make now?" asked Cooney.

"I'm matriculating. Dedicating all my time to enlarging my knowledge of mankind. Because, like I said, it's not about money," explained Border.

"Surely you have a job somewhere . . . working at the Kwik Chek, flipping burgers at Wendy's, sweeping up the college gym?" pressed Cooney.

"I have an assistantship. I help teach some of the classes," Border said.

"That's what? Seven bucks an hour? Six?"

"Eight-fifty," Border said.

"Canadian?" asked Cooney.

"What are you getting at?" asked Border in a threatening tone.

"Nothing. I was just wondering how much longer you'll be working on your master's thesis," said Cooney.

"As soon as I . . ."

Cooney interrupted, "But, of course you haven't even started it yet. You still need to pick a location to use as your model, if I understood you right. And what good is a master's without a PhD? That must be on your list as well, right?"

"Of course. Pure academic immersion, untainted by mundane variables, is essential to ensure that one has a clear mind and therefore can think with a worldview," stated Border.

"Whew," said Cooney, "it all sounds pretty expensive to me." He caught a glimpse of Chalk and Fiona bent forward listening to Border's answers. They were particularly interested in his comments about money. Cooney assumed the parents were financing their bright boy's education.

He was also acutely aware of the BSE (bovine spongiform encephalopathy) quarantine on Canadian cattle and of the dire straits it had created for many cow-calf producers like the Chalk Line Ranch.

"I guess Straight could lend you some money," offered Cooney. "He's already won over $35,000 this year, U.S. But if I was in the advice-givin' business, which I'm not, I would think you better start trolling for a woman with a job."

CHAPTER 14

May 2, Sunday
Rodeo, Canadian Style

RODEO IS REAL LIFE. THEY DON'T CALL IT OFF BECAUSE IT'S RAINING.

It should have been a short two-hour drive from Buffalo to Maple Creek, but the pouring rain slowed them to a crawl several times. Myra and Tyra intended to spend the entire weekend cowboyed up, and all four fit semicomfortably in the boys' crew cab.

The crowd was light due to the weather, but the show went on. Tyra and Myra sat in the open bleachers with slickers on and hats pulled down. It was still drizzling when Art Undertow climbed to the announcer's box:

"Ladies and gentlemen, welcome to the Cowtown Pro Rodeo right here in the shadow of the Cypress Hills, Maple Creek, Saskatchewan, where the west begins! Home of the Maple Creek Hotel, the *Maple Creek News,* and the Maple Creek Open, Canada's premier stock dog trial competition, where the dogs are beautiful and the sheep fight back!

"Aren't we thankful for the rain!" he boomed.

The crowd responded wetly: "Yes. Thank you, our dear Lord in Heaven, for the bounty of thy gift of moisture. Amen."

"If it's any consolation to the bronc riders, this little sprinkle makes the arena softer."

There were bigger rodeos going on in the States over this weekend, but Maple Creek and Taber were where Straight began his career, and he tried to support them by entering every year. It meant a lot to the home folks to have a local boy-made-good come back, especially if he was ranked in the top fifteen in the PRCA. Cooney wasn't chopped liver either!

Our heroes had the advantage of being able to watch the bareback riding. Doing so gave them an idea of how the horses could buck in the mud. It was a sloppy mess. To its credit the rodeo committee dragged and raked and turned the wet arena dirt the best it could. But horses slid, cowboys skidded, chute help ducked, judges dived, and the crowd went wild, all to a visual symphony worthy of any mud slide four-by-four dirt bike jamboree.

Steer wrestling—or bulldogging, as it is also known—in the mud was the pinnacle of absurdity. The dogger, on horseback, raced down the arena just a few feet behind a six hundred-pound steer, who was flinging mud and water like a monster truck trying to get unstuck. Before the dogger even reached for the steer to make his jump, the right side of his body from boot toe to eyebrow was solid brown.

Then he leaned off his horse, grasped the steer's horns, and leaped, planting his heels in the arena mud to try to stop their forward progress. Each one looked like a snow plow comin' through fifteen acres of chocolate pudding.

Finally, when the steer had slowed enough to get some leverage, the steer wrestler was obligated to throw him to the ground. This put them in the awkward position of being beneath the thrashing beast when he fell.

After each run the dogger would try to stand and acknowledge the crowd. The crowd cheered, but it was hard to watch. One was reminded of the La Brea tar pits.

When saddle bronc riding came, Straight was the first one out of the chute on a journeyman bronc named Long Reach. The horse came out, bucked as much as he felt he owed the stock contractor, then quit. Straight's style allowed him to look good on any horse he mounted, good or bad. Straight always got *his* points. However, if the horse was weak, erratic, disabled, or a full-blown bad actor, Straight couldn't make it look any better than it was. And it took a good effort by horse and rider to score well. The judges gave them a combined sixty-three points.

Cooney's style differed from Straight's classic "rock and fire" style. Cooney went all out—hook 'em, hang and rattle—every time. He never rode "not to lose." He could ride a bad horse and make him look like a bobcat with a firecracker tied to his tail. His "all or nothing" attitude endeared him to the crowd but put him at a disadvantage with some of the judges who revered the purity of the traditional ride. Audience appeal had no bearing on the judges' score . . . most of the time.

A steady rain had begun by the time Cooney had Pecos Bill in the riggin' chute. She was a big, powerful, twelve-year-old mare who had the book of bein' a dead head or a whirlwind, one or the other. Like when you throw a Tater Tot onto a hot griddle, you've got no idea where it's goin'! She hated her name.

Straight was beside Cooney to help him get down when he was on deck. Rain was pouring off the front of their hats. Straight was wearing his yellow slicker, but Cooney was shivering in his long-sleeve shirt and protective vest.

"Shake it off, Cooney," said Straight. "Take a deep breath."

From behind Straight put his hands on Cooney's arms and rubbed them up and down roughly. The stimulation created some warmth and relaxed Cooney enough that he quit shaking.

Cooney reached up and pulled down the rag that his black hat had become. He felt water in the seat of his pants. *Okay*, he thought, *take your best shot, you old snide. We're goin' swimmin'.*

At the fringe of his concentration he heard the chute boss tell him he was up. He leaned back against the cantle, felt the rein come tight in his left hand, and saw the back of Pecos Bill's shaggy head swing toward the arena. Cooney's neck tensed as he gritted his teeth and nodded.

The chute gate flew open, Cooney's legs straightened out in front of him, and his spurs hit the rock-hard neck muscles of Pecos Bill as she wheeled to her right and catapulted into the muddy arena!

Pecos Bill was powerful enough to suck her big feet out of the mud and change direction. She would have quickly disrupted the rhythm of most good saddle bronc riders, but Cooney set his own rhythm, made her dance to his tune, and it was a pleasure to watch. During one outlandish half-gainer with a twist Cooney appeared to be standing in the saddle seat, ballet dancing as Pecos Bill gyrated beneath him. He seemed to skitter above her like a horse-fly. All went well . . . until the end.

Just as the whistle blew Pecos Bill slid off a hind leg and went down onto her right side. Cooney bailed out backward over her right rump. He hit the mud, and she rolled over him.

People in the crowd rose in unison and groaned.

Pecos Bill struggled, stood up, and then trotted toward the gate. The rider could not be seen. Several cowboys sloshed out to help. The paramedics were racing into the arena. People in the crowd saw Cooney's right knee rise, then his left. They breathed a sigh of relief and sat down.

One cowboy had Cooney by the arm and was pulling on him. Cooney was trying to push himself up with his other arm. Finally he stood, pulled up erect like someone was standing up a fence post. Unfortunately, he could not dislodge his boots to keep his balance and fell face-down in the opposite direction.

The cowboys to the rescue were laughing so hard that it took them a minute to get Cooney right again and another minute to get him unstuck.

The loyal crowd couldn't have had more fun at a bullfight or a ten-car pileup at the Indy 500.

People in the stands were breathless with laughter, temporarily unaware of the rain, as Cooney was dragged toward the fence. As a fitting climax, one of the cowboys came back to dig Cooney's right boot out from the scene of the crime, return, and present it to Cooney in front of the chutes like a trophy. The crowd gave him a standing ovation.

The judges gave him an eighty-four, which was even better!

At the close of the day Cooney Bedlam held the lead in both saddle bronc riding and bull riding.

CHAPTER 15

May 27, Friday
Pica Has Interview in Denver

WHILE STRAIGHT AND COONEY WERE SWIMMING IN THE ARENA IN MAPLE Creek, Saskatchewan, Nova Skosha had picked Pica D'TroiT up at Denver International Airport and driven her to the Marriott Tech Center Hotel. They had dinner at the hotel restaurant and discussed plans for the big interview the next day.

At 9:45 a.m. on Friday Nova opened the door for Pica and followed her into the conference room, where Turk Manniquin stood to greet her wearing an off-the-peg Armani suit and vest in amber, an off-white silk shirt, golden sunset tie, and Lamborghini slippers, size 14. His head was shaved, and he wore a gold stud in his right earlobe.

He walked the length of the sixteen-foot conference table and offered his hand. Turk was 6'7" tall. Pica was 5'3" barefoot. Add an inch and a half for her Ariat Fat Boy boots.

"I am so pleased you could come to Denver and visit with us. Nova has told me a sufficiency of you. You are more than I expected," he said in his slight New Orleans Creole accent.

"You, too, sir. Much more than I expected, I mean, I guess, I was all, I never thought that you'd be, like, a giant, hey!" she said.

He laughed. "I wonder if you would stand up on this conference table and walk to the other end."

Pica looked up at him and thought, *It's his table.* She swung a leg up and stepped on, walked to the other end, and turned around.

"Now what?" she asked.

"I want to know if you can whistle," he said.

She placed her thumb and forefinger together, slid them over her teeth and under her tongue . . . and blew. It was a glass-shattering, Mach-splitting, bell-ringing, mind-piercing, soaring, triumphant tintinnabulation that made dogs scream, eyeballs burst, and elk run for cover two miles away.

Turk's skull was vibrating as if it had been struck by a twenty-pound tuning fork! He shook his head slightly and looked up at her. Pica smiled a smile that spread across her face like raising the blinds in a dark room. Her eyes said, "How's that?" She gave him that crawl-up-your-back look that had earned her the appellation "Pica, with a long *EYE* and capital *TEASE*."

"My goodness gracious, sweet baby James, you have got lips! Brandi lips, Jolie lips, Sister, Slide-on-Over-Here Congo lips . . . What a Light-up-the-World, Fourteen-Carat, Radioactive, Plutonium, Call the Dogs, and Put Out the Fire smile you have got! You have a mouth full of lips.

"Please allow me to help you down and to thank you for the runway performance. It made it so much easier for me to picture you." He took her hand, and she jumped off the table.

"Are you French?" he asked as he gestured for her to sit down. "I ask because I come from the French Quarter of New Orleans and have French in my blood."

"Canadian mostly," she answered. "My grandfather was descended from the French trappers of like, thousands of years ago, or hundreds . . . anyway, that's, ya know, where the 'D'TroiT' came from."

"When I first saw your name I thought it would be pronounced 'DE-TROY,'" he said.

"It is in Quebec," she said, pronouncing it "KEE BECK."

"As you know, we are looking for a female to represent our company and specifically a new product, COWBOY KISSES, an extreme lip balm for extreme athletics. The job would entail traveling, all at our expense, particularly to rodeos and athletics events. We would be using your likeness in our advertising.

"Have you done any modeling?" he inquired.

"No," she answered.

"Were you a . . ." He searched for a description, "a cheerleader, prom queen, thespian, that sort of thing in high school?"

"No-o-o," she laughed. "See, I was, like, a tomboy. I rode horses, packed into the wilderness, hunted, fished, did some cow work. I didn't have time for, ya know, girlie things." It went unsaid that she also had sproingy reddish hair, freckles, a giant mouth, and not much meat on her bones until the summer between her junior and senior years.

"We would like to have you do a photo session as part of the interview. That okay?" he asked.

"Sure," she answered.

"Okay, good. Any questions?"

"You'd need to know that I wouldn't be able to work for you much in the fall, particularly October, November . . . hunting season, you know. Dad will need my help."

Turk thought a moment. "Well, let's see how the photo shoot comes out. We can discuss details if it looks like you are our choice."

On Monday morning the photos arrived at Turk's office by messenger. The fifty color pictures included Pica puckering in an evening gown, a cowboy hat, jeans, western shirt, low-cut jeans, tank top, cut-off jeans, bikini with cowboy boots, applying LIP LASTER, sitting with legs crossed in a dress, in shorts, over-the-back shots, bosomy shots, close-ups of the face, eyes, mouth, and teeth but none of her in the buff. She had refused.

File Blitzer, Nova, and the secretary were examining the pictures with Turk.

"They've got her too made up," said Turk. "She looks like a doll somebody painted lipstick on."

"It's the rodeo queen look," said Nova. "It's too much, too fancy. She's too small to carry all that dazzle."

"That's right," said Turk. "In person she's got her own dazzle. She doesn't need bling."

"Look," said Turk, "this one here is the best picture in the lot." He passed around the photo.

It was a shot of Pica from the knees up wearing a tan canvas jacket with a corduroy collar. She had her hands on her hips holding the jacket open, a black V-necked pullover T-shirt, old hip-hugger jeans, no belt, and small silver concho earrings. Her reddish-blonde hair in natural curliness was teased out behind her head and sparkled with highlights. Some of the sprinkles had fallen onto her face and creamy white chest. A delicate silver pendant hung on a thin chain around her neck. Her head was slightly cocked, and her mouth, teeth, and lips, glistening with Light Rose–colored LIP LASTER, were asking "Why?" The pretty blue eyes looked right at you with just the right combination of allure and mischief.

This photograph had captured that look. That capital *Tease* look. She was absolutely mouthwatering.

"How about those lips? That mouth," said Nova. "It's artistic. Like there is an invisible line. Your eye immediately hits those gleaming teeth, then follows the pendant right down the front of her shirt."

"What do you think, File?" asked Turk.

File was slow to speak. "Well, she is a looker. Not as photogenic as some. I'd have certain reservations. One, her lack of photogenicity. Her, shall we say, lack of sophistication, maturity, her Valley Girl teenage vocabulary. Will she be able to go on the road and take care of business? She's already said she couldn't work full-time. Seems like we should keep looking."

"You mentioned you had a girl that might be worth interviewing," said Turk. "I have those pictures you gave me somewhere . . ."

"I just happen to have another set right here, sir," said File, handing Turk a folder containing an extensive portfolio displaying the wares of Oui Oui Reese. Including one of her in an off-Broadway play wearing nothing but a top hat and cane.

CHAPTER 16

May 28, Saturday
Pincher Creek, Alberta, Supper and a Do

JUNEAU D'TROIT, A SHORT, RUDDY-FACED OUTDOORSMAN IN A WESTERN HAT, wool shirt, and lace-up hunting boots, stood in the waiting area outside Customs at Calgary International Airport. As soon as Pica saw him, she waved. A warm feeling swept over him, leaving goose bumps.

"Dad!" she said, dropping her bag and backpack. She gave him a big hug.

"Is this all your stuff?" he asked.

"Yes, yes . . . it was so cool, Dad," Pica said. "They interviewed me and, like, made me walk like a model, did a *long* photo shoot. I was all, like, posing in all these clothes."

She talked as they walked to the parking lot, telling him all the details. He had not seen her this excited for a long time. After they were in the car and past the payment kiosk, she continued. "And, Dad, you know what they liked most about me, I mean, besides my personality, of course?"

"What?" he asked, enjoying her vivacity.

"My lips! My mouth and my teeth! My big mouth and fat lips that I practiced squeezing tight and sucked in all through school. Can you believe it! Can you remember how I used to pose in front of the mirror trying to hold my lips so they wouldn't be so gross?"

He remembered well. He also remembered that sometime during her senior year in high school she quit being self-conscious about her big mouth, fat lips, sproingy hair, and shortness. That transition coincided with her discovery that, like her brothers, she could ride bucking horses.

"So, do you have the job?" he asked.

"I don't know. I know they are interviewing others, but they made a big deal about me rodeoing and being athletic."

She paused for a minute.

"Dad, I never, ya know, dreamed too big. I was all, if somebody said I'd spend the rest of my life packing, cooking at hunting camp, riding horses, I'd go, ya know, that would be all right with me. Like I told them, even if they picked me I couldn't work for them during hunting season. I'd, like, be with you. I told them that, but, Dad, I wish, I really hope they'll give me a chance, hey."

Juneau kept his eyes on the road.

He loved his sons, he adored his daughter. The boys helped with his business because they could. She helped because she wanted to be with him.

Unable to look at her because his eyes were welling up, Juneau said, "Peter, Paul, and Perrier are coming home today And the Ag Society is having supper and a do at the Community Hall tonight. Lick Davis is going to do a program, and there's a dance after."

"All right! I could stand kickin' up my feet!" she said.

"Gord is back," he said neutrally.

"Oh, no!" she groaned.

"He's not so bad, Sweetie," said Juneau.

"I know, I know, it's just that . . . aw, you know the deal as well as me."

WELL, WE, THE INTERESTED READERS, DON'T KNOW, BUT WE CAN GUESS. GORD IS MORE THAN LIKELY A CHILDHOOD SWEETHEART WHO IS STILL CARRYING A TORCH FOR PICA. THAT IS TRUE (IN THIS BOOK OF FICTION). HE IS ALSO A STABLE, HARDWORKING, RUGGEDLY HANDSOME COWBOY WHO IS PRESENTLY A TEACHER AT OLDS COLLEGE, TEACHING AGRI-BUSINESS MANAGEMENT.

HE WOULD BE CONSIDERED A GOOD BET, A GREAT CATCH BY MOST FEMALES WHO ARE LOOKING FOR A STABLE, PREDICTIBLE FUTURE, A GOOD FATHER FOR THEIR CHILDREN AND A RESPONSIBLE BREADWINNER.

IF HE EVER HAD A WILD OAT, HE PROBABLY SEWED IT IN HIS PIGGY BANK AS A THIRD GRADER AND INVESTED IT IN A HIGH-QUALITY PEN AND PENCIL SET FOR HIS FUTURE DESK.

IT TAKES A LOT OF DISCIPLINE FOR A WOMAN TO MARRY A MAN LIKE GORD.

HE WAS BEIGE. PICA WAS FLUORESCENT PINK. BEIGE WILL GO WITH ALMOST ANYTHING, AS YOU KNOW, BUT FLUORESCENT PINK DOESN'T.

Not too far down the road, our heroes were resting up between rodeos. They were both up the next night in Taber, Alberta, a two-and-a-half-hour drive from Buffalo. Straight's sisters had been planning to go to the big doin's in Pincher Creek, three-and-a-half hours away, for weeks, and they invited Cooney and Straight to go along.

"I'm going to pass," said Straight. "I promised a couple of old high school friends I'd come see them. You go ahead. Tyra and Myra would love for you to go with them."

"Lick Davis is gonna be there," said Cooney.

"I know. Tell him I said hello and ask him if it's okay that I use some of his poems. I've got to give a speech to the Rotary Club in Clovis next week. Anyway, I'll see you in the morning. Have a good time!"

Myra, Tyra, and Cooney pulled into the Pincher Creek Community Hall parking lot in Myra's car at 5:56 p.m. Both girls were decked out in cowgirl chic: Tyra was wearing black Lucchese high-top boots with a cow skull inlay, Cruel Girl jeans tucked in the boot tops, one of Straight's trophy buckles on a bling belt, and a retro western shirt with roses on it. Myra had on cowboy-cut Wranglers, a tight red cheetah print shirt layered with rhinestones, a big concho belt, red boots, and a furry vest. Between them they wore enough hair spray and lip gloss to taxiderm a small mule!

The sisters had ironed one of Cooney's shirts for him, and he had shaved. Otherwise, his jeans were wrinkled, his boots were unshined, and spatters of mud still speckled his black hat. But his Birmingham Bullnanza belt buckle glowed like the headlight on a locomotive!

After they were in the community hall, hair glistening, faces on, and anticipation shining in their eyes, they found a table at the back and saved three seats together. Tyra and Myra disappeared into the crowd, which was enjoying the social hour before supper. It did not cross Cooney's mind that he was in "Pica" territory. Not putting two and two together. Of course, after last week in Miles City, the two and two together sure didn't add up to him and Pica!

"Aren't you Cooney Bedlam?"

Cooney turned to see a foxy-looking woman with jet-black hair pulled back from her face and held with silver combs.

"Yes, ma'am," he said. "Sure am."

"My friend told me you won the broncs *and* the bull riding at Maple Creek. She's a barrel racer," the lady said.

"It might not be me after tonight," he said, "but when we left last night we were winning."

"I'm Tickle," she said, extending her hand.

Cooney took it. It wasn't soft. Matter of fact, Tickle had a bit of a hard look about her. He guessed she was older than he was, early thirties maybe, and she was wearing tight black jeans, frilly western shirt with a fancy yoke opened three or four buttons, red lipstick, and dangly earrings to match her combs. She had an empty glass in her hands.

"Could I get you a drink?" he asked Tickle.

"I was hoping you'd ask," she smiled up at him.

While they were standing in line for drinks Lick Davis appeared.

"Cooney!" he said, offering his hand and noticing Tickle standing close by him.

"I'm Lick Davis," he said to her. "Cooney and I have stirred a few hornet's nests together!"

"Tickle," she said, "nice to meet you."

Lick, who didn't hear as well as he used to, thought she said, "tickled" as in "tickled to meet you." He remembered discussing Cooney's confused feeling about a woman, but no name came to mind. Maybe this was her. And it didn't make any difference to him anyway. He briefly told the story of how they gathered a wild cow in the mesquite of Arizona. He had them laughing.

"Did that lady ever call the law?" Cooney asked him, "the one whose kitchen we tore up?"

"And lawn and living room!" laughed Lick.

A local rancher came up and captured Lick's attention; Cooney and Tickle moved up to the tables in the balcony for supper. Afterward the house lights dimmed, and Lick stepped to the stage and started his performance.

Cooney tried to soak up some of the poetry, but it was hard to concentrate as the empty plastic glasses of rye and water began to accumulate. Not to mention the tactile attention of Tickle, practicing barrel racer and student of saddle bronc riders.

By the time the dance began our lovely couple had already slipped out to the parking lot.

"My car is over there," tipsy Tickle said, pointing outside the circle of light that shone from the building.

It was a Volvo station wagon old enough to have the sleek design of a cheese box. The back seat and storage area seemed to be filled with horse tack, sacks, buckets, hay bags, and cardboard boxes. It smelled like the saddle room at a riding stable. The faint aroma of Absorbine Jr. clung to the interior.

Cooney slid in on the passenger side. It was cramped; stuff was piled up against the back of his seat. He managed to get the seat back to recline about 30 degrees. There was a center divider with a short gear shift sticking up between them. Tickle slid into the driver's side. No lights came on when they opened the doors. The headliner was gone, as was the dome light. The bottom side of the roof was exposed, as were the steel braces that spanned the width overhead.

She rolled down her window, he, his.

"Sorry 'bout the mess," she said. "I'm an animal freak." She shook her hair and belched lightly. "Whew! I'm a little dizzy. Roll down your window, too, Cooney. Let's get some air in here!

"Are you hot, Honey? Let me help," she said, then reached over and unbuttoned his shirt.

"How 'bout you?" he said, reciprocating.

"Hope you like black," she said, fanning herself.

Next thing you know, she had climbed the transmission housing between them and was pawing at him like a dog diggin' up a bone! Passion swelled its neck and began displaying its rutting colors. If you ever wondered how it feels to shed your skin like a snake, try re-creating what Cooney and Tickle were doing in the Volvo that evening in the community hall parking lot at Pincher Creek.

Elbows got whacked, knees got scraped, boots got scuffed, joints got bent, muscles got strained, ankles got sprained, plus rug burn, alfalfa rash, and wedgie chafe.

Cooney found himself balancing on top, kissing her fiercely, when he felt a cramp in his neck.

He pushed himself up with his arms. She was looking up at him intensely, her hair loose and her lipstick smeared. He was sweating. Holding himself above her, letting the evening breeze cool their exposed skin, he returned the look. Then slowly, gently he lowered his head to kiss her. She closed her eyes. He closed his eyes. Their lips touched with the delicacy of two rose petals bumping each other in a glass bowl.

A big, wet, slurpy tongue slathered his right cheek from his jawbone to his hairline. He opened his eyes. A dog the size of a triceratops was two inches from his face. "Woof" was all it said.

Cooney reared back violently, banging his head on the exposed roof brace, knocking him out cold! Tickle, who managed to get the passenger door open and crawl out from under the unconscious Cooney, saw him hanging out of the car like the hide of a three-toed sloth strung across the shoulders of a yeti.

She screamed and ran into the dance hall.

Less than a minute later she returned with two paramedics, her ex-husband, and his family, all of whom knew her and would be discreet. They followed her as she was trying to tuck in her shirttail. "I don't know how bad he's hurt; I think he's bleeding, but I . . ." She was trying to undo a silver comb from her tangled hair. Her shirt was buttoned up wrong. "There he is," she said. They ran up on the vehicle and rounded to the passenger side.

Cooney lay flat on his back beneath the open car door. His right foot rested in the window, his left foot at an awkward angle, still in the car. His left pant leg had caught on the gear shift, preventing him from sliding completely out.

His head was spinning, the band was playing far away; he could feel the gravel beneath his head and see a night full of stars. Suddenly Tickle was standing over him pointing. She looked as if someone had colored her outside the lines. He squeezed his eyes tight, then opened them. She was in full color and clear as a bell.

The paramedics bent to assist him. They were palpating his arms and legs and examining his head.

He could hear Tickle explaining to the crowd, "It's Cooney Bedlam, Peter. I know, don't say it. We were just having a good time." Cooney moved his head to see the faces of those bent over him. It was as if the Angel of Bad Timing was following him around; Pica D'TroiT, his long-distance obsession, was staring down at him.

Tickle stepped in front of Pica, blocking his view. "Cooney," she said, "this is my ex, Peter . . . Peter D'TroiT."

Cooney's mind dredged up the everlasting debate concerning creationism versus evolution.

Surely, he thought, this isn't just bad luck. It couldn't be the result of random collisions between hydrogen and oxygen and nitrogen atoms, haphazard coincidence, or an indiscriminate roll of the dice. Surely this is part of a master plan. How else could he continue to leave such a lasting bad impression on the girl he was trying to impress?

In spite of a splitting headache and a suffocating heart, he laughed and sagged against the hard ground. God has a grand sense of humor.

Cooney woke at noon with a thick tongue, a stuffy nose, and a deep, pounding headache. It was just as well, he reasoned at some primitive level. If he felt worse on the outside than the inside, it might help dull the broken heart receptors.

Myra and Tyra had laid him out on the floor in Straight's room when they had come in about 2:30 a.m. They might have undressed him, too. He didn't care to know. He was in his shorts and socks. His jeans were neatly folded over the back of a chair, and his shirt hung on a hanger behind the closet door. Even his boots were standing soldierly against the wall.

He let his mind drift back to last night, Lick Davis, Tickle . . . what was her last name? Oh, yeah, *oh, no!* The gauzy face of Pica floated through his brain like a black and white newsreel of Marilyn Monroe loving the camera, then the film disintegrated like it was melting.

He had sporadic memories of beating off the paramedics, who called him ungrateful in Canadian profanity, which resembles American profanity except the queen is involved.

The Line sisters had left him in the back seat of their car, and he must have slept all the way home because he didn't remember riding in the car or arriving here . . . where he was, staggering around their empty house looking for a headache remedy.

AT ONE TIME ALTERNATIVE SCIENCE ADVANCED A MONEY-MAKING SCHEME THAT INVOLVED WHAT THEY CALLED BIORHYTHMS. EVERY HUMAN, THEY POSTULATED, IS SUBJECT TO THREE RECURRING INTERNAL TEMPOS THAT RISE AND FALL LIKE SOUND WAVES. THEY ARE YOUR EMOTIONAL STATE, YOUR PHYSICAL STATE, AND YOUR MENTAL STATE.

HOW YOU ARE FEELING DEPENDS ON THE POSITION OF EACH STATE: STRONG, AVERAGE, OR WEAK. THESE WAVES CAN LINE UP SIMULTANEOUSLY OR OVERLAP. THEY RISE AND FALL INDEPENDENTLY OF EACH OTHER.

IN COONEY'S CASE, HE SEEMED TO BE MIRED IN A TAIL-DRAGGING EMOTIONAL DITCH AND A MENTAL FOG WITH LESS THAN TWO DAYS' VISIBILITY, BUT HIS PHYSICAL BIORHYTHM—HIS STRENGTH, BALANCE, TIMING, AND REFLEXES—WAS BANGING ON ALL EIGHT CYLINDERS!

WHICH HELPS EXPLAIN WHY HE TOOK SECOND MONEY IN THE SADDLE BRONC AND WON THE BULL RIDING THAT NIGHT AT THE TABER, ALBERTA, PRO RODEO, WHICH ADDED $1,100 TO HIS WORLD STANDINGS IN BOTH EVENTS.

ACT II

CHAPTER 17

May 31, Tuesday, Day after Memorial Day
Oui Oui's Interview
with Turk and Company,
Denver Tech Center

OUI OUI REESE DIDN'T JUST WALK INTO A ROOM; SHE SUCKED THE AIR OUT of it. When she arrived in the conference room, it was as if a door had blown off a 757 at 35,000 feet, and everyone took their last breath in unison. If God had wanted to sculpt a prototype for Sophia Loren, Raquel Welch, Lynda Carter, Salma Hayek, or the Amazon version of Christina Aguilera, he would have chosen Oui Oui.

For her interview with Turk this fine morning she was wearing a sleeveless, low-cut, tight-waisted, calf-length sheath dress with a slit up the front that ascended to the timberline, high-heeled shoes, an amber ring on her right hand, and matching dangling earrings. No necklace marred her vast expanse of tanned skin.

She had auburn locks that fell past her shoulders, long lashes, brown eyes, and perfect teeth. A curl fell on a naked shoulder. She had the poise of an executioner, the heart of a black widow, and the confidence of the biggest crocodile in the pool.

SO HOW, ONE MIGHT ASK, DID SHE GET HOOKED UP WITH SOMEONE LIKE FILE BLITZER? BECAUSE, DEAR READER, INSIDE THIS FLAWLESS BEAUTY BEATS A HEART AS DEEP AS A BOTTLE CAP.

Many women know the secrets of seduction and practice them, even unintentionally. Many women also know how to drive a car. But when you are a woman who has a current driver's license *and* the anatomical equivalent of Corvette Sting Ray in the garage, you have a definite advantage picking up prospects.

The concept of mutual love and respect was one Oui Oui did not understand. It never crossed her corrupt little mind. Men were to be used. They were always a means to an end and never the end in itself.

Oui Oui did have other traits, such as envy, deviousness, jealousy, duplicity, ambition, narcissism, and a finely tuned radar for the obvious or unspoken lust of *Hominus hairyleggedus.*

"This is Oui Oui Reese, that I've been telling you about," introduced File as proud as punch.

Turk's first reaction was, "Wow."

"It is such an honor to meet you, sir," Oui Oui cooed. "I have enjoyed following your career with the Denver Nuggets, and I'm so happy for your success as a fashion designer, esthetic fashions, I'm referring to.

"I have used your Pit Stop deodorant for years when I'm skiing, hiking, playing tennis, golf, dancing, water polo, so many times. It has saved me embarrassment because I'm so athletic, I guess, I need strong protection. I even wear it when I anticipate having strenuous . . . relations where perspiration might inhibit my free spirit, if you know what I mean."

She looked up into his eyes. She stood at 5 foot 9½ inches tall not counting the three-inch stiletto heels on her shoes. Turk was not looking at her eyes; he was watching her breathe. She noticed. It was going exactly as planned.

"Well, let me offer you a seat, and we can have a nice visit," he pointed toward the conference table.

"Why not over there?" she suggested, pointing at a cozy corner with two arm chairs and a sofa. "It looks so much more comfortable."

"Sure, why not?" agreed Turk, ushering her to one of the arm chairs.

She and Turk sat in the arm chairs facing each other. Nova scooted a chair over from the conference table.

Oui Oui Reese obviously was the perfect woman to represent OVER THE TOP ATHLETIC COSMETICS. She knew how to modulate her voice, was photogenic, knew how to dress, had studied modeling and elocution, had done acting, TV broadcasting, was single, and easily could have been a chorus girl in Las Vegas, a model for *Vogue,* a movie star, a centerfold for Snap-on Tools, or a magazine cover girl for *Low Rider!*

The interview went smoothly, if a bit formal on Turk's part.

As she took his hand to say goodbye and give him a kiss on the cheek, she slipped him a small card with her cell phone number. "Call anytime" she had penciled on it.

Oui Oui left the room, taking the oxygen with her. File followed in her wake.

"My goodness gracious, great balls of fire, Jerry Lee Lay-It-Down Lewis, is there a hurricane named after her yet?" Turk shook his head.

"She is . . . too perfect, too well spoken, too . . ." Turk said.

"Too plastic," interjected Nova. "She is like a windup Barbie Doll."

"But how in the whole wide world can I turn her down?" Turk asked her.

"Well, if I may say, she has too much of everything. Not even human, but a graphic arts depiction from *Roger Rabbit*! I could see her as our representative if we were selling beer, but . . ." Nova paused, trying to convey her reservations without offending her boss. "What I thought we were looking for was authenticity, the real thing."

"You must admit she makes a smashing first impression," said Turk with a sideways grin.

"That she does," agreed Nova. "But how long will it last?"

Turk looked at her, puzzled.

"She wore me out already," said Nova. "I believe she would be pretty high-maintenance."

—~—

As File opened the cab door for Oui Oui in front of the building, she trilled: "Oh, Filly, Filly! What do you think? How did I do? Did I seem too nervous, too pushy? He has been around, but I could see he was impressed. I tried to think like I was business woman, just a normal business woman applying for a job as a bank vice president, or maybe as an ambassador to, you know, some foreign country like Sweden or Saskatchewan . . ."

"Get in the cab, Baby," said File. "You did fine, fine. Listen, I've got to get back in there to close the sale, so to speak. But I'll call you as soon as I can. You just go on back to your apartment. Maybe we could cook in tonight?"

She looked up at him from the cab with provocative pupils and purred, "If I get this job, Fee Fie Foe, I'll be so hot you'll be able to cook your brauts on my front range."

File could smell the smoke.

File had been after Oui Oui's holy grail since he'd discovered her hostessing in a bar at the Atlanta International Airport last spring on his way to a baseball game in Florida. She had dangled it, dragged it across his trail, left tracks through the wilderness with it, and yet it had remained just out of his reach. Her affection, that is. She was not prepared to give it lightly. Unless, of course, it was business.

— ·~ —

Turk, Nova, and File had a spirited discussion that lasted for three hours. They reviewed the photographs, they read Oui Oui's bio and press kit, they looked at video of Pica riding broncs, they hashed over the pros and cons of each and compared.

"The decision is mine to make, ladies and gentlemen," said Turk finally. He lifted one of the photos of Pica's enormous smile.

"Our cowgirl gets a chance. Let's get to work. Nova, call her. Let's get her down here for some . . . lessons! She has six months to make her bones."

At 6:30 p.m. File was comforting a distraught Oui Oui in her apartment.

"I don't know what he could have seen in her," Oui Oui was venting. "If she's as bad as you say, how could she possibly have done a better job than me? Answer me that, File! How could you have let them do it? She's an amateur, a horse bucking rider, for the sake of . . ." She threw a plate of M&Ms across the room. It hit File on the arm. He didn't think it was deliberate, but he was thankful nonetheless that it was a paper plate.

"Look at this!" she stood up, striking a hands-on-hips seductive pose. She strode like a model to the door, spun on her heels, and marched back. "Look at these!" She shimmied and shook. File actually placed his hand over his heart, feeling it fibrillate.

"Can she do *this?!*" Oui Oui screamed, then did six consecutive cartwheels in a row circling the small living room, a 360-degree backflip followed by a leaping split. "Can she? Can she? No! And yet you let them give her the job!

"They are talking national television, File Fink! Print ads! Live appearances!"

"Oui, Honey . . ." File tried.

"It's 'Oui Oui'! Not 'Oui'!"

"Oui Oui, listen . . ."

"Why should I listen? Huh? You won't even fight for me, for my chance at the big time."

"Six months is not that long," said File.

"Sure, it's not that long, to you! To me it's a lifetime, a missed opportunity, a ship in the night, a . . ."

"Wait. Hear me out," he said and waited for her to settle down.

"A lot can happen in 180 days," he explained. "I will be helping set up her schedule, doing her PR, often going with her and with Straight, her male counterpart. I will be in a position to control her activities. Her interviews . . . so, you see, if she doesn't perform well, screws up, misses dates, makes flubs, eventually, meaning after the finals, they will be dying to dump her, and you, my sweet little kitten with a whip, will be waiting in the wings, ready to step in and save the day," File explained.

"You mean," she studied him, "something could happen along the way to poor little Pica, what a stupid name, poor little Pica, a pothole, a brick wall, a booby trap . . . that would . . ." she paused, "I think I see."

Chapter 18

May 30, Monday, 11:00 a.m.

On the Road

Straight was at the wheel of the big Dodge pickup. Cooney was slouching on the passenger side, dog tired but unable to doze off. Neither had said much since they had bid goodbye to the Straight family and hit the road. They were 40 kilometers north of the U.S. border, headed south on Alberta Highway 41.

Straight's mind was clearing family cobwebs from his short-term memory and beginning to think about his new responsibility as spokesman for OVER THE TOP ATHLETIC COSMETICS. He was deliberately submerging any thoughts about his mini-riding slump. Even thinking about it, he imagined, would make it worse.

Cooney was bobbing up and down through his mental and emotional strata from comatose to jittery, but no matter where he stopped, Pica was there haunting the layer.

Myra and Tyra had not known about Cooney's obsession with Pica when they helped salvage him Saturday night and packed him home. They knew only that he had gotten mixed up with Pica's ex-sister-in-law, Tickle, and made a mess of himself. It was only when on Sunday morning Straight had made mention to his sisters that Cooney had a crush on Pica that they realized how badly Cooney had pooped in the buckwheat.

"I screwed the goose again Saturday night," said Cooney above the singing of the tires on the asphalt.

"My and Ty told me," said Straight.

"I can't seem to do nothin' right around her," moped Cooney.

"What I don't quite understand is how you got so deep, so infatuated, or whatever you call it, 'cause you've never even had a date with her . . . or have you?" asked Straight.

94

"No," answered Cooney.

"So how did you get so . . . I mean has she ever said anything to you or written? Have you two been exchanging e-mails or late-night phone calls?"

"No."

"Well, how do you know how she feels?" asked Straight.

"I don't."

"Wouldn't it help to know if she liked you? Seems like that would a natural thing to find out. 'Cause, if she thinks you're a . . . if you're not her type, you could just forget her and quit kickin' yourself around," offered Straight.

"It's not that simple," said Cooney.

"Looks pretty simple to me," said Straight. "If she thinks you're lower than the bottom of a posthole, you're wasting your time, worrying about nothing."

"You don't understand . . ." said Cooney.

"It's not that hard to understand," said Straight. "Just open your eyes!"

"You don't know nothin' about it!" said Cooney.

"I know that when the beer can's empty, suckin' on it won't quench your thirst."

"What does that mean?" demanded Cooney.

"Just that there ain't no peaches on that tree, least none for you," said Straight.

"You are sure getting poetic for someone who's never read a book."

"Ya know, I don't care what you do. If you want to make a fool of yourself over some girl who can ride broncs, have at it. But you better look in the mirror and keep your mind on business," said Straight.

"Yeah, well, I guess you can sure teach me a thing or two . . . Let's see, how much did you win this weekend?" mocked Cooney.

That arrow went right to the heart. Straight blanched. The air went out of him.

"You shot low and got me," said Straight.

Neither spoke. Our heroes knew each other well enough to know how to make the jabs hurt.

"Listen," said Cooney, "I'm sorry. I didn't mean anything. I'm just so tied up about her . . . Pica. I can't describe what's going on inside me. I think about her all the time. And you're right: I got no reason to. She's never given me one bit of encouragement; I wouldn't have a clue what she thinks about me. I feel like dog meat.

"It would be wonderful to just put her out of my mind and have a normal day, but she won't let me. She haunts me. Have you ever been in . . . in love?" he asked.

95

"I think I'm too practical," said Straight thoughtfully. "There's plenty of girls that I find attractive. I've dated a lot, in school, anyway, but none of them ever stole my heart, as you would say. So the answer is 'No,' I guess. I don't even know what love is."

SUMMER LOOMED AHEAD FOR OUR TWO HEROES. IT WAS ALWAYS A GOOD TIME FOR FULL-TIME RODEO HANDS. THEY HAD THEIR SCHEDULE PLANNED OUT AND WERE ENTERING UP AS THEY WENT. BUT BOTH OF THEM HAD DEVELOPED SERIOUS DISTRACTIONS. I GUESS RODEOIN' CAN BE JUST LIKE REAL LIFE.

CHAPTER 19

June 27–July 4, A Particular Thursday, June 30
Greeley, Colorado

IT HAD BEEN A MONTH SINCE NOVA SKOSHA HAD CALLED PICA TO INFORM her that OTT had picked her to be their female spokesperson. They had offered her $25,000 plus all expenses for a trial period to extend through the National Finals Rodeo in December. In other words, Pica had six months to become the image for LIP LASTER. Pica vowed to take it seriously. They had flown her back to Denver for five days of makeover, lessons, and propaganda. Her first appearance had been as a part of the OTT booth for the final three days of the Reno Rodeo. Straight was there only one day, so the rest of the time she was the main attraction.

Reno had not gone as well as Pica had hoped. File Blitzer, her road manager, had arranged for her to do an interview with the local television morning show. The cab driver who was to pick her up was ten minutes late, then couldn't find the television station. By the time Pica finally came racing into the interview room, her hair was a mess, her breath was bad, and she was having a bout of stomach cramps. The show was nearly over, and File was pacing and making excuses to the show's producer.

Pica was on the air less than ten seconds, managed to smile and say thanks. Afterward neither the on-air personality nor the producer had spoken to her. File just shrugged his shoulders and told her these things happen.

OTT had also sent a package to the hotel in Reno that included some monogrammed shirts and three hundred new promo photos of Pica, her smile blazing. After she'd signed and given out half of them at the rodeo grounds she noticed the printer had spelled her name "Pike." She was upset, but File told her to keep signing, that they would get the spelling corrected in the next batch.

She buckled down and made it through the weekend. When she called her dad and told him about the late interview and misspelled promo photos, he said, "Darlin', sometimes ya get bucked off."

On Monday, June 27 she boarded a plane with File and flew to Denver. He went home to his apartment in Boulder, and she drove a rental car to the Ramada Hotel in downtown Greeley, an hour north of Denver. She was going to spend the week in the OTT booth at the Greeley Independence Stampede.

File planned to meet her the next day, and they would open and set up the booth.

To Pica's great relief Tuesday went well. File had brought a new OTT poster that showed her and Straight side-by-side, actually back-to-back, arms crossed, one leg straight, the other bent as if each was leaning against a wall. Their bucking saddles were at their feet. Their hats were pulled down, and her smile shown like that of the Cheshire cat. They were posed against a white background.

From a distance their silhouette on the poster looked like a two-headed cowboy, legs spread wide, arms cocked and ready to draw *pistolas* . . . or if you were an old livestock inspector, it looked like the Death Head brand!

It read:

OVER THE TOP ATHLETIC COSMETICS EXTREME TEAM
LIP LASTER "FOR PROS WHO SWEAT"

It was a tasteful, artistic poster that clashed with the brazen, all-out post-modern splashy artwork that beckoned to teens and twenty-somethings from competing print ads. It was also evident to the "real" cowboy crowd that the two models were the real thing.

OTT was helping sponsor the Greeley Independence Stampede Rodeo Queen Luncheon and Fashion Show at the Clarion. Pica was set up to make a presentation and be recognized as a sponsor. She was expected to give a short speech, which File had prepared for her. He also told her that at 8:00 a.m. Thursday morning a fashion consultant, a friend of his, would be by to pick her up and take her shopping. Pica was not expected to model in the fashion show, but File wanted her to "knock their knickers off!" At 8:00 a.m. on the dot Pica's hotel room phone rang.

"Pica D'TroiT?" asked a woman's formal voice.

"Yes, that's me," said Pica.

"I am Sachet LaNewt [rhymes with 'Chevrolet Ka Poot'], your fashion coordinator. Shall I come up or wait for you in the lobby?"

Pica looked around her room. Clothes were dumped on the extra queen bed. The other was unmade. A scatter of magazines, papers, signing pens, promo photos, business cards, scribbled notes, rental car keys, hotel keys, and change covered the writing table and dresser. Boots, socks, towels, jeans, and undergarments were strewn on the floor. She could not see the bathroom from her position by the phone, but she could imagine the scene postbath, postmakeup, posthair. Did she flush?

"No, I mean, yes, I'll be right down."

Pica had spent most of her young woman years working outside. As a result she had not developed her own sense of style. Being around the house, hunting, or doing chores she wore her hair in a bun or pigtails, wore hiking boots, too-big jeans, and a flannel or wool shirt. She could easily be mistaken for a young boy.

During her few months with Lionel Trane and at the occasional social functions she tended toward "cowgirl sexy." It was a variation of "juvenile mall trash," that is, hip-hugger jeans, tight short-sleeve baby tee, lots of cleavage, bare midriff, and pout. She had never really graduated socially from "high school parking lot rebel." Her immaturity was a factor in Lionel's ending of their relationship. Her sometimes-flirty manner was a means of overcoming her insecurity.

Sometimes she overdid.

This morning she was wearing Justin ropers, khaki Wrangler Riatas, and a button-down Oxford shirt with the OTT LIP LASTER logo. Her hair was pulled back and pinned so that the sides were sleek, and her naturally curly strawberry blonde hair billowed out behind her.

As she stepped off the elevator a hefty woman rose from the waiting area and approached her.

"The preppy look! How metrosexual," the woman gushed. "However, Dahling, it is not quite what we're looking for in a star!"

Sachet LaNewt seemed substantial to Pica, who, at 5' 4" wearing boots, was at least four inches shorter than she. Sachet had a pretty face, brunette hair streaked with gray and pulled back, large tortoiseshell glasses, sensible clunky shoes, support hose, and rather heavy foundation makeup. A white ruffled collar rose from beneath her jacket and was buttoned at the neck.

She was a busty woman with a thick waist and wide hips. At first glance one would be reminded of a frumpy older aunt and not a cutting-edge fashion maven. Pica was reminded of Robin Williams in *Mrs. Doubtfire.*

"I am Sachet LaNewt. Mr. Blitzer has engaged me to prepare you sartorially, so to speak, for your appearance at the Rodeo Queen Luncheon and Fashion Show."

"I'm not supposed to be in the fashion show," said Pica defensively. She had been petrified that they would ask her to model.

"I know, Dahling, I know, but . . ." Sachet raised a finger, "you will be a visiting celebrity. Your company is helping sponsor this event. It is my job to see that you make a lasting impression."

"Yes, but," Pica stammered, "remember, they are all queens, rodeo queens, Miss America types, beautiful, who can . . ." she added with respect, "rope and ride with the best of them."

"Honey, can we talk in the car? We've only got three hours to transform you. I've got a thousand-dollar makeover budget for the morning, and I guarantee you will light up the room!"

On the drive into downtown Greeley, Sachet quickly concluded that Pica had very little knowledge of or allegiance to any particular style. She was just another victim of the "every clothing manufacturer's" latest fad.

Through a prior arrangement the store owner had arranged to open an hour early to allow Ms. LaNewt and Pica some privacy. A well-lit office space served as the fitting room.

Sachet knew exactly what she wanted: black Calvin Klein ultra-low-rise jeans, stiletto Las Vegas cowboy boots with Swarovski crystals, bright orange tops, pointed toes, and a narrow sole. The belt matched the boots.

Instead of a blouse, she selected for Pica a padded halter top with a three-inch tiger-striped waistband that tied in the back. The bra portion was made with polyester sequin fabric that hung from around her neck like shiny silver teardrops. Even as short-waisted as she was, Pica was still showing four inches of bare midriff.

Streaking across the small of her back was the top of a silk lace thong in pale yellow that brazened itself above the pants line.

Bling included large orange ceramic hoop earrings, a choker necklace of black pearls, and a ring on her right middle finger sporting an oval black stone as big as a silver dollar.

Sachet selected a crushable, floppy Nashville/Santa Fe dishrag straw hat with a tiger-striped scarf as a hat band.

After the clothes fitting the two women went to an avant-garde beauty salon, where Pica's long hair was straightened, waved, ratted, and sprayed so that her face was framed by a wild mane. Black and orange sparkles were sprinkled in her hair.

Dark eye shadow and off-red lipstick with a black outline were applied. A silver navel ring was glued on, and as the pièce de rèsistance, a temp tat artist drew "RODEO RAGE" horizontally on her right arm and "LIP LASTER!" vertically the length of her left arm.

The hairdresser, who herself had black and white streaked hair, pierced eyebrows, and a gold tooth, stood back and studied Pica.

"I don't, like, well, ya know, I'm all, so, down with it!" the hairdresser gushed. "Movie star mania, cowboy goth, so hot, so cool, so up, absolutely hectorful. Are you, like, performing around here?"

Pica herself was not sure. She felt like a *kachina* doll or, worse, a kewpie doll. But Sachet kept up a running rave: "Stunning, stupendous, sexy cowgirl, so . . . *cow girl growl!* You will shine!"

As they stepped out onto the sidewalk that brilliant Colorado morning, Sachet dragged an Australian ankle-length oil-skin duster from the back seat and draped it over Sachet's shoulders. Sachet stepped back to admire her. "When they unwrap you, Honey, you'll cause a riot in the firehouse!"

Sachet punched her cell phone, waited, then spoke. "Mr. Blitzer, this is Sachet LaNewt. LaNewt," she repeated. "The fashion coordinator for Ms. D'TroiT." Another pause. "Right! Now . . . your prize is ready. We shall meet you in front of the hotel in twelve minutes. Excuse me a moment." She cast an admiring gaze at Pica and said with a dramatic flair, "She is so beautilicious I must catch my breath."

Pica gave into the praise, conceding that Sachet must know, and spread out a smile so brilliant it blinded a passing motorist!

At five minutes past noon the exchange was made on the sidewalk. File was speechless. Pica was smashing. She would have turned heads at any ultrahip art gallery, jazz bar, or bachelor party in New York, Soho, Paris, or Benihanas anywhere! Maybe not anywhere. For a moment File had begun to doubt that having Oui Oui Reese, aka Sachet LaNewt, prepare Pica for her queen luncheon debut was a good idea.

But, of course, it was not his idea. It was Oui Oui's, and she was a past master of sabotage.

In the conference center ballroom, the rodeo queen program director, Loretta Length, was addressing the audience, who sat at round tables on each side of the banquet room. The stage and runway were built of four-by-four-by-eight-foot risers arranged in a T. The runway split the room, allowing the watchers a good view of the models.

The podium from which Loretta spoke was on the stage. She was doing the welcome, introducing celebrities. File and Pica slid in the backdoor and worked their way to their sponsor's table.

". . . And we'd like to welcome a new sponsor for our Greeley Independence Stampede Rodeo Queen Luncheon and Fashion Show, marketing coordinator File Blitzer and Miss LIP LASTER, Pica D'TroiT!"

Pica watched File stand and wave. He gestured for her to do the same. She stood up. Several eyebrows shot up in unison as if saluting a passing general! Pica had shed her duster. Need I say more?

Consorcia (pronounced "CON-SOR-SHA") Ti rose from her table and discreetly worked her way into the adjoining room. Seven young women were in various stages of being costumed.

She walked over to the tall, twenty-year-old raven-haired woman called Contempla. Contempla was the reigning queen and Consorcia's daughter.

Contempla was an exotic beauty, having inherited her mother's patrician Hispanic features and her father's Oriental eyes.

Bold colors had been Contempla's choice for her ensemble today. But the style conformed to the strict guidelines established in the world of rodeo queen contesting.

Her dress was a black and yellow lambskin with four-inch fringe on the long sleeves and hem. A modest scoopneck set off a tasteful silver necklace.

The hem of the skirt reached halfway between the ankle and knee, covering the top of the boots, which were black ostrich with yellow stitching. She wore a Gist belt buckle as big as Hulk Hogan's.

A black felt western hat displaying her tiara sat like a purring cat above her luxuriant mass of shiny black hair, which shone like an oil slick on rolling waves.

"*Mija*," spoke Consorcia conspiratorially, "you will not believe! Into the room there walked the OVER THE TOP lipstick girl. She is looking like a *puta*, Father forgive me, you will see, I cannot be believing it.

"She is being a disgrace to the *banquete*. So I think I should warn you so you will not make an exclamation upon seeing it!"

"It's okay, Mama," said Contempla. "Nothing can shake me. I am a professional . . . but I will warn the royalty so they won't be shocked. You go on back and sit down."

Contempla turned to the first runner-up, her princess: a blonde from Fort Collins wearing a lavender-purple pigskin dress with silver piping and fringe. She, too, wore a black hat on her cotton-candy hair. Beside her stood the queen of the Cheyenne Frontier Days Rodeo. She wore a turquoise and rustic pink version of the other queens' dresses.

"Mama says the OVER THE TOP LIP LASTER girl is here. But she is not the little barn cat that she appeared to be when I saw her passing out samples in her booth this week," said Contempla to her fellow rodeo royalty.

"What do you mean?" asked the princess. "I sneaked by yesterday, and it looked like she was wearing her brother's clothes!"

"Mama says, and you know Mama." And they all did. She was the ultimate stage mother.

"She is dressed like, in Mama's words, a call girl!"

"At our fashion show?" said Miss Frontier Days indignantly.

Within ten minutes all seven of the royalty were in high dudgeon that someone—and remember that any "someone" can be competition—could actually invade their domain and distract attention from their worthy purpose of promoting professional rodeo.

"Maybe your mother's exaggerating," said a large redhead bedecked in tan and white with black accessories.

"Maybe so," conceded Contempla. "I know I spoke to her, Pica, I think is her name, at the booth OTT has at the rodeo. She was nice enough, maybe even a little shy."

"Well, you make a lot of us a little shy," said Redhead, acknowledging what they all secretly felt in Contempla's presence. She was actually destined to be Miss Rodeo America, Queen Isabella, or Jude Law's leading lady! Contempla was in a class by herself.

Out front a sirloin salad was being served along with cheddar baguettes and a choice of wine or lemon water. As the audience members began garnishing and picking at their lunch, Loretta Length filled them in on the history of the Greeley Independence Stampede Queen Contest. She herself had worn the crown.

Then followed a slide show of past queens and a summary of the contest guidelines for dress, the equestrian competition, and the talent portion, including how judging points were awarded.

Then the seven queen models were presented by last year's queen with a detailed description of their attire. Photographers from the *Greeley Tribune,* the *Denver Post,* the *Fence Post,* and *Pro Rodeo Sports News* snapped pictures like polite paparazzi. The rodeo queen royalty was the height of rodeo fashion: glitzy, western, and elegant, a cross between a Cadillac showroom and a Quarterhorse sale.

After the parade the royalty returned to the stage to enthusiastic applause. The sponsors were invited to say a few words from the podium by way of congratulations. Reps from Wrangler, Montana Silversmith, Justin Boots, Pace salsa, and B & W Trailer Hitches each spoke and shook each queen's hand.

"And next, from our new sponsor, OVER THE TOP ATHLETIC COSMETICS, I would like to introduce Pica D'TroiT!"

At least she pronounced it right, thought Pica. Her mind had been elsewhere during Loretta's lengthy running commentary. She had practiced the short remarks File had written out for her. She didn't give much thought to her appearance. Sachet had said Pica's job was to make a splash. Pica trusted File. He was supposed to know how these things work.

Pica rose from her seat to polite applause. She left her duster on her chair. But as she approached the runway to ascend, the clapping faded into a cavernous silence. Pica was concentrating on her speech and being careful not to trip. She walked the length of the runway toward the podium, and every click of her high-tone boot heels reverberated in the room.

Camera noise and flash were at a minimum. The press was unsure what was happening as the audience watched her tight-lipped. Loretta had been reading her notes through half-glasses and didn't exactly see Pica until she was ten feet from her and closing in!

Lips, teeth, navel, buckle, cleavage, and hat burst upon Loretta's professional composure as if she had opened the door to a chemical toilet and found Cirque du Soleil in the middle of Act II!

Loretta reacted physically to the overload. She grabbed her throat and gasped!

Pica kept coming, oblivious to her reception, the silver sequins on her headlights swinging jauntily with each step as she bounced across the stage.

Pica extended her hand. Loretta gave her a weak smile, then gestured to the microphone.

"Good afternoon to all the rodeo royalty and your committee. I would like to thank you on behalf of OVER THE TOP ATHLETIC COSMETICS and our LIP LASTER for extreme conditions."

Pica sounded relaxed, but she was quite nervous. She smiled and took a breath. "We are glad to be a part of the great rodeo tradition and the contribution these glamorous women make to our cowboy heritage.

"It gives me great pleasure to give each one a necklace bearing a solid gold LIP LASTER dispenser as a token of our respect." Addressing the audience, she said, "And there are samples for each of you here at the table."

Pica presented a small beribboned sack containing a lipstick-like dispenser on a necklace chain to each member of the royal company as they stood poised in a line on the stage.

Pica was shorter than all but one of the royalty. Each one gave her a thin smile or a fake one, shook her hand, and said "thank you." Even though the queens seemed to loom over her like a mountainous skyline of hats and hair, every eye in the audience remained glued to Pica's skin-tight, ultra-low-rise Calvin Klein jeans, bare back, and loosely tied halter top.

Contempla was the last in line. Pica looked up at her and said with a self-conscious laugh, "I hope I'm, like, doing this right. It's really cool to be here."

Contempla was taken aback for a fraction of a second. An expression of disbelief flashed before she could catch herself.

Pica saw it immediately and stepped back, but Contempla's face was frozen in a smile again. Pica swiveled, turned on her high-voltage smile, and strolled down the runway. Cameras chattered like freezing dentures.

She kicked on the high beams and lit up the room.

There was a very short and tentative applause, leaving so much tension in the banquet that it was a wonder that oxygen masks didn't drop from the overhead. An uncomfortable silence reigned until suddenly the photographer from the *Fence Post* said, "My, oh, my!"

Caught by surprise the crowd giggled, then relaxed.

"Thank you . . ." Loretta looked through her half-glasses at the paper she held for a name. "Thank you, OVER THE TOP SPORTS! Now, our next sponsor . . ."

File slipped Pica out the back before the banquet ended. She returned to the hotel and changed into her Twenty X jeans, a long-sleeve button shirt, a bronc riding buckle she had won, and sensible Justin Ropers, a type of flat-heeled plain boots. She was on duty at the booth by six o'clock.

The fallout from Pica D'TroiT's appearance was mixed. The queen committee wrote letters to the PRCA and OVER THE TOP SPORTS complaining of inappropriate dress and behavior, lack of respect for tradition, and ignorance of rodeo etiquette. Mean letters to the editor appeared in the *Greeley Tribune.*

All four papers that covered the event ran variations of the same runway picture. The *Fence Post* ran a full page of photographs: one group shot of the queens and three views of Pica on the runway. The *Denver Post* had her on both the society page and the sports page. This did not please the queen committee.

Contempla listened to the disgruntled, disapproving, carping comments that ensued the next few days, but something puzzled her. In her brief moment of intimacy with Pica, she got the distinct impression that the outrageously dressed ingenue was clueless about the riot she was causing. Her innocence did not seem feigned.

Contempla had noticed one other thing when she had glanced down past Pica's black pearl choker and melons: a belt buckle inscribed "Pica D'TroiT, Champion, Saddle Bronc Riding." It was new.

CHAPTER 20

August 5,
The Republican River at
the Willa Cather State Historical Site

THE FIRST TIME COONEY SAW PICA'S PICTURE ON A LIP LASTER POSTER it was a jolt. His mind immediately replayed the Technicolor visual of her face looking down over the bucking chute in Tucson and blasting him with a smile and crossed eyes.

The poster had been tacked on a wall behind the grandstands at the Livingston Round-Up during Fourth of July rodeo. Matter of fact, posters were everywhere that week—in Red Lodge, Montana; Cody, Wyoming; Molalla and St. Paul, Oregon. Since then the posters had begun appearing at all the rodeos, in western stores, magazines. In some Pica posed alone and in some with Straight.

Because of the publicity campaign obligations for LIP LASTER, Straight was now flying directly into about half of the rodeos returning from media appearances. Pica was often with him.

It appeared to Cooney that all the media effort was working. Many cowboys and rodeo spectators wore the brightly colored hard-plastic LIP LASTER dispensers hanging around their necks on breakaway chains, and Straight saw Pica almost weekly at some promotional event or in the LIP LASTER booth. It was common for Straight and Pica to be seen together in photos and on posters, even in person at events. After two months it was beginning to wear on Cooney.

Straight was sensitive to Cooney's feelings. He tried not to even mention her name unless Cooney brought it up. Then, when he did, Straight stuck to the facts: "Yes, it was fun, yes, we ate together, yes, she's still on tryout 'til the finals. No, she didn't . . . ask about you, that is."

Long drives, long waits, and long nights were all opportunities for Cooney's mind to imagine, think, relive, wish, and worry. He was having trouble sleeping. He was usually traveling solo. He had plans to hook up with Straight at the next rodeo.

Somewhere between Sidney, Iowa (August 3–6) and Dodge City, Kansas (August 3–7) on Highway 281 south of Hastings, Nebraska, his mind swimming with piranhas, Cooney caught a fleeting thought of something Lick Davis had told him. It was that night after the wild cow chase and several tequilas. He tried to remember it, then tried to forget it, but it gave him no peace. He decided to call Lick.

Cooney pulled off the highway onto a dirt road. Several cows were grazing in the adjoining pasture. Signs designating the REPUBLICAN RIVER and WILLA CATHER STATE HISTORICAL SITE were visible from the spot he chose to park.

He shut off the engine, looked up the number, and punched it in. The receptionist answered, "Posthole Poetry Company, may I help you?"

Lick wasn't at home, but the receptionist had just talked to him in a motel in Cortez, Colorado, where he was entertaining that night. She gave Cooney the number.

"Yes?" answered Lick in a businesslike manner.

"Lick Davis?" asked Cooney.

"It's him," said Lick.

"This is Cooney Bedlam."

"By gosh!" said Lick with obvious pleasure. "What a treat to hear from you. I wanted to visit with you more after the speech in Pincher Creek, but I was signin' books and visitin,' you know how it is. I looked for you after, but it was pretty late, and you had left. Anyway, where are you now?"

"I'm on the road. Actually I've just pulled off road. I'm in Nebraska on the way to Dodge City. Me and Straight are both up tonight. He's flyin' in from St. Louis, I think. He's been busy doing promotions for LIP LASTER."

"Yeah," said Lick, "I see his picture everywhere! But I wonder if it's takin' away from his riding . . . I know there's plenty of time left in the season, but he keeps slipping in the standings. But you! You're on a roll! What are you, second or third in the bull riding and in the top ten in saddle bronc? Man, yer hot!"

"Yeah, that's about right," said Cooney. Cooney was actually sixth in saddle bronc, third in bulls, and sixth in all around. Straight was thirteenth in the saddle bronc.

"So, how's your poetry writing?" asked Lick.

"I'm writing some, but . . . I'm more writing sad love song stuff. I can't sing or play, but these sad love poems keep boiling up, and I write and lay awake at night. The words keep coming, and I have to write them down. It's drivin' me crazy. I get about three or four hours of sleep a night. I've started smoking, drinkin' a little more . . . I just can't get this girl out of my mind.

"And I'm jealous, and she doesn't even know me! I'm losing it."

Lick Davis listened to this agonized confession. He remembered unrequited loves from his own life. It was easy to be philosophical now that he was happily married and aged, but old loves are like healed-over wounds. They no longer hurt, but they leave scars as reminders of life's skirmishes on the battlefield of human feelings.

Lick Davis was veteran himself, with several broken purple hearts earned in the love wars. But the man on the other end of the phone was still on the front lines in heart-to-heart combat. It was obvious he was wounded.

"Is it that same girl you alluded to when you were down here at my place?" asked Lick respectfully.

"The same. The very one," Cooney answered.

"Did you have a fight?"

"No."

"Are you still together?" asked Lick.

"No. I mean we've never been together."

"What!" said Lick. "Well, how can you be . . . jealous, or possessive. If you've never, ya know, she was never yours in the first place?"

"That's just it," said Cooney. "I want to take her out, get to know her better . . ."

"Well, why don't you just ask her out?" said Lick.

"I've somehow managed to turn her off. I mean, she kinda came on to me, once . . . Or I think she was, but since then, it seems when I've had a chance to meet her or make contact, something comes up, and I make a complete fool of myself."

"Like what?" asked Lick.

"Like sending her a suggestive e-mail before I hardly met her," said Cooney.

"That works with some girls," said Lick.

"Then I threw up on her boots," said Cooney.

"Well, I've never seen that work with a girl," said Lick, trying to keep from laughing out loud.

"This last time she caught me sloppy drunk and unconscious with her brother's ex-wife. I was at Pincher Creek, yeah, when you were there. That's why I didn't get back to see you. But see, I never connected that was her hometown. I wound up . . ." Cooney rambled on through his tragic tale.

Lick began laughing. By the time Cooney finished with the paramedics and Straight's sisters catching him in the kitchen the next day in his underwear, Lick was bent over and wheezing with delight.

"Cooney," said Lick, gasping and trying to regain control, "if I was you I'd try and tell her the story . . . or just shoot yourself!

"I learned a long time ago that we make mistakes . . . all of us. Unforgivable mistakes. We don't do them on purpose; it just happens. When I was sixteen and just driving I followed a cute girl all over town in my car. It was me and some other guys. We were cool, we had a car, typical high school studs. She finally pulled over. She had another girlfriend in the passenger side. I jumped out, sauntered over to her car, my buddies right behind me. She rolled her window down. I noticed some strange handles on the steering column. "Cool wheels," I said. "How'd you girls like to go to the dance?" just as I noticed she had no legs.

Lick went on: "I have two friends, brothers. One of 'em's wife had cancer and was not expected to live. I wrote a sincere letter of condolence to the couple, assuring them they were both believers, that they would be together again someday. I sent the note off and said a prayer for them. Three days later I get an e-mail saying that she had died. Problem was, I had mixed up the wives. I'd sent a letter to the wrong couple!"

"What did you do?" asked Cooney.

"What could I do? I called them both, apologized, not that the other wife had died, but that I had got it wrong. By the time I had explained the whole chronological screw-up and asked the nonwidower brother to forward the letter on to his brother, we, all three of us, well, four counting the surviving wife, were laughing and crying together.

"See, sometimes you mess up, despite good intentions, ya just mess up. It's the cowboy's greatest excuse and the only one that works."

"I don't know," said Cooney. "I don't think she'll even speak to me."

"Do you ever see her?" asked Lick.

"Everyday, it seems. On some poster or magazine. She's the LIP LASTER girl, for cryin' out loud!" said Cooney.

110

"You mean the one who's on all the posters with Straight?" exclaimed Lick.

"The self-same, dyed-in-the-wool, twenty-four-carat, steel-jacketed, double-barreled, smile-like-a-refrigerator-openin'-in-a-cave-at-20,000-leagues-under-the-sea, luscious, lovely, now-appearing-nightly-in-my-dreams LIP LASTER girl!" reeled off Cooney in a burst of pent-up prose.

"My gosh," sighed Lick. "I kinda figured she and Straight had somethin' goin', you know, have more than a professional relationship." Then he realized he might have misspoken and followed weakly with, "But I'm sure they're not, 'specially since he's got to know that you've got a crush on her."

Cooney let the silence settle.

"Yer in limbo, my fine friend," said Lick. "Love is like a crawfish trap: easy to fall into and hard to find your way out of. Bein' the love advisor that I am, I am torn because it strikes me that your state of constant agitation is related to your stellar performance in the arena.

"Would you give up your chance at rodeo stardom and poetry prestige for a long shot at a gorgeous Canadian gosling you hardly know?"

"Faster'n you can spell *propitiation*," said Cooney.

DEAR READER, WE ARE BACK TO SQUARE ONE. AT THAT FINE LINE BETWEEN ADORATION AND STALKING. IT IS A STORY OLD AS SAMSON AND DELILAH, ROMEO AND JULIET, KATHARINE HEPBURN AND SPENCER TRACY, WINSTON CHURCHILL AND THE BRITISH CITIZENRY.

LICK DAVIS, COWBOY COUNSELOR AT LARGE, HAS ALLUDED THAT COONEY'S EXCELLENT PERFORMANCE IN THE RODEO ARENA MIGHT BE RELATED TO HIS STATE OF CONSTANT AGITATION. IT IS WELL ACCEPTED THAT SONGWRITERS, NOVELISTS, AND POETS WRITE THEIR BEST LOVE BALLADS WHEN THEIR LOVE LIFE IS IN THE POTTY. TRAGEDY, HEARTACHE, PAIN, AND SUFFERING BRING OUT THE UNSELF-CONSCIOUS CRIES TO BE HELPED, TO HAVE PEACE OF MIND, AND TO BE LOVED BACK.

IS COONEY'S SEARCH FOR PERFECTION IN FRONT OF A ROARING RODEO CROWD MERELY A PLEA FOR ADULATION TO FILL THE SPACE BETWEEN HIS EARS SINCE HE CANNOT FILL THE VOID BETWEEN HIS VENTRICLES?

COULD IT BE THAT THE ONLY WAY TO KEEP THE LOVE-HUNGRY BUG OFF HIS BACK IS TO FEED THE THRILL-HUNGRY BUG IN HIS BELLY?

TO SHED THE TORMENTING SHE-FOX OF LOVE, HE RIDES LIKE THE HOUNDS OF HELL.

It was as if Cooney had just admitted he was going to jump off a cliff and hope for a miracle on the way down.

"If that is the case, my young amigo," spoke Lick, "you are beyond my help. Call me along the way when you pass through those clearings when you can see daylight. Adios."

"Goodbye," said Cooney.

Cooney snapped his cell phone closed and sank back into the pickup seat.

His mind began to whirl:

I fell in with a roper, but she threw me for a loop.
I tried to pigeon hole her, but she up and flew the coop.
I thought I had her figgered, but what happened don't add up.
I thought that I was tougher, but she whipped me like a pup.
Love is like a jagged cracker all crumbled in the soup,
And even Humpty Dumpty has admitted he's been duped.
Can a fancy-dancy lipster ever fall for Bronco Bill,
Or is she bound to sort him like a baleen seines a krill? . . .

Cooney placed his palms flat against his temples and pressed. "Stop it! Stop it!" he screamed at himself.

Cooney opened his briefcase and looked at the Baggie that Lipo Conrad, better known as Star Child behind the chutes, had given him a week earlier. Lipo was a New Age bull rider who meditated, practiced yoga, and did incantations. He claimed Indian ancestry, though he still looked like the same stereotypical blond beach boy who had written "Surf the World" under "ambitions" in his Santa Monica high school annual.

Lipo had noticed Cooney's agitated state and had given him some of his magic elixir. Cooney had been afraid to try the Star Child Stress Potion, but on this hot afternoon he had reached a desperate point. He had never tried any illegal drugs, not even marijuana.

Cooney took a pinch of the dried, leafy mix from the Baggie, rolled a smoke with the cigarette papers Star Child had been gracious enough to include, and inhaled deeply. Tensely he awaited some reaction. After two minutes: nothing. He took another long drag and blew out the smoke. Then another . . . he felt a tiny buzz in the back of his head. He lay back against the seat and looked languidly out the open window on the driver's side.

Another long drag; the rolled paper crumbled in his fingers. A small pinch of the leaves fell into his palm. He looked at them bovinely, then popped the remains into his mouth.

As he chewed he dully took in the scenery. Where was he? Was he a Republican? If not, did he have the right to be on their river? One of the cows began to levitate. He drooled in amazement. In the basement of his brain, where the fuse box became a Hydra, a connection was made.

Many times he'd been out checking cows for his grandpa, following a fresh cow track, and then suddenly it would disappear! The levitation explained it all. It was a life-changing experience.

Then the Republican sign began to rock like a boat. Three doctors—he guessed they were doctors—were rowing the boat toward the other sign. They were after Willy's catheter. Cooney knew what a catheter was; he'd had surgery before. Only he was not aware that catheters were kept in a historical site. Just his luck to park beside it. Now they were going to park it in him!

"There's nothing wrong with me," he said as he clumsily got the door open and fell to the dirt. "They're coming! They're coming!" Cooney crawled on his belly under the barbed-wire fence into the cow pasture. *They can't get me here,* he thought with relief.

He sat up, sort of. The field was full of cows. He had to think a minute what they were. But one said, "I'm a cow. Be not afraid. Cows do not eat bronc riders."

"But," he said, "I am not a bronc rider. I am a lion creeping through the savannah to come and milk you. I am a snake on the lawn looking for a croquet ball. I am a catheter in a field of urethrae. I am a mosquito sneaking up on a pork chop."

Suddenly he felt ants crawling on his body. They were in his boots, down his back, and up his pant legs. He pulled off his boots, got out of his pants and shirt, and rolled himself in the tall grass. As soon as the cool air freshened his skin, the itching stopped.

He lay there on his back staring up at the light blue Nebraska sky. The occasional cloud painted its way across the canvas. He was overcome with joy, then the giggles, then melancholy, then exhaustion, then sleep.

In his dream he was kissing Pica. Her luscious lips pressed against his. The palms of her hands lay on his forehead and chin. She was moving his head gently to place her lips precisely on his. He could feel himself responding to her ardor. As his mind rose from the swamp mist into clarity, he probed gently with his tongue. He could feel holes in the picket fence of her incisors.

He thought to himself that she hadn't shaved for a day or two . . . or were those his whiskers? And . . . he didn't chew Copenhagen. It was certainly a surprise to find out that she did. The strong smell of fish enveloped him, then suddenly she pinched his nostrils closed and blew a hot breath into his mouth.

A confluence of feelings surrounded him as he reached up to run his fingers through her hair only to find that she had apparently gone bald since he'd seen her last.

Cooney opened his eyes and looked right into the cloudy eyes of Loyal Dimwiddie.

Cooney pushed Loyal off him and scooted back through the grass like a scuttling crawfish. In his haste he dragged his white Jockey shorts right across a fresh pile of cow manure. He stared up at Loyal in terror.

Loyal had been fishing the river, as he did often since he'd retired. He had a catfish the size of a cocker spaniel, already gutted and cleaned and in a cooler in the back of his pickup. He made his own stinkbait out of garlic and chicken liver with just a sprinkle of seasoning salt. His secret ingredient was Elmer's glue. It held the bait together well, but it was hard to get off your hands.

Loyal was in the process of having all his teeth pulled once and for all so he could get dentures, but he was in that awkward stage between the initial excavation and "Say, 'Cheese'!" And he'd had a cold fried-egg and onion sandwich with Miracle Whip for lunch, then a big dip of Copenhagen.

Loyal had seen the stranger's pickup pull in and just assumed it was a weary traveler stopping for a nap. It was only when he had packed up and driven by the vehicle on the way home that he had noticed the open car door and had seen the nearly naked body out in the pasture.

At first Loyal thought the pilgrim might be sunbathing. But the open, unlocked pickup with a computer and other valuables lying in the seat led him to suspect a problem. He walked to the fence and called many times. The body never moved or gave an answer. Clothes were scattered about. Loyal climbed through the wire and approached the body. He could not see breathing, but then again, his eyesight wasn't all that good. A touch or two with his boot toe and a prod with his finger elicited no response.

As a last resort Loyal spit out his chew, took off his hat, wiped his hands on his overalls, and began to apply mouth-to-mouth resuscitation.

What happened after that cannot not be summed up very tidily. Suffice it to say Cooney was incoherent, Loyal didn't stay, and a curious cow ate the evidence.

CHAPTER 21

August 15, Monday
Boise Airport

STRAIGHT AND PICA HAD SPENT TWO DAYS SHOOTING A ONE-MINUTE television commercial for ESPN 2. The shoots were long; they said their lines over and over, posed and smiled, and earned their wages. They were both tired.

Pica was vaguely aware that Cooney would be picking Straight up at the Boise airport, and when Straight offered her a ride, she declined. She could be civil, but she didn't want to be in the car with Cooney Bedlam. He gave her the willies.

Cooney had killed three hours napping in the Boise airport parking lot, waiting to pick up his partner. He woke with a start when his phone rang and headed toward the baggage claim. There he saw Straight just coming out the door with his war bag and briefcase. Pica D'TroiT was with him. She had even given Straight a quick peck on the cheek and hurried off toward File Blitzer, who stood by his rented Cadillac Eldorado Biarritz waiting on the curb.

Now Straight and Cooney were headed west on Interstate 84 toward Caldwell, Idaho. Cooney was driving and tumbling in a green storm cloud of jealousy, frustration, humiliation, and lovesick blues.

"Git it out, whatever it is," said Straight. "I've about had it. Ever since Pincher Creek when she wrote you off you've been takin' it out on me."

"Knock it off," warned Cooney.

"No, you knock it off. I can't make her like you. I've told her you're a good guy, but you've pooped in the buckwheat so many times, there's not much I can say. Doin' it with her ex-sister-in-law had to be the high point of stupidity.

"I've put as many good words in for you as I can. When I mention your name she just holds her hands up and covers her ears!"

"I saw her kiss you," said Cooney darkly.

"Where?" said Straight.

"Right there at the door, back at the airport."

"Oh, man. You are losing it. We work together, for crying out loud! I like her, she likes me. We spend lots of time together, but it's business."

"Yeah, right," said Cooney sarcastically.

"What are you getting at?" asked Straight.

"Nuthin'. I'm just beginning to feel like your butler, your chauffeur. You fly all over. I drive and bring your riggin'. You'd think you were some high-class calf roper that needs his valet to haul his horses to the next show," griped Cooney.

"It's only a gear bag and saddle," said Straight. "Besides, I pay half the gas. Look, Cooney, I'm sorry she doesn't like you. I wish she did. Sure make my life easier! You're hard to be around. That might be what's hurting my riding."

"Now it's my fault you're in a slump?" shot back Cooney.

"No, I didn't mean that . . ."

"So, because I'm driving all over the country waiting on you like some celebrity athlete, you can't seem to spur a bronc? I'm breaking your concentration, am I? Maybe it's the bright lights and TV spots. You're living the high life with your big endorsement, and I'm picking up your laundry?" Cooney's tone was ugly. "Maybe you're just feeling guilty."

"Quit pushing, Cooney. I'm wore out."

"All that posing and smiling must be exhausting," said Cooney.

Straight bent his head back against the seat, stretching his neck. "Anytime you wanna split, just say so. I can't take much more of this."

JEALOUSY FEEDS ON A FERTILE IMAGINATION. ITS MEDICAL EQUIVALENT WOULD BE HAVING A HEAD-SPLITTING MIGRAINE. ITS ARTISTIC EQUIVALENT WOULD BE COVERING A STATUE OF SADDAM HUSSEIN IN PIGEON DROPPINGS. AND ITS MUSICAL EQUIVALENT WOULD BE CASTRATING PIGS IN A METAL BUILDING.

JEALOUSY IS A SMOTHERING, PERVASIVE FOG THAT SLITHERS IN LIKE A PROPANE GAS LEAK AND CLOUDS THE MIND. IT IS ALSO OUT OF BOUNDS, AGAINST THE RULES, USUALLY UNFAIR, AND CANNOT BE CURED WITH REASON.

IN THE END IT IMPLODES, DESTROYING THE AFFLICTED, OR VANISHES OVERNIGHT TO EVERYONE'S EVERLASTING RELIEF.

STRAIGHT IS TRYING TO BE PATIENT, BUT HE HAS HIS OWN
PROBLEMS, AND JEALOUSY HAS COONEY'S HEART IN A VISE.

"They've got me a room at the Holiday Inn Express," said Straight as
they pulled off the freeway into Caldwell. "It's got double beds."

"I think I'll just drop you off and park behind the arena . . . sleep in the
camper," said Cooney.

"You can leave your gear in the truck. But . . . thanks anyway."

CHAPTER 22

August 15, Monday Evening
Caldwell, Idaho

COONEY SLEPT FITFULLY FOR AN HOUR, THEN GOT UP AND WALKED OVER TO Victor's, a fine dining restaurant and bar at the edge of the fairgrounds that housed the rodeo arena.

Unbeknownst to our blurry hero, File Blitzer, duplicitous road manager for Straight and Pica, had surreptitiously picked up Oui Oui Reese at the airport that morning, and the two of them had slipped unobtrusively into Victor's dining room and sat in a corner booth.

"So, Sweeto-muss," Oui Oui was cooing at File, "when is little Pica Poot going to fall on her face? I'm getting anxious. You know I'm already planning my wardrobe for the national finals. I've got this cute little see-through knit tee with an unborn calf-hide bustier, black and white, hair side out, that will knock your socks off. I brought it to model for you this evening.

"I'm thinking OTT LIP LASTER girl, *Vanity Fair* cover or maybe *Stud, GQ, Esquire*. This is gonna be big." She rubbed her buxomness against his arm. "Of course, I'm not wearing it now. I'm not wearing anything now," she purred.

File felt a catch in his chest. She had just plugged in his toaster.

"Soon, Baby, soon. That little trick with the whoopee cushion in Vernal, the toilet paper stuck to her saddle during the grand entry in Calgary, the bogus e-mail about her secret love child with the commissioner . . . It's just that she's getting determined not to let her pitfalls stop her."

"I'm getting impatient, Mega File!" Oui Oui fumed, then turned plaintive. "I want this for both of us. I'm not just thinking of myself, Smooky. You'd be happy if I was happy, right?

"Maybe we're going at this from the wrong angle. Something in her past or private life that could be revealed. Start a rumor that she's a member of PETA, doesn't like rap music, or takes steroids?

"We need to exploit her weakness," she concluded.

Well," said File, "there is this one thing. I don't know how we could use it, but I've heard she has a stalker. Not really a stalker but some rodeo clodhopper who has a crush on her and she hates him."

"How do you know?" Oui Oui asked.

"I've overheard Straight and Pica talking. He's Straight's rodeo buddy. I've seen him occasionally, but I don't know him. Straight keeps trying to defend him, but Pica doesn't want to hear it. Maybe we could get a wedge in there somewhere . . ."

Oui Oui's infinitely devious mind began plotting. "Like maybe frame her for a crime . . . the two of them plan some scheme . . . some scheme that interferes with . . . cheat another rodeo rider's chances, they get exposed . . ."

Oui Oui sipped her wine and looked away in thought.

"My gosh!" said File, pointing at Cooney. "There he is!"

Just at that moment Neville Schneer, sports columnist for the *Owyhee Avalanche Weekly*, stepped to their table. "By gosh, aren't you File Blitzer?" exclaimed Neville.

"Well . . . uh, yes . . . Yes. I am he," said the startled File. "Do I know you?"

"Maybe not, but I know you," smiled Neville. "You are Pica D'TroiT's manager, if I'm not mistaken."

A thunderhead rolled across Oui Oui's expressive brow. File caught her expression and paused. He gave her a conspiratorial smile and said, "Road manager would be the exact title."

"I'm covering rodeo week. I have a column in the paper. How is Pica doing? Does she like her new position with OVER THE TOP ATHLETIC COSMETICS?"

"It's taking her some time to get adjusted. She was pretty green when she took the temporary job of road rep," said File.

"You mean she's just on trial, so to speak?" asked Neville.

"Yep," said File.

"Well," said Neville jokingly, "I guess she could go back to riding saddle broncs."

Neville glanced over his shoulder to see Cooney getting up. "Hey, Cooney, how ya doin'?"

Cooney eased over to their table.

"I'm File Blitzer. I'm the road manager for your buddy Straight." File offered his hand.

"Cooney Bedlam," said Cooney genially. "I've seen you around. Straight says you do a good job."

"Thanks. Say . . ." File directed his comment to Neville. "Did you hear that Pica is going to exhibition a bronc this week?"

"No! Wow! That should be a crowd pleaser!" exclaimed Neville. "There's a background story on her I remember that talked about her rodeo skills. You don't see them competing in pro rodeo. I wonder if they could. Can a woman ride as good as a man?

"Cooney, what do you think?"

Cooney knew he'd better keep his mouth shut. He just shrugged his shoulders.

Oui Oui sensed an opportunity. She didn't know for what exactly, but she played a card. "Well, I personally think it is silly. Of course, girls can't ride bucking horses as well as a man. If they could . . . they would! Or else why don't they?"

"They don't," said Neville, "because the men won't let them belong to the Professional Rodeo Association."

"That's not true," said Cooney.

"It's like letting women play in the pro basketball league. They'd get creamed!" added Oui Oui. "Besides, they all look so butch. Don't you think so?" she asked Cooney.

"Think what?" asked Cooney

"That women should keep their place. You see it everywhere, in college, in grade school, girls playing football. Wearing the pants in the family. Now the feminists have taken over rodeo. Where does it end?" Oui Oui was on a roll. "Do you think it's fair for women to get paid more than men if they can't do the same job? Do you, do you? I've about had it with those hairy-legged women trying to prove they can ride better!"

"I guess I don't think about it much," said Cooney, suddenly uneasy with this loud woman. "You just don't see 'em, so even if it is allowed, it's obvious that women can't ride broncs as well as men, or we'd see a lot more of them. They're good at other things: roping, barrel racing, baking cookies, and having babies."

"Oops," said Neville. "My tape just ran out."

"I gotta be goin' anyway," said Cooney. "Nice to meet you, ma'am, boys."

Cooney headed back to the contestant parking area at the back of the rodeo grounds. The lights were on in the arena, which caused him to change directions to see what was going on. A cherry picker parked in the arena was extended, and a workman was replacing one of the big lights. Cooney noticed movement behind the bucking chutes and walked over.

Out of the dark shadows Pica D'TroiT strode and literally ran into Cooney. "Oops. Sorry!" she said, then realized into whom she had crashed.

"My gosh!" was all Cooney could say.

She raised her eyebrows and chuckled. "I was hoping I'd get to meet you someday."

Across Cooney's brain paraded visions of him barfing on the sidewalk in Miles City and being flat on his back in Pincher Creek. "Me, too," he said. "At least on a day when I was able to talk."

She looked at him kindly. Finally she said, "I've always sort of hoped you weren't as bad, as uh . . . as . . . help me out here, Cooney, from your first e-mail I assume you are a man of words."

"'Sorry' would be my first choice, if it was me. You hoped I wasn't as sorry a human being as it appears I am every time you see me."

"That might be a little harsh," she said.

"Oh, I don't know. Truth is, I . . . I've been intrigued, I guess, since the first time I saw you," said Cooney.

"Behind the chutes at Tucson," she stated.

"Yeah, when you stared at me and crossed your eyes. In my mind I keep playin' over all my slipups and major faux pas. Thinkin' how stupid I must look to you, when I really just wanted to get to know you. I get fuzzy. It makes it hard to keep my mind on my business."

"Looks like you've been doin' good," she said." Ranked in the bulls and the broncs."

"Yeah, I can't explain it," he said.

"Straight is worried about you," she said.

"I'm not proud of that. He's got enough on his mind tryin' to do all that publicity stuff and rodeo, too. I'm not helpin' much. I've not been a very good partner. I need to make it right with him. Word's out that you're gonna exhibition a bronc this week?"

"Yessir," she said. "That's what I was doing here tonight. Checking out the chutes."

"You need help gettin' down?" Cooney offered.

"Thanks, but Straight has offered to help. I think it will be after the bronc riding Friday."

"Well," said Cooney, "it was nice to talk to you. It really was. Good night."

At 10:00 p.m. that night, Lick Davis's message machine came on. "You have reached Lick Davis and the Posthole Poetry Company. Nobody's here right now, so the javelina is checking this machine. You can leave your message, but talk slow 'cause he has trouble makin' his *m*s and *n*s. Something to do with cloven hooves, I think. Or you can try back during business hours, nine to five Cowboy Standard Time. Thanks . . . [*click*] . . ."

"Lick, this is Cooney Bedlam. I had a nice conversation with Pica tonight. I didn't insult her or throw up on her shoes or nuthin'. Maybe things are takin' a turn for the better, and I'll get a break!

"Take care, amigo. Adios!" he said. "I hope I'll be seeing you around."

Chapter 23

August 17, Wednesday
Caldwell Night Rodeo

When the *Owyhee Avalanche Weekly* came out on Wednesday, the headline on Neville Schneer's column read: Girl to Ride Bronc at Caldwell Rodeo! Not All Cowboys Are Impressed!

Cooney Bedlam, a ranked saddle bronc rider, was quoted as saying, "It's obvious women can't ride bronc as good as men . . . they're better at baking cookies and having babies."

After Cooney had had his short, uncomplicated conversation with Pica, his attitude improved mightily. He'd placed fifth in the bull riding the night before. He'd drawn Crash Bar in the saddle bronc riding for that night, and he was pleased with the draw. He had made an effort to be more pleasant to Straight, had rode his bronc on Tuesday, and taken fourth. They had helped each other get down onto their respective bucking beasts. It felt like old times, PPI (Pre-Pica Infatuation).

The two of them stood behind the bucking chute. Crash Bar stood beneath them wearing Cooney's bronc saddle. All three were waiting tensely for the team roping event to finish. "The only thing I wish I could tell you is how to set your rein. Most of the guys who got bucked off left it too long. Crash just holds his head back, and they flop right out of the seat. I admit I've tried to outguess him. I took it short and got lucky twice. But if you leave it short, and he bogs his head, it's *sayonara*, baby!" counseled Straight, who'd drawn Crash Bar before.

"Six of one or a bird in the bush," malapropped Cooney.

"You could try somewhere in the middle," said Straight. "But you won't do that. I know you. It's all or nuthin'." He smiled.

When the bronc in the chute ahead of them went, Cooney straddled his horse. He eased down as Straight kept a hand hold on his vest, ready to pull

123

Cooney out if the horse acted up. His boots found the stirrups, and he held them back like a jockey. Cooney took the soft, loosely braided rein with his right hand and pulled it straight along the neck and over the pommel. With his left hand he reached down and gripped the rein.

Straight watched to see where Cooney took his grip. "A fist," he observed aloud. Then Cooney measured one finger. He was leaving a short rein. *All or nuthin',* thought Straight.

Cooney glanced quickly up at Straight and said, "Gotta try it."

The next few seconds became a whirlwind of gate ropes being moved, the horse's head being steadied, legs being cocked, hat being pulled down, rein being lifted, body being flexed, and head nodding!

Bang! The gate swung wide. Crash Bar arced into the sky; the crowd cheered! At the apex of the leap, when Cooney was at his greatest distance from the Earth, he considered for a microsecond that he would know, when Crash Bar's front feet hit the ground, whether or not he had guessed right on the length of rein.

If the big horse held his head up, like Cooney had bet, it would be smooth sailing. He would have considered the other option, but he ran out of microseconds.

Crash Bar came down on his front feet and stuck his head between his knees, and Cooney was catapulted into the loamy Canyon County dirt! It was not a graceful landing. He actually did a complete flip to land face down.

CHAPTER 24

August 19, Friday
Caldwell Night Rodeo

PICA'S SCHEDULED EXHIBITION BRONC RIDE HAD RAISED THE LEVEL OF excitement for Friday night's performance. In the days since Neville Schneer's column had come out, she had done four radio and television interviews locally in the Treasure Valley. The first, a 6:45 a.m. on Channel 7's *Morning Show*.

Just to clear the air, women are not prohibited from competing in the U.S. PRCA, but the prohibition is widely believed because so few women participate. However, it is true that women are not allowed to compete with men in the Canadian Pro Rodeo Association.

The night before the *Morning Show* the producer had read Neville Schneer's column and had prepped the on-air hosts. A summary of the interview went something like this:

"We understand that women are not allowed to compete in the saddle bronc . . . bronco? Am I saying it right? . . . riding contest, yet you have won prizes for riding these wild horses?"

"That's right, Lauree, but it . . ."

"That must really chap . . ."

"Great pun, Lauree!" teased the male co-host.

"Oh, 'chaps,' ha, ha. That must really make you feel totally discriminated against."

"Well, it's not that they aren't allowed . . ." tried Pica.

"Have women, cowgirl women protested? I mean they should. One of the cowboys, Cooley Beldam, was quoted as saying 'women can't ride.' Pretty insensitive, if you ask me. Chauvinism is alive and well!"

Turning to the camera Lauree struck her serious pose, which involved pursing her lips and raising her eyebrows. "What say you, girls? Let's show up at the Caldwell Night Rodeo tonight to support Pica D'TroiT, lady bronco buster!"

Two more radio and one television interview took up the cause. File had located a copy of Schneer's column and the inflammatory quote for Pica to read.

". . . Better baking cookies and having babies! Can't ride broncs!" she responded in disgust, then turned the hurt inward. Had he really said that about her? Was it before or after their brief encounter Wednesday night? *Two-faced, conceited,* and *lying* were her top three adjectives. She concentrated her rage into psyching up for the big ride that night.

Pica tried to call her dad but was unable to reach him. But she knew what he would have said: "Be smart. Don't get distracted. Keep your mind right side up. Otherwise, you'll prove his point."

That night twenty-five or so redneck good-time girls protested for women's rights to ride. The carried a few signs and a few beers and were thrilled to perform for the local TV stations that were filming the minihappening.

Needless to say, Pica's appearance at the OVER THE TOP ATHLETIC COSMETICS LIP LASTER booth created a mob scene.

Pica was the only one who seemed to see no humor in the hurrah. She and the local activist director of the National Organization of Easily Offended Women.

After the rodeo had begun, the announcer made the protesters part of his patter.

At the conclusion of the saddle bronc riding he called for a prerecorded drum roll. "And . . . now what we've all been waiting for! An exhibition bronc ride by OVER THE TOP'S LIP LASTER GIRL! The one, the only, our own queen for a day, from Pincher Creek, Alberta, Canada, our neighbor to the north! Welcome Pi-Ka Deeee-Troy-Tuh!"

As prearranged, Pica came galloping into the arena posting the OTT flag. She was wearing her buckin' horse chaps, a long-sleeve buttercup-yellow satin shirt with light green yoke and cuffs sporting dark fringe, and a furry Larry Mahan hat that had come out of the chute with her more than once. Her strawberry-blonde tresses trailed like turbulent golden smoke.

The horse she was riding was a magnificent palomino stallion tacked out in black and silver gear. They made a complete circle, then whirled to the center of the arena, did a 360-degree roll each way, backed ten yards, then the stallion reared up like Trigger!

Every horseman in the crowd, from backyard owner to dressage trainer, got goose bumps.

There was no doubt to anyone in the grandstands and behind the chutes that this girl could ride.

As Pica gathered up the big stallion and controlled him around the arena and out the gate, the announcer primed the pump. "We have a real treat tonight. The Caldwell Night Rodeo has invited Pica D'TroiT, OTT's LIP LASTER girl, to exhibition a saddle bronc. Pica hails from Pincher Creek, Alberta, and comes from a family of good Canadian bronc riding brothers.

"For you ladies who have come tonight to support Pica . . ." The protesters cheered as if he was Pat Sajak. "And saw the news today . . ." Boos interrupted his attempt to inform. "We're going to give her a chance to prove him wrong!" Wild cheering broke out.

"Pica is going to ride Crash Bar," intoned the announcer, "one of Cervi Rodeo Company's best bucking horses. Matter of fact, two nights ago this horse bucked off Cooney Bedlam, national finals qualifier and presently third in the world standings." A chorus of loud, extended booing came from those in the audience who made the connection between the insult and its author.

"Dropping down in chute number 4. Her LIP LASTER partner, past world champion Straight Line, is helping Pica get set."

"You sure you don't want the vest?" asked Straight, referring to the padded safety vest most rough stock riders wear nowadays.

"Nope." She bit off the word, her body tight as a spring.

"But . . ." Straight started.

"Don't worry about me, Straight. I know what I'm doing."

She was thankful she had continued to carry her bronc saddle in her camper. Because of her small size, it would have been difficult to borrow one.

The horse fell back a little. Straight, who had his hand around her belt in the small of her back, lifted her six inches above the saddle.

The horse settled again. Pica dropped down onto him instantly and leaned back.

AH, DEAR READER AND RODEO FAN, THIS IS THE FUNNEST, NOT FUNNIEST, FUNNEST PART OF WRITING RODEO NOVELS. DOES SHE RIDE CRASH BAR? DOES SHE GET BUCKED OFF? IS COONEY WATCHING? WHAT WILL BE HIS REACTION? NOT TO MENTION THE REACTION OF TURK MANNIQUIN, HER EMPLOYER, AND OUI OUI REESE, HER NEMESIS. SO MANY RAMIFICATIONS, SO MUCH RIDING ON THE NEXT 8 SECONDS.

AND WHAT WAS CRASH BAR'S PART IN THE DRAMA? JUST TO DO
HIS BEST, FRIENDS. HE WINS EITHER WAY AS LONG AS HE DOES WHAT
HE IS FED TO DO: BUCK OFF THE RIDER OR HELP HER GET A GOOD
SCORE. IT IS A SIMPLE AND HONORABLE OCCUPATION, THAT OF BUCK-
ING HORSE. IT IS ON A PAR WITH MAILMAN OR A PRISONER ON THE
HIGHWAY LITTER PATROL.

Pica knew the book on Crash Bar. She had to make the same decision
as Cooney had the night before, that is, how much rein to give the horse.
Straight had warned her about Cooney's gamble—that he had gripped too
short and had been pulled out over the top. Pica's resentment told her to do
the opposite, but she had a secret. She always took a booth break during the
saddle bronc riding to watch. Cooney was her favorite bronc rider. He took
chances and "rode the fire out of them," as critics were wont to say. That was
her preferred style as well.

At the last second she slid her grip a full fist width up the rein, shorten-
ing it. She lifted her arm and nodded her head. Straight started to say, "You
sure?" But it was lost in the cacophony of the audio man's explosion and the
crescendo of the crowd.

Crash Bar did her a dirty. He raced two steps into the arena before he
broke in two! But he was going too fast to get his head very low. Pica rang
the rowels along his side. He rose as she swung her legs forward to reset the
spurs on the side of his neck.

Two good bucks, and he wobbled on the downbeat toward his left. Pica
got off center of her saddle. She held to him a fraction of a second longer
with her left spur. It was enough to regain her balance. The last four seconds
she rode him like a wildcat trying to open a Christmas gift.

At the whistle she did a flying dismount in the style of Neatsfoot
Hawkins, former world champion saddle bronc rider.

WHICH LOOKS EASY TO A SPECTATOR, BUT TRY IT YOURSELF OFF THE
FENDER OF YOUR CAR AT 20 MPH NEXT TIME YOU GO TO TOWN.

The crowd's reaction was as expected. Pica's collateral had squared itself,
algebraically speaking.

She took bows for a full minute, pointed to the booth, blew everyone a
sumptuous kiss, and left the arena the new rodeo "It Girl."

Cooney and Straight had watched her exhibition ride from the catwalk behind the chutes.

"Man, she pulled that one outta the fire!" said Cooney.

"Yes." Straight agreed. "Not too high on style points, but ya gotta give her credit."

"She took a short rein, didn't she?" asked Cooney "Did you tell her to do that?"

"No," answered Straight, "it was her idea. Oh," Straight said. "I told her I'd get her saddle. I better go grab it. I'll be back to put you down on your bull."

Pica was headed toward the arena exit when she looked up to see Straight's backside climbing down and Cooney watching her. He gave her a big smile and a thumbs-up. She returned him a slit-eyed glare, did an eyes-front, and disappeared.

A cowboy standing near Cooney saw it all. "I guess that will teach you to keep your mouth shut."

"I didn't say anything," said Cooney, puzzled.

"Only that girls can't ride buckin' horses. That's all. Just insulted half the human race. Probably will get you blackballed from the Buckle Bunny Hop and hung in effigy on *Oprah*."

"What are you talkin' about?" asked Cooney.

The cowboy explained.

Cooney shrank inside.

CHAPTER 25

Last Ten Days of August
Pica's Story

OVER THE NEXT TWO WEEKS PICA DID NOT MAKE A SINGLE RODEO BOOTH appearance. She was too busy. She had her picture in *Sports Illustrated*, *USA Today*, and the *High River Regional*. She appeared on *The View, Ellen DeGeneres Show, Larry King, Tonight Show*, and ESPN. Cooney rode four bulls and four saddle broncs and placed in the money five times. Straight worked the OTT booth next to cardboard likenesses of Pica, answered questions about her, and gave away her autographed posters. He was beginning to show definite symptoms of anxiety and depression. He dropped to sixteenth in the world standings.

At 7:30 a.m. on the day after Pica's famous ride, Lick Davis had been sitting on the south-facing veranda watching the monsoon clouds jostle around in the sky. When the family and friends phone line rang, Lick answered, "Yes?"

"Lick, it's Cooney Bedlam."

"Cooney! Are ya callin' to invite me to the wedding?"

"Oooo, no," moaned Cooney. "I think I have brought down the wrath of Amazon dot Estrogen on my sorry self."

"Tell me about it, Son," said Lick, relishing the opportunity to manipulate young minds.

By the end of the sad tale Cooney had tears in his eyes. So did Lick, but his were tears of hilarity. Lick had actually covered the speaking end of the receiver with his scarf to avoid disruption of the narrative.

"So by the time I showed up at the club where the dance was, a bunch of irate girls chased me back out the door, throwing beer on me and calling me names."

"Like what?" Lick managed to choke out.

"Common bred, second string, no dice, diaper bag, bad draw, goat colon . . ."

"Goat co . . ." Lick was gasping. Finally he gained some semblance of control. "First off, I'd say in her eyes you are lower than whale scat in the Marianas Trench. Is there anything else you could possibly do to make her opinion of you worse?"

"Maybe shoot some baby seals," offered Cooney, "or call for a tax increase on orphanages."

"Cooney, do you ever get the feeling that this romance isn't meant to be?"

"I don't give it that kind of thought," said Cooney in love. "I've just got it in my mind that we could . . . be friends, I guess. I wrote this last night after I got tarred and feathered in the bar. If she only knew how I feel, get to know the real me.

She's the passion that I ride for, she's my clarity of mind.
She's the breath of open spaces all my life I've tried to find.
I've been captured by her tiger, I'm enraptured by her lamb.
She defines my whole existence and revealed the Who, I am.

Lick let that eloquent statement hang in the atmosphere for a respectful moment, then spoke. "Cooney, there are men doing life in prison on less evidence than we have showing you are guilty of screwing up royally. It is apparent that you are in felony denial.

"There can be two approaches: One, wait patiently 'til hell freezes over and hope she forgets your transgressions, or, two, exacerbate the wound and hope that a new wave of inflammation will overcome the chronic revulsion she obviously feels for you."

"Maybe you could explain," said Cooney.

"If you wait you won't make it any worse than it is. And if you chase her you might could miraculously break right through to her heart," explained Lick.

"Sounds risky to me," said Cooney.

"Dang right," said Lick, "but so is ridin' bulls, fallin' in love, and tryin' to peel a grape with an electric sander."

They talked a long time and eventually got around to Straight's riding slump. Lick gave Cooney some ideas that might help both him and his friend. In particular, Lick referred them to a witch doctor.

Meanwhile Pica has a case of Cooney. It feels like a chronic dry cough or maybe a blackberry seed stuck in your teeth. To make matters worse, she has no one to whom she can vent her spleen because she's been whisked away on a two-week media blitz. It is exhausting. She has called her dad several times, but her Cooney affliction is not a good subject for a father-daughter conference.

Ten days into the tour, at the Atlanta Marriott Hilton, she finally cracked.

Nova Skosha, the OTT publicity director, had been sharing escort duties with KroAsha LaTourre. KroAsha was Turk Manniquin's older half-sister from Baton Rouge who was occasionally hired to help OTT in special situations. She had a knack for dealing with sensitive, high-care celebrities and had spent the last four days with Pica. This particular night they were staying in a suite with two adjoining bedrooms. They were dreading a 4:00 a.m. wakeup call to do Atlanta Public Radio. At 11:30 KroAsha heard Pica crying.

"What's the matter, Baby?" said KroAsha as she sat down on the edge of Pica's king-size bed.

Pica was curled up in the fetal position, weeping, her back to KroAsha. KroAsha laid a hand on Pica's hip, then hefted herself onto the bed, sitting up against the headboard. She continued to gently massage Pica. Then she began to sing in her husky Satchmo voice:

"I hear birds singin', wind in da trees, crickets are clickin', da hummin' of bees, and I say to myself, God's in Heaven today . . ." lullabying Pica, chasing discontent and worry from her mind.

Pica rolled over and snuggled against KroAsha. Then she laid her head in KroAsha's lap. The crying stopped; her breath became regular.

"Is all dis be drainin' you, Honey? Or is it somethin' else be botherin' yo' sweet little mind?" asked KroAsha.

Without lifting her head Pica asked, "Have you ever tried to fight not liking somebody?"

"Tell me 'bout it, Sweetie," KroAsha encouraged.

"There's this guy. I thought I really liked him, but he just keeps making me mad. It just seems like he is giving me every reason to think he's a jerk. Why can't I see that? It's like a giant sign warning me, but every time I try to go to sleep he crawls from that corner where he stays in my brain and floats to the top, and I get funny feelings and angry feelings. I toss and turn, lay there thinking 'til late at night."

KroAsha could tell Pica something about love. Forty years old, two daughters over twenty, neither married and both pregnant. All of them victims of loving men who felt no obligation to stick around.

But she remembered the long nights, tossing and turning and hoping and plotting. She never had a relationship that lasted more than two months. Then, to see her daughters follow in her footsteps. She'd shed tears many a night, crying herself to sleep.

"Tell me more," KroAsha said kindly.

Pica poured out her heart for fifteen minutes about her run-ins with Cooney.

KroAsha got to laughing so hard that she nearly smothered Pica! Finally, through exhaustion or frustration or survival instinct, Pica's tears turned to laughter. Spent, she leaned back on the headboard and relaxed.

"Well, Darlin'" said KroAsha, "it sounds like y'all have never had a decent conversation, much less a good, pucker-up, tongue-lashin', four-alarm kiss! And that first e-mail he sent, dat by the way, you quoted to me p-xactly, don't fit wit da rest of his sorry behavior. Either he didn't write it his ownself, or . . . the god of bad luck is smilin' on dat po' boy!

"If it was me, dat's what I would want to find out first! Is he really capable of dat kind of feelin's he done spelt out fo' you in cyberspace, or is he shallow as the army of 'love 'em and leave 'ems' that have followed me home my whole life?"

KroAsha realized that her girl-talk companion had fallen asleep with her head resting on KroAsha's shoulder. She waited several minutes, then carefully slipped from the bed and e-mailed her boss and half-brother, Turk Manniquin.

BOSS MAN,
   Our little girl is mentally and physically drained. I would suggest an immediate weekend in the Bahamas. Maybe three days of no phones, no interviews, no pressure. We've got CNN in four days, three different interviews. She's tough, but we've put a lot on her little shoulders. We better take care of her. Let me know,
   Yo faithful rosebud, KroAsha.

CHAPTER 26

August 21, Sunday Morning
Detour to Goose Valley

ON LICK'S ADVICE, COONEY AND STRAIGHT PULLED INTO THE PARKING area of the tribal police headquarters of the Goose Valley Indian Reservation just south of the Idaho-Nevada border in town of Owyhee. They didn't need to be in Washington State until Wednesday afternoon, so they had a couple of days to kill. The morning was starting to heat up.

"You sure about this?" asked Straight. "I tried to check it out on the Internet, and there is no listing under 'Roanhorse, Aroma Therapy' or 'Stone's Soul Cleansing and Aroma Therapy Trading Post.'"

"Trust me, Lick knows this guy from way back and thinks he can probably change your luck," answered Cooney. *And maybe mine, too*, he thought. What Lick had really said was that "Straight has his head up his butt about being a celebrity, and somebody needs to pull it out for him. Give him a new point of reference."

They walked up to the counter in the police station.

"Can I, uh, help you?" asked an Indian officer seated behind a desk.

"Yes, please," said Cooney. "We're tryin' to find a man named Stone Roanhorse."

Officer Sherrill Em stood and walked to the counter opposite Cooney and Straight. She was in her mid-forties, solidly built with jet black hair. "Is something wrong?" she asked.

"No. He's just been recommended to us," said Cooney.

"For his therapeutic treatments?" she asked.

Cooney looked at Straight with a nod. Maybe Lick did know what he was talking about.

"Well, I'm not sure ... A friend told me he could help us ..." Cooney started.

"May I ask who?" interrupted Sherrill.

"Lick Davis is his . . ."

"Well, kiss my Native American . . . heart!" she said, startled. A vision flowed through her mind of a mustachioed cowboy asleep on her couch, ol' Al, and a mixed-up girl she knew twenty years ago.

"You know him?" asked Cooney.

"Uh, yes . . ." she paused. "Where does he live now?"

"Arizona, down on the border," he said.

"Do you know if he married that woman, that woman that was called Teddie Arizona?" she asked.

Cooney looked at Straight and asked, "Do you know Lick's wife's name?"

Straight thought a moment, then replied, "I'm not sure."

"Sorry," said Cooney. "Anyway, Lick said we should see Mr. Roanhorse. Does he have a phone?"

"Yes. He has a cell phone, but he, uh, doesn't answer it. But you can drive to his trading post. That is what he calls his house."

Sherrill gave our two needy bronc riders directions, and forty minutes and three wire gates later they pulled up to a cinder-block building brightly painted with palm trees, turtles, and an Indian chief smoking a pipe. There were also a dozen or so vehicles in various stages of dilapidation parked around the yard and a corral with two horses.

Stone Roanhorse appeared in the doorway. He was a shrunken, big man. His face was lined with wrinkles, and he was wearing red flip-flops. "Gentlemen," he greeted them, "I wuz hoping you would come by. Did you bring any chardonnay or Skoal or smoked oysters? I am having a strong sensation of craving for those smoked oysters."

"No," said Cooney. "We might have some Cheetos in the camper, but we cleaned out the rig this morning. Wait, we've got twelve boxes of freeze-dried crab jerky. One of the vendors gave it to us. All you add is water. You reckon that would work?"

"The jerky sounds tasty, but those Cheetos, you know they make your fingers orange and sticky, and it is hard to roll a cigarette with sticky orange fingers. So, is that the reason you have come to my trading post and therapy sweat lodge, to bring Cheetos?"

"No, no. We have come upon the recommendation of my friend, Lick Davis, so that you can change the bad luck of my bronc riding friend, Straight Line, here. Lick speaks very highly of your ability," explained Cooney.

"Ah, Lick. I have never known his last name. He is a close personal friend of my blood brother, Al Bean, who passed out permanently one or two years ago. They buried him, but sometimes he speaks in my dreams. Is Lick still living on this side?" asked Stone.

"Yeah, he's fine. In Arizona," said Cooney.

"Did he ever marry that woman that he and my brother Al saved from the helicopter cavalry?"

"I dunno," said Cooney. "I know he is married is all."

"Humm." Stone went into a thoughtful mood, then revived. "So, what is it that I can do for you?"

Cooney explained his Pica problem, and Straight confessed to his riding slump. Stone listened patiently, then pronounced, "I can save you both. Using a unique combination of nutritional supplements, breathing exercise, and an ancient Anastazi aroma therapy, it may be possible to realign your magnetic luck hydrants.

"I have treated many famous people in Hollywood who suffered from rider's block. You may think that only the brain is afflicted when the block strikes a rider, but it is often more than just constipated composition. It is important to free the indoles and skatols that are trapped within the alimentary pipelines coursing through the body," obfuscated Stone.

"What does that have to do with bronc riding?" asked Straight, beginning to have doubts.

Stone seemed stumped for a moment. "Ah," he said, "you thought I said 'writer's block.' What I really said was 'rider's block.' They are maligned simultaneously along the nervous pathways, and it is an easy mistake for you to make. By merely altering the location of the candle flame I can free the blockage from both brain and bowel."

Our two cowboys appeared confused.

As possibly are you, reader. Remember that Stone is practicing the modern art of perception over reality. Though he is not a medicine man, he speaks as if he is one. His livelihood depends on being able to convince the patient that ancient therapies and abandoned treatments that have been relegated to the quackery graveyard and were never approved by the FDA are what you really need to be well again.

At this point Stone resorts to his most convincing exhibit of proof, his ace in the hole: a celebrity testimonial . . .

"Do you trust Lick?" asked Stone.

"I guess," said Straight.

"Then there you have it! Would Lick . . . what was his last name? . . . lead you down the path to personal injury and ruin? No! I tell you, Lick will tell you, you will leave your rider's block here in the soot on the top of the sweat lodge! You shall ride to victory on the wings of a new confluence!" pronounced Stone.

"But first we must obtain the proper natural ingredients for our change of direction."

Stone stepped out onto the wooden pallet that served as his doorstep. "You," he nodded to Straight, "go to Mountain City and return with forty-eight candles, four heads of cabbage, a five-pound bag of Anastazi beans, broccoli, Brussels sprouts, a case of sparkling carbonated water, and a six-pack of tequila, any brand will do."

"Your friend and I will begin preparation for the fire."

Cooney followed Stone around behind the house. A respectable distance away was gathered a cluster of car bodies arranged in the manner of a down-sized Stonehenge.

"I guess you've been to Alliance," chuckled Cooney.

Stone was stonefaced.

"Never mind," said Cooney.

The car collection turned out to be Stone's sweat lodge. The car bodies formed a circle sixteen feet in diameter. A pit four feet deep filled the circle . . . if a pit can fill a circle. Sturdy, peeled lodgepole pine rails supported the roof like a teepee, conjoined at the center. A smoke hole the size of a basket ball filled the peak . . . if a hole can fill a peak.

The roofing itself was a colorful mishmash pattern of blue, brown, and silver plastic tarps, saddle blankets, bed sheets, quilts, Superman capes, dresses, kilts, down coats, coveralls, and one very large piece of orange shag carpet.

Stone led Cooney down earthen steps into the lodge. It was cooler than Cooney expected for such a warm August afternoon.

A fire pit lay unflamed directly beneath the smoke hole. The pit was shaped like a keyhole, the handle being lined with bricks that supported a thirty-six-inch-by-eighteen-inch grill for cooking.

Animal skins covered the floor. Cinder blocks were scattered like icebergs in the Bering Sea, each supporting several candles.

CHAPTER 27

August 21, Sunday Evening
In Stone's Sweat Lodge

Two hours later Cooney, Straight, and Stone were lying around the fire on large bean-bag chairs. Each wore only a hair-side-out goatskin loincloth and a cowboy hat.

They had drunk a flagon of powerful prune punch, chewed a little peyote, and dined on Stone's ritual stew. It was heavy on Anastazi beans, cabbage, and fruit high in fructose.

Stone's conversational voice had taken on the timbre of a professorial chant: "... the hieroglyphics of prehistoric Egyptians shows them using what in the Native American healing arts is called *puk tu chee,* in white man lingo a 'virtual' colonic irrigation. Not a real hosing, simply a gaseous cleansing. According to ancient cave paintings we, too, once practiced the live-time fireman's flush like they do today in Ojai, California. But it was just too messy. Maybe if we could have rented a drive-through carwash or even a fountain we could have pulled it off, but we have chosen to cleanse our innards with natural gas."

Straight was paying attention to the lecture, but the picture of Stone sitting on a propane tank bobbled his mind for a moment. Or maybe it was the gas bubble just to the left of his navel.

"... It is to dispel bad humors that reside in you that prevent you, He Who Talks With Stumbling Lip [referring to Cooney] from choosing the right words to say to achieve consummation of a certain beautiful maiden. Or ... in your case, He Who Rides Like Mating Wombat [referring to Straight], does not allow the coordination of your motor skills needed to ride a bronc like an eagle rides the current," explained Stone.

An explosive flatus rocked the room, punctuating his point and fluffing his loincloth. *Kaboom*! Poof!

Straight jumped, and Cooney flipped backward off his bean-bag chair.

As candle flames were unfluttering and getting back to normal, Stone remarked with enthusiasm, "Oh. A very good start."

He passed around another cup of powerful prune punch and Valium. "We shall reach into your inner depths, unlocking your reticence, permitting your visions to be verbalized and explored."

A sneaky slipstream whistled out from underneath Straight like a cobra from a snake charmer's basket. The whistle ended with a whip-cracking *screeeeee! Snap!*

"Ooo, He Who Rides Like Flapping Sock! That is what we call 'A Lee O,' the writhing eel! Look at the candles around you. They are now drawn back, looking down their noses at you. It is a good sign. Soon you will get a glimpse of your vision."

Whack! Thummmmp! Three candles blew out in front of Cooney.

"Speak to us, Stumbling Lip!" encouraged Stone. "Your words will become Metamucil to the ears of succulent maidens. Here, drink more punch!"

The next ten minutes descended into a cacophonous orchestra pit of tooting, tumultuous, turbulent tubas, trombones, and trumpets, stuttering saxophones, and fleeing piccolos. Candles closed their eyes, covered their wicks, and held their noses. Some flickered and flamed out, others, braced with a zephyr of methane, kicked on, and relit their smudged, waxen partners.

"Can you feel the spirit of our Pharaoh of Phlatulence, the Master Blaster, the Trigeminal Titan of Throaty, Throbbing Thurifiers, the one, the only Toot in Common? Can you feel him moving inside you?" asked Stone. "Let him speak through you! Three, two, one!"

To the untrained ear one might have been reminded of an extended crash between two bugling elk and a dirt bike.

Attracted by the noise, one of Stone's dogs trotted down the steps, barked, sniffed the air, and shook his head as if he had a bee in his ear. Then he raced back the way he had come.

Straight rose in a trance from his poof pillow. He stumbled but caught his fall. At the apex of his three-point stance, his innards under great pressure, a summer squash-shaped cloud of gas was released. The cloud struck a clutch of candles. The sweat lodge lit up like a moonshine raid!

Sparks and flashbulbs of fire crackled through the heavily charged atmosphere. Spider webs in the roof crannies ignited.

Straight stood at attention, looking up at the smoke hole. Stone was reminded of his favorite movie, *A Man Called Horse.*

"I can see Pegasus," said Straight in a breathy voice.

Stone let a silence linger, then said, "Is he bucking?"

Straight stared more intently through the smoke hole and said, "He is bucking. Very smooth. Up and down, rock and fire. He would be beautiful to ride."

"Can you reach him?" asked Stone politely.

Straight tried, then shook his head.

"You must try. Release yourself from the tightness that holds you back. Cleanse yourself of the fecowhiffs that bind you."

Straight strained. Slowly he began to rise. Pots rattled on the grill, candles lay sideways, and Cooney's hat blew off as Straight mounted to the sky like a rocket lifting off Cape Canaveral. He disappeared through the smoke hole.

Cooney was unfazed. He had partaken of the tequila. He was . . . Mellow Yellow. Seconds, minutes, or hours passed, he didn't know. To Cooney it was a timeless interlude until Stone spoke.

"She is here," he said.

"What does she look like?" asked Cooney politely.

"She is a redtailed hawk with the head of a fox. She has a question . . . which one are you?"

"How shall I answer?" asked Cooney.

"Straight," said Stone.

"He is riding Pegasus," answered Cooney.

"No. Answer her straight," instructed Stone.

"Ah, okay," said Cooney, understanding. "You mean without capitals."

"Yes."

"Then the answer is, I am both."

SOME WOULD CONSIDER HIS ANSWER PROFOUND. SOME WOULD CALL IT INSCRUTABLE. THE REDTAILED HAWK CONSIDERED IT . . . EVADING THE QUESTION. THIS WAS POINTED OUT TO COONEY.

Stone channeled Pica HawkFox: "Who were you quoting in the very first e-mail I received from you?"

Deep inside Cooney an answer assembled and flowed like organ music from his mouth: "The words that passed my lips flowed directly from the soul of my being, circumnavigating all the warnings and signposts that suggested caution: Ego adjustment! Preening, bravado, vanity, common sense, and self-protection ahead!

"I am filled with the wonderment of a sky full of stars, the yearning of a young Mexican house finch that has lost his lover, and the conviction of a cowboy strapped to Cupid's arrow that is aimed directly at your heart.

"If there was a path going in the direction of your affection it is my fervent hope that you would leave some sign that I might . . ."

Cooney faded into unconsciousness.

"He's asleep," said Stone.

"I think it is possible he is the two-sided man who wrote the first e-mail to me," said Pica HawkFox.

A thoughtful pause ensued.

"Thank you for coming," said Stone.

"You are . . ." Suddenly a sharp hiss of air like the relief valve on a venting steam pipe interrupted. "Excuse me!" said HawkFox, embarrassed. "Must have been the caviar!"

"Sheep ovaries," corrected Stone but not out loud.

CHAPTER 28

August 22, Monday
Owyhee County, Idaho

OUR TWO HEROES ROSE AND PEEKED OUTSIDE THE SWEAT LODGE. THE SKY was clear; they were not. Lingering remnants of Stone's aroma therapy and virtual colonic experience popped and gurgled. There was no sign of Stone.

They hosed off the dirt and soot at the back of his house, scraped up their own belongings, and took off. On a particularly hard crease in the gravel road back to the highway they thumped the shocks. It knocked a king-size wind pocket out of Straight's shorts.

READER, JUST A WORD ABOUT THE AMAZING ABILITY OF A SCENT TO BRING BACK A MEMORY IN VIVID FOCUS. WALKING BY A CROWD AT A PARTY AND BEING TAPPED ON THE NOSTRIL BY THE FRAGRANCE OF JUNGLE GARDENIA TAKES YOU IMMEDIATELY BACK TO YOUR HIGH SCHOOL PROM.

THE SMELL OF A DEAD MOUSE IN THE PANTRY BRINGS TO MIND THE FIRST HOUSE YOU RENTED AS A NEWLYWED AND HAVING TO HAMMER AND CROWBAR YOUR WAY THROUGH THE DRYWALL TO EXTRACT THE CORPSE.

THUS, ONE SHOULD NOT BE SURPRISED THAT WHEN THE FAMILIAR SMELL OF INGESTED, DIGESTED, AERIFIED PRUNE PUNCH, CABBAGE, AND ANASTAZI BEANS ENGULFED STRAIGHT AND COONEY, EACH WAS TRANSPORTED BACK TO HIS OWN PERSONAL HALLUCINATION FROM THE PREVIOUS NIGHT.

STRAIGHT FOUND HIMSELF MOUNTED ON PEGASUS, AND COONEY COULD FEEL THE PRESENCE OF A FLYING FOX WAITING FOR HIM TO SAY SOMETHING IMPORTANT.

Straight's effusion was the first of many that particular morning. Fits of laughter verging on hysteria, pounding of the dashboard, revulsion, competition, evaluation for stench and distance, and daydreaming filled the tight pickup cab.

Somewhere down Highway 78 between Grand View and Murphey, Cooney ejected a bolus that actually fogged the windshield. Cooney was on a cloud choking in his own rankosity. Suddenly he found he had driven into the back of a bicycler! The biker seemed to be at the end of a long line of cyclists who were riding to raise money for a charity for victims of hay fever. Each was wearing a yellow ribbon with a red clown's nose sniffing, snuffling, and sneezing in the pollen infested breeze.

The bicycler flipped in front of Cooney and lay flat on the road. Cooney could feel his front tires, then his rear tires bounce over the body and the bike.

Cooney stopped in the middle of the road and ran back to the downed biker.

"Are you all right?" asked Cooney desperately.

"It's here," said the biker through his rough beard.

"Where?" asked Cooney.

The biker took Cooney's wrist and stuffed the attached hand inside his shirt.

Cooney felt the soft rise of a woman's breast.

"Can you feel it?" asked the biker.

Cooney could feel it all. "Yes," he breathed.

"Then you know that you can speak freely."

It was a woman's voice. The bearded biker had become Pica D'TroiT. She put her hand over his and clutched it to her bosom. Her full lips pursed at him. It was like a flower blossoming. He could see her eyes fill with emotion. "Tell me, how you can be both?"

"Winged Fox Face," he began, "I long for you, yet I do not know you. I am overwhelmed by your presence inside me. When I let my heart run with its own feelings it tries to escape from my body. My chest gets so tight I can hardly breathe. I am bursting to say to you every word that will make you love me . . .

"The other me takes over when I face the reality that you are just a dream, a lovely confection, a picture on a poster that is beyond my feeble ability to attain. I'm in a game of Texas hold 'em with a seven and a deuce. I realize I can win only in my imagination."

She pressed his hand tighter; he leaned his face closer. Her inviting lips touched his. They were hairy. He was eye to eye with the bearded biker!

Straight sat straight up in the passenger seat to see the pickup crossing the opposite lane and heading toward a big turnout. Straight grabbed the steering wheel and aimed toward a large pile of road gravel.

Cooney came awake and hollered! The rig skidded to a stop, their own dust cloud overtaking them.

"What's going on?" yelled Straight. "What's that in your hand? My gosh, it looks like . . . it is. It's one of Stone's loincloths! Whoa, man, this is too much. Get out. Let me drive. I think you must have fell asleep at the wheel."

"I was . . ." Cooney started but then looked puzzled. "She came to me in a dream."

"Who?"

"She did, Pica. She came on a bicycle. It's fuzzy, but it was good. She wants me to . . ." he paused.

"To what?" asked Straight.

"I don't know. Except it was good. That's the main thing. I'm gonna e-mail her. That's what I'll do."

"Fine," said Straight. "Just let me drive."

CHAPTER 29

August 25–27
Kennewick, Washington,
to San Juan Capistrano Rodeo

THE WEEK HAD TURNED BUSY FOR COONEY AND STRAIGHT. THEY WERE BOTH up in the saddle bronc riding in Kennewick, Washington, on Wednesday. Cooney had bucked off, and Straight would eventually split third place. Cooney had ridden his bull but finished out of the money.

On Thursday they drove to Bremerton, Washington, across Puget Sound from Seattle. Cooney got hot and placed well in both the saddle bronc and the bulls. Straight's good luck continued, and when they left for California Friday afternoon he was leading in the saddle broncs. They wouldn't know how well they had placed until the all the performances were over that weekend.

The Seattle airport long-term parking area looked like a good place to lose your car. Cooney stuffed his war bag, which contained his rodeo gear, with a change of clothes and a dop kit.

Nothing was folded neatly.

Straight, in contrast, carried a suitcase with five starched shirts, two extra pairs of Wranglers, folded hankies, two silk scarves, underwear, socks, a hat brush, nose hair depilatory, and an iron. In his war bag he made sure he had a box of latex gloves, rub-on insecticide, a small bag of prunes, and a plastic container of flavored dairy coffee creamers.

They boarded flight 6988 to Los Angeles, which arrived at 5:55 p.m., then took a rental car to San Juan Capistrano, thirty miles south of the airport. San Juan Capistrano, residence of the homesick swallow, was host for the Rancho Mission Viejo Rodeo. Two of the richest rodeo days in the country. An "invitation-only" rodeo, if you will. Only the top thirty contestants in each event were invited. Each contestant had one chance at the big money. Fifteen were up on Saturday, fifteen on Sunday.

Its setting is unique. It is held on the show grounds east of town. Everything from the candelabra to the manure fork is brought in and assembled for the two-day event. The Rancho Mission Viejo Rodeo raises and donates hundreds of thousands of dollars to the community each year.

A grandstand for general seating is available on one side of the arena, but for the equestrian aristocracy of this generous community, nothing is spared to assure them that their platinum-level admission price will be worth it. They are hosted in an elaborate tent-covered viewing pavilion with three tiers of tables on the opposite side. Self-serve lavish dining, colorful sponsor pavilions, easy access, doilies in the portable toilets, single-malt scotch, *añejo* tequila, live-action television, gratuitous waiters, gracious hosts, and the best combination of cowboys and stock that money can buy make even the most strung-out real estate speculator feel like royalty. Queen Elizabeth would feel right at home.

The first-class accommodations are arranged so the most discerning can rest their elbow on a fine linen tablecloth and sip *vino de pais* while watching a bulldogger miss his steer and get crinkled like a paper cup under the tire of a passing Porsche Boxster.

Straight was entered in the saddle broncs on Saturday. He would do the OTT booth duty Sunday. Cooney drew his bull on Saturday and his saddle bronc on Sunday.

At 5:10 p.m. Saturday afternoon Straight leaned over a big blond monster of horse called Dos Semanas. He was pumped. He had ridden "Dos" three times, made money twice. Cooney was beside him on the catwalk.

Straight was straining, holding his breath, squinting his eyes.

"What's the matter?" asked Cooney.

"Nuthin'."

"You got a bellyache?" asked Cooney.

"No. I'm just . . . psychin' up," said Straight. About then a strangled toot escaped his Wranglers.

"Can you smell it?" asked Straight with a straight face.

"What? Yer gas?" asked Cooney, wrinkling his nose.

"Yeah. It's what's working, I think. The smell is supposed to take me back to the trance I was in at Stone's sweat lodge. When I rode Pegasus."

"What makes you think that's what's working?" asked Cooney, confused.

146

"I did it in Kennewick and Bremerton. Both times. Both times I rode good. It has changed my luck, Cooney. I mean it!" explained Straight with the seriousness of an ATF man reading you your rights.

"Well, I kin smell it all right, if that's what you're talkin' about," said Cooney.

"Good! I've been eating prunes, lots of fruit," said Straight, satisfied.

"Yer up in two," said Cooney.

Straight climbed into the chute and was soon in position, legs cocked, left arm lifting on the rein, and concentrating. Cooney was holding loosely to the back of Straight's protective vest. The nod came. The gate swung open. The big horse pivoted to his left and catapulted into the arena, leaving a pocket of noxious gas in the space he had vacated.

Straight extended his legs with a snap, and his spurs caught on either side of Dos's powerful neck.

Riding big horses is a different experience than riding small ones. If you are an equestrian you can relate even if your horse isn't bucking! For starters, you're so much higher off the ground. Whereas a small, quick horse can wiggle underneath you, shoot out from under you, and change directions like a water skipper, a big one just shrugs his shoulders and puts you into orbit. You often feel like you're sitting on top of him like a frog on a car hood. There's nothing to wrap your legs around.

And the impact of something so big hitting the ground sends seismic waves radiating up from your tailbone to the back of your skull, compressing your vertebrae and smashing your discs to the thickness of a Canadian dime. It's how bronc riders pull muscles, tear tendons, and get hemorrhoids.

But Straight was on him like kudzu on a telephone pole. His rowels were there every time Dos peaked. He was never out of position, out of passion, or out of purpose.

From the spectator's vantage point the ride was not as exciting to watch as some. The big horse was smooth and seemed to roll like a big wave on the open sea. But if you put sound effects to his rhythm, it would be like a wrecking ball banging on the side of an oil tanker ten feet below the water line.

They finished together, Dos and Straight, like the end of a symphony. The whistle blew. Straight swung gracefully from the back of the bronc to the pickup man, then dropped to the ground. He walked away from the smooth landing to the polite applause of the crowd. The judges scored it eighty-four points. By the end of the first day Straight was tied for the lead. He couldn't have done better on Pegasus. Thank you, Stone.

If saddle bronc riding is a profession, bull riding is a job. Saddle bronc is a Cadillac Escalade SUV; bull riding is a two-year-old Dodge three-quarter-ton four-wheel drive with a cracked windshield and a winch on the front of a hand-made bumper. Saddle bronc is clean shaven; bull riding is Yosemite Sam. Saddle bronc is Straight Line; bull riding is Cooney Bedlam.

Cooney had been climbing steadily in the bull riding ranks as the summer progressed. He was in the groove. After helping Straight with his saddle bronc he dropped behind the chutes to get ready for the bull riding. From his war bag he unpacked his purple chaps. There were still visible mesquite scrapes on them from his cow-catchin' fiasco with Lick Davis down in Benson. He put on his short-top bull riding boots. They had knife cuts in them, a patch on one toe, caked mud, and were a dull dirt color. They looked like a giant condor had eaten a bull rider and barfed up the indigestible parts.

His spurs, which stayed on his boots, were situated and tied on with strips of leather. He was still wearing the shirt he had on when they had departed the Seattle airport. He was saving his other one in the war bag "for good."

Cooney draped his bull rope over a top rail, put on a left glove, and began rosining the handle and the tail of the rope. A no-slip grip was his objective. The rosin got hot and sticky. He checked the bell that was tied on the section of rope that lay against the bull's belly.

Bull riding is not as complicated as saddle bronc riding. Nor as predictable, safe, intelligent (if you ask calf ropers), easy (if you ask PBR fans), or organized (as in, "I have a plan").

If you could categorize the predictable modus operandi of all the saddle broncs that are respected and used in the PRCA rodeos, the differences between them could be measured in microns.

On the other hand, the differences in the "books" of the best bulls in the PRCA are measured in cowboy body lengths. Most bucking horses color inside the lines. Most bulls eat the coloring book.

Cooney's draw this afternoon was a Falling U Rodeo Company bull named Cotton Ball. He was a short, all-black, wide-horned bucker with a skunk stripe down his back and a white switch on the end of his tail. He would give you a good ride, but he knew how to use his wicked horns.

The time came. Tension built. Soon Cotton Ball was in the chute in front of Cooney. With Straight's help he pulled the tail of the bull rope through the loop on the other end and brought the tail back up on the left side.

The left palm of Cooney's rosined leather glove lay snuggled underneath the braided handle of the bull rope. Coordinating the setting of the grip with the moment the chute director would give him the sign, Straight pulled the slack by hauling on the tail of the rope like a sailor pulling up an anchor.

"Good," said Cooney.

Straight laid the tail of the flat, braided rope into Cooney's palm on top of the handle. In a flurry of activity Cooney took the tail of the rope, wrapped it around the back of his hand, twisted it in his palm, and pulled the tail of the rope up between his little and ring fingers. He closed his fist, pounded it with his right hand, shook the tail out of the way, scooted up on his left hand, looked at the bull's poll, and nodded his head.

It took Cotton Ball only two quick jumps to get into his plan. His front and hind legs pumped up and down like a seesaw as he spun in a tight circle to his left, into Cooney's hand. What the bull lacked in size and power he made up for in velocity—rpms.

Cooney sat perfectly balanced on Cotton Ball's fulcrum as the bull rose and fell, whirled and spun. Cooney's legs worked automatically, his left squeezing on the inside, his right spur reaching and grabbing as if in synchrony with the bull's choreography. He kept his upper body over his rope and used his right hand like a tightrope walker's gyroscope.

Watching from the stands it didn't look very smooth. The jarring of the hooves and the jerking of the centrifugal force seemed to be whipping Cooney around on top of the bull. But in the driver's seat Cooney was anticipating each pound and pull, each crash and acceleration, and was able to keep his seat.

Mind you, it wasn't easy. It took a strong left arm and legs like steel springs to hold himself in the center of the centrifuge. But when everything was working right he could have been sitting on a lazy Susan in the eye of a hurricane.

Outside his vacuum he heard the buzzer. Cooney released his grip, thinking the bull might pull out of his counterclockwise turn, straighten up, and allow him to bail out on the left side. Cotton Ball, however, was not done. Cooney's right shoulder hit the edge of the wind tunnel and was slammed back. His butt slid rearward, as did his legs, but his hand didn't come free.

Cotton Ball's head end pitched down, and his rump rose up, catching Cooney's body and throwing it forward! Cooney's hand came loose as he cartwheeled across the bull. He landed in a sitting position between the horns, a juicy hood ornament. The bull's powerful neck muscles flexed and launched our hapless cowboy into orbit!

Cooney's back hit the rump of the bull. The bull kicked high and sailed Cooney off the bull's tailhead into a complete backward flip. A moment captured on high-speed film showed Cooney in midair, four feet off the ground, parallel to it, in the flying-Superman prone position, eye level to the departing bull's upraised tail.

The picture would become famous in rodeo bloopers, *America's Funniest Animals,* and *Animals First! Magazine* under its popular feature, "Serves You Right!" The picture was captioned "Eye to Eye!"

In the wink of a bull's eye Cooney completed the remaining 180 degrees and landed on the back of his head in the soft arena dirt.

Snorty Ruefelt, rodeo bullfighter, handed Cooney his hat and dusted him off. "That was one of the best!" he said.

"Did I make the whistle?" asked Cooney.

"Who knows?" said Snorty. "But you did make a memory! That's what they'll be talkin' about on the way home tonight."

CHAPTER 30

August 27

San Juan Capistrano, Party Time!

"EIGHTY-FOUR!" ANNOUNCED THE ANNOUNCER.

Through the panels Cooney saw Lick Davis waving him over. It took Cooney a few minutes to gather his bag and shake hands, but he made it around to the plush accommodations side.

"Great ride," said Lick, laughing. "Meet some of my friends."

Lick led Cooney into one of the good-size tents. A bar was set up at one end.

It was a loud crowd. The ladies and gentlemen who peopled the place were dressed cowboy fancy. The men wore high-dollar boots, good straw hats, long-sleeve western shirts, and clean Wrangler jeans, and although they didn't look like rodeo hands, many wore fancy trophy buckles that they obviously had won rather than bought.

Their female counterparts, mostly wives, were women who knew how to shop.

"Make way, boys," hollered Lick. "There's a champion comin' through!"

Cooney was surrounded by an appreciative crowd. "What a ride!" "You made history!"

"Give him room!" "Get him a drink!"

Lick stepped up onto a chair. "My friends, allow me to present a close personal friend, a first-class bronc rider, and, as you saw this afternoon, one of the few bull riders who has mastered the bassackwards cartwheel dismount just to thrill the crowd, Mr. Cooney Bedlam!"

A huge cheer swelled from the watchers.

"Raise yer hand, Cooney," suggested Lick.

"Gentlemen," yelled Lick, "one more thing. Our special guest is in need of some raiment enrichment. Witness, if you will, the tattered tunic, the annihilated habiliments, the ragged garment, the wardrobe laid to waste ..."

Two defense attorneys were scribbling down Lick's text for use in their next trial.

"In other words," continued Lick, "our young lion needs to borrow a shirt!"

All eyes scrutinized more closely the wrinkled rag that partially covered Cooney's upper torso. The shirt he was wearing had torn horizontally just below the pocket line from the button to the center of his back. The right sleeve had come loose at the shoulder seam and hung limply from his elbow. And there was a visible streak of cow—make that *bull*—manure running unbroken down his right front from his chin to his shirttail.

In the blink of an eye at least four men were taking off their shirts and offering them to Cooney.

Cooney looked at Lick. "I can't take these guys' shirts. I got another one in my war bag here."

Lick laid a hand on Cooney's arm. "Take 'em," he said quietly. "Let 'em treat you right. They know what they're doin'."

Each profferer of a shirt made Cooney try it on. Finally one particularly dashing fellow took over and insisted that Cooney wear his. Although Cooney had no way of knowing, it was a $250 shirt from Saville Row.

"Name's Corp," the fellow introduced himself to Cooney. "I'd be honored if you'd wear this one. It was a gift from my great-grandfather, Corpus Luteum the first, Greek immigrant and the first to plant olive trees in the area now known as Clovis. See, that's his brand there on the cuff: CL bar."

"How could I turn down an offer like that?" said Cooney, getting into the mood.

"In return," said Corp, "I'd would like to have yours, worn in battle, as a memento if you could spare it."

"Well, sure, I guess . . ." said Cooney, "but . . ."

"Get me a staff, boys, and we'll make a flag outta this gladiator's shirttail to honor the occasion!" hollered Corp.

Two hours later a group of eight men, including Cooney, had depleted the bar and was still celebrating. Cooney had learned that this tent was the privy of the Piebald Polo Club. Membership was composed of California businessmen, Realtors, doctors, lawyers, farmers, and cowboys who held trail rides, were generous to worthy causes, and liked to have a good time. Maybe like raucous Rotarians but with a bigger budget and no secret handshake.

They were down to actually having conversations. "So," Cooney asked Lick, "is it true you rode a camel at the national finals?"

All the men laughed. "Yeah, tell us about it," they encouraged.

"That was a long time ago," started Lick. "'fore I met any of you guys: 1985. You probably wuddn't born yet."

"I think I was five or six about then," said Cooney.

"I'll just tell you the camel part. There's a book they wrote about it, 'bout that whole year: *Hey, Cowboy, Wanna Git Lucky?*"

"Yeah," said Cooney, "I read it, but I never knew if it was true or not."

"The camel part sure was!" assured Lick. "I rode him from the Oklahoma City zoo to Myriad Arena, right down Main Street, jumpin' cars, duckin' around buses, racing reporters, policemen, runnin' red lights. I nearly ran over the security guard at the contestants' gate to get back of the chutes. He recognized me at the last moment and opened the gate."

"Were you really naked?" asked one of the men.

"Nope. I had on somebody's underwear. Actually, I can't remember if it was mine and a pillowcase for a wild rag . . . but I can remember I was only thinkin' one thing: make the bell, get to the church on time. It was my last chance. I couldn't miss it. I didn't want them to turn out my bull."

"And you rode him," said Cooney with respect.

"Yep, I got lucky," said Lick.

One of the men started in on a story, and Cooney turned to Lick and asked, "I've had a couple people ask me, including an Indian policewoman, if you married the girl that you rescued from the Las Vegas mafia. I don't really know that story, just the legend. You mind tellin' me if the lady I met in Benson was her?"

"Naw, I don't mind," said Lick. "Her name was Teddie Arizona, and, no, I didn't marry her. After the rescue, as you call it, I stayed in Las Vegas for a couple years. She put me up in a fancy apartment in town. But she was real mixed up, and I was in a mental slump. We became a burden on each other. She started goin' to a psychologist, and I started drinkin'.

"Truth is, I asked her to marry me, even bought a ring. When I asked her, she broke into tears and said no," said Lick. "I packed that next mornin', borrowed a car from a guy I knew, and left town."

"What happened to her?" asked Cooney.

"I think she stayed in Vegas, started her own business. She inherited, or got in a divorce settlement, some pretty good money. Don't know if she ever got married again," said Lick.

"Where did you go?" asked Cooney.

"That's another story, Cowboy," said Lick. "How 'bout another tequila and prune juice?"

CHAPTER 31

August 27, Saturday Night
The Llama Ride!

"THAT CAMEL STORY SHOULD BE IN *GUINNESS WORLD RECORDS*!" SAID LESS Oriole. "You ever been on a camel since then?"

"Nope, can't say as I have," said Lick.

"Hey, boys, I've got an idea," said Less.

"We better go," said all the others who knew Less and didn't really want to be a part of any of his ideas.

"No! Wait! This is great! Let's have a race. We'll re-create Lick's camel race! Cooney, you're a good kid, and you know we love ya. We wouldn't do anything to lead you astray, but how could you pass up an opportunity to have a camel race with Lick? A re-creation of one of rodeo's greatest events!"

"Lesster," said William Bill, one of the few remaining who still had any modicum of restraint, "this doesn't sound very wise."

"Well," said Lick, "I've done dumber things than that. Less, what's your plan?"

"DONE DUMBER THINGS THAN THAT?" WHAT A GREAT RATIONALE TO EMBARK ON A TRAIN WRECK. THERE ARE PEOPLE WHO WALK A LITTLE CLOSER TO THE EDGE THAN MOST OF US. AND I DON'T MEAN WHEN LIVES ARE AT STAKE OR WHEN THERE ARE BATTLES TO BE WON. I MEAN JUST TO SEE WHAT'S THERE.

YOU KNOW THEM. THEY MAKE YOU UNCOMFORTABLE. YOU CAN LET THEM INTO YOUR BOX, BUT YOU WOULDN'T DARE GO INTO THEIRS. IT'S JUST GOOD SENSE TO KEEP THEM AT ARM'S LENGTH. IT SHOULD BE NO SURPRISE THAT A SIGNIFICANT NUMBER OF THESE EDGE WALKERS ARE DRAWN TO BULL RIDING.

COONEY IS GETTING DANGEROUSLY CLOSE TO LICK.

Our band of merry revelers was unable to locate any camels for the "Midnight Ride of Lick and Cooney" or "Loony," as it quickly became called. But these were resourceful men, and they soon located a fellow Piebald Polo Club member who raised llamas, the next-best thing.

At 11:00 p.m., down a long driveway off Camino Capistrano, a group of men was standing in a cyclone-fenced corral explaining to Federico Dedos why they needed to borrow his two fastest llamas for a race.

Lick was pumped. He had gone over the edge and was inciting the crowd to riot.

"We could all ride one!" he crowed. "Feddy, how many llamas do you have? Looks like ten or twelve here. Whattya say?"

Less was living a dream. "I need a big one, Federico! Gimme yer best!"

"Now hold it, boys," said Federico. "These are valuable llamas, and I don't know if I've got racing insurance."

"Whattya worried about?" asked Corp. "You probably beat some poor ol' wool-weaving hippie from Hemet outta them. For ten cents on the dollar."

"You don't know that!" said Federico indignantly.

"You probably still owe her for them. You do, don't you?" said Corp.

"Come on, Feddy," said Less. "You know we won't hurt them, but just to be fair, we'll put up collateral. Corp, you and Bill Bill, cover it. Just say, 'We swear to cover it,' and we will pay you back for any damage done to the llamas."

"Ah, that's okay," said Federico. "I'm thinkin' we should have a little bet on the side as to who wins. But this little corral's not big enough to have a race."

"Feddy," said Less, "this is the Midnight Ride of Loony, which is the reenactment of Lick's camel ride at the national finals. It is in honor of rodeo fans everywhere!

"Here's the plan. There's nine of us, ten countin' your son. So we send Bill Bill down the street to the Boomerang Swallows, where the front door will be the finish line. Everybody that rides will get a haltered llama and start right here in this pen. Your boy can open the gate, and out we go.

"First one through the Swallows door gets the pot."

"How 'bout a hundred apiece?" said Federico.

"Here's three hundred," said Corp. "That's for me, Lick, and Cooney."

"Well, here's five hundred," offered Lick, "to sweeten the pot!"

"I can . . ." started Cooney.

"Put yer money away, Son, it ain't no good here," said Federico.

Bill Bill took the money, jumped into his car, and drove to the bar. It was full of rodeo fans and cowboys in town for the festivities. Bill Bill made the announcement, and the contents of the bar spilled out into the street. Traffic was light, and a couple of corners were covered to provide safe passage.

Twenty minutes later, at 11:44 p.m., Bill Bill got the call from Federico's son, F-2, that the gate was about to be opened. Several cars full of onlookers had driven down from the Boomerang Swallows to see the start of the race.

Between Federico, F-2, and each jockey, they managed to get a halter, with a lead rope tied back around to make reins, on seven llamas.

A WORD ABOUT LLAMAS: NASTY.

THEY ARE BIGGER THAN ALPACA, ANTELOPE, AND WOMBATS AND SMALLER THAN COWS, OLD SOWS, AND HARLEYS. WEIGHING IN AT UP TO FOUR HUNDRED POUNDS, LONG LEGGED AND LONG NECKED, THEY CAN STAND FLAT-FOOTED AND LOOK OVER THE TOP OF THE AVERAGE MAN'S HEAD.

THEY ARE QUICK TO ANGER, TO KICK, TO SPIT, PAW, RAM, WHACK, ORGLE, NECK WRESTLE, AND MOUNT ANYTHING THAT MOVES. AND THEY ARE HARD TO RIDE. NOW BACK TO MY STORY.

Llamas have a thick coat of wool, which is helpful when getting onto them and hanging on for dear life.

The corral was now surrounded by a crowd. Onlookers lined the mile-and-a-half roadway to the finish line.

Some of the bystanders who had livestock experience helped the riders get mounted.

In addition to Lick and Cooney, others, including Corp Luteum, Feddy Dedos, Less Oriole, Hubcap Longevity, Hookworm Shields, and Jack Handle, were entered up. I know: That's more than seven, but Hubcap had agreed to run along beside Jack Handle to keep him upright, so they each counted as one-half.

F-2 had his hand on the gate, watching for the moment when all seven riders were up and ready. It took two or three men on the ground to keep each llama contained. F-2 could whistle. Not a tune, but a noon o'clock whistle in a factory town. He laid his fingers to his lips, and *they were off!*

Out of the gate was Lick in the lead! His llama was trotting, and it was painful to Lick's skinny buttocks. He tried to lie back with his boots out in front of the shoulders. His balance was good, but the llama's back was not very wide. Besides, he still held in one hand a large plastic glass of tequila and prune juice (the bartender stocked it in his honor)! He leaned forward to try to urge the llama to run.

Less Oriole shot by him. Lick's llama immediately switched into a cow gallop trying to keep up. All of the llamas soon caught the spirit. The first casualty was Hook Shields, appropriately, when he hooked his left boot toe on the gate post, lost his balance, grabbled the top rail, and swung himself off the llama, then smacked into the gate! It was a Wile E. Coyote moment. However, his llama continued on with the pack.

Corp lost control on the first right turn onto Camino Capistrano when his llama, whom he had named Gilroy in honor of his hometown, turned abruptly, and Corp sailed off the left front quarter. Corp somehow managed to hang on to the rope reins. Gilroy dragged him several feet, then, realizing what was impeding her progress, turned back up the rope to the scene of the crime.

Corp, thinking he was winning, grabbed the halter on both sides of her head and started to pull himself up. When he was nose to nose with Gilroy, she pursed her cloven lips and spit a fetid, bile-flavored slanger all over his face! He fell over backward like a Mace victim, screaming and rolling in a large, uneven circle.

Federico was giving Lick a run for his money. They were both up on big males. Federico knew how to pick 'em. What he didn't count on was that the two males were neck and neck in the pecking order and would fight at the drop of an Inca.

Feddy and Lick were soon in a heated effort to keep the two apart and still make progress.

Feddy, always ready to hedge his bets, had strapped a light English saddle around his llama.

While the two llamas were ramming each other and neck wrestling, Feddy, on the right side of Lick and slightly behind, grabbed him by the collar. He leaned into his left stirrup to position himself to pull Lick off the back of his ride. To his chagrin his saddle slid sideways 90 degrees.

Lick's head was now pinned to the back of his llama. Feddy was nearly airborne. He looked like one of those bulldogging pictures in midjump. He had a hold of Lick with his left hand, the rope rein with his right hand, and was squeezing his legs as tightly as he could around his llama. It was amazing that he covered almost twenty yards in that position.

It was then that the two llamas swerved to the curb, each passing on opposite sides of a lamp post. It was curtains for Feddy. He performed a horizontal jackknife in an attempt to evade the collision. Unfortunately, the iron post left a message on his belly that read SAN JUAN VALLEY ELECTRIC COMPANY, but in mirror image.

Cooney was hangin' on for dear life. He had ridden lots of wild beasts but usually under more controlled conditions. He was watching Less Oriole, who had taken the lead, whoopin' and wallopin' his llama down the edge of the street next to the eight-foot plastered wall that surrounded the mission. *Thank goodness llamas are sure-footed*, thought Cooney, *'cause Less is floppin' all over him.*

Sticking out from the mission wall, eight feet off the ground, was a clay pot in a wrought-iron frame. Long-flowing flowered vines grew from the pot and descended toward the sidewalk. It was a long shot, but Less was up for it. After all, he had once bulldogged an army tank. He grabbed the vine with both hands, intending to swing up onto the top of the wall.

In his mind he was envisioning Zorro pulling off a coup that would overshadow any boring llama race. However, the hundred-year-old wrought iron that was cemented into the adobe was no match for 220 pounds of mass going at the velocity of 20 mph. Let's see . . . 220 pounds (mass) x 20 mph (velocity) = collision, contusion, concussion, confusion, and calamity cubed!

Lick and Cooney were on opposite sides of the street from each other. The sidewalk was lined with yelling, screaming spectators. They had formed a V that would funnel the racing llamas to the front door of the Boomerang Swallow. Cooney could hear the cheering. People were shouting his name and rooting for him.

"Take him out, Cooney!"

"Coo-Nee! Coo-Nee! Coo-Nee!"

In that split second he went competitive! Up 'til then it was just a joke. Some horseplay. Granted, it was way outside the box . . . but he was in a race, and Cooney didn't like to lose.

He started putting his heels to his llama, leaning forward, coaxing him to go faster. They were less than twenty yards from the door when Lick pulled up on Cooney's off side. Lick looked in Cooney's face and smiled a crazy smile.

"Here," said Lick, stretching his left arm across the chasm and offering a plastic glass half full of tequila to Cooney.

Cooney couldn't help but laugh. He reached for the glass.

Lick, in a move that left everyone breathless, grabbed Cooney around the waist like he was a pickup man and slid on behind him just as they crossed the door jamb! Into the chaos they rode!

The crowd literally fell back. Just as our two mounted champions slid up to the bar on four even-toed ungulate hooves, a tall, red-haired man rose from the crowd and tried to jump on behind Lick. He missed. But Lick's original llama, still hot on the trail, crashed through the door and leaped!

158

A NOTE ABOUT LLAMAS, AND I QUOTE: IF A LLAMA IS AGITATED, IT WILL LAY ITS EARS BACK. ONE MAY DETERMINE HOW AGITATED THE LLAMA IS BY THE MATERIAL IN THE SPIT. THE MORE IRRITATED THE LLAMA IS, THE FARTHER BACK INTO EACH OF THE THREE STOMACH COMPARTMENTS IT WILL TRY TO DRAW MATERIALS FROM FOR ITS SPIT.

THE MALE IS CALLED A MACHO. AN "ORGLE" IS THE MATING SOUND OF A MACHO WHO IS SEXUALLY AROUSED. THE SOUND IS REMINISCENT OF GARGLING, BUT WITH A MORE FORCEFUL, BUZZING EDGE. MALES BEGIN THE SOUND WHEN THEY BECOME AROUSED AND CONTINUE THROUGHOUT THE ACT OF PROCREATION.

LLAMAS MATE WITH THE FEMALE IN A KUSH (LYING DOWN) POSITION, WHICH IS FAIRLY UNUSUAL IN A LARGE ANIMAL. THEY MATE FOR AN EXTENDED PERIOD OF TIME (TWENTY TO FORTY-FIVE MINUTES), ALSO UNUSUAL IN A LARGE ANIMAL.

SOURCE: WIKIPEDIA.ORG

"Look out, Sheriff!" cried his deputy, but it was too late. Cooney's llama shot on by as Lick's agitated llama arrived. He reared up on his hind legs and slid into the red-haired sheriff's shoulder, pushing him to the ground.

Cooney and Lick, still double-mounted, were propelled farther in, slicing between the bar and the crowd like an edge trimmer. Lick grabbed a guardrail that delineated the cocktail waitress' station at the bar and locked on! With his right arm still around Cooney's waist, Lick slicked them off the back of the racing llama like they'd run under a hanging bough!

They landed on their backs, on the bar, still entwined, where they crashed and stuck.

Cooney looked back over his shoulder and handed Lick the plastic cup. "Sip?" asked Cooney.

"Yer my kinda man," said Lick and took the last swallow. A deep orgle punctuated the dramatic moment.

An hour later Cooney and Lick were able to slip out the door. The hard-core partiers were still going strong, the less-discriminating of either sex were finding each other, and the ones who knew where to draw the line had gone home.

The night was balmy and beautiful. The proximity of the ocean added a little moisture to the air.

Cooney had planned on sleeping in the pickup camper back at the rodeo grounds, but Lick changed his mind: "Come on home with me. I've got a nice room for the weekend. Got two beds, and we'll find a ride to the rodeo tomorrow. You can catch me up to date on your poetry and that girl with the big smile you been pining after."

They sat in lawn chairs out by the pool. Cooney was drinking a bottle of water. Lick's room had included a cheese and cracker basket with a bottle of wine. Lick indulged.

"I'm gettin' over her, I guess," Cooney said. "She's getting so much publicity now. I saw her on TV, *People* magazine. Don't think she'll ever look back."

"You can take a certain amount of credit for her success, from what I hear," laughed Lick.

"That thing about 'women can't ride' was taken out of context. Well, not really. The truth is I wasn't sure that women could enter in the PRCA. Turns out they can," explained Cooney.

"I guess that's an honest mistake," said Lick. "I didn't know it when I was ridin'. So, how you handlin' losin' her?"

"Ump, that hurts. I never had her in the first place. Only in my mind. And I still got this . . . oh, this crush on her. Best way to describe it. Sounds juvenile. It even feels juvenile, but I never had a crush on anyone before."

"You'll get over it. You can still dream about her, but another one will come along. You don't have to forget Pica, but when you find the right one your heart settles down. The memory of old crushes fades."

"That happen to you?" asked Cooney.

"I'm not sure what happened to me," said Lick, "except I was in the right place at the right time, and the right women showed up, and when the new wore off I knew I had found the love of my life.

"If you can see past your sexual cravings for her, enough so that you can sleep at night, it makes life easier. If you believe in God you can just step back and leave it in His hands, so to speak. Whatever will be will be. The older I get, the more I realize that I, myself, am not necessarily in charge.

"That's the only explanation I have for findin' my wife. It's either that or just dumb luck, and luck hasn't always been my best friend."

The two cowboys stared up at the night sky. The city lights didn't block out all the stars. The depth of infinity made itself known.

"There's nothin' standing between you and the farthest star you can see, Cooney. You've got your whole life to get there. Take your time," said Lick.

That night they both slept in the king-size bed. There hadn't been two queen-size beds as Lick had thought. No matter, they'd both slept in campers, sheep camps, and bad motels. Sleep was sleep. Lick snored, and Cooney put off thinkin' about Pica. He finally drifted off.

CHAPTER 32

September 6, Tuesday, 1:00 p.m., Day after Labor Day Miami Airport

"WILL YOU COME WITH US, PLEASE, MISS?" SAID THE CUSTOMS AGENT.

Pica looked at File, who was with her in the Customs declaration line. He shrugged his shoulders. She followed the agent, who carried her suitcase, into a small room, where they were joined by another agent who closed the door behind her.

"Please sit down, Miss," the first agent directed.

The two agents began to empty her suitcase onto the table.

After muffled snippets of conversation and serious grunts, they addressed Pica. "Is this yours?" They held up a Ziploc bag holding brightly colored feathers.

"No," she answered, furrowing her brow. "Where did you get them?" she asked.

"They were sewn behind the liner in your bag," they said.

"Let me look," she said.

"Don't touch them, please," an agent admonished.

"I have never seen these before," she said.

"And I guess you are unaware these feathers are from the endangered Glandular Y Cock, one of the rarest parrot species on Earth?" continued the agent.

"What would you estimate underground collectors would pay for this small bag of feathers, Earl?" Agent No. 1 asked of Earl, aka Agent No. 2. "Two thousand, five?"

Earl nodded seriously.

"I . . . It's not . . . Is this a joke?" Pica asked, the panic rising in her voice.

It did not help that a few paparazzi were waiting outside the Customs area when File came through the doors without Pica. He was recognized by one of them and was stopped.

"Where is she!?" they clamored.

When they settled down File explained that she had been briefly detained in Customs and would be out shortly. He went off to get a limo.

By six o'clock that evening the press had begun to think that they had been hoodwinked and that Pica had slipped by them. But at 6:15 File reappeared and explained to them that Pica was still unavailable but that nothing was wrong.

"Is she ill?" one reporter asked. There was clucking speculation that her trip to the Caribbean had been to prevent a nervous breakdown. Other questions tried to narrow down what medical problem she might have.

File suggested that the reporters go home and that he would clear it all up in the morning. He went back in the Customs office, leaving the reporters to hone their own reports, which would include quotes from fellow reporters who served as unidentified sources.

Pica was alternately baffled, scared, mad, distraught, and curious. The Customs officers left File and Pica alone in a small room to talk.

"How serious is this?" asked File.

"They talked about, you know, jail, many-thousand-dollar fines. I was all, I don't know how they got there. They told me, like, it's probably worth $5,000! Feathers of the Y Cock! I've never heard of it!"

"Are you sure it was in your bag?" asked File.

"Yes! It was like, my big bag, but I didn't smuggle that stuff, File. I don't know, like, somebody had to be trying to sneak it into the United States. Later they'd steal my bag or whatever . . ." She began crying. File noticed she had fallen back into her Valley Girl speech habits.

"I'll get a lawyer," said File. "But I'll need to call the office."

The look on Pica's face said it all. She looked like she had just run over her good dog.

<hr>

At the headquarters of OVER THE TOP Nova Skosha was in her wreck-control mode. She was quizzing File over the phone. "When did KroAsha leave?"

"On the plane I arrived on. She's not in the office today?" File asked.

"No, but I'll catch up with her. So, you met Pica at the hotel. When was that?"

"Two-thirty, I guess. Maybe three. I talked to her on the phone. She was going to the beach, so I took a nap. We met for cocktails . . . I had one anyway and dinner. She was upbeat, looked good . . . she'd gotten some sun."

Nova continued, "Have you got any idea about the contraband?"

They talked several more minutes.

"Okay," she said, "if there is a way to keep this out of the press, that will be our first priority. You stay down there. I'll get the lawyers on it, but they might not get there 'til tomorrow. Let's see, it's already 6:00 p.m. in Miami . . .

"Just do what you can, File. I'll get with Turk and let you know. If this explodes I'm guessing Turk might want to interview again for a LIP LASTER girl."

"Let's just see what happens," said File. "Maybe there's some simple explanation, and it will blow over as quick as it started."

Disembarking in Miami from the 7:15 p.m. flight from Nassau, a robust woman in breezy tourist clothes, floppy hat, and sunglasses passed by the four reporters still waiting for Pica to appear. She pulled the only female reporter off to the side and asked her if the police had captured the girl who was smuggling endangered species.

The reporter perked up. "What do you mean!?" she said, trying to appear nonchalant to her competing paparazzi.

"There was gossip at the airport about someone on the last flight smuggling animals or animal parts. Apparently the Customs people here in Miami were in contact with the officers in Nassau."

"Who are you?" asked the reporter.

"Jane Doe," answered the woman. "Gotta go!" She disappeared into the crowded concourse.

File was in the hall outside the Customs office. His cell phone rang. "Filo, folly, Filomine, baby mine! Where are you, Filomew?"

File explained what happened: that the lawyer wouldn't get there until tomorrow, that Pica was actually being held under suspicion, and that the local police were on their way to take her down to the city jail.

"I dropped a little spark to the waiting reporters," she said. "We should have a bonfire by morning!" She laughed loudly.

"Honey, Honey, Sweetie, Sweetlips," cooed File, "I will be staying here overnight . . . I could find you a place to rest your weary head tonight, and we . . ."

"Oh, Filomagic, I'm so sorry. I've got an 8:30 flight to Denver. Besides, it is not a good idea to be fraternizing . . ."

"I promise no frater would be involved," he pleaded.

"You're so funny, Filofunny, but if this works and she's dropped like a hot potato, I'll be waiting in the wings. Oh, Filey, Filo, luscious Filo, my lips are quivering in moist anticipation of your kissy, kissy, your tender manly touch just above my knee . . . *Foooey, foooey,* Baby, Baby, I just can't wait!"

"Oui Oui, you drive me crazy," he whined.

"I'm your widdy widdy baby! See you in Denver, Smooch!"

CHAPTER 33

September 8, Thursday
Moses Lake, Washington,
On the Road

STRAIGHT PULLED OFF INTERSTATE 90 INTO MOSES LAKE, WASHINGTON. Since the Rancho Mission Viejo Rodeo ten days before our heroes had made Walla Walla, Ellensburg, and Dillon. Both were riding well and making a little money. Today they were on the way to Puyallup, Washington, where both were up tomorrow in the saddle bronc.

Cooney was filling the gas tank when Straight strode out to the truck carrying a newspaper. On the front page, above the headline, in the top right-hand corner was a head shot of Pica D'TroiT. The caption read, "Lip Chick up Crick! See Sports Section B1."

Straight handed it to Cooney, pointing at the picture.

Cooney's jaw dropped. He let go of the gas nozzle. Straight grasped it as it wobbled.

Cooney flipped to section B.

In the unflattering photo, Pica was holding her hand up to ward off paparazzi. The shirt she was wearing was wrinkled, and her hair was flattened in back. A stern-faced policewoman accompanied her in the photograph.

The two-column article described Pica as an overnight sensation, firebrand for women's rights, bronc-riding cowgirl, atypical beauty, LIP LASTER girl, and smuggler of endangered species contraband.

It said that she was being held in the Miami-Dade County jail until bail could be arranged. Because she was Canadian she was a strong flight risk.

The article continued outlining the whirlwind tour she had been on and the charges against her.

An accompanying article described the Glandular Y Cock, a tropical version of the magpie, that had been imported to the Caribbean in the '30s by fans of Ernest Hemingway all the way from his Idaho home.

The article took all of the wind out of Cooney. For several days he had been making progress putting Pica behind him. He turned to Straight and asked, "Do you know anything about this?"

"Nothin', Cooney," he said. "She was supposed to be on this big PR tour. I didn't know she was in the Caribbean. Last I heard of her was an interview last week on Public Radio, I think.

"I'm sorry, Cooney. But it's better to learn this kind of stuff about her now than if you ever got involved."

Cooney squinted his eyes. "You don't really think she did this, do you? I mean, how could you?! You don't even know her!"

Straight looked Cooney squarely in the eye. "You don't either, partner. You don't either."

That gave Cooney a moment of pause. "No," he said, shaking his head. "No. I don't believe it. She just wouldn't do it. It's a mistake or, worse, she's being framed."

"By who? And why? She's not rich . . ." said Straight.

"Do you think you could call OTT and find out where she is?" asked Cooney, "Maybe find out what's going on."

"I'll try, but I'm gonna see File tomorrow. He'll be setting up the booth in Puyallup. You ready to go?"

"Yeah, I guess so."

In the ensuing hours Straight got through to Nova Skosha, the OVER THE TOP ATHLETIC COSMETICS celebrity recruiter. All she could tell Straight was that Pica was still in custody and that OTT had sent a lawyer to Florida to protect its interests. Charges were being prepared by the U.S. Customs Service.

Cooney was beside himself. That night he e-mailed Pica five times offering to help. He received no response. He tried to reach Lick to talk. Not home.

"Settle down, Cooney," Straight said with some sympathy. "This kinda stuff takes time. I didn't mean to be so hard on her. I'd be real surprised if she really did that smuggling, but the truth is I don't know either. That's some serious criminal activity. But I can't think of any reason somebody would try to trap her. Or maybe the smuggler just slipped the stuff in her luggage and planned to steal it from her when they got through Customs."

"I'll keep trying from my end. File will be here tomorrow. He was with her when she was arrested. He might give us a better picture.

"And . . . maybe it would be better if you stayed in the background. If you get to bugging File he might clam up, you not being with the company and all."

"Okay," said Cooney, taking a deep breath. "Tomorrow's gonna be a good day."

"That's right," said Straight. "We got horses to ride."

As for Pica, the next three weeks of her life were a nightmare. Turk Manniquin of OVER THE TOP ATHLETIC COSMETICS put up a $500,000 bond, and, in an unusual international agreement, Juneau D'TroiT, Pica's father, gave the U.S. government a lien on his ranch and property as collateral to allow Pica to come back home to Pincher Creek, Alberta.

Oui Oui Reese was offered the position that Pica had held with OTT. Within ten days she began working the LIP LASTER booth at rodeos with Straight. File was still the front man.

Cooney was confounded. His crush on Pica, his absolute belief that she was innocent, his intense desire to help her, and her refusal to even answer his e-mails kept him roiling inside.

Straight was keeping his eye on the ball. He did his job in the booth and rode broncs like his life depended on it.

CHAPTER 34

September 26, Monday

Oklahoma City Airport, Cooney Goes to Alberta; Straight Goes to Denver

STRAIGHT DROVE UP TO THE SECOND-LEVEL DEPARTING PASSENGERS AREA at the Oklahoma City airport and parked. He and Cooney had competed in the rodeos at the Amarillo Tri-State Fair and the Oklahoma State Fair. Both placed in the saddle broncs at Amarillo and got skunked in OKC.

Cooney had set his mind that if Pica wouldn't return his e-mails, he'd just go see her. He was booked on an early morning flight to Calgary. Straight was perplexed and concerned over Cooney's overreaction to Pica's problem. He listened and didn't encourage him one way or the other. He himself had never been in love, so how could he possibly understand? It's like expecting a male obstetrician to tell you how it feels to have a baby: Something's wrong with this picture.

"Okay, thanks, Straight," said Cooney. "I'll be flyin' in to Omaha on Thursday. I'll see you then. I'll give you a call or maybe e-mail you along the way to keep you posted. I'm gonna rent a car and drive to Pincher."

Straight just looked at Cooney.

"Ain't you got nuthin' to say?" asked Cooney. "Like this is the stupidest thing you ever saw, or what do I think I can do when she's already got lawyers and relatives, givin' her advice . . . and she won't even answer my e-mail, and for all I know she still thinks I'm God's gift to the Losers Club."

"Nope," said Straight. "I just wish I knew somebody I cared that much about. It must be a deep feeling."

"It is," said Cooney. "It gets you down inside." A pause. "Okay," said Cooney, blowin' out his breath, "I'll see ya."

WE CAN TAKE A MOMENT HERE, DEAR READER, TO COMPRE-
HEND THAT THIS GIANT BALL OF NERVOUS, SCARY, BREATHLESS,
SOUL-BARING INTERCOMMUNICATION EXISTS BETWEEN JUST TWO
HUMANS, OUTSIDE EARSHOT OF THE REST OF THE UNIVERSE. ONLY
STRAIGHT KNOWS WHAT IS DRIVING COONEY, AND HE CAN'T DEFINE
IT. IF COONEY'S PLANE CRASHED AND STRAIGHT HAD TO EXPLAIN
WHY COONEY HAD BEEN ON A FLIGHT TO CALGARY, HE'D BE HARD
PUT TO DO IT. THE FIRST QUESTION WOULD BE, "DID SHE KNOW HE
WAS COMING?"

Straight had a meeting in Denver with OTT. Straight dropped Cooney off at the curb of Will Rogers International Airport to get checked in, then parked their pickup in the long-term lot. He had a later flight scheduled to attend a meeting in Denver with OTT.

Oui Oui's addition to the OTT traveling program had been a hit. It was like having a *Playboy* bunny LIVE! in the booth! She attracted attention like a lightning bolt in a microwave. Her attire was revealing, bold, sexy, and seduc-tive. She walked that fine line between lovable and lascivious, between titil-lating and bawdy, between your grandmother kissing you on the cheek and someone running a tongue up your midline navel to chin! Oui Oui had noth-ing to do with rodeo, cowboys, tradition, the PRCA, or education. She was simply the musky scent a mountain man would daub on his trap. It drove them beavers crazy! She was so good with the drooling boys who came by the booth to gawk and get autographed photos. Not Straight's, mind you, but hers.

But behind the scenes Straight had noticed that she and File were get-ting close: confiding, touching, acting very familiar. She had several *noms d'amor* for File that Straight overheard: Filey, FiloMan, Filomatic, Filly Fi Lo. When Pica had been the LIP LASTER girl, Straight, Pica, and File would often eat together, visit about the booth activities, their future. Now, as soon as the show was over Oui Oui would head to the motel alone. File would stay and close the booth and find his way back to the motel by himself. Oui Oui always complained of tired feet, stupid fans, bad motel breakfasts, how hard she worked, on and on. She was constantly pressing File to get her first-class tickets, more per diem, a bigger clothes allowance, a personal trainer, and a lady-in-waiting.

Yes. She was truly obnoxious, selfish, and imperious in real life, but when the spotlight hit her she became the most beautiful, sensuous, charming orchid in the hot house! She could turn it on.

This last weekend Straight had accidentally come upon File and Oui Oui discussing Pica's "problem," as it had come to be called. File was whining that Oui Oui wasn't being very generous with her time considering all he'd done for her.

Straight stopped in midstep when he heard the word *Caribbean*. File and Oui Oui suddenly noticed his arrival and immediately changed the subject. A memory snapped into Straight's brain of Cooney saying maybe Pica had been framed.

CHAPTER 35

September 27, Tuesday, 9:00 a.m.
Pincher Creek, Alberta

COONEY DROVE INTO THE SCENIC LITTLE TOWN OF PINCHER CREEK, THE gateway to Waterton Lakes National Park. The town had a bit of a European feel. Switzerland, maybe, except for the abundance of three-quarter-ton, four-wheel-drive pickups with iron grill guards and steel toolboxes that occupied every other parking space.

Cooney went into the local veterinarian's clinic on the outside of town and inquired as to the whereabouts of Juneau D'TroiT's place. "You a hunter?" asked the lady behind the counter.

"Yeah, of sorts, I guess," smiled Cooney.

"West on Highway 3," the she directed. "Probably five miles. If you reach Cowley you've gone too far. It's on the south side of the road, maybe a mile back towards the mountains. D'TroiT's has a wooden sign. You can't miss it."

Less than thirty minutes later Cooney turned at the sign. The house, outbuilding, and corrals were set back from the road. The house was a two-story, wooden structure with fresh paint and a small front porch with a small lawn surrounded by a split-pole fence. It sat in a stand of large poplars, quakies, and pines. A creek meandered through the surrounding fields and furnished drinking water for the stock in summer.

He heard a loud buzzing coming from the back and drove toward the sound. A tall, lanky man with ear protectors and safety glasses was cutting boards from a twelve-foot-long piece of pine tree trunk on a thirty-six-inch electrical circular saw. Cooney parked where the man would be able to see him approach.

When the man saw Cooney he finished the cut he was making, then shut off the saw.

It whined to a stop.

Suddenly the quiet of the morning enveloped Cooney. He could hear the birds chirping, the man's footsteps in the gravel, the ticking of his engine cooling. A cow dog cautiously crept closer.

"Howdy," said the man.

"Howdy," said Cooney. "I'm looking for the D'TroiT ranch."

"Are you with the press?" the man asked suspiciously.

"Do I look like I'm with the press?" asked Cooney.

"Well, I don't look like the prime minister's valet either, but I could be," replied the man.

"Are ya?" asked Cooney.

"No. I'm the famous Uncle Firmston who serves as the guardian of the gate to protect the pestered Princess Pica from paparazzi."

"You have found me out, my good man. I am not a reporter but merely a friend who is concerned about the princess and seeks permission to see her," confessed Cooney.

"You would not be that Lionel character, would you?" asked Firmston.

"No. Unfortunately, he is a much better bronc rider than me," said Cooney. "I am merely a friend who wishes to offer comfort."

"Is she expecting you?" asked Firmston.

"I'm afraid I made the hasty decision to hunt her up before I was able to contact her," said Cooney. "Perhaps you would be kind enough to tell her I have come calling."

"Tell me, have you studied Shakespeare?" inquired Firmston.

"It was not my good fortune to be taught his plays. And you, Mr. Firmston, are you a student of the titan of the Thames?" asked Cooney.

"No," said Firmston, "I have no official training either. I am just a humble word manipulator, a practitioner of the sleight of vowel, a consonant concoctor, and, I fear, on this beautiful Tuesday morning . . . I have met my match."

"So," said Cooney, "does this mean you will lead me to the majesty in question?"

"She is in the tack room as we speak, sorting the camp gear for the upcoming fall hunting season. You may find her thus occupied."

"My thanks to you, kind sir. I shall recommend you to the prime minister the next time he and I are trying on socks."

Cooney was feeling more confident after his playful conversation with Uncle Firmston. He walked across the farm yard to the tack room, which was actually an enclosed part of a large open-faced barn shed.

He heard a radio playing country music and the occasional noise of things being moved around. From under the shed roof he could see in. A large window facing the east side allowed the morning sun to light the room. He could see a woman in jeans and a work shirt bending at the waist, pulling something from underneath a work bench. She was straining. She bent down to get a better grip when Cooney said, "Maybe I could help?"

Pica straightened to 90 degrees quickly and whacked the back of her head on the bottom of the work bench. She fell back onto her backside, slapping her head against the board floor with a thunk.

The brim of her well-worn hat bent flat and slid down to cover her nose.

For a moment she lay flat on her back in snow angel fashion at Cooney's feet. His confidence escaped him as if he had been punched in the stomach.

She peeled her hat back and looked up at the person standing over her. He saw her expression grow from surprise to recognition to anger.

She rolled to her right side and got her left foot under to catapult herself upright and regain her footing. Unfortunately, she hooked her right boot in a strap on a harness. Her attempt to rise was aborted, and she fell into his legs, knocking him backward across the door jamb and landing in his lap.

Her head was on his chest, her arms reaching out, her body pinning him to the floor.

"I . . . I didn't expect this joyous a welcome," he stammered.

"You . . ." she began. "How dare . . . you . . ." Then she started to make strange huffing noises, then muffled cries that rolled into choked laughter, uncontrollable heehaws, hysterical hoots, finally exhausted gasps, heavy breathing, and a long whistling sigh.

She lay on top of him in that same position for what seemed a heavenly hour to Cooney but was really only twenty-three seconds.

In that brief interlude, his engine room took over the conning tower. The fiery glimpse of her black pupils, the ascending display of her parted prehensile lips, the riveting view straight down the front of her shirt as she rose from the floor . . . nearly blinded him! They replayed in his mind like a slot machine coming up grapes, roses, and melons.

The collision and subsequent engulfing were tumultuous. He felt as if he were melting when she finally relaxed her entire weight onto him. Then he realized she had begun to cry.

He wrapped his arms around her and held her until she brusquely pushed herself off of him.

Tears glistened on her face. She gave him a hard glower. "You are the last person I . . ."

Cooney raised a hand in protest, then put his index finger to his lips, indicating silence.

"No," he said, his brain taking control again. "I am the *first* person you need and the *last* person you should turn away."

She stared at him. Then her visage softened slightly to a less-suspicious pose. "Why?" she asked.

"Because I believe," he began, ". . . because I *do* not believe—for a second—that you are responsible for the wreck you are in."

"But you," she said with distaste, "why you? You've done nothing but embarrass me . . . and yourself."

The spirit of Stone Roanhorse rose in Cooney, and he said, "The answer is, I am both."

Without knowing why she understood, she did—immediately.

CHAPTER 36

September 27

Pincher Creek, Alberta, on the D'TroiT Ranch

PICA STOOD, ABSENTMINDEDLY PICKED UP A SHOEING RASP, AND LEANED against the bench. Had Cooney been alert to her every nuance, he might have interpreted that as a defensive maneuver, but he was too empathetic to take it personally.

"So, what are you doing here?" she asked.

"I came to help you," he said.

"What do you think you can do that's not being done already?" she asked.

Cooney had given considerable thought to this very question. He responded. "Since I know you are innocent, probably framed, then the first thing we have to do is find out who did this to you."

"What makes you think . . ." she started.

He interrupted her, "Because I'll bet you a loonie that not a single person, including your lawyers, the OTT, your family, or your friends has lifted a single finger to begin the chase."

She stared at him.

"Have they?" he pressed.

"Well, no, I guess. They've been mostly, like, worrying about my bail and court hearings," she said.

"Exactly," he said. "And you are stuck up here, lyin' awake nights, wondering what's gonna happen. Probably goin' crazy, I'll bet."

"So just what do you, like . . . think you can do?" she asked.

"Right now nobody's doin' anything to find out who's trying to frame you. If I make one phone call, I'll be doin' more than them."

"I think that OTT is trying to help me, hopefully," she said.

175

"It's my opinion that OTT is covering its own butt. They've laid you off, shipped you far away, hired Oui Oui Reese to take your place, and never looked back," he said a little cruelly.

"Their lawyers are working . . ."

"When was the last time you talked to them?" Cooney asked.

"Couple weeks ago, maybe?" she replied.

"Listen," he said. "Since you got arrested, or since I read it in the papers, it's all I can think about. I don't know if you need me, but I need to help you, so I can sleep. Two heads are better than one. I'm thinkin' that if you were an innocent mule for endangered species smugglers, we would have to go to the place you left from, that island, or whatever it was.

"That would mean you were a random choice, and they planned to rob you when you got back to the States. You can do some Internet searching for smugglers, particularly of that kind of stuff. If you come up on a good lead, we . . . or I can go down and start digging.

"But," he continued, "if that was *not* the case, instead, someone specifically wanted *you* to get caught with contraband . . ."

"What?" she said. "Who would want that to happen to me?"

"That is the million-dollar question," he said. "I think that's where we start putting our heads together."

Two hours later they were sitting on the front porch. They had been talking like two teenage girls. Each feeding off the other. She'd gotten them some coffee. They had established a bond.

"Cooney," she said, "I don't know what to say. None of my lawyers or the OTT people have even discussed any of this with me. How you knew . . . I mean, this is exactly what I should be doing, finding out who's behind all this."

She studied him as he sat in the old lawn chair, letting the silence have a turn. He had taken off his hat. His straight, dark-brown hair spread out over his ears like wings—hat hair. He also had brown eyes and latte-colored skin. It was obvious he hadn't put on a clean shirt or jeans this morning, nor were his boots shined. Only his belt buckle shined. It was new. "Saddle Bronc Champion."

"Cooney, can I ask you a question? Why did you say women can't ride bucking horses?"

He felt a little blurp in his stomach. "What I said was although women are allowed to ride in rough stock events in the PRCA, you don't see many of them doing it. So, logically it's because . . . well, they find it hard to, uh . . . *compete,* ya know. It doesn't mean there aren't exceptions to that observation. You, obviously, but for the most part . . ." Cooney realized he was babbling. "I can only chalk it up to bein' stupid. I've got no excuse.

"I can tell ya that I'm sorry it happened. I'm sorry I even talked to that jerk of a reporter. I've been paying for it plenty, but there is nothing I can do to go back and change it. If I could I would, but sometimes ya just mess up. You don't mean to, you're sorry you did it, but the damage is done. You just gotta buck up, take the flack, and go on."

He looked over at her to see if his explanation made any sense.

She was thinking about it. Also about his throwing up at her feet in Miles City. Of his hanging out of her ex-sister-in-law's car passed out and half-naked. The thoughts were enough to give a woman pause.

"That's a pretty buckle," she said, avoiding what could have been an ugly conclusion to the nicest morning she'd had since her arrest.

"Thanks," he said. "Snake River Stampede, Nampa, Idaho."

"I haven't been paying attention to the rankings. How are you and Straight doing?"

"Straight's coming back steadily," said Cooney. "He was in a slump, but I'm still bettin' he'll make the finals."

"And you?" she asked.

"I'm settin' good in the broncs and the bulls," he said.

"I like to watch you ride," she confessed. "You really hang in there and hook it to 'em. It's like you never let up. Really aggressive."

"I saw you ride Crash Bar in Caldwell," returned Cooney. "It was a beautiful ride. No, it was more. It was a spectacular show, which put me in my place and did more for women's rights than all the woman generals in the U.S. of A. Marines!"

She grinned at him.

Cooney was invited to lunch. Afterward he decided it was best that he depart before he somehow managed to make a mess of his visit. "I've got lots to do," he told her. "I'll be talking to you or e-mail everyday to keep you informed."

She didn't walk him to his car, just waved from the porch.

After Cooney's car had disappeared down the lane and back out of sight, Pica remained standing on the porch.

Uncle Firmston came out and stood beside her. He lit a cigarette.

"Uncle Firmy, you know you should quit smoking, hey," she said.

"Yes, I know. Kind of a burly Yank ya had for lunch," he noted. "Did ya feel how hard his hands were? A workin' man's hands."

She remembered the rough palm of Cooney's hand on the back of her neck while they were . . . well, on the floor in the tack room and she was on top of him. That, she realized, would be hard to explain, so she just let Uncle Firmy's comment go unanswered.

CHAPTER 37

September 28, Wednesday
Denver Airport

As Cooney's big jet landed at Denver International Airport his mind was racing. After he had debouched he called Straight on his cell phone. They were to meet after he landed, then they had a three-hour layover and then a flight to Oklahoma City to pick up their truck and head to Omaha.

Straight was in a bar near gate B29, sitting in a corner near a large picture window. They could see the anthill activities of the ground crews as airplanes came and went.

Cooney sat down and immediately began pouring out his story about Pica and his plans to save her. "Let me get a beer," he said. "You want something?"

It was then that Cooney first paid enough attention to realize that Straight was not right. "What's wrong, amigo?" he asked, suddenly concerned.

Straight stirred his rye and Coke with a straw. "I've got other problems. I'm sorry about Pica, I'm glad you got things straightened out with her, but I . . ." he took another draw on the straw.

"The big meeting this week about replacing Pica also put me on notice. They are liking Oui Oui as the LIP LASTER girl, at least some of them are. They are thinkin' rodeo authenticity is not nearly as valuable as sex appeal. Which means Pica's out. Then it came up, 'How's it going to look?' for the booth, for me, really, if I don't make the finals."

Cooney felt a catch in his heart. Straight had been steady on the course toward his dream, which was to capitalize on his bronc riding ability and use it to become a rodeo media personality. Three months ago his dream was coming true. Now it appeared he might lose it all. "Nothing more for me," said Straight in answer to the first question.

Cooney went to the bar and picked up a draft beer. Suddenly his whole life was complicated.

He was an intelligent man, but sorting out these problems left his mind fuzzy. But first things first: He owed Straight. More than he liked to think about. For three years his riding buddy had coached and commiserated with him. It had paid off. Cooney was the best he had ever been. Okay . . . he took a deep breath and returned to the table.

"Partner, the first thing we need to do, before Pica, before OTT, before the booth, the girls, the truck, or your miserable brother, is to get you ridin' like you know you can. I need to think on this, but we'll do it.

"I've got to go to the john and make a call or two. The plane doesn't leave for two hours. If you're not here when I come back, I'll see you at the gate," said Cooney.

❧

"Posthole Poetry Company. May I help you?"

"Lydia, it's Cooney Bedlam. Would Lick be around?"

"He's takin' a nap in his new hammock. Can I have him call you back?"

"I'm in the airport between planes. Any way you can . . . I need to talk to him kinda bad."

"All right. Let me see what I can do. I'll put you on hold."

Thirty seconds later Lick came on the phone. "Hey, Cooney, what's up?"

"Howdy, Lick. Thanks for talking to me. I'm in a squeeze here, and I need some help sorting it out. Ya see . . ." Cooney laid out his confusions.

"Humm," said Lick. "I think the first thing I'd do is get Straight some mind-bending drugs."

"What?" said Cooney.

"Not illegal drugs. But he needs uppers, some mood-altering, calming medication. He sounds like he's depressed. Xanax is one that comes to mind. Believe me, I got depressed once. I didn't know I was, but I finally went to the doctor and told him I couldn't sleep, didn't eat, cried at odd times. He gimme these pills, I took 'em for two days, and rose from the doldrums like a Phoenix."

"Where do you get 'em?" asked Cooney.

"Yer in the airport, right? Where are you headed?"

"Omaha."

"Great. I know folks everywhere. Let me make a call or two. Then I'll call you back, and you can pick them up when you land. I've got some ideas on Pica's problem, but we can talk about that after Straight gets straight."

"Thanks, Lick," said Cooney.

CHAPTER 38

September 29–October 1
Omaha Qwest Center

On Thursday in Omaha Cooney was up in an Xtreme Bull Riding event, which also counted toward the PRCA standings. It was limited to forty selected bull riders who qualified to enter based on year-to-date winnings. The entry fee was $185. One go-round with the top twelve qualifying to compete in the final go-round. Winner could make upward of $5,000.

The regular Omaha rodeo featured the requisite events: bareback bronc, saddle bronc, bull riding, tie-down calf roping, steer wrestling, and team roping. Each event had one go. Cooney entered both the saddle bronc and the bull riding. Straight entered the saddle bronc.

Straight's mood had definitely mellowed after Lick had arranged for them to pick up a few pills from a friend in Council Bluffs who had recently gotten divorced at age fifty. He told Lick he would be glad to give a couple of days' worth to a friend in need. The arrangements had been made.

Since their aroma therapy and virtual colonic under the tutelage of Stone Roanhorse, Straight had begun to regain his riding karma. The fact that he had come from twenty-second and out of the running to nineteenth since then looked good to him, but to OTT, he was still a long shot to make the finals with only a month to go.

Straight had a good draw for the Saturday night performance. Klackamas Jack was big, powerful sorrel gelding. His book said that he could be inconsistent on occasion. Maybe take a nose dive to the right, so one had to be alert to him changing course in midair.

Straight's attitude was great. He had taken the Xanax as Cooney had instructed for two days, but he hadn't had one since Friday morning. He was pleasant in the OTT booth on Friday night, while Oui Oui had been upset

180

that her room had a view of the railroad yard. And the lotion in the hotel room smelled like deodorant soap. Klackamas Jack thundered into the bucking chutes with the other broncs. Nebraska was as much cowboy as it was corn. Those eastern Nebraska and western Iowa farm boys liked the rodeo. And the Qwest Center Arena was full.

The first saddle bronc slammed out of the gate! Straight, up next, dropped down in the chute, rein in hand, thighs pressed against the swells, boots in the fiberglass oxbows doubled back along the side, hat pulled down, the rein hand raised almost straight-arm taking the slack, body back, back bowed. Then the bowlegged, bullet-proof Buffalo, Alberta, bronc rider in the black hat gave the nod . . . and the door blew open!

As Straight left the chute, his last lifeline to fall away was Cooney's fingertip on the edge of his vest.

Cooney, standing on the catwalk, was three feet off the ground. The top of his hat was therefore nine feet above the arena floor. At the peak of Klackamas Jack's launch, the top of Straight's hat was three feet above Cooney's eye line.

Cooney watched Straight snap his heels right out over the flat of the neck, rowels landing in the crease along the top of the shoulders where they parked, his boots pushed hard against the stirrups. So hard that it lifted Straight's body out of the saddle seat up against the cantle. You could see daylight between jeans and leather. His legs were maximum extension like the jaws of a bear trap waiting to scissor closed. Man and beast descended. The arches in Straight's boots took the full force of the impact when horse and man hit with the Earth.

As Klackamas Jack reloaded and began to launch again, Straight leaned against the swells and brought his dull rowels back along the neck 'til they reached the cinch. *Good drag,* Cooney noted.

They found the rhythm. Straight and Klackamas. Rock and fire, ridin' the stirrups and the rein, light as a feather in the saddle seat. Grace under power. Cheetah, jaguar, Lamborghini. A Greyhound 240Z. Smooth, suave, the epitome of "just exactly right."

Klackamas never tried any tricks; he just poured his all into it. From the stands it looked so easy. And it was, as long as horse and man and rein and spur and footing and hoof and muscle and tendon stayed in harmony. Fifteen hundred pounds of feng shui.

"Man, oh, man," thought Cooney an instant before the 8-second buzzer jarred the spectators. "That is what it is supposed to be like."

Straight and Klackamas scored an eighty-nine. The crowd loved it. Straight took the lead with only six bronc riders left to go for a purse of about $15,000 to the winner.

Straight went back to the catwalk to help Cooney get down onto his draw.

"Great ride," said Cooney as they were checking the back cinch.

"Yeah, well, thanks," said Straight. "Let's see if you can beat it. You've got the horse that can."

In the next nine minutes before Cooney nodded his head to ride Sky Walker as the last man out, the wisp of a thought kept floating through his mind. It never completely formed, but the gist of it was: *Straight needs to win this for his confidence, for his job, for his shot at the finals. And I am the last man standing between him and the championship buckle. But . . . I couldn't . . . Straight would be devastated if he thought . . . How could I even consider . . .*

In the middle of the muddle Cooney called for his horse. He was on autopilot. He rode ol' Sky Walker. But he failed to mark him out. Straight took the buckle and the check. Cooney didn't mean to disqualify himself . . . did he? In the deepest part of his own heart, he didn't know.

CHAPTER 39

October 1, Saturday Night
Omaha after the Rodeo Party

STRAIGHT, IN A GREAT MOOD, WAS IN THE OTT LIP LASTER BOOTH AS the crowd leisurely departed the big auditorium. Many stopped to visit, get samples of LIP LASTER lip balm and autographed pictures. For the first time since Oui Oui had begun appearing in the booth, Straight was getting as many requests for photos and autographs as she was. There was one point when no one was waiting to get Oui Oui's autograph, and Straight had five people waiting for his. It wasn't because Oui Oui had become lax in her personal appearance. It was just that the number of rodeo fans equaled the number of cleavage connoisseurs.

Back in her hotel room, which conveniently connected to File's, Oui Oui was simmering as she got ready for the invitation-only party planned for that night by the Omaha Rodeo Committee

"Did you see that? Straight had more fans than me!" she fumed.

"No, no, Oui Oui Baby. It just seemed that way for a minute because . . . because several were holding back. Waiting out of sight for your line to shorten. They were actually in it, they just didn't know, and it seemed that way."

"Do you really think so?" she asked, not exactly understanding what he said.

"Yeah, they love ya, Baby. Nobody can touch you. Besides, you're gonna knock 'em dead at the party tonight."

"Oh, Filey, Filofrenzy, you always say the right thing. I just woochy, woochy, woochy you."

"Maybe when the party's over we could have our own private party up here," he crooned. "You could model that little exotic package you got in the

183

mail from Barbados." File was referring to the very source of the rare feathers that had caused Pica's downfall.

"Oh!" she said. "Oooooo! I could wear that to the party!"

File cautioned her, "Remember, we'd be better off to keep that out of sight for a while."

"Oh, File!" she said, petulantly pursing her lips. "Nobody will know. Nobody even knows what the Tooting Pavo Real is anyway!"

"That is the Tetuchtan Pavo Real," said File, correcting her gently. "Endangered feathers have been in the press a lot. It might be taking a big chance."

"You really think there will be an authority on endangered peacocks at a cowboy party? Lighten up!" she said slyly, "because . . . if I wore it to the party, there's nothing to stop me from giving you a private fashion show after we come back to the room.

"You know I want to make you happy. Please let me wear it. Please, please, please, pleeeeeese, Filomantic, Filovely, Filamour."

Twenty minutes later Oui Oui Reese walked into the crowded ballroom filled with men dressed in jeans and suit coats, women swooshing in long dresses or tight jeans, and waiters with trays of hors d'oeuvres and Champagne. She crashed the party like an icebreaker going through the Northwest Passage. The crowd would heave up, step back, then re-form in her wake.

She was wearing a halter top made of two upraised fans of the most *fluoredescent* feathers imaginable in nature's studio. It was as if a swan had been painting the ceiling with every color of sherbet she could find: lime, blackberry, raspberry, cherry, mango, melon, metropolitan, sunflower, Godiva dark chocolate, and John Deere, and . . . it had dripped onto her downy breasts. The infrastructure, neck strap, and back tie were made of tightly braided grass, as was the lining that separated her skin from the feathers.

Like drones attracted to the queen bee, a swarm of men moved within her circle of pheromones. Just as one of the attendees handed her a Champagne glass, she felt something bite her!

She fluffed her skirt and deliberately avoided touching where the little sting remained.

"Of course, I'd be thrilled to have my picture with UUUU!" she gasped, eyebrows raised in surprise as she felt another tiny bite underneath the left fan of feathers.

"Ooo, pardon me," she said. "The Champagne must've . . . Ow!" she said, this time reaching up and scratching above her seventh rib.

Oui Oui got control of herself. "Okay," she said, "who would like a picture with the LIP LASTER girl?" A gentleman stood on either side of her.

"How 'bout an arm around each of them?" asked the photographer who had been hired by the rodeo committee just for this party.

"Of course," she smiled like the seventh siren. She was taller than both men. Each seemed to nestle under her protective arms. "Smile!"

Just then there were simultaneous bites on the abaxial sides of her halter top! Instinctively she reached to scratch them, but in doing so she jerked the surprised committee members across her chest and banged their heads together!

It was the first of many photographs that would be passed around at rodeo committee meetings for years to come. The photos would eventually be included in a special historical scrapbook in her honor.

Other photographs included one with her left hand raised like the Statue of Liberty, right hand underneath the left fan; another with her left hand inside the right fan like Napoleon; another with her right hand over the left fan as if she were reciting the Pledge of Allegiance; one with both arms crossed over her chest, fingers scratching madly, a grimace on her face; another with her bent at the waist shaking them as if she were trying to get crumbs out of her cleavage; one, particularly festive, with her upending a Champagne bottle into the right fan; and, finally, one with her lying on a round banquet table face down, arms spread wide, legs bent up at the knees, wiggling wildly as if she were polishing the table top with the feathers!

Needless to say, after she had run out of the ballroom, through the hotel lobby, and down the hallway screaming at the top of her lungs and clawing at herself, she reached her hotel room door before File did. He had both keys. He came racing up and swiped the card.

As soon as the green light blinked, she smashed him into the side of the door and careened through the room and into her bathroom.

File heard the door slam and the shower come on. He knew it was going to be a long night.

CHAPTER 40

October 1, Late at Night
Omaha, Cooney Calls Pica

COONEY CALLED PICA FROM HIS HOTEL ROOM IN OMAHA AT 11:30 P.M., AN hour later than it was in Pincher Creek. She was in her bedroom, sitting at her desktop computer.

"I've been trying to find out about these endangered species," she said, "the smuggling business and all.

"These feathers . . . they are quite the deal. They are, like, the most popular bird item to be sold. The birds, parrots, actually, live in the jungles of Venezuela. They've been hunted nearly to extinction. The governments and museums and bird people, I guess, are trying to protect them . . . Which only makes them more valuable, hey."

"Where are you learning all this?" asked Cooney.

"Internet. It's everywhere! So, anyway," she continued, "like, I saw several related stories about the Customs Service catching smugglers. There are lots of color photographs of ornaments and headdresses and ceremonial stuff made out of these feathers. One of the articles was about this professor who is an expert on exotic bird poaching. I'm going to try and contact her."

"That's a start," said Cooney. "We've haven't got much done down here yet. Straight had some trouble, but he got over it and won the Omaha saddle bronc championship!"

"Oh, good. He's such a good guy," she said with compassion. "I worried about him, about hurting his feelings when I went on the media blitz, and he didn't get invited. He deserves a break, hard as he works and all."

Cooney had a fleeting thought that she might have some regret about *him*, too, about hurting his feelings, because it was his verbal faux pas that catapulted her to fame in the first place and he who had borne the scorn of the media and the feminist world. However, she apparently had nothing more to say about his suffering, so he changed the subject.

"On a side note, the girl that has taken your place in the LIP LASTER booth created a scene tonight at the sponsor's party. I hate to wish anyone bad luck, but it was so hilarious!" Cooney started to laugh.

"Well, I don't know her," said Pica, "but I remember I had several pie-in-the-face moments when I first started with OTT. That queens banquet I did in Greeley. OTT even hired a woman who had tried to make me more, like, sophisticated. It was awful. And I didn't even know I was humiliating myself 'til afterwards. So, I feel sorry for her. Oui Oui Reese, right?"

"Yup," said Cooney. "Oui Oui got some kind of bugs or stinging nettle in her fancy bikini top, and she couldn't have broke the party up more if she'd yelled 'Fire!'"

"Any word from the lawyers about your court date?"

"No, except that it won't be anytime soon. It's an international crime . . . Gosh, I can't believe I said that. I'm an international criminal."

"Don't think like that, Pica," said Cooney. "You're not guilty. You know that, and so do I. And there's probably lots of folks who know you who know you couldn't have done it."

"Yeah, but, the, like, you know, the press. They keep trying to get interviews. There's even photographers who have come down and hid out trying to get pictures of. They found one in an old hunting magazine of me in camp sharpening my hunting knife. It was on the front page of a national rag, hey, a gossip magazine," Pica took a breath.

"Don't let it get to ya. You didn't do it! And we are going to prove it. So, remember that," said Cooney with force. "And there's one other thing that you should remember."

"There is?" she said.

"Yeah," he said.

She waited. He spoke not.

"Well?" she prompted.

"Uumm," he said. "I, uh, I just want you to know, you don't owe me anything for this."

She literally held the telephone receiver away from herself and looked at it quizzically.

Should I invite him to call collect next time? she thought.

CHAPTER 41

October 18, Tuesday
Denver, Colorado, Meeting at OVER THE TOP ATHLETIC COSMETICS Headquarters, Denver Tech Center, 10th Floor

TURK MANNIQUIN SAT AT THE END OF A LONG CONFERENCE TABLE WEARING a custom-tailored Italian suit made by Caraceni in silver-blue with sleek black lapels. It went well with his Calvin Klein eggshell-colored turtleneck and silver Gucci loafers with black tassels. His black bald pate reflected the ceiling lights. He wore no bling. He was pushed back from the table in a large padded-leather office chair with leopard-skin seat. The other chairs were similarly made but with a zebra pattern.

He was tapping a yellow pencil against his cheek, thinking.

To Turk's right side at the table sat Nova Skosha, in her black bobbed hair and black pants suit. The only appurtenance to her austere attire was a soup spoon–size seashell inlaid with turquoise hanging around her neck. Beside her in the next chair File Blitzer waited subserviently, as a vassal awaits his liege.

"Well," began Turk, "we need to make some decisions about our LIP LASTER COWBOY KISSES campaign. It has certainly taken a detour from our original intent. Our two stars have dimmed. One is under indictment, and the other appears to have lost his spark.

"But in their place we now have a spokesperson that appeals to the eighteen- to twenty-year-old testosterone burners. That's a far cry from the metrosexuals, male and female, that we set out to reach.

"I'm not complaining. The initial product made a big splash in sales with national attention, following Pica's bronc ride and the feminist tour that ensued. Unfortunately, sales dropped like a rock after her arrest. Oui Oui's commercials have stopped the decline. Sales aren't climbing yet, but at least they've stopped falling."

Turk looked around the table. His staff waited respectfully to ensure that he was finished talking.

"It's significant that the demographics have changed since Oui Oui got on board," said File. "The last survey indicates our new base follows professional wrestling, martial arts, and X-Box more than rodeo."

"Not exactly the more sophisticated GQ, Outdoor magazine type we aspired to reach," observed Turk, "but is it a bad thing to now be competing with Budweiser and Colt 45 for the attention of our redneck homeboys? Nova, what do you think?"

"Are they mutually exclusive?" she posited. "Does it have to be one or the other? One of the risks we ran marketingwise was to use real athletes as spokespersons. Granted, our rodeo stars do not have the broad celebrity appeal of Tiger Woods or A-Rod, they were not in our budget, but Straight and Pica have the cred of authenticity. And for a moment there it looked like we had struck gold with Pica. But any team owner who's had a player arrested, accused, and convicted of drug use or dog fighting or philandering knows that sometimes you choose wrong.

"We could have started with actors playing cowboys. It's easier. They aren't real people. If they get caught in some mischief, we just hire another actor. Just run a new Marlboro man into the game. But it's safer.

"If you recall, Pica just sorta came along. Fell into our laps and made us set up and take a good look! More than any of us expected. I think she would have achieved considerable notoriety, good notoriety, if . . ." Nova paused. "I know we've hashed this over a million times in the last few weeks, but I still can't believe she planned the smuggling. It's just so out of character with the fairly innocent, or at least naive, girl that I spent so much time with."

"File," asked Turk, "what do you think about the whole LIP LASTER COWBOY KISSES marketing campaign as it stands today?"

"Well, Boss," started File, "personally I'd say it's time to move on. Kiss the cowboys goodbye. Put Oui Oui in a bigger venue. There's nothing wrong with the professional wrestling. They always rank high in the cable ratings. Set up a booth at the NASCAR track. Let Oui Oui pour wine on the winner's head, pose in front of muscle cars, put LIP LASTER on Kyle's lips. Instead of COWBOY KISSES it could be NASCAR KISSES, maybe a tie in with NASA, call it LIP BLASTERS, or get the drywallers' endorsement,

LIP PLASTERS, or the fishing show *LIP CASTERS,* or the PGA LIP MASTERS TOURNAMENT, the ecumenical council LIP PASTORS; we could sponsor a hunger strike, promote LIP FASTERS, but I think I'd start with the WWF, the World Wrestling Federation. Call it LIP RASSLERS."

File saw that Turk was having trouble digesting his radical solution, so he hedged it by saying, "Of course, I know we saw something in the rodeo setting that we liked," he said, changing his tack, sucking up to Turk because COW-BOY KISSES was Turk's personal idea. "If we feel the need to continue with the rodeo theme, at least through the national finals, we could promote some spectacular finale, an awards ceremony where Oui Oui mounts . . ."

The top bulldogger, thought Nova.

". . . a stallion and rides around the arena," File continued, "or she sings the national anthem wearing sort of a Wonder Woman suit, maybe a cape, with lots of fireworks . . ."

They talked for another hour, tossing out scenarios, molding, discarding, assembling, and finally came up with a game plan. Turk summarized: "Pica's out. Even if she didn't do it, she's finished. Tarnished, I'm sorry to say. I thought she had what it took.

"Straight's probably not going to make the finals. Only a month away. If he makes it, his presence in the booth might draw a few more fans, but if he doesn't . . . we won't need him in the booth. Nova, I'll give you the dirty job of telling him.

"So it looks like Oui Oui is going to be our big attraction at the finals," concluded Turk. "She's here in Denver, isn't she, File?"

"Yessir," File replied, rigid with glee.

"Why don't you and she give some thought about how we can use her best in the rodeo venue," said Turk. "Then both of you come here to the office at eleven o'clock tomorrow morning. We'll consider our options."

File departed to dispense the good news to Oui Oui. Nova Skosha lingered. "Turk," she asked, "do you think that Pica really smuggled those feathers into the country?"

Turk shook his head noncommittally. "Truth . . . I just don't know. Our lawyers did some deep diggin'. Seems our sweet little bronc rider shot a guy one time. On a hunting trip. There was an inquiry, but she was a juvenile, so the records are not public. It had to do with a mountain lion or grizzly bear . . . anyway, protected animals were involved." He sighed, "She was hard to read."

"That she was," agreed Nova. But in her mind she was beginning to have some doubt.

Nova had a dirty job to do. She'd done dirty jobs before, and putting them off did not make them easier. Straight had come to Denver to coordinate schedules. He was staying nearby with Cooney. She called him at his hotel and invited herself to lunch.

"So, with Pica being out of it and you not making the finals, it kind of leaves a big hole in the 'real athlete' endorsement campaign."

"There's still a chance I'll make the cut," Straight reminded her.

"Believe me, if you make the finals, we want you in the booth, for sure," encouraged Nova. "But in case, Turk want to be prepared to take another direction."

Neither ate much. Straight said, "Nova, I think there's something going on with Pica. I'm convinced she was framed, or a professional smuggler used her as an innocent mule."

"What do you mean, 'framed'?" asked Nova.

"If she is innocent and it wasn't a professional criminal, then it had to be someone who wanted to hurt Pica. Or at least get her out of the way. Maybe somebody who wanted." Straight paused for effect, ". . . her job."

Nova's eyes narrowed, "You mean . . .?"

"I can only say that I've accidentally eavesdropped a little and heard some suspicious talk."

CHAPTER 42

October 19

On Highway 90 between Houston and Beaumont

COONEY AND STRAIGHT HAD SPENT THE NIGHT IN A MOTEL NEAR THE Denver airport after the OTT meeting going over their itinerary. Their main goal was to qualify Straight for the National Finals Rodeo.

During the previous two weeks, Straight had ridden Klackamas Jack and won enough to stay in contention for qualifying. He and Cooney had contested at the Silver Spurs Rodeo in Kissimmee, Florida, the Heart O' Texas Fair and Rodeo in Waco, and the NILE ProRodeo in Billings, Montana.

They were hot. Cooney was locked in a tight three-man race for second place in the saddle bronc with winnings to date, all within $2,000 of each other, close to $100,000. He was also in solid second in the bull riding at $120,775.

Straight had won money in both Waco and Billings. Enough to bring him within $1,700 of the saddle bronc rider in fifteenth place, a rookie from Utah.

Two weeks of rodeos remained. By stretching it they could fly Denver to Houston to do the Trinity Valley Exposition in Liberty, Texas, on October 19, fly Houston to Denver to Rapid City on October 20, fly Rapid City to Denver to do the Fort Collins Qualifier at the Fort on October 21, then fly Denver to Medford, connecting in Portland, on Sunday morning to ride in the Wild Rogue Pro Rodeo in Central Point, Oregon.

It was a killer schedule: Wednesday through Sunday, 6,000 miles, $2,500 each airfare, not counting hotels, rental cars, and entry fees. It left Straight little time to work the LIP LASTER booth that first weekend. File didn't seem to mind.

They pulled out of Houston's George Bush International Airport on Road 1960 headed east toward Liberty. Straight had told Cooney about OTT's intentions to drop his sponsorship if he did not qualify for the finals. That goal lay beneath all the other conversations.

"Anything new with Pica?" asked Straight after they got out of heavy traffic.

"She's supposed to be diggin' into the smuggling business. Maybe give us a clue where to turn. You remember when you told me that Oui Oui and File were talkin' trash about Pica? We need to be following up on them. 'Cause they sure got motive. Making her a star."

"I agree," said Straight. "I've been thinking: If those two are in cahoots, then they had to somehow buy those feathers from the poachers and hide them in her suitcase. How would someone know what kind of endangered stuff they would need and then where to get it?"

"I can't get my mind around it," said Cooney, "and we're too dang busy right now to."

"I know," said Straight, "and Pica's sittin' up there by herself."

"I'm stayin' in touch with her," said Cooney. "She's all right, right now. It's just that she has to wait for the lawyers to do their stuff. They are supposed to be looking into the source of the contraband."

"I've got a good feeling we'll get her out of the mess," said Straight. "Just like we'll get through this wild week."

"Are ya ready?" asked Cooney.

"I am," said Straight with certainty. "I am."

Straight's future hangs in the balance, as does Pica's. Of our three heroes, only Cooney has the odds on his side. If this were a movie, the scene would be a rear-view shot of the big Dodge pickup with a camper shell headin' down the road toward a fuzzy blue-sky Texas horizon with an old Garth Brooks/Chris Ladoux rodeo song sailing in their slipstream and broken notes dancing in the bronc rider's backwash.

Like Willy says, "On the road again!"

CHAPTER 43

November 15, Tuesday, Five Weeks Later On the Road to Alberta

STRAIGHT WAS DRIVING. THE BIG DODGE LONG-BED WITH A CAPRI CAMPER shell was a popular rig with the cowboys. The Capri had room to sleep and to hang your clothes.

The previous forty-eight hours had been rough for our Buffalo, Alberta, bronc rider. Not qualifying for the NFR, being informed by OTT that he would not be needed in the booth in Las Vegas, and now dreading his brother's expected insincere sympathies, to wit: "Gosh, Straight, I'm really sorry you're not good enough at the stupid sport of rodeo to even make fifteenth place. Maybe you could deliver propane for UFA or get on the Provincial Motor Vehicle Bureau, something that doesn't demand much and has a good retirement plan."

Our two heroes were headed north out of Great Falls, Montana, on Interstate 15. Straight was in the "cowboy up" mode. Stoic acceptance of his setbacks. His indigestion was acting up, nagging him to periodically pop an antacid. The sky was bleak, a bluish-white washed-out ceiling pressing down on a vast doormat of earth the color of the bottom of a shoe.

Cooney was sensitive to the fragile tension within the cab. He himself had qualified for the NFR in both broncs and bulls. That, in itself, generated a leg-shaking nervous buzz, but in addition, Pica had invited him along on a five-day hunting trip with her family. He had not seen her since he had paid her the surprise visit.

"You want another piece of chicken?" asked Cooney.

"No, thanks. I'm good," said Straight.

"Yeah, you are," said Cooney.

"What?" asked Straight.

"Good," said Cooney. "You are good. You're a good man, a good friend, and . . . a good bronc rider."

"Yeah, sure," said Straight sarcastically. "Didn't even . . ."

". . . Made the finals five years runnin'," interrupted Cooney. "Won it all one year, taught me how to ride better."

Neither spoke for half a minute.

"Okay, okay, I get it," said Straight. He had actually placed sixteenth in the total annual winnings, $2,100 out of qualifying. His dream of "endorsement" income had gone up in smoke. Until it happened he hadn't realized how important it was to his self-esteem. He was a man with a plan . . . he had it all worked out.

"My life plan hit a brick wall," he mused and kinda laughed. "A big brick wall. I must have taken my eye off the ball."

"Why don't you come with me to Pincher Creek? I'm sure they can squeeze in one more," said Cooney.

"Thanks, but I've got to go home and face the music, see the folks," answered Straight.

"Maybe Brother Lard Butt won't be there," said Cooney.

"Oh, he'll be there all right. He wouldn't miss this for anything," said Straight.

"You can handle him," said Cooney. "Just take 'em all out to dinner, pick up the tab. See if he offers to get the tip! Practice forgiveness and mercy to all that offend."

"What?" said Straight.

"Forgiveness and mercy to all that offend. A Bible quote, I think," Cooney repeated.

"Where'd you come up with that?" asked Straight.

"My old Sunday School teacher," Cooney explained. "There was this kid. He was on the high school rodeo team. He left some anonymous notes to Miss King, the new computer teacher, and signed my name. They were pretty graphic. He even tried to imitate my handwriting. It was good enough to get me in trouble. I got suspended. Shook me up!"

"I'll bet," said Straight.

"I explained to Miss King that it wasn't me, but I couldn't prove anything. All I knew was I didn't do it, and I was pretty sure who did. It was eating me up. So Mr. Blair, my Sunday School teacher, had a talk with me. He told me, 'Practice forgiveness and mercy to all that offend.'

"The heart of the matter was the guy who sent the notes knew I didn't do it. I knew I didn't do it. And God knew I didn't do it. And no one else mattered."

"And you believed it?" asked Straight.

"I still do. And I still ask God to change that kid's heart every night in my prayers," said Cooney. "And your brother, why do you think he puts you down?" asked Cooney.

"Sibling rivalry, I guess," said Straight.

"How 'bout jealousy? Vying for the attention of your folks or your friends," said Cooney.

"Jealousy!" said Straight. "I don't think he's ever been jealous of me. He's so smart! He's big and good-looking!"

"Maybe it's not jealousy, but somethin' sure keeps him jabbin' at you," said Cooney. "But it doesn't make any difference what it is, he's trying to offend you. And if you actually practice forgiveness and mercy towards him you are suddenly above all the pettiness and the insults he aims your way. His arrows don't stick.

"You realize how childish it seems. 'Cause you know what he is doing, he knows what he is doing, and God knows what and also why. And no one else's opinion matters. It changes the level of the water for all the fish in the pond."

Straight puzzled this last allegory but let it slide.

Cooney changed the subject. "Have you decided if you're comin' to the finals?"

"No," said Straight. "I've kinda put off thinking about it, hey."

Cooney said, "Things are heating up 'bout Pica's problem. If we get a break we might need a hand. Pica talked to Nova Skosha about checking out some angles."

"If I can help, you know I'll do what I can," said Straight.

CHAPTER 44

November 15, Tuesday, 2:00 p.m.
Lethbridge, Alberta

PICA HAD BORROWED THE FAMILY SUBURBAN FOR THE TWO-HOUR DRIVE from their place to Lethbridge, where she was meeting Cooney. Straight was dropping him off there on his way home to Buffalo. Her thoughts were fluttering around in her head like birds in a cage: Miami, OTT, Cooney, Nova Skosha, camp supplies, Cooney, Barbados, Cooney.

The weather was overcast. Old snow piled up along the highway shoulders. The temperature was below freezing, but sun was forecast for tomorrow.

Her impression of Cooney, or at least of his good side, had risen through their corresponding e-mails. He was very good with words. She could savor them when they were printed out. He seemed to have a logical mind as they discussed the possibility of a frame job behind her smuggling arrest. Cooney had convinced himself that somebody deliberately planted the contraband in her suitcase to get her into trouble.

Pica continued to stay in communication with Nova Skosha, but she could not frankly discuss what she and Cooney were thinking. After all, the suspects were still on the payroll!

She made an effort to keep her expectations about Cooney's character modest. Every time she imagined him slipping his hand underneath her reservations, she forced herself to picture him on the sidewalk in Miles City barfing on her ankles! It brought her back to reality. She made a mental note to be friendly but formal, to stay in control. Her arrest had made her only stronger, more determined to take care of herself.

For her "pick up Cooney" ensemble Pica had chosen tight Wranglers, Fat Boy turquoise boots, and a long-sleeve camouflage hunting shirt buttoned almost to the neck. Her wild strawberry-blonde hair was pulled back and stuffed underneath a worn-out tan Ruger baseball cap. It was like she started to get dressed up, but the higher she got, the less convinced she thought she should. Of course, it probably didn't matter. Cooney had shown no sign of being very fashion conscious anyway.

Two hours after dropping Cooney off in Lethbridge, Straight turned into his folks' driveway and pulled up to the house. Forewarned by his cell phone call, members of his family were all standing on the porch to welcome him. Chalk and Fiona, his father and mother, stayed put, but his sisters, Tyra and Myra, raced down the steps to meet him. He barely got the door open, and they were squeezing and kissing him, patting his back and hugging his neck. Any trepidation or shame he might have felt about disappointing them disappeared.

His mother actually gave him a short, tight hug, then regained her formality. His father gave Straight a firm, manly handshake and said, "We're glad to have you home, Son."

While the girls were fixing Straight's room, Chalk mixed a rye and Coke for himself and one for his oldest son. They sat in the living room in stuffed chairs inherited from Fiona's folks. Late autumn sunlight shone in the windows on the west side of the room. It was cozy. "I'm sorry you missed the cut, Straight. Your mother and I, she follows you on the Internet, realize how close you came. We were pleased for your endorsement with OTT. You've done so well with your rodeo. Way more than most who try.

"And," he said, "you'll be back next year. As good as you are, you will only get better. Is there anything your mother and I can do to help?"

Straight was used to his father's encouragement. It was never a slap on the back, or "buy you a beer" sort of good cheer, just an accountant's assessment and a "look on the bright side" attitude. That, in spite of the terrible year Canadian cattlemen were having due to the loss of export sales to the United States and Canada's crippling opportunities to market cull cows.

Straight was fully aware of the financial impact that BSE had on his family's ranch. He felt a brief chest squeeze thinking of his OTT cancellation. But his dad was right about riding broncs. He had come within one good ride of making the finals. It just wasn't in the cards this season.

Still, he had won over $49,000 and earned another twenty-two grand representing OTT. He wanted to tell his father the numbers, just to brag a little, but didn't. His dad knew his rodeo winnings anyway. His mother would have kept track.

"Thanks, Dad. I guess I did okay. I should be grateful for the run I had. You're right, I've got a few more years before I have to think about givin' it up." What went unsaid was the real expectation of both men that Straight would be the one to take over the ranch if he wanted. Later Straight planned to offer some money, a buy-in, or a loan to his folks. He just wasn't sure how they'd take it. They were stubbornly proud and might be insulted.

"Dad, how 'bout I take the family out to supper tonight? I need to celebrate. It would be my treat."

Chalk looked at his son, about to say, "No way. We'll pay our own way . . .," then realized that Straight's gesture would lend well-deserved status to this fine young man they had raised. He said, "We would be pleased to. I'll just tell your mother."

Meanwhile, about 200 kilometers west and south . . .

Cooney laid down his spoon and pushed back from the table. Mr. Juneau D'TroiT was telling hunting stories to the two other guests at the table, a well-to-do couple from Montreal. The gentleman, Dr. Lorenz Nuen was in his fifties, in good health, and loved to hunt. His wife, Angelique, was a trophy wife and pretty handy with a gun herself. They were repeat paying customers. This year they were here for five days. Their intended prey included elk, mule deer, bear, mountain lion, and maybe a mountain sheep.

"So," Juneau D'TroiT was saying, "we'll leave tomorrow morning at five, hey. Two-hour drive and a four-hour pack trip to our camp. Might even get in a short scouting trip tomorrow evening.

"Firmy and Pica will set up camp while we take a look." D'TroiT looked at Cooney. "Cooney here will . . . I'm not sure . . . get firewood, help out, pitch in." He paused. "He's Pica's friend. He won't be hunting."

Dr. Nuen seemed relieved that Cooney wasn't hunting. Less competition. They had paid several thousand dollars and assumed first-class privilege.

"Pica and I will both be taking photographs of your hunt. All part of the service!" Juneau said, smiling.

In the day and a half since Cooney had arrived, Pica had been schooling him on the business end of a hunting guide's life. During that time they had also talked about her smuggling arrest problem. But in spite of the proximity of pheromones and ample opportunity, nary a kiss had crossed their lips!

And, yes, it was hard on Cooney! He was constantly on his best behavior, to the point of deferring to her obsequiously on occasion. It did not flatter him. The battle within him raged, waged by the devil of temptation and the angel of restraint.

Even Thursday night after supper, when he called her "Patty" instead of "Pica," he blushed, and she looked hurt. He realized what he had done and feebly attempted to explain. "Patty, oh . . . Patty was my dog . . ." the word slipped out before he could stop it.

Her jaw dropped. She was aghast. Her eyes narrowed. "Wha . . . What?" she stammered.

"I . . . I mean," he literally blanked out her name. "P . . . P . . . Patty was a . . ."

"If you say 'good dog,'" Pica threatened coldly, "you go immediately back to square one."

They were standing in the mudroom about to put on their jackets and go out to the barn to finish packing the gear. In that moment he felt like a fledgling paratrooper standing at the edge of the door with nowhere to go but *jump!*

He picked her up, sat her down on the washing machine, slid his hands up her back, pressed one against her neck, and kissed her large, lovely, beckoning mouth.

Time stood still.

She was the texture of a rose petal, the resilience of a ripe peach, the tang of Tabasco, the tenderness of a truffle, and although her lips never parted, he felt like she had swallowed him whole!

She placed a hand on his neck. Their lips didn't press so much as caress. The pressure lessened, then returned again and again like waves upon the shore. The inside of her lower lip sensed the searching tip of tongue, teeth parted, tips touched and retreated, then the lingual explorers separated as softly as the moon slips behind a cloud.

They experienced a labial eclipse.

Cooney was encompassed by rapture. Pica, in a breathless dream puff, thought, *So, oh, my, that's how it's supposed to feel.*

Cooney stepped back to look at her. She sat on top of the old Kenmore washer, a box of laundry soap on the shelf behind her. His eyes held hers. Her cheeks were flushed, pupils dilated, wild reddish hair frizzing a halo, and that mouth. That inviting, tantalizing tulip of temptation waiting like the docking port on the international space station yearning for *Challenger* to come coupling her way.

"Never," he said, "have I drunk from such a deep well."

She stared into his eyes, searching for a familiar dock, a pier, a coat rack, a parking space, an embrace to use as a corner of commonality on which to build a relationship. Alas, her boat seemed to be adrift.

"Pica," said Juneau, poking his head in from the kitchen. "Better put in a couple bottles of Champagne."

"Okay, Dad," she said without looking at him.

Juneau started to say something, took in the scene, and ducked back into the kitchen. He closed the mudroom door behind him, smiling for the little girl he loved.

Somehow our two star-crossed lovers realized that something had passed between them. They slowly got themselves gathered and without a word put on coats and hats and walked out to the barn.

CHAPTER 45

November 19, Saturday, Midday
Hunting Trip

TWO DAYS LATER COONEY FOUND HIMSELF IN HUNTING CAMP WITH UNCLE Firmy, having a little shot of rye after a cheese sandwich lunch, while Pica and her dad were out guiding the Nuens. The conversation got around to the hunting clients they were hosting.

"Ah, yes," said Firmy in his best W. C. Fields imitation, "the Nuens. We have guided them before. The missus is quite demanding, hey?"

"Well, it's nothin' to me," said Cooney, "but she's not very nice to Pica. I don't mind pickin' up after 'em. Shoot, she even asked me to shine her hunting boots! I said I didn't bring any polish. What color are they anyway? That's not real alligator skin, is it? And Angelique? Whoever named her got it square backward; it should be 'Devilique' or 'Medusa-Eeek'!"

"'Seduca-Eeek,' more like it," laughed Firmy.

By 3:00 p.m. the two men had nursed down half a bottle of rye. Firmy would later say it was already opened when they found it. He had begun to regale Cooney with what one could call only "B-roll Shakespeare." "So, you see, my limping prince, you find yourself merely a footman at the toe of Angelique, Cinderella's step-Nazi. She has been compared in literature with the Loch Ness Anaconda, the Hooker of Notre Dame, Mercury's heel, Napoleon's Waterloo, Custer's Big Horn, and Al Gore's Ralph Nader. After she has drawn you into her web, there are few men—and I, my young knave, am not one of them—who can resist her sulfurous jungle gardenia charms.

"And should the occasion arrive, you would do well to remember that her bite is poisonous ... so be aware."

"Ah, wise counsel," Cooney replied in kind. "I can see from the drool on your tunic you have given this much thought. Now, I, on the other hand ..."

Cooney sat up slightly and looked in the direction of the trail to the north. The clearing was lit by the sun. "Kind sir, does that look like a bear to you?"

"I would answer your query thus," said Firmy. "If it is not a bear, what else could it be?"

Cooney squinted and pulled his hat down slightly, showing his eyes. "Sasquatch," he said, "it could be Sasquatch. Or Little Bo Peep with hairy-leg syndrome. Maybe a pilgrim tarred and feathered with mutton fat and a pillow."

"I don't know," said Firmy. "Looks like a bear to me."

"Do they normally come so close to camp?" asked Cooney.

"Get my rifle," said Firmy. "It's in our tent under my cot."

Cooney arose, slipped into the big four-man tent that he, Firmy, Juneau, and Pica shared, and located the 30.06. He cradled it in his arms to exit and ducked through the tarp cover door flaps, then tripped over a ground peg, knocked the safety off as he fell, and . . . kablooey!

The big rifle boomed! Immediately the box of pint-sized butane canisters exploded in the Nuens' tent: the Nuens' twelve-by-twenty-foot, heavy-duty, steel-frame, puncture-resistant, deluxe Alaknak tent! It billowed, then burst into flames!

Cooney rose to try to rescue something, anything, from the conflagration! Firmy managed to kick him as he went by.

"Don't!" yelled Firmy. "Nuthin' t' save, hey!"

Cooney stuck his head inside the burning tent flaps and quickly retreated but still managed to catch his hat on fire!

An hour later nothing was left in the Nuens' pile of ashes but skeletons, shards, shells, and smoldering clumps of the aluminum table, Lafuma reclining chairs, hammock hips, a Phillips environmental toilet, Zodi hot camp shower, Sheepherder stove and pipe, splintered butane bottles, bed frame, the twisted remains of a Browning .450-caliber bear gun, and the handle of a riding crop made out of the seven-inch tusk of an African warthog!

One drawer was filled with the melted remains of Motorola walkie-talkies, a Garmin GPS Map 60CX, a custom-made knife with the Nuen coat of arms carved on its narwhal ivory handle, a Terrafix personal locator, Silva handheld compass and altimeter, Leatherman Seclusion 3D folding knife gadget, and a set of six Surefire high-pressure Xenon flashlights.

Needless to say, anything vaguely cloth was ashes. Granted, they were Gore-Tex, Thinsulate, Hertgers, Pendleton, Meindl, Denali, Pronghorn,

Danner, Columbia, Cabela, L.L. Bean, Scent-Lok, Silent Weave, waterproof, Under Armour, super-mesh, super-light, super-strong, and super-duper performance cammo apparel ashes, but ashes none the less.

Unspent cartridges, unused bottles of hair care products and makeup, and a heavy turquoise-and-silver squash-blossom necklace would be identified later when the ashes were sifted through.

"I should be going now," said Cooney, serious as a root canal.

"What? And leave me to take the blame? I'm actually here on borrowed time! I've got two DUIs already. It wouldn't do to be arrested for 'hunting under the influence.'"

"I've got it," said Firmy. "We take our guns, go out like we're hunting, and just sort of drift back into camp when they do. We can claim it was a bear attack!"

"With a gun? A bear with a gun?" asked Cooney.

"Okay, okay, it was a mysterious hunter who wanted our . . . our food! No, guns . . . no . . . how 'bout we say that it was a bail bondsman from California, and he was carrying your picture with a warrant for your arrest because you . . ." Firmy was withering under Cooney's gaze. "Well, okay, not so good, but we'll think of something."

Forty-five minutes later Cooney was sitting under the ledge of a large rock twenty feet off the trail, pondering whether to stick it out or head for home, when Mrs. Nuen came walking by.

"Hey," he said.

"Oh! It's you, Cooney," she said. It was the first time he had heard her call him by name.

She wandered over to him and sat on his rock. "*Je suis fatigue*," she said in French. "My muscles ache. Would it be possible for you to apply a little massage to my shoulders?"

"Where are your husband and the D'TroiTs?" he asked.

"They shot a big elk, according to them anyway, and it was over a farther ridge. I decided to walk back. They didn't need me."

"Weren't you worried about getting lost or eaten by a bear or something?" he asked.

"*Petit chiot*, I may look like a rich man's toy but I am a hunter's daughter. I can handle myself in the woods . . . and elsewhere," she said and turned her dark brown eyes on him.

"So," she asked in her French-accented English, "are you and that teen-age blonde bomber shell-in-the-rough an item?"

"An item?" asked Cooney.

"Are you engaged, spooning, courting, playing footsie, doing it after dark?" she elaborated.

"No! no," he said, not wanting to besmirch Pica's reputation. "I just came up to visit."

"So, how does this feel?" She licked her finger and traced a wet line from his right ear under his mustache and gently pulled down his bottom lip. His heart skipped a beat. It was like being licked by an anteater.

"Do you know what is behind this big rock?" she asked.

He shook his head no.

"Follow me," she invited and rose.

"What about . . ." he started to say the obvious as he pushed off the rock after her.

"He's twenty years older than me, and shooting the elks is what turns him on . . . Not I."

"Gosh, Ma'am," he stammered.

"You are not worried about the buckskin cheerleader, are you?" she asked.

"Well, yes, no . . . I'm not but . . ."

"Do I smell smoke?" she asked, wrinkling her nose.

Cooney's mind was immediately brought back to his most-pressing problem: the tent that lay destroyed back in camp. To distract her he quickly said, "So, where do you hurt, exactly?"

By the time Cooney had begun to think of a way to explain the fire in camp to Angelique, she was sitting yogalike on his heavy coat. Her shirt was unbuttoned. Cooney was kneeling behind her on his knees, hands up under her shirttail, kneading his heart out and all the while trying to think about baseball!

"Oooo," she groaned, "unbuckle that retaining strap, Coney Island, to give you more freedom."

He obliged. She straightened up, then laid back against him and slid forward so her head rested in his lap. She lay on her back, looking up at him. "How about massaging my aching shoulders and the shooting muscle? I've been carrying that rifle all day."

I hope she likes it, thought Cooney, *the rifle, that is. It's the only one she has left!*

Her shirt was wide open, but her white, lacy B-cups covered the positive and negative poles of her estrogen battery.

"Umm, that is so wonderful," she said. "Anything I could do for you?"

Cooney mustered what was left of his resolve. "Yes, Mrs. Nuen . . ."

"Angelique!"

"Yes, Mrs. . . . Angelique . . . I need a serious favor. I wasn't quite truthful about Pica. I've got a . . . something, some feeling for her, but I keep messing up and turning her off."

"I could give you some lesson on how to turn her back on," Angelique purred.

"No, oh, no, not that kind of messing up . . . I keep, well, like today. I was sitting there by the fire with Firmy, and he sent me to get his rifle. Apparently, he, which I didn't know, kept it loaded, in case of camp invasion, I guess, but anyway, I stumbled, and the gun went off and hit our box of propane bottles, which exploded and caught the tent on fire."

"Well," said Angelique, "they can always get a new tent." She assumed the big four-man tent that belonged to Juneau was the one that had been immolated.

"There was stuff in it," Cooney went on. "Ya know, guns and personal items."

"They are mountain men, Cooney boy," she said. "Their stuff's not worth much. So, then what can I do to help you with your 'mussing up,' as you say?"

"Maybe you could just shake off the burnt tent. Tell 'em it's no big deal. Accidents happen, et cetera," he explained. "I think if you don't get mad, then they might think I'm not as stupid as I seem to be. That would help me out a lot."

"I guess that would not be too much to ask," she acknowledged. "In return, how about you slide down on this big coat and let me loosen your sore muscle."

Rock and a hard place. Obviously the strong feelings Cooney has for Pica would preclude any dalliance that might occur with this older, though supremely seductive siren sitting in his lap.

However, the devil on his shoulder could easily justify a lusty participation (faking it, he could tell himself) by pointing out that the price of earning Pica's trust might ironically involve satisfying Angelique's itch.

We, as author and reader, are holding out for his ability to resist temptation. But in doing so, we must consider the consequences of spurning Angelique. For instance, it could easily result in a cancelled hunting trip, loss of future business, bad blood between Juneau and Cooney . . . and, in the end, goodbye Pica.

HE IS BETWEEN THE DEVIL AND THE DEEP BLUE SEA. BUT, BECAUSE I AM IN THE WRITER'S SEAT, A MIRACLE IS STILL AN OPTION TO HELP HIM OVERCOME ANY POSSIBLE CHARACTER FLAWS.

Cooney didn't move. She looked up at him suspiciously. Cooney was frozen! Eyes wide open, his mouth a large O!

She brought her gaze down to where his rested and saw a bear as big as a Volkswagen! It was within rock-throwing distance!

"Don't move," she said, as cool as gazpacho in the shade. She slowly reached to her right and behind to locate her octagonal-barreled Blaser K 95 Stutzen .30-06. In trying to retrieve it, her right sleeve fell off her shoulder and impeded her motion.

"Pull it off," she whispered. Cooney slipped the loose-fitting cuff over her hand and peeled off the sleeve.

In one steady movement she raised the rifle, sat erect, gently jacked the bolt to load the chamber, thumbed the safety off, and said, "Whattya think, Coney Island?"

"If it was me I'd shoot him 'tween the eyes," said Cooney.

"A tough shot, *mon ami*. I think the heart would be better. A word of caution: I hope you can run or climb. Ready?" And before he could answer she squeezed the trigger!

The crack of the bullet was immediately followed by a growling wail! Then a second shot!

"Run!" she screamed.

Cooney rose and stumbled! She passed him, and they were sprinting through the high brush and pine trees to the trail to camp!

CHAPTER 46

November 19, Saturday Afternoon
The Bear Attack

PICA'S FATHER HAD ASKED HER TO HEAD BACK TO CAMP AND CHECK ON MRS. Nuen while he and Mr. Nuen stayed to cape and gut the elk and strap it onto the pack mule.

As Pica approached the camp in the late afternoon, she smelled smoke. The mule she was riding smelled it as well and required some controlling. No smoke was visible, but she sped up anyway. Something was wrong.

In a short three minutes she trotted into the camp. The tent was still smoldering in the corners. Skeletons of nonflammable infrastructure stood in place as if somebody had burned down a playground. Struts, stays, metal poles, gun barrels, braces, and a $249 Woodsman Axe lay in the blanket of ashes.

A woodwind of snores snuffled and snorted from the four-man tent. She recognized Uncle Firmy's emanations. Suddenly, close behind her, back in the trees she heard two rifle shots three seconds apart and the roar of a wild animal!

Pica glanced at the four-man tent. The snoring continued. She levered a cartridge into the chamber of her Ruger .44-caliber lever-action rifle. Coming toward her out of the forest was the clatter and respiratory noise of running beasts!

She shouldered her gun. Bursting into the clearing was Angelique Nuen, as bareback as Tarzan! Her hair flying out behind her, her eyes wide open, and her mouth screaming!

Pica, with lightning reflexes, dropped the barrel of her gun. Her brain was trying to process what was happening. Mrs. Nuen was being chased? *A bear*, Pica thought and immediately swung her rifle back into firing position. In the next two seconds she took in the crashing, brush-breaking thunder and a bone-chilling growl that sounded as close as her next breath!

Hot on the heels of Mrs. Nuen came, in all his glory, Cooney Bedlam, pounding after her like some famous quarterback taking the field. At this juncture, Pica lowered the rifle again.

"Don't shoot!" yelled Cooney. The deafening animal growl came so fast that it almost drowned out his voice. "Shoot!" he said. By then he was twenty feet in front of her, and the bear, who had just appeared, was about twice that distance behind him.

Pica raised her rifle again. In those microseconds as she pulled up on the bear, she could see he was bleeding. Fresh, red blood covered the bear's chest and arms. With the nerve and skill of a professional hunter, she let the arc of her gun sight rise past the bloody chest and stop right below the chin. She fired.

Her bullet severed the spinal cord between cervical vertebrae 4 and 5. The massive beast pitched forward with momentum, rolled sideways, and skidded another ten feet. Pica could see his eyes from where he lay less than ten feet away. As she watched, life left them as if someone had closed the Venetian blinds. He was dead.

Firmy stepped from the tent and rubbed his eyes. Mrs. Nuen, as yet to remember her nakedness, stood like a wild woman, arms hanging down holding the rifle across her waist, gaping at the bear. Cooney had fallen and come back to one knee. His gaze, too, was locked on the dead beast. Pica, in her hunting cap and fluorescent vestment, still held the rifle to her shoulder, pointing at the bear.

It would have made an interesting Charlie Russell painting.

It could be entitled *Nude in Hunting Camp* or *Bearly Nude* or *Nudely Bear*. But, alas, no one was there to take the photo, and each participant has a different picture forever implanted on his or her brain.

———

Because Mrs. Nuen—Angelique—had bought an out-of-province license that included bear, and she had shot him first, it was logically her kill. Firmy, Pica, and Cooney set about skinning the bear while Angelique busied herself in Juneau's four-man tent, dressing, cleaning up, and dropping the level of the rye.

Within an hour Juneau and Dr. Nuen arrived with their elk. Completing the skinning, dressing, and preparation of both animals took two more hours. Everyone was aware of the tent ruin that was as obvious as a dead mule in a car trunk, but they were so busy that no one had time to address the issue.

Firmy and Pica managed to put together a nice meal of fresh elk steak, potatoes, and bear paw dip. They ate around the fire, sitting in camp chairs or on coolers. Pica and Juneau assumed that Angelique had burned down the tent and waited patiently for someone to say something. Coincidentally Dr. Nuen thought his wife had done it as well. Angelique's afternoon was filled with a Technicolor collage of feelings: roars, rubdowns, gunpowder, the scent of man, whispers, explosions, pursuit, fear, bear blood, butchering in the wild, and vodka! The burnt tent wasn't on her radar.

Firmy helped Pica discreetly rearrange the four-man tent for the Nuens so that when they had enjoyed one more cognac for the road and were ready to retire, they went comfortably. They were both snoring within minutes.

Cooney sat with the D'TroiTs around the fire.

"So," said Juneau, looking at Firmy, "how'd it happen?"

"You'll never believe," said Firmy, lighting his pipe.

"Somehow I thought you'd say that," said Juneau. "Did lightning strike on a clear day? Did Angelique rosin her bullwhip and create so much friction she set the tent on fire? Let me guess: You went over to search through her pack for Copenhagen and unwittingly stepped on a land mine she had placed at the door, and it exploded?"

"No, my clever but innocent brother," explained Firmy. "I merely fired my gun accidentally and hit the propane canisters we had stored in their tent."

Cooney listened to Firmy take the blame. It embarrassed him. He remembered what he almost did with Angelique to cover his tracks. All for the sake of impressing a girl.

He thought of President Clinton, who had lied about his adulterous adventures and brought impeachment down upon himself. Pica can take it, he thought to himself, and if she can't, I'd rather her think of me as a fool than a liar.

"That's not true," said Cooney.

Firmy gave him the slant eye.

"I can't let you take the blame, Firmy. I know you mean well, but," Cooney turned to Juneau, "it was me who blew up the propane tanks. I was getting a gun out the big tent, tripped on the tent cord, and pulled the trigger."

"What were you getting the gun for, anyway?" asked Juneau.

"There was a bear, probably the same bear Angelique shot, standing just outside the camp. Just me and Firmy were here."

"Yep," said Firmy. "A big sonuvagun. It was the same one, all right. I coulda shot 'im with my eyes closed. So close he was."

"Yes," said Juneau. "That bear will make the trip for them. And that she shot it will keep them coming back, I'll bet. It's good size and will make a beautiful mount."

"Mr. D'TroiT," said Cooney, "I can pay for the tent and the camping stuff, their guns that were burnt up. I'm havin' a good year, and I can afford to do it."

"Thank ya, Son. We'll see. They might have insurance, hey? And if they don't, we might have some," said Juneau. "One way or the other it will all come out in the wash.

"I know you are trying to help Pica with her smuggling charge. She tells me that's why you are here . . . just to help. I hope you know how much that means to her mother and me. Your faith in her innocence makes us that much stronger."

Cooney snuck a look at Pica. She had a soft look on her face, but her eyes still showed a little puzzle. Cooney knew it had something to do with her memory of him running out of the brush chasing a half-naked Angelique. He still didn't know what he was going to tell her.

Half an hour later the time came. Juneau had asked the two of them to go check the mules on the picket line.

Cooney laid a hand on her arm. They stopped in a small snow-covered clearing lit by the half-moonlight. "Pica, I'd like to try and explain to you about this afternoon. It wasn't what it looked like . . . not exactly, I mean. I . . ."

She stopped him. She put a finger to his lips. "Cooney, sometimes being around you is so bizarre. There must be a side of you that . . . attracts calamity. I am so, so mixed up about how to feel about you. It's like being around a jack-in-the-box. I, like, never know who's going to pop up.

"So, here's how I'm going to deal with it. I'm not going to ask why you came running out of the woods chasing a naked woman . . ."

"Well, not naked, just . . ."

"With a naked woman I'm not going to worry about it," she said firmly. "You get a pass. No questions asked. Okay?"

"You need to know that nothing . . ." he started.

"No explanations. I do not want to know. It is not going to be an issue between us," she said.

"But . . ." he said.

She put her finger on his lips again and shook her head sideways. The highlights in her hair sparkled in the moonlight. Her skin shone. Her eyes were hooded. It took his breath away.

He felt butterflies in his chest; the urge to speak arose, but he restrained. They held hands 'til they were within sight of the camp.

HOW OFTEN DOES THAT HAPPEN? UNCONDITIONAL FORGIVENESS.

Act III

CHAPTER 47

November 25, Day after Thanksgiving
Philip, South Dakota

CROCUS RINK, MOTHER OF COONEY BEDLAM, STUCK HER HEAD INTO THE living room and asked, "Anybody need more coffee?"

Cooney, his stepfather Cline, Aunt Trinka, cousin Sherba, older sister Ellie, her two kids, and husband looked up from the football game on the television. Cline and Ellie both held up their cups. "I'll help," said Sherba, rising and heading into the kitchen.

It was the day after Thanksgiving, and Cooney had been sleeping and lazing about, resting. He still had a little restive tickle in his chest every time he thought of Pica.

The National Finals Rodeo started Thursday, December 1, and ended Saturday night, December 10, and he had qualified for the finals in both saddle bronc and bull riding. He was driving by himself. Straight had not qualified. His OTT presence was not needed, so he had chosen not to go. Pica was virtually "under house arrest" due to the smuggling charges she faced. But Cooney could do it alone. He was brought up by this fine family to be responsible for himself.

Although it would have been nice to share the trip and the rodeo with someone, he was still pumped. This was his best season finish ever, and he was going to make the most of it. Lick and his wife were coming, and they planned to meet up. Cooney got him seats with the rodeo participant families.

At the beginning of the second half Cooney's cell phone rang. The ring tone showed that it was Straight. *Probly callin' to encourage me*, Cooney thought.

"Straight," said Cooney, "how . . ."

Straight cut him off: "Cooney, guess what? No, don't guess, I'll tell ya. I'm going to the finals. Yep, Slidell broke his leg. Was skiing in Colorado and broke his leg. Shoot, he was in sixth place."

"Fifth," said Cooney.

"Okay, fifth, but he's now eliminated, and I'm movin' up! Can you believe it? I was already resigned to not qualifying. Ready to jump in next season . . . But now I've gotta get tuned in again. Man, oh, man. What luck, hey?"

"I'm pullin' outta here on Monday," said Cooney. "I could sure use some company."

"Any chance Pica would be able to make the trip?" asked Straight.

"Nope. The law has got her pinned down."

"Sorry," said Straight, "but if she doesn't come I won't have to clean out the truck! I'll be talking to you, hey. Oh, and Nova Skosha has already called and said I'm back in OTT booth! It's almost too good, Cooney."

"Naw, you deserve it, amigo," said Cooney. "I couldn't be happier if it was me! See ya this weekend!"

<hr>

Meanwhile back in the mountains west of Pincher Creek, Pica D'TroiT was slicing potatoes for the hunting party that was in its third day of a five-day trip. She, Firmy, and Juneau had taken a pair of teenage boys and their father hunting for elk. She had been out of cell phone range and had had no contact with Cooney, much less the civilized world.

She wished she could be with him. Especially at the National Finals. She winced back a tear at not being able to be there to see him ride.

In another part of the Rocky Mountains several states south, Oui Oui Reese was sipping warm cider in the lounge at the bottom of the ski run in Vail, Colorado, where Turk Manniquin had given her a week at his personal townhouse apartment, all expenses paid. At her table were two ski hunks drinking off her tab and feeling her out . . .

File, who, Turk assumed, had only a business relationship with Oui Oui, was not included in the coverage. The closest room File could get for under $180 a night was in Wheatridge, Colorado, a Denver suburb. So he chose to stay in his small apartment on the southeast side of Denver.

He wanted to drive up every day to make sure Oui Oui was all right, but she asked him not to.

She needed peace and quiet before her tour de force ten-day performance at the National Finals Rodeo in Las Vegas, Nevada. It would catapult her to the stardom that they both believed in their hearts that she deserved.

CHAPTER 48

November 24–November 30

In Cyberspace

November 24, 11:30 a.m.
LL.mans@featherduster.com
University of Florida
Department of Biology

Dr. LeMans:

I have been searching the Internet for someone with knowledge of endangered tropical bird species. I hope you will be able to help me or direct me to someone who can.

My name is Pica D'TroiT. I was arrested September 6 in Miami for smuggling feathers of the Glandular Y Cock from Nassau in the Bahamas. I am out on bail and restricted to my premises here on my family ranch in Pincher Creek, Alberta, until the hearing, which is still not even scheduled.

I am innocent. Someone planted the feathers in my suitcase. I am assuming it was someone who intended to use me as a "mule" and recover them from my luggage once I had passed through Customs. The feathers had been sewn in the lining without my knowledge before I left Nassau in the Bahamas.

This is all speculation on my part.

For reasons I cannot divine, the lawyers of the company I was working for, OVER THE TOP ATHLETIC COSMETICS, don't seem to be doing anything. Therefore, I am making inquiries myself, and I'm hoping you will take me seriously.

There must be an expert or authority somewhere in your world who is an authority on the smuggling of endangered birds and their feathers. I'm not worried about getting even or suing, but somebody in your wide circle of interest must know the kind of people who did this to me.

If I were able, free to do it, I would make the trip to Nassau myself. But . . . that's not possible.

Please, please, please help me. I don't know where to turn.

Pica D'TroiT
Pincher Creek, Alberta
Telephone

November 28, 8:47 a.m.
Pica D'TroiT e-mail

Dear Miss D'TroiT

I remember your arrest. You are a famous young woman, if I am right. A rodeo rider, as I recall. You made the national news for a few days. Forgive my skepticism, but, of course, you are innocent. That's what they all say.

Although I am not directly involved in the criminal process of pros-ecuting smugglers, I have had occasion to be an expert witness. Your case is probably under the jurisdiction of the Wild Bird Conservation Act and CITES, the Convention on International Trade in Endangered Species. These are federal laws with deep and convoluted rules and restrictions. It is not surprising that your lawyers are mired up to their wallets.

First I would like to talk to them, maybe get a couple of character references I could contact, and then I will visit with you on the phone. If I feel that you truly were "framed," then maybe we can pursue it further.

Sincerely, Dr. L. LeMans

November 28, 10:59 a.m.
NovaSkoska@OTT.com

Nova,

I am in contact with an expert on tropical bird smuggling. I had to send her a list of character references. I hope it was okay that I named you. Also she, the expert, Dr. LeMans, wants to talk to my lawyers. I gave her their names, but they don't return my calls, so I don't expect they'll be much help.

Hope all is well. It's cold up here and . . . oh, nothing, I just miss you, hey.

Pica

November 30, 9:01 p.m.
Cooney@e-mail.com

Cooney,

First, we're so happy for Straight getting to go to the finals. All of Alberta is thrilled! About my case, I've been working the Internet for help to do some digging into the business of endangered bird smuggling. I found one lady, after e-mailing five other good prospects that turned out to be fruitless. Anyway, the lady, Dr. LeMans, said she would check me out and if she thought I might be telling the truth, she would try and help.

It is so humiliating to be treated like a criminal, like a thief. I'm trying to be tough, but some nights I feel like screaming. I get mad at the lawyers; they keep saying there's nothing they can do until a case is brought. Nova still speaks to me, but I haven't heard from Turk or File . . . I know they are busy; finals are starting tomorrow. I wish I was there to cheer you on. I know you'll do good, both of you. You guys take care,

Your biggest, kissingest fan, Pica

CHAPTER 49

December 1, Thursday
Las Vegas, Wrangler National Finals Rodeo

IT WAS THE FIRST NIGHT OF THE NATIONAL FINALS RODEO, AND THE CROWD was humming. The spectacular ten-day show routinely sold out every night. A blizzard of commerce circled around the big event for the full ten days. Two huge trade shows as well as many smaller ones were set up to appeal to those who revel in the world of the cowboy.

Every year in the three weeks before Christmas, the city of Las Vegas went all out, filling its theaters with country singers, the biggest stars money could buy, and redecorating the casinos in cowboy high style.

If you had an interest in agriculture, horses, three-quarter-ton trucks, turquoise, leather, western art, western clothing, jewelry that cost more than the world champion cowboy would make this year, or boots so beautiful and well fitted that putting them on felt as if you were slipped your tootsies into a chocolate mousse, Las Vegas had your number. Any eye-pleasing, taste bud-tickling, spine-tingling overindulgence you could imagine was as close as the limit of your Visa card!

At the center of the whirlpool of pumping commerce were the cowboys. The Thomas and Mack Arena (on the UNLV campus) afforded most of the nightly sixteen thousand fans a good view of the ropin', ridin' gladiators. The big four-sided screen that hung above the arena showed close-ups in the box and over the bucking chutes plus the subsequent action. Several postperformance presentations at certain hotel-casinos and daily trade-show booth-signing opportunities gave fans a chance to get an autograph.

Most of the sky boxes were filled with corporate sponsors and their guests. These national sponsors, many of whom have been involved for years, were the difference between rodeo in Las Vegas and a team-roping practice in the covered arena at the Adams county fairgrounds. The vast majority of PRCA members would never set foot in a sky box during the rodeo, but there was always the hope that someday they'd be invited.

In contrast, an invitation to the Gold Card Room was the ultimate acceptance. Gold Card members were rodeo contestants who, over the years, proved themselves worthy of being included. Many sky box invitees would never set foot in the Gold Card Room, although there was always the hope that someday they'd be invited.

An hour before the rodeo, our two heroes, Straight and Cooney, found themselves in the locker room, sitting in their bucking horse saddles on the floor, legs outstretched, checking the fit, the feel, the seat, the swing. They were surrounded by bareback riders whose event opened every rodeo.

Twenty minutes before the first notes of the National Anthem would ring out, the contestants were herded together and put onto horses to ride in the grand entry. They were introduced by states. Cooney went with South Dakota, and Straight went with Canada.

The grand entry is a performance that you would never see in the "professional sports" where the contestants belong to the owners.

"Too risky," the owners would say. "Someone could get hurt, too much money at stake. Are you crazy? There must be over a hundred cowboys and cowgirls racing around that little arena, most on strange horses, at a dead run, carrying sixty state flags! And the noise! And the laser lights! The smoke and explosions! All waiting for one of those spooky cayuses to jump the track like a loose coal car on a runaway train! They'd go down like dominos!

"What if a rider fell off?" would say the football, baseball, basketball coach, manager, or owner. "He could be trampled or kicked or knocked out. Not for my quarterback, no way, or my goalie, or my light heavyweight! I'm savin' them for good."

But in rodeo a wreck is not an issue—something organized sports simply wouldn't understand.

Cooney and Straight had had a lot to talk about on their drive down to Las Vegas. They'd hooked up at Salt Lake City and left Straight's pickup at the ranch of Lou Fielder, a retired bareback rider. Cooney was trying to encourage his buddy to "relax and enjoy it." Straight tried, but it wasn't his personality. He was going to think through every ride, every contingency. It was just his style. He was also listening to self-help CDs: "How to Be a Better Whatever," "Charisma for Dummies," "Fine Tuning Every Nervous Twitch." If you're going to have them, put them to *use!*

And, truth be told, Cooney had an undercurrent going on inside, too. It was called "Pica D'TroiT." He finally had gotten to first base with her, but between first and second there was the big, thunderous, threatening cloud of Pica's legal problems. Every time he'd try to think about what he could do to help her, his mind would wander to the back of a bull. He finally conceded to himself that even with their e-mail correspondence, his mind was on riding.

Cooney and Straight had arrived on Tuesday, November 29, two days ago. By 6:00 p.m. Thursday night they were pumped, excited, bearing down, and buzzing.

CHAPTER 50

December 1, Thursday Night
Las Vegas, First Performance of the Finals

THE FIRST NIGHT OUT OUR HEROES DREW UP GOOD. STRAIGHT WAS THE first saddle bronc rider out of the chute in the first performance. Most in the audience who followed rodeo enough to subscribe to the *Rodeo Sports News* were aware of the good luck Straight was blessed with to be here. No one had wanted Slidell to get hurt, but if anyone got moved up, Straight was well known and likable.

Cooney finished the regular season in the number 2 position in the saddle bronc with $251,320, only $5,045 out of first place. He was standing eighth in the bull riding with $88,468. And to top it off, that put him in the running for the title of "All Around Cowboy"! To qualify for this last category a performer must earn over $1,000 in at least two events. Cooney got 'er done!

Straight qualified in the saddle bronc in fifteenth place with a total of $54,027. He was just proud to be there.

It would come to pass that ten days later the world champion saddle bronc rider would win $278,169.

In other words, a performer could win well over $40,000 at the finals alone. The National Finals Rodeo average competition stands alone to be won or lost at the NFR. The bronc rider who goes into the finals in fifteenth place could actually win the NFR average. It still might not be enough to earn him the world championship, but it is a prize to be treasured and grants lots of braggin' rights to be in the record books.

In the three weeks between the last rodeo and the NFR, the lull that fans have is different than that of the performers. Ropers will continue to rope, fine tuning every nuance of horse, rope, steer and man, studying, as it were, right up to the final test.

Rough stock riders have to weigh their physical readiness, alertness, mental state, and psychological attitude against the chance of being injured before the finals just practicing!

Cooney continued his routine stretches and weight lifting. He rode with the confidence of an actor who was taught "when you have a line down pat, forget it!" Don't worry or practice too much.

Straight, on the other hand, worried about everything. He went over each ride endlessly in his mind, even got his hands on rodeo blooper videos to examine the riders for flaws.

He also kept practicing his voice lessons. He had bought several self-help tapes lately on "sales presentation" and "audio and video vocalization training" designed for those who wanted to be professional on-air radio or television personalities. Speakin' of which . . .

"It's shoah a treat to see Straight Line make the finals, even if it 'uz bad luck for Hi Slidell. We wish y'all the best, Hi. You'll be back," announced Layer Pie, an Alabama backyard team roper and scrap iron collector who was calling the action for XM Rodeo Radio.

"Rat on, Layer, you've been wrong a lot, but yer rat this time," agreed Skim Slayton, his partner back home in a small Internet bluegrass program. And now both were broadcasting live from Las Vegas!

Skim was also the designated color man. "Straight hails from Buff'lo, Alberta which is 'bout as far as Buff'lo, South Dakota, or Buff'lo, New York . . ."

"Or Buff'lo Beeyill," added Layer. "Anyway, as I was sayin' when I was so crudely interpreted, Straight, or Straighten, as his friends call him . . ."

"His friends don't call him 'Straighten,'" said Skim.

"Wayill, that's what I call him," said Layer.

"Which proves my point . . ."

"Yup, Straight is first outta the chute tonight . . ."

"I believe, if y'all had noticed," pointed out Skim, "we already done bucked out fifteen bareback riders, so Straight is certainly not the verah first outta the chute tonight, as you so colorfully put it, when I am 'sposed ta be doin' the colah and y'all jis' read the statistics . . . which y'all do so wayill, like knowin' that you shoulda have said, 'Straight is the sixteenth cowboy to buck outta the chute tonight.'"

"He's up on a previous saddle bronc of the yeah, Miss Conception," intoned Layer. "If Straight ever wanted to prove he was worthy of bein' invited to the finals, this heah is the time."

"I was thinkin'," said Skim. "It's time for smoke. All you kiddies light up! Whenever I want a good, flavorful smoke that doesn't stain yo' fingers or make ya cough up big ..."

Suddenly over the radio there was a loud crash, the sound of microphones being pounded, speakers screeching feedback, and a racket like a swing set falling down a stairwell! It lasted five seconds. Layer had accidentally kicked Skim's folding chair out from under him.

"Welcome back, ladies and gentlemen, to the live coverage of the National Finals Rodeo brought to y'all on XM Rodeo Radio. This is your announcer, Layer Pie, heah to bring y'all the play-by-play. My colah co-announcer apparently has stepped out fo' a smoke."

Down at the chutes Straight Line was astraddle Miss Conception. She was not a big horse, but she could kick the lights out! Ride her, and you were in the money.

Cooney was holding her head steady while Straight measured the rein.

"X and four," said Straight as he measured with his fist, thumb, and four fingers.

"X and four," confirmed Cooney. It would allow the horse to take a little more rein because she had the tendency to bury her head between her knees when she bucked. Too short a grip on the rein would pull a rider right over the top.

In a few quick, well-practiced movements Straight was reared back, legs cocked at the knees ready to snap, rein held high, and eye on the back of the horse's head.

Straight gave a glance over his shoulder at Cooney, who loosely held the back of his vest. Straight made a quick smile and an easy nod, which were read correctly as "I don't know how or why it happened, but we made it."

Cooney actually chuckled. "Show 'em how!" he said.

The gate swung open like the lid comin' off a trunk full of dynamite!

Every bronc ride is like a fingerprint. No two are exactly the same. Straight Line was was a classic saddle bronc rider, and Miss Conception was a classic saddle bronc.

They arced out of the chute like a centaur springin' off the high dive. It seemed they were in the air a full two seconds. Miss Conception had a pow-erful kick at the top of her arc that appeared to propel her farther down the arena. Straight never missed a lick. He popped his arm and pistoned his legs like the drivers on a locomotive. You could almost hear the expulsion and see the steam!

The hat on his head was steady as the bead on a rifle. The action was so good that it gave Layer Pie, up in the Rodeo Radio booth, goose bumps.

"Boy, that's the kind of ride that makes a catfish hold his breath," said Layer.

"I couldn't have said it bettah, Layah, even if I wuz the colah coordinator. Which I am, so I'll jis' say it again: 'You couldn't hold yo' breath bettah, even if you wuz ridin' a catfish!"

"Wayill said, Skim," said Layer.

"You said it," he said. Then, "Look at theyat!"

At the buzzer Straight had taken off his hat, fanned the horse, and then bailed out! He landed on his feet, hat in hand, then threw it high into the air.

"My good smokin' red-eye gravy," exclaimed Layer. "He mawked an eighty-seven point five! What a way to start the Wrangler National Finals Rodeo saddle bronc riding!"

"An eighty-seven point five!" said Skim. "That takes the lead in the NFR saddle bronc ridin'!"

"Not to diminish that fine ride, Skim," said Layer, "but I guess even a fifteen score woulda prob'ly took the lead at this stage uh da game."

Fourteen more saddle bronc rides rolled in and out of the chutes. Four riders bucked off. The next-highest score was an eighty-five by Shelby Truax, who came into the finals in fourth place with $146,445. Then the chute boss was standing in front of chute 3.

"Ladies and gentlemen," spoke the rodeo announcer over the din of booming music, sound effects, and the undertone of spectator noise, "in chute number 3, standing second in the world, from Buffalo, South Dakota, Coo-oo-oo-nee-ee-ee Be-e-e-ed Lu-u-u-u-m!"

If Straight was an engine on the track, Cooney was a derailed box car coming off the edge of the Grand Canyon! He rode all-out every time. He was not afraid to get bucked off; he was always trying to win, as opposed to "not lose."

"Furious" would be the best description of Cooney's riding style.

His draw was Silver Belle, a middlin' to large dapple gray mare who had started life as a filly in Porum, Oklahoma. Broke to ride, she had spent a year in Hitch's Feedlot in Guymon checkin' pens until one day she decided she'd had enough of the mud and dust and had a change of personality.

Not wanting to get any of his cowboys hurt, the cattle foreman took her to the sale with the warning that she was not a kid's horse.

The Maid Brothers Rodeo Company bought her to use as a saddle horse because of her size.

After getting her back to the ranch and finding they could not saddle her, they ran her in the riggin' chute and forced her to dress as a bareback bronc. The brothers found out what she was good at!

That first year the riders rated her one of the five best bareback broncs.

Two years after that she switched to saddle bronc riding and found a home.

In addition to being good sized, she was quick and unpredictable. She was now nine years old and in her prime.

Straight helped Cooney get down onto Silver Belle. Her book was well known. Both Straight and Cooney had drawn her, but only Straight had scored well. That "unpredictability" meant that she didn't always come out of the chute nice and clean, line out, and start bucking.

"Okay," said Cooney, "I'm givin' her a little slack." He adjusted his grip on the rein. "Any ideas?" he asked Straight.

"Just be ready, partner. She can come from outta nowhere."

Cooney leaned back, glanced into the arena, then back to the horse's poll, stretched his shoulder, moved his arm position slightly, and took a tight-lipped, concentrating breath. He was like a model posing for a photo. As soon as body, mind, and heart lined up perfectly, he froze! Through gritted teeth he said, "Let's ride!"

Silver Belle's first move out of the box was an almost 180-degree swing back to her left! Instead of propelling herself out of the chute by leaping into the air, she had swung her body around as if she were in a reining pattern. Cooney's spurs shot out and caught both sides of her neck just as her front feet hit the ground! Her body was twisted so far to the left that her front end and hind legs were not parallel. Then, in a split-second move she swung her front legs back to the right a full 90 degrees! She looked like a cutting horse at the top of its game. Cooney's spurs held their position, though the unexpected move caught him off balance.

All that kept Cooney in the seat was the fact that he was left-handed and rode with his right. That gave him a slight edge. The whole right side of his body was rigid and rock hard. His muscles were locked in position when the gyroscope fell off the edge of the table!

The muscles in her powerful hindquarters flexed in a crouch . . . then came unwound! Horse and rider entered the arena atmosphere six feet above the ground! As they climbed upward Cooney's arm reached out above the neck, and his upper body moved forward, almost over the swells, as his dull rolling rowels glided backward in an arc along the flanks. A perfect demonstration of the "rock" as in "rock and fire"!

225

She was a quick horse and got in a lot of up and downs during their short 8 seconds. As seen from the stands Silver Belle was putting on a show. Even with her changing directions twice more unexpectedly, Cooney hung on and kept spurring. He looked like a helicopter trying to land on a bouncing dune buggy in the Baja 500. All that seemed to be in contact between man and beast was the rein in his hand and the bottom of his boots in the oxbow stirrups. There was so much daylight between his seat and the saddle that migrating ducks could have flown between them!

"Furious was right!" It described the ride: exciting, explosive, and furious.

At the buzzer Silver Belle was just coming down. She must have deliberately leaned to the right because Cooney unceremoniously sailed out head first over the swells and into the dirt, performing an awkward somersault before crumpling in a pile of chap leather and smashed felt.

"By the buckskin on my breeches," exclaimed Skim Slayton, "I believe she done nat on purpose!"

"How you come up with them pithy gesticulations, Skim, is beyond me. You jus' have a way with woods."

"Looka theyah! A sebundy-nine! I don't b'lieve it! Why, them Yankee judges, they . . ." complained Skim as Layer Pie pushed the mute button on Skim's microphone.

CHAPTER 51

December 5, Monday
Fifth Performance of the
National Finals Rodeo

December 5, 10:14 a.m.

Dear Pica,

Since you wrote I have visited with one of your lawyers and a Ms. Nova Skosha with OVER THE TOP ATHLETIC COSMETICS. The lawyer was noncommittal on your culpability, but Ms. Skosha is convinced you are innocent of the charges of smuggling "limbs or pieces, living or dead, whole or in part" of the endangered species, commonly called the Glandular Y Cock.

I put in a call to a contact that is familiar with the "illegal trade" in the Caribbean. He is not recognized by the feds or academia, yet he has been helpful to me in the past. He is aware of a transaction last fall wherein a feathered garment was shipped to a buyer in the U.S. This is third-hand but originated from the person who made the delivery. It was in September, according to the source.

My intermediary is making subtle inquiries about the seller, potential buyer. Nothing solid yet, but I'll keep you informed.

y.t., Dr. Laurel LeMans

December 5, 12:24 p.m.

Dr. LeMans,

Oh, my! I don't know if it would be the same person . . . shipping to the States, I mean. Whoever did it actually hid them in my suitcase. But any news keeps me optimistic. Thank you, thank you, thank you!!!!!!!!

Pica

❧

December 6, 1:28 p.m.

Pica,

News. According to my intermediary, a package containing a feather halter top made from the Tetuchtan Pavo Real was smuggled into the States and hand-delivered to a party in Denver, Colorado. Second-hand information said that the recipient was a voluptuous woman who had a French name. I hope this helps. I'll keep tracking, but it is tricky business down here.

Dr. Laurel LeMans

❧

December 6, 1:42 p.m.

Dr. LeMans,

This gives me an idea! Thanx!

Pica

❧

December 6, 1:51 p.m.

Cooney,

I just heard from Dr. LeMans, the bird expert. You'll never guess who was delivered a package containing a halter top made from endangered bird feathers. In DENVER, NO LESS! Not the Glandular Y Cock, but something called the Pavo Real. But the timing was about the same time I was traveling back to the States from Nassau. Plus . . . they have hearsay that the recipient was a good-looking woman with a French name. Ring any bells?

Pica

December 6, 12:14 a.m.

Pica,

Sorry I didn't get your e-mail quicker. Rodeo, ya know. Straight and I both rode tonight. He finished third, me fourth. Pretty tight. I rode my bull.

But wow! In a collision of coincidences . . . after the Omaha Rodeo last fall Straight and I went to a party that ended in a spectacular conclusion involving a voluptuous woman wearing a halter top made of fancy feathers! That voluptuous woman, who might be a ten, only if you are a one hundred, is standing in your booth at the NFR right now and, according to Straight, starring in the big OTT party following the last perf. We're close, Pica. What can I do to help?

Cooney

December 7, 6:47 a.m.

COONEY!!!!!!!

> *This is it! Get me her hotel and room number, if you can.*
> *I'll be out of touch for a while. Leave it on my e-mail.*
> *Cooney, whichever one you are, I'm owing you big-time.*

My Lps Kss yr Hrt
P D'TT

A handwritten note left on D'Troit's kitchen table:

December 7, 10:52 p.m.

Dad,
> *I love you. I'm doing what I have to do to clear myself. I'll be gone maybe two weeks. You can't know where I'm going. I know you are liable for me, no matter what, but I have information about the smuggling charge and must check it out.*
> *Just know that I am in no danger. I can take care of myself thanks to you. You are my mountain, my rock, and it hurts me to have to keep you in the dark. Oh, Dad, I love you so much . . . Please*

This first draft was thrown into the trash at the Pincher Creek bus station. The note that Juneau D'TroiT found on his big chair in the living room Thursday morning read simply:

Dad,
> *I love you. I'll be gone maybe two weeks. Please trust me. Don't forget to give Thunder Jack his Bute paste.*

> *Your daughter, with love*

CHAPTER 52

Oui Oui's Background to Bring Us Up to Date

WAY BACK BEFORE OUI OUI'S PAST GOT CHECKERED SHE MADE ACQUAINTANCE with a flashy import-export dealer from the Caribbean island of Barbados. Oui Oui had been on spring break from San Jacinto Junior College in Houston. She and two other girls had driven to Fort Lauderdale, Florida, to celebrate. It was in Fort Lauderdale one tequila night that she had met Hurtado Herman Huachuca.

A REMINDER TO READERS WHOSE SPANISH IS CONFINED TO "ENCHI-LADA" AND "TACO BELL": THE LETTER *H* IN SPANISH IS SILENT, THE LETTER *U* IS "LONG," AND THERE IS NO LETTER W. SO PHONETICALLY HIS NAME WOULD BE SPELLED OOR-TA-DO AIR-MAWN WA-CHOO-KA.

He was thirty-five years old then. She was eighteen and ripening.

He whisked her away on his 106-foot motor yacht from Fort Lauderdale to his luxurious villa on the leeward side of Barbados and entertained her for a week. He collected many things besides pretty conquests. He had a collection of hallucinogenic dried tropical fruits, beautiful soft hides from the mighty jaguar, and jujus made from the feathers of tropical birds.

Senor Huachuca allowed Oui Oui to luxuriate in the feathers and jaguar hides and even to taste some of the mind-bending tropical fruits.

The idea that these items were rare, verboten, and valuable made Oui Oui tingle inside. Senor Huachuca dressed and decorated her with his treasures, and she posed in discreet but seductive positions for him to photograph.

At the end of her spring break he returned her to St. Petersburg in his yacht. He could not gift her any of his illegal bounty, he had told her, but he invited her to come back and visit again sometime.

Once a year until she was twenty-five she always found time to give him a call. They would arrange for her to fly down and spend a week. She became acquainted with his staff, his chefs, his gardeners, his pilots, chauffeurs, and the captain and crew of his yacht. She also was on speaking terms with two gentlemen, Feliz and Trueno, who served as his bodyguards.

"Why do you need bodyguards?" she asked Three, as she called him—three *H*s.

"In my business I often deal with certain items that may be approved by one country and, how you say, outloud by others . . ."

"'Outlawed,'" she corrected carefully. Three was sensitive about having his English-is-a-second-language corrected.

". . . So I sleep in dormancy when I feel their presence. They are quite correlated in what they do," he explained unintelligibly.

He was always generous with her. Oui Oui had a nice collection of pretty things, although Three was very cautious about entrusting her with illegal contraband. Eventually there came a time in their relationship when she became consumed in pursuing her quest for stardom and didn't make it down to see him. Three sent her cash occasionally, but she always tried to pay him back. "No, no," he'd say, "just come and see me."

Last August 30, when File had been notified about Pica D'TroiT's breakdown and unscheduled layover in the Bahamas, he had immediately rushed to Oui Oui's apartment in Denver to tell her the news.

She was furious! "It's just another way to get attention! Everyone will be worrying, 'Oh, oh, I hope it's not serious. She's so sweet,'" Oui Oui mimicked. "'Let's get her on Larry King, Dr. Laura, or *The View*. Maybe Barbara WaWa could do an exclusive.' . . . That slimy little two-legged bench sitter! And to top it off, she's not even American! Can you believe it?"

File ducked as a plastic glass, two couch pillows, and a bag of jelly beans filled the air! But the storm went out of her as quickly as it had come. "Oh, Filo, Filo, Filoptic, whatever shall we do? . . . Every time we try and do the right thing . . . like when I lent her my comb, it always comes back to haunt me."

"Listen," said File firmly, "maybe we can turn this into something good. Sort of make oil out of oatmeal."

"Oil out of oatmeal? What does that mean?" she shot back.

"You know, clams outta crabcakes, hay outta sunshine, dinero outta tortillas."

"You mean rainbows outta rain?" She sought for the right phrase. "Like, turn lichens into luck?

"Ducklings into swanlings? Pica into powder?"

"You got it, Baby," said File enthusiastically. "Like what if Pica got stuck down there in the Caribbean and couldn't get back? Maybe she commits a murder, is picked up for prostitution, or is arrested for smuggling drugs or ..."

Oui Oui interrupted, "Or arrested for smuggling jaguar hides or ... wait ... feathers."

"Feathers?" said File. "No, it would have to be something serious like stolen diamonds or forged banknotes."

"Feathers, Filoman," she said, "rare, protected, illegal exotic bird feathers."

"Where in the world ..." objected File.

"I think I know just the person to call," she said with a bit of a grin.

It had been three years since Oui Oui had seen Three. He could not come to the States because he was listed as a sneaky, crooked, half-baked feather fondler and self-important paranoid peyote dealer by the U.S. Customs Service. But she could see only the good in him.

The night after File's revelation, Thursday, September 1, Oui Oui's plane landed in Miami. She flew the shuttle to the Nassau airport and was picked up by Feliz, one of Three's personal bodyguards. He delivered her to Three's yacht.

She had explained her dilemma to Three and said that she had to be back in Miami by Monday with the goods. "No problema!" he said and set the wheels in motion. She kissed him and kept his wheels in motion for the next three days!

In selecting the ideal contraband they selected three jujus made from the feathers of the Glandular Y Cock. Little fetishes like shoo flies or key-ring bobs or fancy earrings. Simply a gather of feathers no more than four inches long banded together at the top with delicate metallic thread. Smaller and much lighter than an old shaving brush.

File, surreptitiously working in concert with Oui Oui, had made arrangements to arrive in Nassau on Monday evening, September 5, to spell KroAsha, who was staying with Pica. KroAsha left that evening. She and File crossed paths at the airport and exchanged news. KroAsha had assured File that Pica was back on her feet and ready to continue her round of media appearances as the flashy, feminist, athletic woman bronc rider who had captured the interest of the media so completely.

As soon as KroAsha boarded her flight back to Denver, a large, busty woman with big sunglasses wearing ill-fitting Bermuda shorts and carrying two large name-brand paper bags came around the corner and bumped into File. She spoke quickly from underneath an unstylish straw hat with fruit in the band: "Here," she said, handing him a small box. He took it and kept walking.

A cab ride soon found File checking in at the resort hotel where Pica was registered. He left a message on her room phone, then called Oui Oui: "Hey, Babe."

"Oh, Filio, Felio, Folio, I am so buzzed!"

"It's gonna work," he said joyously. "It's brilliant. I haven't opened the box but . . ."

"It's endangered feathers," she described. "Real light, flat, easy to hide."

"I'm thinkin' I could put it in the lining of one of her bags," he said.

"Right, and there's a small packet of marijuana. Just rub a little on the bag that you hide the feathers in. Their dogs or chemical sniffing machine will pick right up on it. Plus my friends are gonna make a little call to Nassau airport security just after her plane leaves for Miami and alert them. The locals will call their counterparts in Miami and voila! Our little Canadian ragweed is down for the count." Oui Oui sighed, "It's the right thing to do, isn't it, Filoflow? I mean, she stole the job from me, so I'm just, you know, just getting what I deserve."

"Yes, yes," File agreed, "you don't worry about her. She'll get what's coming to her. Speaking of which, I might be able to slip out this evening, a little wine, a little moonlight . . . my plane doesn't leave until tomorrow at one-thirty. We could . . ."

"Oh, Fily, Fily, Fily, you know how much I'd love to. It's just that . . . well, my friend down here, I've already promised . . . ya know. But it's you I love, Filovaceous, only you. I'm only doing this for our future. You know that. And we have to make sacrifices. Gotta go, Fi Fi."

"Okay. Good night," he said wistfully.

The next morning File's dream girl was back on the yacht completing her week in the sun.

"*Un momento, mi Toro,*" said Oui Oui. She took one more look in the mirror, swung open the dressing room door, and entered the yacht's plush salon wearing a halter top made of feathers from the Tetuchtan Pavo Real, spiked heels, a jaguar thong, and a Glandular Y Cock fetish behind each ear.

Bright flashes popped as the camera followed her as she prowled sensuously back and forth in front of a grinning Hurtado Herman Huachuca, sugar daddy and fairly good amateur photographer. "Buena, buena," he exclaimed, "*maravillosa, espactacular, se parese de una leona abrazando una quetzal! Eyii!*"

Fifty nautical miles from the yacht, while Pica was taking her last lazy hours on the Nassau beach, File "inviggled" his way into her room. Stealthily he inserted and sewed the two feather jujus under the lining in her big, hard-sided bag and rubbed it with marijuana. The setup was complete.

CHAPTER 53

December 8, Thursday, Midday
South of Waterton Park, Alberta

Five miles south of the Canada-US border in Glacier National Park, Pica D'TroiT looked down on Montana State Highway 17. It was a sunny day and very cold: minus-9 degrees centigrade at midmorning. Pica was warm as toast, as determined as a brass section marker, and as strong as a Chinook comin' off the Rockies!

She was headed for a scenic rest stop three more miles south of her position on the west side of the highway. She didn't have the specifics of her plan worked out, just the general outline, but she was confident it would work. Adrenaline still stoked her progress as she marched on, staying near the tree line along the highway to travel surreptitiously.

She purposely pushed the painful pangs of guilt behind her . . . her father . . . how could she hang him out like this? He had put their ranch up as collateral. What would happen if she didn't . . . didn't what? Prove herself innocent? Even if she did find the smugglers, would her father still forfeit his bail because she had left the confines of her parole, the ranch?

Can't think about it, can't think about it, can't think about it . . . then she saw the rest area.

It was not bustling, but six vehicles were parked in front of the viewing area and three more near the washroom area. An old, well-used, flatbed truck was parked in a handicapped space with the engine running. It had a Montana license plate. The metal dump bed was full to the top of the sideboards with something. A blue tarp hid the contents.

Next to it was an SUV with a pod on the top for storage. The family who belonged to the SUV was standing by the low cable fence that defined the edge of the scenic viewing area: mom, dad, two kids, Pica noted. *I could hitch*

235

a ride with them. But . . . maybe they wouldn't be comfortable picking up a stranger . . . even, she thought, *one who looked like a college kid on Christmas break.*

Then, looking at her image in the SUV's tinted rear window, she realized she *didn't* look like a snow bunny just bumming around! She was wearing her old hunting jacket, scuffed backpack, nylon pants with blood on them, a ratty fur cap, felt-lined boots, and snow goggles. Her appearance brought to mind a brain-washed terrorist on her way to blow up a theme park. And she was packing a Ruger KP 141 .357 magnum revolver with a four-inch barrel under her jacket.

She looked over at the idling flatbed. To her it had the advantage of her not having to be seen and of her being able to avoid socializing. However, as any woman reading this knows, hitchhiking, especially stowing away, holds a real danger.

SUV or flatbed? The family members seemed to be gathering for a snap-shot. They'd be back to the car very soon. She could just wait and ask them for a ride. SUV or flatbed? The truck engine still growled. Its driver or drivers? Men? Man? Man and woman? Old? Young? Samaritans or sadists? She felt the hilt of her skinning knife and the bump of the pistol under her coat. *Can you take care of yourself? Absolutely,* she decided. She stepped behind the truck, slid under the tarp, and crawled in.

Her heart was pounding. She realized she was holding her breath. The greasy canvas tarp allowed in very little light. She sat frozen in place and absorbed her surroundings. Her back was up against something firm, almost bony. A piece of furniture? She peeled off her right Thinsulate skiing glove and reached back just as the driver's-side door opened with a metallic screech! Pica's hip pockets came up off the metal floor as she jumped in fright. The door slammed! The transmission ground as it sought reverse, followed by a tinny rumble and jolt—both signs that the truck was backing out of the parking space.

Acutely aware of the vehicle's every move and direction, Pica sighed with relief after she was sure the truck was headed south. Highway 17 would connect to Highway 89 across the Blackfeet Indian Reservation to Cut Bank and eventually to Great Falls, which would be her jumping-off place to Las Vegas. Exploring her surroundings, she laid a bare hand on the sofa or what-ever it was. It felt like horse hair. As she felt farther she soon realized it was not a horse-hair sofa but rather a dead horse. Not long dead, either, because it was not frozen, just cool on the surface.

She rolled to her side. There was less than a foot of clearance between the floor and the tarp, though the tarp was quite flexible and flapped lightly as the truck ran down the highway. Pica ran her hand up to the horse's head and hit a sticky, crusty slick of blood.

She reached over the back of the horse next to her and felt another. *Oh, well,* she thought, *in for a loonie, in for a liter. I don't know, and I don't care.* She closed her eyes and drifted into the first sleep she'd had since two mornings ago.

CHAPTER 54

December 8, Thursday, Noonish
On a Side Road off Highway 89 near Browning, Montana

PICA LURCHED OUT OF HER SLEEP WITH A BANG! THE TRUCK HAD HIT A drainage cut in the dirt road and bounced. She was tossed around but soon got her bearing. She felt the flatbed gearing down and ascending a slight incline up a snow-packed gravel road. The truck pulled into what she assumed was a driveway, followed it, maneuvered, then backed up and stopped. The driver's door opened, but the truck engine was not turned off.

She lay there sharpening her senses. She was in quiet place. No sounds of traffic or the bustle of a town. Voices came in and out but were unintelligible. Footsteps in the snow came her way. There was no way to slide out of sight. The bungee cords holding the tarp down were popped off, but to her surprise no one lifted the tarp.

She heard the clunk of a gear engaging and the whine of a heavy winch. The truck bed began rising at the front! She had no place to brace her feet, plus the horses began pushing against her. At 45 degrees everything started moving to the back of the truck bed!

Pica slid out on her side, hit the deck, and rolled out from under the avalanching horses! A stiff limb caught her between the shoulders and knocked her down. The third horse, whose carcass was solid with cold, bounced beside her as she ducked away. It rocked back and lay gently across her right leg.

It all took place in less than five seconds. Then the winch stopped.

Pica had not screamed nor said a word. The driver, who was operating the winch from a switch just behind the cab on the truck frame, never saw her. But the heavy, blackhaired Blackfeet man standing on the other side of the truck was staring at her. He looked over at the driver, then back at the scene before him.

AH, DEAR READER. I AM SURE MANY THOUGHTS RACED, OR AT LEAST SPEED-WALKED, THROUGH HIS MIND AS HE WATCHED THE SCENE UNFOLD. NOT THE LEAST OF WHICH WAS, *DID SHE COME WITH THE DEAL? AND HOW MUCH MORE WOULD IT COST?*

Pica shook and tried to raise her head just as the driver stepped around the corner. He screamed! Hit falsetto, sounding like the Ink Spots attempting a yodel! Grabbed the side of the truck, then fell to his knees holding his chest! It was beautiful.

Pica squinted her eyes and said, "Spiral?"

"Pica?" he asked.

In the next few minutes Spiral Keets, independent businessman, lifted the horse off her leg with the winch, collected $125 from the Indian man for the carcasses, and, with Pica beside him in the truck cab, headed toward the junction of Highway 89 and Highway 2 that went to Cut Bank, Shelby, and Interstate 15.

Spiral started talking: "I can't believe my luck. Just like in a fairy tale or a movie, ya know, like a romantic comedy where you are Sandra Bullock, and I'm Tom Cruise and, like I'm a sports agent, hey, and you're a policewoman whose tough and can fight, but Tom gets you in a pageant thing, and we're both on a bus that we can't slow down or stop because the bad guy will set off a bomb which can release a meteor or an earthquake or a giant tidal wave, and we're on the *Poseidon,* hey, in the perfect storm, and we're trying to free Willie . . ."

Pica was immediately taken back in time. What she remembered most about Spiral from their middle and high school coincidal matriculation was his exuberance—excessive exuberance and earnestness.

"Man," he continued, "what luck. What if you had crawled in the back of another rendering truck or in front with a logger or maybe a meth addict who had just murdered his wife, or sister, ya know, or ex-wife, even, or maybe you would have met a nice family who could have taken you with them, maybe kidnapped you, even though they looked innocent to start with. Even their children would have been kidnapped earlier but now were under the influence of the . . . something effect when the Black Panthers or the rubber underground, or whoever, the Weathermen who were also women, but what the . . . hey? What if you have been tricked by the family, and you'd become their slave? Whew!"

"Where you going?" she asked.

"Cut Bank. I live in Cut Bank. I have a green card. Oh, I make it back to Pincher pretty often. Mom and Dad keep an eye on me, but, as you can see, I've started my own business. After the States passed the horse slaughter ban I figured, what are all those backyard, city-type people gonna do when they can't get rid of the horses they have?

"I talked to a vet. He said a hundred dollars to euthanize them, hey? Then whattya do with a dead horse? Bury it? . . . big backhoe expense, rent a hole somewhere to put him in? Hire somebody to take him to the dump!

"So, I set out to make it work. And the kicker! Guess what?" He stared at Pica. She stared back. "Recycling!" he said and waited for overwhelming complimentary response.

"I've got a list of six people now who will pay for dead horses. Ya know, dog trainers, one guy has two half-wolf pets, likes to train them with real meat. I'm workin' on a zoo in Conrad . . . it's not a big one, but if I can furnish them meat for, like, a mountain lion exhibit or wild boars . . . They'll eat anything, them boars. And that last guy where we just dumped the three horses, I'm not sure what he wanted them for, but I can tell ya, he sure had his eye on you!"

"Spiral," she said, "I just want to thank you . . ."

He interrupted, "I'm glad to, I'm glad to. I told you, it's my lucky day. Anyway, I also am spreading word that I can euthanize horses right at their place and haul 'em off!"

"How do you . . ." she started.

"Forty-five-caliber S&W. That's when I can get up close. Sometimes I've had to use my .30-30. Forty-five is great if you hit the brain the first time, and I'm a pretty good shot. But if, ya know, they're in the corral and hard to corner, I can do a heart shot or even a head shot, hey.

"I've even thought up a name for my company. You know, paint it on my truck, maybe a ball cap. How's this . . . Heaven's Helper . . . Equine Demise and Disposal?"

"That's great," said Pica.

"Ya know," said Spiral, "I've never held it against you when you wouldn't dance with me at the eighth-grade graduation party. I was just a kid. No job, no sophistication. You were cute. Not very well developed, like Amber, I mean, but still, you could tell you were a girl and . . ."

"I'm sorry if I hurt your feelings," she said.

"No, naw, you didn't. My mother said it was my braces. But it wasn't a big deal. Sure, I cried a lot, actually cut myself . . . accidentally, I told everyone, but it didn't matter. I just lived for the day when my braces would come off and I could ask you to dance again."

Pica was having mixed feelings between having hurt him so deeply and thinking, *I could be in the back seat of a station wagon having conversation with a functional family.*

"You remember the Mexican Beach Party?" he asked. "I think we were juniors, had a Mexican theme?"

A vision hit her like a cyclone! A specter walking toward her dressed as the Aztec Pyramid of the Sun carrying a large bowl of guacamole dip and a pour-on dipper full of the blackened green substance.

She was wearing a brand new, bought-for-the-Mexican Beach Party western blouse, with lace and a bit of a low neckline. It was unclear in her memory whether the lights went out or somebody did a table dive or the Pyramid of the Sun was pushed from behind, but she went over backward, and the bowl of guacamole hit her décolletage like a pie in the face!

She was humiliated!

For months after the incident Spiral had written her apology cards. Store-bought ones, handmade ones, ones in cookies, cakes, boxes of candy, and flowers, begging forgiveness. Finally her father and Uncle Firmy had made her see the humorous side of the whole thing. At their insistence she had written Spiral back, thanked him for the flowers, and forgiven him.

She received a thank-you letter weekly for a couple of months, and then he was mollified.

"Yes," she said. "I remember the Mexican Beach Party . . . and the guacamole dip," she said. "I finally saw the humor in it."

"I was so embarrassed," Spiral said. "Mother said I should write you an apology, so I did. I think somebody pushed me that night. I still relive it in my mind. I tried to write my version of it, but I don't know who pushed me, so I can't finish the story. I must have five or six boxes full of my notes and speculations. It still keeps me up at night.

"But then I got to thinkin', hey, it could be a movie! Somebody good write the screenplay, maybe I could be cast as the narrator. I'm imagining Renée Zellweger playing you, sort of the funny but good-looking character, who knows? But in the movie that somebody, an evil somebody, pushed me, and I, you and I could spend the entire movie trying to find the guilty party, the one who pushed me. Matthew McConaughey could play the role of me, the wounded, innocent victim . . . I could be injured in the fall. A little artistic license.

241

"We'd keep the villain, the bad guy's identity unknown until the very end when we find guacamole dip on a broom handle hidden in his basement."

Spiral paused. Then, "Whattya think? Pretty good, hey?"

She looked at him warily.

His features softened, and he spoke, "Pica, this must be fate. I can't tell you how often I've fantasized about you and I. How could something like you sliding out of my Heaven's Helper truck just be an accident . . . a coincidence?

"I don't want to rush you. It's all so new, so sudden, but I believe you and I are destined to . . . to, to be a part of each other's lives."

"How far is it to Cut Bank?" she asked quietly.

CHAPTER 55

December 8, Thursday
Still on the Trail with Pica

SPIRAL CONTINUED TO DRONE ON, EXPLAINING IN DEPTH HIS DREAMS FOR their future.

The droning of the truck tires and the driver soon had Pica, in spite of herself, remembering long-suppressed memories of her high school days. She had been a late bloomer. Not physically but socially and emotionally. She had resisted acknowledging her feminine side.

She had been sixteen the fall that Spiral had "guacoed" her. It had set her back months in her maturation.

Unfortunately Spiral was one of those intelligent but insensitive humans who had convinced himself that if she only knew him better, she would like him more. He had persisted in trying to explain and apologize. In self-defense, she agreed to go steady with Albert Chrz that Christmas of her junior year.

Albert was an outdoorsman, a junior like herself, and they established a comfortable relationship. It centered around hunting seasons, the movies, school functions, and some fairly innocent making out. But secretly, selfishly, she was aware that being with Albert solved her Spiral problem.

Pica never shunned Spiral or refused to say hello; she just avoided any possibility of close encounters. That was how their relationship stayed until they all graduated high school, and Spiral went off to the University of Calgary.

Albert's romantic drive outgrew Pica's, and they split amiably. He subsequently married and now had two children.

She had not thought of Spiral or Albert since graduation. But apparently, as she sat in the cab of the Heaven's Helper rendering truck, pressed against the passenger door listening to Spiral Keets pour out his deepest feelings, the

243

torch he carried for her still burned brightly. All she could think of was that Spiral needed psychiatric help!

She began to feel vulnerable.

"This is too much," Spiral was saying, halfway to himself, as they drove on eastward. Highway 2 was dry. The sky was overcast, and snow covered the country on both sides of the road.

"It's not a coincidence that we have been reunited after all this time . . ." he rambled on in this vein as Pica weighed her options.

She thought about telling him she was married, had kids, was with the FBI, was an escaped felon (which was actually closer to the truth), had become a nun, was with the Canadian Game and Fish Department, or even had a dreadful contagious disease. But she was not a good liar or actress. She usually chose direct action as her modus operandi.

"Can I borrow your cell phone?" she asked Spiral.

"It's not working," he said. "I tried earlier. The battery's dead. No charger in the rig here."

"That's okay," she said. "Spiral, would you mind pulling off the road for a minute?"

He looked at her with concern. "Are you all right, Pamyka?"

"Pah-my-ka?" she asked.

He looked at her with the tiniest embarrassment. "It's my pet name for you. How I think of you in my heart and mind. Pah-my-ka, as in 'My Own Pamyka.'"

"Oh," she said. "I just need to get out for a minute."

"Sure!" he said. "Nature calls. I understand. How 'bout this bunch of trees here, hey? You go first, ladies first and all, ya know."

She did and returned to the truck and climbed inside.

He excused himself and walked into the edge of the copse humming "Pincher Creek Wrangler" from one of Ian Tyson's albums.

When Pica could see his backside amongst the tree trunks, she slid behind the steering wheel, quietly put the gearshift into second, and hijacked the rendering truck!

Sixteen miles to Cut Bank, the coldest spot in America, according to the Talking Penguin that served as the town's statue. She had her foot to the floor and was doing 65 mph! The heavy metal bed banged and rattled, the engine roared, the tires sang a heavy drone, and wind whistled through the leaky windows.

Four cars headed west passed her as she raced across the Blackfeet Reservation. Approaching Cut Bank she watched for a large parking lot. IGA and Albertson's side by side loomed on her left. She pulled in between them and parked on the fringe.

It would be unkind to take the keys, she thought. So she didn't.

Now what?

A handsome blonde woman strode out of Albertson's automatic doors marked EXIT. She looked at the high clouds and light blue sky that formed the winter's roof on the Hi Line. Then pulled her fur-lined jacket closed around her neck against the twenty-degree weather. As she cut across the striped lines she noticed a warmly dressed woman wearing a small backpack staring at the rear of the blonde's two-month-old riptide-blue Cadillac Escalade four-wheel-drive SUV with the pewter interior.

There was a sticker on the back window that read LCA WILD ANIMAL SANCTUARY.

The blonde punched the electronic key that she held in her gloved hand. The taillight blinked just as she said, "Can I help you?"

Pica jumped in surprise. She turned and looked at the blonde woman, who was a couple of inches taller than she. "I . . . I . . ." Pica stammered. "Your plates . . . your license plates are Nevada."

"Yes," said the blonde. "I know."

"I'm thinking of going there myself," said Pica, looking meekly up into the blonde woman's face. Pica noticed that the woman was older than she was, but her hair was a sparkling blonde.

She had very few wrinkles, but what was most unusual was that she had one blue eye and one brown. Also that her fur coat was very expensive.

"Blue sable," said Pica, refurring (sorry) to the collar on the woman's coat.

"That's right. Why Nevada?" asked the blonde.

Pica paused, then replied, "It's personal."

"A man?" the blonde asked.

Pica didn't yea or nay.

"Leaving or chasing?" asked the blonde matter-of-factly.

Pica, who had not met the woman's gaze, looked up at her. "Both," she said.

It wasn't a lie, Pica rationalized. She was being chased by Spiral, and was she really looking for Cooney? Maybe she was.

The blonde woman relaxed her shoulders and studied Pica. Then she reached out and gently pulled the cap's ear flap, coat collar, and string of reddish-blonde hair back from Pica's face. The fresh scrape across her cheekbone and left eyebrow looked black against the cold, pale, freckled skin.

Pica said, "I fell off a truck."

"Sure ya did, Honey," said the blonde. "Sure ya did."

Just then a high-wheeled four-by-four with big mud and snow tires and a deer guard across the front bumper wheeled into the parking lot off Main Street! It slowed, then sped up in the direction of the Heaven's Helper one-ton rendering truck.

Pica turned quickly and saw Spiral's long face through the passenger-side window. He was leaned forward and pointing to his truck!

"That's him!" Pica said with fear in her voice.

The blonde took Pica firmly by the elbow, opened the back door, and pushed her in. "Stay down," she said.

The blonde stood by the driver's door, fumbling her keys as she tried to get a look at the man who had scared the girl.

Spiral jumped out of the high-wheel pickup and advanced on his ugly one-ton. He opened the door, looked in, then made a complete circle of the vehicle checking in the dump bed, between the frame, and under the hood. Satisfied, he looked around the parking lot, noted that none of the shoppers was Pica, and advanced on Albertson's.

The blonde slid under the steering wheel, started the car, and pulled out of the parking lot. She reached back and patted her passenger. Pica sat up.

The blonde spoke to Pica's reflection in the rear-view mirror. "I'm Teddie Arizona. Who are you?"

CHAPTER 56

December 8, 9:32 a.m.

Innercom Hotel, Las Vegas

THE RINGING PHONE WOKE OUI OUI. SHE PUSHED THE BLACK VELVET EYE mask back on her golden brown locks and reached for the bedside telephone. She placed the receiver to her ear and said, "File, I've told you . . ."

"*Perdon*, Senorita," said a man with a Spanish accent. "It iss not that. It iss me, Feliz, Feliz de Barbados, de Senor Huachuca."

"Feliz?" she said, sitting up against the headboard. "Is Three all right? He's not hurt or . . ."

"No, no, Senorita. He iss *muy fino. Pero*, he hass sent me on to here to help watch for you. I mean, *cuida a su . . . su seguridad.* He hass write a note for you to get from me. So I am here at the hotel, *bajado*, es waiting for you. I haf come from the airplane this mornin' from Miami."

"Feliz, can you, do you mind waiting for a few minutes, let me get dressed? I'll meet you by the reception desk at," she looked at the clock, "ten o'clock, please."

"Bueno, Senorita. *A las diez.*"

"Goodbye."

"Adios."

She thought about calling File immediately but then realized she would have to explain more to him about the Caribbean trip she'd made last September than she had so far. *I'll talk to Feliz first, see what's up*, she decided.

At the appointed time Oui Oui walked up to a slender, handsome Latino wearing a cheap suit, straw fedora, and wing-tip loafers. He had a rather prominent bump on the bridge of his nose and a well-kept mustache.

She was wearing a baseball cap, tennis shoes, tight jeans, and a loose, long-sleeve sweatshirt. "Follow me," she said. Soon they were seated in an obscure booth in the back of one of the show bars. The stage was empty this time of the morning.

She was reading the letter that Feliz had delivered. It read:

My little cappuccino, mi leona feroz,

> *I am sending Feliz with the message. I have heard through the grape juice that a certain well-known expert* de plumas, *de feathers, from the Chunited States iss askin' about a certain person who was captured in the* aeropuerto *de Miami with the goods.*
>
> Mi espia, *my espy is tellin' me that the liddle mule, the little burrita, she is knowing that you* recibio un paquete, *a certain package hand-delivered to your door.*
>
> *How does she know? Sometimes it iss that the espys are working two ways. It is jus' business. But she has connected you to the, the giffs. So,* este es un aviso, *a warning to be on the outlook. This ragamuffler could be seeking your position in order to do you harm. I am worried for you.* Entonces *I am leaving Feliz to stay with you, for your safety. I was lookin' on the Internet and Gugled you and know where you are this week, which iss why Feliz is there.*
>
> *With much confection.*

Oui Oui looked up from the computer printout page. "Do you know what this is about?" she asked Feliz.

"Maybe some things, but not other things," answered Feliz. "El Jefe *dice que* that I should take the letter back after you read it, and he wants for me to stay in the hotel room next to you and to guard your body."

"I think I will keep this," said Oui Oui, looking at the letter.

"No," said Feliz. She looked up, leveling her low-browed, threatening look that normally scared the hired help. Her lips froze where they parted when she saw his expression. His deep eyes drilled her, demanding undivided attention. She could see the angle of his jaw close slowly as his eyes became slightly opaque. It was Al Pacino as the Godfather taking the measure of a man. "Do not ask me to disobey El Senor Huachuca . . . effer."

She gathered up her wits quickly. "Sure. Sure, Feliz. It's just that we're so . . ."

The stare of Feliz did not change. It was deadpan. He did not release her eyes.

248

"Right," she said, taking a deep breath and handing him the piece of paper. "Right on."

Ten minutes later back in her room Feliz was watching Oui Oui explain the story to File: "So that's it. Somehow my Caribbean source found out that Pica knows, or at least suspects that we are somehow involved in framing her for smuggling. I don't know how she could think that! I mean, as well as we've treated her, tried to help her, before we framed her, I mean. I was beginning to feel like her big sister. I tried to give her tips on foundation, skin care, her heels . . . her heels were so hard, scuffed, like the bottom of a dog's foot."

"I know, Baby," said File, "but now is now. You know what they say: No good deed goes unpunctured. Are you thinking she might actually be coming down here . . . to Las Vegas . . . to ruin your debut tomorrow night? It can't be. I've got two—two, mind you—two agents from Hollywood that are coming to that party."

"Oh, I don't know what . . ." then she stopped herself. "File. That girl is not going to ruin my party! Feliz is here. He is going to move into your room next door."

"Well, where am I . . ." he said.

"We'll find something." She went on, ignoring his interruption. "We don't know if she will be trying to catch me in the hotel room or at the rodeo or shoot me or arrest me or what."

"We don't know if she is actually coming here," said File. "She may suspect something, but remember, she is confined to her family ranch in Canada, by law. Do you think she'd break the law?"

"Not a doubt that she'd break it," said Oui Oui. "You could make a telemarketer phone call and say . . . no, no . . . I'll make the call. You still have her cell phone number?"

"Yes."

"Dial it," she ordered. He did and handed his phone to her.

She listened to the message, and hung up. "See if you can find the number at her home ranch. Ask Straight. He might know.

"Right now we are going to be on full alert. You can go down to the booth this afternoon. I'll wait here. Feliz can keep an eye out for suspicious activities. I'll bet you still have some promo photos of Grimy Girl. Give one to Feliz so he can know who to look for."

"If she shows up," said File, "she won't recognize Feliz. She might not even know that I am involved. Do you think she would use violence?"

249

Oui Oui pondered. "Yes. I believe she would. She is an outdoors person, good with a gun, a hunting knife, stalking in the woods. The use of physical force would not be out of the question. Regardless, I think it is me she is after. We will just make a point for one of you two gentlemen to be with me at all times . . . at least 'til tomorrow night is over.

"Feliz, you may get moved in if you wish. File, see if we can get a sense of whether Pica-Smyka is still in Alberta or absent without leave. Now, if you two will excuse me, I am going back to bed."

CHAPTER 57

December 8, Thursday, Midday
On Interstate 15 in Montana,
In Teddie Arizona's Car

TEDDIE ARIZONA EXITED THE ALBERTSON'S PARKING LOT AND DROVE EAST out of town headed toward Interstate 15. "Are you hungry?" she asked the still-prone body in her back seat. There was no response. Pica had fallen asleep.

They reached Shelby, where Teddie Arizona stopped at a convenience store, gassed up, and got coffee. There she picked up Interstate 15 and headed south. Somewhere between Shelby and Great Falls, Pica stirred and woke.

"Mornin', Sunshine," said Teddie.

Pica groaned.

Teddie didn't say much for the next few minutes. She let Pica come awake on her own. When Pica did, she dug her cell phone out of her shirt pocket and checked the messages. The first was from Cooney, who gave her the hotel and room number in Las Vegas of Oui Oui Reese. The second was a call whose phone number she thought she recognized— File Blitzer. That call was a hang-up. There were six calls from her dad.

Pica had deliberately refused to make any calls on her cell phone. She wasn't really knowledgeable about the technical abilities of cell phones. Could people trace her calls if they were eavesdropping on Cooney or File or Straight? She chose to remain cybersilent. She was on her way to Las Vegas, wasn't she?

It was the day of the eighth performance of the National Finals Rodeo.

The lady who had given her a ride was still headed south, Pica guessed by the sky.

Finally Pica spoke: "Thank you for helping me."

"It's nothin', Darlin'," said Teddie. "Violent men are like a D-Con truffle in a box of candy. Anywhere is better than where they are. I hope you didn't leave any children behind."

"No. I'm not even married," offered Pica.

"Well, good, I guess," sighed Teddie. "Have you ever come close?"

"Not really," said Pica. "I've got one now that is really confusing me. I've only even kissed him!"

"Yer kidding me!" said Teddie. "You don't even know how he is in the sack, and he's got you all a-dither!"

"I'm all a-dither, as you say, about a lot more things than him."

"Ah," said Teddie. "Yer not pregnant, are you?"

"No. No chance really," said Pica.

"You mean with him . . . or with anybody?" Teddie asked.

"I've never been 'officially' all the way with anybody," said Pica.

Teddie Arizona took all this in and puzzled on it.

"So," Teddie said, changing the subject, "you say you are heading for Nevada?"

"Did I?" Pica asked. "I guess I am."

"Someplace in particular?" asked Teddie.

"Las Vegas," said Pica.

"Ah," said Teddie. "Las Vegas. Sin City, the place of dreams, the home of magic, alcoholism, and the National Finals Rodeo!"

Pica remained still.

"Almost twenty years ago I had a ride with a cowboy," mused Teddie Arizona. "I had a bad marriage and tried to escape it and . . . well. I guess that cowboy saved my life. He actually asked me to marry him. I didn't. I was mixed up, so was he. It never would have worked, but I believe I was truly in love. But betting on him was like betting on a crippled horse.

"I came into a lot of money, built a wildlife sanctuary . . ."

"I saw the sticker on your back window," said Pica.

"Yeah, the LCA . . . stands for 'Lick, Cody, and Al.'"

"'Lick'?" puzzled Pica. "I've heard of a Lick, Lick Davis, cowboy poet. He's been to . . ." Pica started to say "Pincher Creek," then stopped herself. She was an escaped criminal in the eyes of the law. *Zip yer lip, Darlin',* she said to herself.

"Yep, that was him," said Teddie. "When I knew him he wasn't famous. He was just a burnt-out cowboy on a winter camp in Idaho. Anyway," she said, "our paths crossed. We had a close relationship, but neither of us was very stable. He finally got his act together, took a job with a veterinary drug company, and started doing cowboy poetry.

"I fell into money, as I mentioned, and became involved in protecting endangered species. I've made a life in Las Vegas. Lick eventually got married, had kids, lives out in the sticks somewhere, and now tours the country entertaining.

"I've been to a show or two of his. I would have never guessed he could be so funny . . . or responsible."

"Are you married?" asked Pica.

"No. Well, not really. There was this deal with a casino owner but . . . It was marriage, but it wasn't love," Teddie answered.

Pica ooohed.

"No regrets, Kid. Lick did ask me. I've always treasured that. It probably wouldn't have worked, but at least he asked me. I turned him down. Deep down I still know it was the right thing."

Silence nudged in between them. Pica drifted back to sleep. Teddie Arizona kept her eyes on the road.

"Where are we?" asked Pica after waking.

"We, my dear, are coming into Helena, Montana," said Teddie Arizona. "I figgered we could freshen up. Get a coffee or a pop and . . ."

"How far is it to Las Vegas?" asked Pica.

"Close to a thousand miles from Cut Bank. But I flew into Billings. I have some development property there and Fort Benton. I was just making a wide circle to see what was movin' and shakin'. Are you in a hurry?" asked Teddie.

Pica was still playing her cards close to the vest, but she thought she better know if this ride was gonna peter out and if she should try another. Her thought was to get to Las Vegas before the finals were over. More specifically, before Oui Oui checked out of her hotel. Pica wasn't sure what she would find there . . . proof of her own innocence? More than likely the proof she was looking for was in Oui Oui's apartment in Denver, but . . .

"I don't guess so. I was hoping to be there by Friday night," hedged Pica.

"Well, that works for me. I've got tickets to the rodeo finals, but I kinda quit going. Too much pizzazz for this ol' party girl," she laughed. "We'll spend the night in Billings and fly out tomorrow. Private plane, you know. I've got a little business in Billings tomorrow morning. We can leave by noon and be in Vegas by five o'clock Friday. That be okay?"

Pica considered telling this nice woman the truth. There was no way Pica could check into a hotel or use her cell phone. But she was too tired to worry about it now.

"I can help drive," offered Pica.

"It would be even better if you just helped with the conversation. I'm doin' all the talkin'," said Teddie.

"Sorry," said Pica. "I just don't feel like talkin' much."

"I'm sorry, Darlin'. You must have a lot on your mind you're tryin' to work out. I don't mean to be prying. You just do what you need to." Then Teddie added, "But, if you wanna air out some of your worries, I'd be glad to try and listen."

AS LUCK WOULD HAVE IT—AND AS I HAVE SAID BEFORE, IT SOMETIMES DOES—IT TURNS OUT THAT TEDDIE ARIZONA HAD A TOWNHOUSE IN BILLINGS. THERE WOULD BE NO EVIDENCE OF HER MYSTERIOUS COMPANION'S PRESENCE ON THE TRAIL FROM MONTANA.

CHAPTER 58

December 9, Friday Night
Ninth Performance of NFR

"BIG EXCITEMENT HEYAH IN DA SADDLE BRONC, SKIM," BEGAN LAYER PIE, XM Radio Rodeo broadcaster, to his color commentator, Skim Slayton. "Foah contestants have ridden all eight broncs so far and are within fifty-six points of each otha' for the average."

"Yessuh, Layer. You said it right. And speakin' of right, I am enjoying a cool, refreshing bottle of Alabama White Delight . . . the light beer with a wiff of white lightnin' all home brewed right outside of my hometown of Cullman jus . . ."

Layer punched Skim's mute button. "As I was sayin' befo' you-all speakin' 'bout yo' uncle's garage business, which I thot I 'splained theah ain't no advertisin' on our XM station."

"Pa-leeze do not misencalulate my intentions," protested Skim. "I am fully awayah and, if you remembuh, that public service announcements are appropriately appropriate *since* you and I nevah, I say, neva have made a dime."

"Within fifty-six points!" said Layer. "Furst in the saddle bronc average with 632 points is Cooney Bedlam, who is also now standing fourth in the bull riding average. Straight Line, the Cinderelly story of this week, is second in the average only three points behind Cooney. Shelby Truax from Geyser, Montana, at 602 total on eight broncs is third, and in fourth place for the NFR average in the saddle broncs is Arizona cowboy Clancy Schmidt."

"That's all gonna change tonight," said Skim.

"Wayal, how perceptavous of you, Skim. That's why you-all gets the big bucks around heyah."

"Thank y'all, Layah. So, speakin' of colah, Alabama White Delight is sho . . ."

The mute button made no sound as it engaged.

Straight and Cooney were back in the dressing room stretching, pulling, reviewing, redoing, winding up, unwinding, just getting in the groove. Straight had done several interviews in the last week. The underdog, against all odds, had a chance to win the big one!

Through some unspoken superstition, none of the rodeo cowboys spoke to Straight about his great run. Comin' from the back of the pack, now within reach of one of the gold buckles. No one wanted to jinx his luck.

RODEO COWBOYS ARE FIERCELY COMPETITIVE, MAKE NO MISTAKE. AND I'M SURE THEY BREATHE A SIGH OR A GET A SHIVERING LIFT WHEN THE ANNOUNCER INFORMS THE CROWD THAT ONE OF THE OTHER CONTESTANTS HAS BUCKED OFF OR HIT A BARREL, MISSED A LOOP, BROKE THE BARRIER, OR FAILED TO MARK HIM OUT. BUT TO DISPLAY ANYTHING BUT EMPATHY AND GOOD SPORTSMANSHIP WOULD BE A VIOLATION OF THE COWBOY CODE. REF. CBY CD CH 12 V 16 . . . NEVER KICK A FELLER WHEN HE'S DOWN.

THE OTHER FACTOR AT THIS STAGE OF PROFESSIONAL COMPETITION IS THAT THE LUCK OF THE DRAW HAS AT LEAST AS MUCH INFLUENCE ON THE SCORE AS DOES THE COWBOY'S ABILITY TO RIDE. AND STRAIGHT'S LUCK WAS ALL ACES.

Straight was down on Persimmon Splatters. Because Cooney was up next, one of the other bronc riders was helping Straight. This ninth performance was loosely called "the Bad Pen." The arena was sold out and filled with a crowd who had started following Straight more closely with each performance as he continued to make every ride.

At the OTT booth every night after the show, Straight was on hand to sign autographs, take pictures with dads, make wives wonder why he wasn't married, be a good example for kids, smile politely, and generally give rodeo a good name.

Oui Oui, the LIP LASTER girl, was doing her part as well. Seductively draped in her copyrighted line of trashy western wear called "Cowgirl Growl," she posed for photos, signed autographs, and exuded estrogen like a pollinating ragweed.

Suffice it to say, OTT's booth was packed.

"Next up in chute number 3," roared the announcer, "coming into the finals in fifteenth place nine days ago and now standing second in the average from Buffalo, Alberta, the one and only . . . *Straight . . . Line!*"

The crowd picked up the chant. Barrelman Razzama Tazz conducted the choir. He'd point to one side of the coliseum, and the crowd would shout "Straight!" Then he'd point to the other side, whose crowd would shout "Line!" With each cheer they would speed up like a locomotive pulling out of the station, increasing slowly with each vociferation, until at full cry it sounded like a freight train: "Straight-Line, Straight-Line, Chooka-Chooka, Chooka-Chooka, Straight-Line, Straight-Line, Chooka-Chooka, Chooka-Chooka, Straight-Line, Straight-Line, Chooka-Chooka, Chooka-Chooka . . ."

But there is no glory behind the chutes. You've got to step out onto the battlefield. *Bam!*

The gate swung open. Persimmon Splatter came out like a racehorse, one, two, three, four strides. Straight's spurs stayed rigid on the buckin' horse's neck, then, just like her book said, Persimmon dived to the right and started to buck! Put her nose into the dirt like she was sweeping mines and commenced to pound the earth and the sky!

Straight stayed on . . . but it was not pretty. Persimmon was leaning into the tight right turn, hind feet kicking to the outside, as she circled as if her head was tied to a post! The audience in the front row could see her underbelly each time she fired!

Her first run-and-jump trick usually caught even the best bronc riders and threw them into orbit. It also earned her repeat invitations to the Bad Pen. Many's the video that shows Persimmon's hapless riders landing ten feet away from the buckin' little mare.

The problem for her was that tonight the rider up was hot, primed, and on a roll. Straight Line stuck to her like he had roots. He did slide. He did roll. He lost his hat and all track of time, but he never lost his grip, his balance, or the nerve that it took to hang and rattle with the best that rodeo contractors had to offer.

He made it the requisite 8 seconds and wondered for a split nano where the pickup men were just as she side-passed and punched him into the ground like a lawn dart! He rose and started walking back to the chutes, unsnappin' his chaps while looking up at the giant four-sided scoreboard that hung high above the center of the Thomas and Mack Arena. One of the chute help handed him his hat.

"Ladies and gentlemen," the announcer pronounced at the top of his lungs, "a new leader! Straight Line with a hard-earned, well-deserved *seventy-nine points!*"

"Theyat had to be one of the ogliest bronc rides Ah have evah seen in my life," said Skim Slayton into his microphone.

"Fo' onct in yo' life," said Layer Pie, "I can find no fault with yo' colah analysis."

"Only thing I evah seen worse was the bridesmaids at my cousin's weddin'," said Skim.

"Which cousin's wedding was 'at?" asked Layer. "The bride's o' da groom's?"

"Bo' fum," said Skim.

"I should have sumized it was a family affair," said Layer, conceding his missing the obvious. "Anyways, that means only five men have stayed aboard in this roun' of bad news broncs. Counting Straight, only three have done rode all nine horses *but*! . . . and Ah say it with no personal assprobation on yo' part, Skim, since it is fairly cleah from the tons of fan mail that XM Rodeo Radio has done received this week alone, that we will not be asked back politely to return. They-all be only two mo' times at the NFR, the National Finals Rodeo, dat we, you-all and me, will be honored to announce that de nex' and final saddle bronc rider in this, the ninth and next-to-last performance, is none other than Buffalo, South Dakota's world cham-peen-ship leader, Cooney Bedlam."

"I don' know how you do it, Layah, you-all can sho' pile it on!" said Skim.

The coliseum announcer was making similar pronouncements to the adoring crowd. "Yessir, ladies and cowboys, coming into tonight's performance this next saddle bronc rider holds the lead in the average by a total of three, only three points ahead of his runnin' partner and best friend, Straight Line, who you just watched score seventy-nine to take the lead. What is going on in this man's head, ladies and gentlemen, I can tell you . . . He is thinking about riding this tremendous bucking horse named 'Smokeless Blood Brother,' who has earned his own reputation by having only three qualified rides made on his back in the last twenty-two tries! Put your hands together, clench your buns, and tear the seat cover off your chair . . . *In chute number 5 . . . Cooney Bedlam!*"

The crowd cheered heartily. Laser lights shot through the dust. Sound effects pounded and rumbled 'til the faces of the fans looked like orbital monkeys drawing three *G*s!

The announcers egged on the crowd! Then out came Cooney Bedlam, all 158 pounds of him, on the back of the big bad bay. The gate swung open, and the pair catapulted into the arena.

The next 8 seconds looked more like a bad billiards shot in which the cue ball banks off the rail and knocks the 10 ball through the front window. Or if you've ever seen anyone fall down a set of stairs, a calf get loose in a chicken house, or a dually loaded with sawdust hit a patch of black ice, you'll get a mental picture of the pair's trajectory.

Somehow in the early going Smokeless Blood Brother slammed the fearless Cooney into the concrete wall, then ricocheted across the arena, weavin' and buckin' while Cooney was rockin' and swervin', feintin' and firin', reachin' and liftin', and never lettin' up until they crashed into the far end, ejecting Cooney out over the dumbstruck calf ropers.

These calf ropers were up in the next event and were watching safely behind the metal panels. As Cooney sailed into the knot of ropers and horses, they tried in vain to scatter and avoid the misguided missile.

Cowboys ducked, horses spooked, and ropes tangled as the Tasmanian devil seemed to explode on impact! Cooney knocked one of the ropers off his horse, rolled under another, and bounced off three more 'til he landed on his feet like an Olympic gymnast!

It took about ten seconds for cowboys to get the horses settled and for Cooney to dust off and unscrew his hat. He looked up at the nervous, glaring group around him, tipped his hat, walked over to the metal panel that he'd just flown over, and climbed back into the arena. The crowd was on its collective feet, each person turning to a seatmate and asking, "Did you see that?"

After the "terrorist" was out of their midst, the calf ropers settled back down. They watched Cooney walking across the arena toward the bucking chutes to a continuous standing ovation. More than one roper shook his head, not believing what he had just seen. And they realized once again why they had chosen to participate in a timed event instead of a self-flagellating, pull-my-finger, teeth-rattling train wreck during which you wear a bullet-proof vest, several bone screws, and a felt hat.

But Cooney felt so good. "A seventy-six!" belted out the announcer, "which sends Cooney Bedlam and Straight Line into the tenth and final performance tomorrow night tied for the NFR average championship!"

The last part of the announcer's blast went unheard. It was buried by the uproarious crowd's reaction to the stingy score that the judges had given Cooney: *Boooooooooo!*

CHAPTER 59

December 9

The Ninth Performance Continues

BENEATH THE ARENA IN THE MEDIA ROOM WHERE THEY'D BEEN ESCORTED, Cooney and Straight answered the sportswriters' questions. "How does it feel? Any friction between you two? Who do you admire? What are your chances?"

Some of the answers were revealing: "Don't count out Shelby Truax. Luck of the draw. Yes, my folks are here. I learned a lot from Straight. Cooney helped me get back my game. 'Scuse us, I've still got a bull to ride."

Cooney and Straight had both ridden all nine broncs they bucked out. Shelby Truax had also ridden nine broncs but was twenty-eight points behind the each of the leader's total count. The first criterion to determine the winner of the NFR average was the number of broncs ridden successfully. Second was the number of total points garnered. Third would be money won. Any of the three who failed to ride tomorrow, regardless of his total points, would lose to the one or two who successfully made the tenth round.

They walked back down the hall to the contestant area. "I meant what I said," said Straight. "You did get me back in the right state of mind. Although you might not be able to tell, I've never been so loose."

"Well, your idea of loose is wound pretty tight to me," laughed Cooney.

"And you remember," said Straight, "tellin' me about 'forgiveness and mercy to all who offend'? I told you about how my brother reacted after I had missed the finals. I didn't let it get to me. I just let his jabs roll off and concentrated on the fact that he was my brother ... and that I'm gonna love him no matter what.

"Whatever his reasons for putting me down were not because I was good or bad. If I didn't provoke it, then all the meanness came from inside him. He couldn't hurt me, and it was actually sad watching him try to. I was changed inside, I am changed inside! It's like looking at my life in a bigger picture.

"Anyway, last night he sent me an e-mail. It was . . . uh," Straight swallowed a little catch in his throat, "kind of touching. We've always fought. I was older, more athletic, he was younger and smarter. He apologized. Said he was sorry for being a jerk. Regretted that we couldn't have been better friends growing up. Congratulated me for having the try and determination to make as far as I had.

"It was one of the best things ever happened to me, Cooney. The folks have enough problems making everything work without havin' to put up with bickering kids. I'm not sure exactly what caused his change of heart, but something did."

Cooney waited to see if Straight was done talking, then spoke: "He saw the goodness in you, Straight. God gave you a kind heart. In spite of your ambition and funny habits, you're a nice guy. Everybody likes you. You work for what you get and don't blame bad rides on judges or horses or bad luck. And you've always been good about helpin' other guys ride better. I'm the prime example of your coaching. Not only that, my amigo, you are a top hand and one classy bronc rider . . . who, if I remember right, is tied for the average goin' into the last perf."

Straight looked up at Cooney, grinned, and said, "Yeah . . . ain't that somethin'?"

Up in the media box Layer Pie was keeping the XM Rodeo Radio audience entertained while Skim Slayton talked to the vendor selling roasted almonds.

"So that thayah is the completion of da ninth round of the tie-down roping. Da fust foah a duh contestants are from da big state of Texas, with Tuff and Trevor in da lead. Matta fack, nine of da fifteen finalists wuz from Texas, three from Oklahoma, and, guess what, Skim? . . ."

"Huh?"

"Guess what?" asked Layer.

"Guess what what?" asked Skim.

"Wayal, if nine is from Texas, and three is from Oklahoma, guess what?" Layer persisted.

"Day iz all in du oyul bidness? All loud? All have pore taste in clothing? All hate the University of Nebraska?" guessed Skim.

"No," said Layer in frustration. "Two is from the Southeast Conference!"

"Wayal pluck the hairs on my nose!" said Skim, "I am po-leezed. As if dat might add some needed colah to the discussion I wuz havin' wit one of the fine gennelmuns who is helpin' put on dis heah whole shebangs, which is should toasted almonds have cinnamon flavor o' jus' plain?"

"I say," said Layer, "they is yo' nuts. You kin do whatevah you dang well pleeze!"

"I am glad, Layah, dat you and I kin finally agree on sumthin's. Now, if I may address the nex' big issue, Cooney Bedlam. All knows he is in a dream race wit his podna' Straight Line but . . . and I repeat a big but, Cooney is not done yet. He has another bull to ride still comin' up tonight."

"So true, my wise and summacious conflagrator," said Layer. "Cooney is, as of las' night, tied with Izzy Bosun for fourth place in the average after eight bulls. A good ride tonight will keep him in contention for some all-around money, too."

"Wayal said," said Skim. "Kayah fo' some toasted almonds? These are, uh . . . catfish flavuh."

Cooney drew Dirty Dudley of the Flying Ewe Rodeo Company. He would come in the second chute load. This round was called the "eliminator round," the equivalent of the saddle bronc "Bad Pen."

Only two bull riders out of ten so far tonight had completed the 8-second ride by the time Cooney's turn came. Cooney was left-handed and rode with his right. Every bull in this eliminator round was picked because of its reputation of being hard to ride.

PAUSE A MINUTE, READERS, AND EXAMINE WITH ME THE PHYSICAL CONDITION THAT THE ROUGH STOCK RIDERS MUST BE IN BY THIS STAGE OF THE GAME. BAREBACK RIDING IS AN ALMOST UNCONTROLLED EXPLO-SION. TWO HIP POCKETS, TWO SPURS, AND ONE GLOVE ARE ALL THAT COME IN CONTACT WITH THE HORSE. IT'S LIKE RELEASING A HISSING BALLOON INSIDE A BIRD CAGE FULL OF PARAKEETS! THE EXERTION IT TAKES TO RIDE A BAREBACK WOULD LEAVE A HUNDRED-YARD SPRINTER GASPING FOR BREATH.

SADDLE BRONC RIDING, ON THE OTHER HAND, IS OFTEN SMOOTH BUT, AS WE HAVE SEEN IN COONEY'S LAST RIDE, CAN TURN INTO BONE-RATTLING DEMOLITION DERBY, REQUIRING EVERY OUNCE OF STRENGTH YOUR ADRENALINE CAN INDUCE.

THEN THERE IS BULL RIDING, POUND FOR POUND REQUIRING THE MOST STRENGTH AND THE MOST QUICKNESS OF ALL THE ROUGH STOCK EVENTS.

COONEY HAD BEEN ON NINE SADDLE BRONCS AND EIGHT BULLS OVER THE LAST NINE DAYS. HE WAS A WALKING ACHE. HE HAD BAN-DAGES ON HIS RIBS, BOTH KNEES, AND ONE ARM, A TOTAL OF THIRTY-TWO SUTURES FROM THREE DIFFERENT WOUNDS. HE HAD ABRASIONS, BRUISES, BLACK EYES, BLISTERS, CONTUSIONS, WOUNDS, JOINT STRAINS, GROIN AND BICEP PULLS, AND A BIG LUMP ON HIS HEAD FROM HIS BAIL-OUT INTO THE CALF ROPERS EARLIER THIS EVENING!

HE WAS, AS SPORTS ANNOUNCERS WOULD SAY, PLAYING HURT.

CHAPTER 60

December 9

Ninth Performance, Cooney's Bull Ride

STRAIGHT WAS UP ON THE CATWALK BEHIND CHUTE 2. COONEY WAS straddling Dirty Dudley as they waited for another bull rider to buck out. Cooney had on his protective vest and bull spurs: Crocketts with star rowels screwed down so they wouldn't spin. The bull rope was pulled through the loop, situated but not tightened.

Dirty Dudley didn't look particularly ferocious, but his size was intimidating: 2,100 pounds of giant braymer bull! He was solid black with short, black, turned-down horns and had a hump as big as a forty-pound sack of Redimix!

Looking toward the bucking chutes from the center of the arena, beginning on the left, was chute 1. Between chutes 4 and 5 was a long gate that gave ingress and egress to or from the arena floor. There were seven chutes in all. Bulls were driven into the left side from the direction of chutes 4 to 1 through a series of tailgates that raised to allow the bulls to pass. Then, as each bull would arrive at his chute, the tailgate would fall behind him.

From the same perspective, the chute gates on the left side opened into the arena by a right-hand delivery. The hinge was on the left side. Chutes 5 to 7 were the mirror image.

Cooney, in chute 2 when mounted, had his left side toward the arena. He rode with his right hand. When he called for his bull, the gate would swing from behind his left shoulder, off the bull's left hip. The bull would have to turn to the left to escape.

Some bull riders had a preference of right- or left-hand delivery, although they were forced to take what they got. Of course, some bulls preferred one over the other as well. Tonight the bull had the luck of the draw.

Applause! The full-throated voice of the announcer was building anticipation for the score of the previous bull rider: "Will you look at that? All you Texans better be on your feet. This is the leader in the aggregate for the average and the leader in the championship battle. Let's see it, it looks, yes, . . . ladies and gentlemen . . . a ninety-one and a half!"

Cooney was down on Dirty Dudley, letting the arena clear from the last man's great ride. He was sitting back off his rope as Straight was pulling it tight. Then Straight handed the tail of the bull rope to him. Cooney was wearing a soft-leather glove on his right hand with a four-inch cuff. The initials "CB" were inked on the cuff. His hand was palm up and slid underneath the braided handle on the rope. He laid the flat-braided tail of the rope across the braided handle, wrapped it around the back of his hand, pulled it tight across the palm again, pulled it tight, and closed his fist. When it was just right, he snugged the exiting tail between his ring and little fingers and pushed it to the front.

Cooney's gloved hand was within an inch of the steeply rising hump. Straight, standing on the catwalk, leaned over Cooney with his right hand on the front of his chest and the left at the base of the protective vest in the small of Cooney's back.

Dirty Dudley made a move forward and a swipe with his head. Straight pulled Cooney's upper body back out of danger. A second later Cooney slid up on his rope, pressing his pelvis and legs hard into the angle of right arm and bull back. That was the pivotal point. If he could stay over his hand he would be in the eye of the hurricane. After the body slid back off the rope, it would become a sail loose at the end of the boom flapping on the mainmast!

Nod! Bang! Jump! Jar! Dirty Dudley sucked in his breath as he leaped forward into the arena! The rope came even tighter around Cooney's hand. His spurs held steady, toes pointed out and lodged just in front of the girth of the bull rope behind the bull's elbows.

At 92/100ths of a second into the ride, Dirty Dudley's front paws hit the ground like pile drivers, pitching Cooney forward over the hump, out of position. In a minisecond the bull was rising from the ground again, starting into a right-hand spin. Cooney's spurs broke loose and began digging at the tough hide as he tipped forward again.

1 66/100th seconds

When his front feet hit the ground this time, the bull's huge body was moving sideways as well as downward. The force of the impact pushed Cooney forward into his hand. Just right.

The forces of gravity and propulsion kept him from sliding sideways. This time his body position was left arm thrown back, chest out, a straight line from his raised fist to his boot toes.

Some bulls spin flat and fast. Dirty Dudley went up and down while spinning like a pump handle on a merry-go-round. Up he rose, veering to the right. Cooney's right bicep and forearm were flexed and hard as he pulled against gravity to keep on top of his rope as they climbed. His body was bent forward to stay in place. Spurs pressed against the hide holding on.

2 56/100th seconds

The up-and-down occurred three times in one 360-degree spin. Cooney was sittin' pretty.

4 77/100th seconds

In the groove Cooney was now spurring constantly, up and down. He had the bull's number.

5 99/100th seconds

On the next ascent Dirty Dudley did a stutter step. On slow motion at a later viewing, it appeared that as his front feet lifted from the ground, he hopped with his hind feet. Just a little hop. No more than six inches. In the time it took to say "tick tock" the seat of Cooney's Wranglers slid back off his rope.

Man and bull were in a climbing attitude. At the peak of his lift, with all four of the bull's feet off the ground, his hind feet flying out behind, his front feet splayed wide, and his massive head flat and level, Cooney, still off the rope, slid to the left, off center, and off balance.

7 12/100th seconds

BAM! CRASH! LEVITATE! STAND ON YOUR HEAD! FLIP CLEAR OVER! HANG UP! GET DRAGGED! GET PUMMELED! EAT DIRT! GET LOOSE! CRUMPLE ON THE GROUND! AND CRINGE!

"That, my friends, is what we call a wreck!" said the announcer, speaking the obvious.

"One good cowboy versus one very large farm animal! Sorry, Cooney, but a no-score. Close but no smokeless tobacco!

"Give him a hand, folks. That's all he's gonna get in the bull riding tonight!"

CHAPTER 61

December 9, Friday
After the Rodeo in the OTT Booth

SURROUNDING THE OVAL-SHAPED THOMAS AND MACK ARENA IS A LARGE, continuous concrete concourse at midlevel. It is filled with venue-owned booths selling beer, popcorn, hot dogs, and a variety of snacks. Also sponsors of rodeo are allowed to have informational booths. The PRCA has the monopoly on selling rodeo-related, officially recognized souvenirs such as jackets, scarves, sweatpants, T-shirts, baseball caps, calendars, buckles, jewelry, and programs.

Space is set aside for autograph signings by those ropers and riders who had won their event that night. The saddle bronc winner's area was sponsored by OVER THE TOP ATHLETIC COSMETICS. Tonight in the booth Straight held the honor. He had invited Cooney to join him. Having both men in the booth was a bonus for the fans. In the same booth at a table next to them but at a convex 90 degrees, Oui Oui Reese was holding court.

Standing by the boys was Lick Davis. He, too, was well known to the rodeo crowd. He was there to honor his friends, Cooney and Straight, at their invitation. He, too, was signing autographs.

"Hey, Cowboy . . . wanna get lucky?" a woman asked Lick.

At the sound of her voice Lick looked over the hat of a kid whose program he was signing.

There was Teddie Arizona, blonde, one blue eye, one brown, toned, dressed like a model from *Cowboys and Indians Magazine*, smilin' and showin' a few lines.

He looked down at the kid, signed the program, patted his back, and said, "Be a good boy and don't forget to eat your candy." The kid looked up at his mother, who was staring at Lick under a furrowed brow. Mother and son walked off.

"Hey, Cowgirl . . . need a ride?" Lick replied.

"I just thought I better say hi and welcome you to Las Vegas," she said.

"It's been ten years, at least," said Lick.

"Yes. Almost to the day," she said. "Since you got married, actually. How's that going?"

"I guess it's the best thing ever happened to me," he said. "I've got an eight-year-old daughter and seven year old son. I've got pictures . . ,"

"No, that's okay," she said.

"I read fairly regular about your wildlife preserve. It's getting big-time. You're doin' good work," he said.

"It keeps me busy and out of the bars," she laughed. It was an ironic comment. One of the reasons why she and Lick had split after two years was alcohol. His and hers. They were made for each other's downfall.

He had saved her life, and she had become wealthy overnight. Neither one, at the time, had a career, motivation, or a plan. She was a depressed, unpleasant drunk. He was a cheerful, irresponsible drunk. She got her act together first and took an interest in investing her money. She gave him a thousand dollars and the boot.

He drove to Elko, Nevada, fell in with the cowboy poets, and found a niche. That was fifteen years ago. He had become a minor celebrity, not necessarily good, productive, or reliable, but well known. Twice, in those days, he had been performing in Las Vegas and had gone by to see her. The last time had been ten years ago.

There was still a relationship then, not like old sweethearts, more like survivors of a sunken ship. But tonight, eighteen years since he had rescued her from certain ruin, a sweet affection seemed to radiate between them as Lick stepped closer. She smiled and gave him a hug. His mind immediately returned to another moment in her arms on the Idaho desert, at night, in the middle of winter.

They looked at each other with humility. They knew one another's secrets and kept them to themselves. The "Hey, Cowboy" and "Hey, Cowgirl" greetings were shiny threads that connected them to a time when they both were at the end of their rope.

"So, how's Al?" she asked.

"He died," said Lick. "Couple years ago. I kept in touch with postcards from places I traveled to. The nursing home wrote and told me. It was too late to go to the funeral.

"Can I buy you a . . ." he stopped. He had controlled his drinking, not quitting entirely. He remembered she had become a teetotaler, joined AA.

"No, thanks. But you can do me a favor. Introduce me to Cooney," she said.

Lick looked over his shoulder at the signing table. There was still a small group hanging around. "Sure," he said. "Just give 'im another minute with the fans."

———

Oui Oui dispensed with the last big T-shirt guy with a red scarf headband. "Yer my favorite, Babes!" he leered. "Save a little for the rest of us!"

"You know you can't handle what you got!" she said, acknowledging the small lady with wrinkles and a "Bull Riders Do It in 8 Seconds" baseball cap.

"Call Feliz," she said out of the corner of her mouth to File, who was assisting them all in the booth.

Oui Oui pulled on a floor-length zebra leather jacket, hair side out with faux leopard-skin collar. It was cold outside.

"He's waiting in the limo line," File said. "You want I should walk you down?"

"It would be nice," she said. "I just don't feel like pasting on one more smile for these schmucks. I feel like I was painted on a linoleum floor and walked over by a marching band.

"Who's that woman with Lick Davis?" Oui Oui asked suspiciously.

"I don't have a clue. Looks like an ol' friend though," said File.

"She's spends good money for clothes, that's for sure. Kinda dowdy but expensive!" observed Oui Oui with a note of envy.

"Let's go," she said.

File laid a hand on Straight's shoulder and said, "I'll be right back. Takin' Oui Oui to the limo."

Straight acknowledged File's message, then looked back to say good-night to Oui Oui. She was headed into the waning crowd like a snowplow.

Two minutes later Lick congratulated Cooney and Straight. Our heroes were tired and wired. "Cooney, there's a lady over here I'd like to introduce you to. She's an old friend of mine."

"Sure," said Cooney.

After Lick introduced Cooney to Teddie Arizona, she took Cooney by the arm, leaving Lick, and walked down the concourse a short distance. She said, "I have someone that would like to see you."

Cooney, in his preoccupied innocence, was thinking the person she was talking about must be disabled, infirm, or too busy to come to the booth.

"I've known her just a couple days, but she has become special to me," continued T.A.

"Is she . . . do I know her?" Cooney asked.

"Ah, here she is," Teddie said as she stepped up to a short woman in sunglasses, a Russian beaver hat, oversize down coat, jeans, and workboots.

The woman lifted her gaze to him, her distinctive lips displaying themselves like peach-colored rose petals on a freckled pillowcase. They took his breath away.

"Pica?" he guessed, but he knew. "Pica."

He breathed deep and experienced a lightness in his head.

CHAPTER 62

December 9

Cooney and Pica Meet after the Rodeo

FIRST WORDS LIKE "WHAT? ... HOW? ... WHERE? ..." HUNG IN HIS OPEN MOUTH.

"I must stay hidden," Pica said without reaching out to him.

"Can, can you come with me? I could sneak you into my room, but aren't ..."

"Please," she said, then looked at Teddie and asked, "may we have a minute alone?"

"Sure," Teddie said and walked back to the booth where Lick was standing.

"I need your help," said Pica.

Cooney was absolutely willing to do anything she asked. "What do we do?"

"My bags are in Teddie's car. She could drop us off at your place."

"Right on. Whatever you say," he said. "Let me tell Straight ..."

"The less people that know, the less will be aiding and abetting," she said.

He looked at her. "You're not worried about Straight, are you?"

"No. It's just that the less people that see me, the better it is for them."

"Okay," said Cooney. "I'll tell him I've got a ride to the hotel. It'll be okay. He and I have different rooms on different floors."

"Good," said Pica, then, "Cooney, you're the only one I trust. Even Teddie Arizona doesn't know the real story. It would be wise to have her drop us off at different hotels, then we can catch a cab to yours. And ... don't even hint to Oui Oui or File you saw me. I'll explain it all later. Okay? I'll wait 'til Teddie leaves and catch her. You meet us at this entrance right behind us."

Cooney nonchalantly wandered back to the booth. "I met somebody, and I'm gonna catch a ride."

"Fine," said Straight smiling. "Me, I'm going home to bed. Today was probably the best day of my life, Cooney. And you'll always be in it. I don't want it to end with me on a barroom floor somewhere or wakin' up tomorrow morning with a hangover and someone I don't even know."

Cooney looked at him as if he'd just declined a huge box of chocolates, a date with Pam Anderson, or a year's supply of Copenhagen. "I guess we have different ways of celebrating," said Cooney.

"See you tomorrow," said Straight.

Cooney walked the few steps to where Lick and Teddie Arizona were conversing.

"There's someone out there for you . . ." Lick was saying to her.

She saw Cooney coming. "Oh, there is, all right. I've got a string full of dandies. About half of them are looking for a trust fund. Not a one of 'em like you. That's good and bad, ya know. But every now and then I get this deep heart-achin' yearning for you, ya good-fer-nuthin' cowboy."

She was smiling. Lick took her in his arms and held her a moment, then released her.

IT'S FUNNY HOW THINGS WORK OUT. JUST GOES TO SHOW THAT PEO-PLE WITH THE ABILITY TO LET BYGONES BE BYGONES CAN ACTUALLY MISS THE PEBBLE IN THEIR SHOE.

With a wave, Teddie Arizona turned and started walking toward the exit. Cooney caught up with her. When they went through the big glass doors he noticed the short girl in the big coat, fur hat, and sunglasses fall in behind them.

＿ ＿

At 10:45 p.m. Cooney heard a knock on the door. He answered it in his jeans, untucked shirt, and bare feet. He had taken a two-minute shower, including washing his hair and shaving.

Pica slid through the open door, dropped her nylon bag, and fell into his arms. Whatever tidal wave had been building burst over the seawalls and down their backs. They fell over onto the foot of the big bed that took up most of the space in the small hotel room. He lay on his back and held her.

CHAPTER 63

December 9–10

Pica and Cooney Plan an Attack on Oui Oui

Cooney held Pica. She began crying. She cried until she was drained.

She had been on the razor's edge of hope, revenge, helplessness, and exhaustion for several days. She had been unable to sleep, even at Teddie Arizona's place. It had been a trip of soaring bravado highs to whimpering, snotty-nosed lows.

She crashed. She allowed herself to crash, to let go, knowing somehow that redemption was within her grasp. She fell asleep in Cooney's arms.

It wasn't what Cooney had expected. In the short hours since she had walked up to him at Thomas and Mack Arena his mind had flipped through the pages of many possibilities. Her loss of control was not one of them. But he was capable of some depth and compassion, and they rose to the top.

He slid out from under her, pulled off her boots, and covered her up to her ears. The television volume was down low. He left it on to help distract him from trying to guess the answers to a bed full of questions. He lay on top of the bedcover beside her in his jeans and finally went to sleep himself. She slept for ten hours with hardly a movement.

Pica woke up to the sound of a door being closed. It took a few moments to gather the whats and wheres of her present situation. In a hotel room, in a bed, fully dressed, in Las Vegas, on the trail of Oui Oui Reese, and Cooney Bedlam was standing at the end of the bed.

"Coffee?" he offered.

She sat silent a moment longer, 'til she booted her consciousness up to speed. "Oh," she sighed, "that would be nice."

He gave her a paper cup of the fancy type available in the lobby. Then asked, "So tell me all about it. What's the plan? What can I do?"

"How 'bout you let me clean up? Is my bag here? Oh, there it is. Then I will tell you the whole story and my plan, hey. We're gonna get her for good."

"What say I order you some breakfast?" he said. "It should be here by the time you're spiffy."

"Spiffy?" she smiled. "I think I can do spiffy this morning!"

It was 10:45 a.m. when the waiter brought up the breakfast. He brought it in, spread it out on the table. Cooney had him leave the plate covers on because Pica hadn't appeared. He signed the check and tipped the waiter extra. He was a good tipper. It was a Lick lesson.

She came out of the bath looking like a pink NRA doll with fluffy hair. From her bag she'd selected her wardrobe. It looked like she was going hunting! Jeans, lace-up workboots, a unisex camo shirt that buttoned down the front, and leather belt with an olive-drab cell phone holster.

Through breakfast he listened to her plan. She had good information that Oui Oui Reese and her connections in the Bahamas had planted, or arranged to be planted, endangered feathers in her suitcase while she was staying a few days in the Caribbean.

"It is also a good possibility that Oui Oui has been delivered smuggled feathers and/or endangered contraband to her home in Denver on occasion," said Pica. "That doesn't sound coincidental to me. I'm making a jump, an assumption," said Pica, "that she is the kind of person who would flaunt these treasures or at least carry some talisman or souvenir of her possessions with her. I don't know, but my only other option is that she has them in her apartment in Denver, but I'm here, and I plan to break into her hotel room. Thanks to you and Straight I have that info.

"I know you want to come with me, but you can't. Don't argue. I know what I'm doing, and one other person to worry about would limit my opportunities. Besides, it would make you an accomplice.

"I will reconnoiter her hallway and wait until she leaves for the rodeo. I assume she goes down at four or five o'clock in the afternoon, but, regardless, it shouldn't take me more than ten minutes to search her bags or clothes for some evidence that she is hooked to the feather smuggling.

"I'm not sure what I'll do with it, but I expect I will see you at the rodeo tonight. I'm too conspicuous to, you know, come talk to you, but just know I'll be watching when they give you that world champ buckle.

"I bought a cell phone from a stranger. In Las Vegas they don't ask any questions if you offer them a little cash. If all goes well I should be able to give you a call by five, maybe six, anyway. So, whattya think, hey?" she concluded.

"You need to know that Oui Oui has a bodyguard," said Cooney. "I don't mean File but another one. Straight said he's met him. He has a Spanish accent. As for your plan, it sounds pretty loose to me."

"It is loose. I call it flexible," she said. "I can cover a lot of conditions that arise."

"You know that OTT, your old LIP LASTER sponsor, is throwing a big bash tonight as soon as the NFR finals are over. It's at the South Point. Straight is back on their payroll and will be there shinin'. You know he's in the lead to win the average. Could be a great night for him. And the star of the show is Oui Oui."

Pica hooded her brow. *Not if I can help it,* she thought, taking a bite of peanut buttered toast.

"Yep," continued Cooney, "Oui Oui is doing a full hour: music, singin', dancin', and who knows what else. Straight thinks it's her shot at stardom."

Pica finished her chewing and reached across the table for Cooney's hand.

"I want you to know how much you have meant to me, how much you mean to me. For never doubting my innocence, for not trying to take over my life or take advantage of my situation.

"I'm not a very trusting person. I've never been in a serious relationship with anyone, just kid stuff on occasion. I can't put into words, pretty words like you can, how I feel. Even right now when I'm planning to do something that may sound ridiculous or stupid, that might take me clear out of your life forever, I still don't know what to say to you." She finished and held his gaze.

WHAT KIND OF HERO WOULD LET THE LOVE OF HIS LIFE GO OFF ON A HARE-BRAINED, DANGEROUS, PATCHED-TOGETHER SCHEME LIKE PICA IS PLANNING ... BY HERSELF? ESPECIALLY WHILE HE WAS "DOING LUNCH" WITH A GROUP OF BUSINESSMEN IN COWBOY HATS.

FIRST, LOYAL READER, YOU MUST CONSIDER THEIR RELATIONSHIP. IT WAS STILL BASICALLY AT THE LEVEL OF A HANDSHAKE. THERE WAS SOMETHING THERE, ALL RIGHT, BUT NOT MUCH TIME HAD BEEN ALLOWED TO PASS BETWEEN THEM TO GET INTO DEEPER FEELINGS. MOST OF THEIR INTIMATE CONVERSATIONS INVOLVED DISCUSSING HER "SMUGGLING CASE."

HE DOESN'T SOUND MUCH LIKE ROMEO, MOSTLY BECAUSE SHE WAS NO SHRINKING JULIET! HE KNEW HE WAS NOT ON SOLID GROUND MAKING ANY DEMANDS. THERE WAS A GOOD CHANCE THAT IF HE "PUT HIS FOOT DOWN" AND ORDERED HER TO STOP, SHE'D TELL HIM TO TAKE A HIKE! SHE HAD TOO MUCH INVESTED IN CLEARING HERSELF RIGHT NOW. AND THAT TOOK PRECEDENCE OVER WHAT- EVER WAS BETWEEN THE TWO OF THEM.

WAS SHE USING HIM? IF SO, THAT WOULD NOT BOTHER HIM IN THE LEAST, BUT MAYBE THAT'S WHAT WAS BOTHERING HER.

"If I were the eloquent one," Cooney said, "I would do everything I could to talk you out of this crazy idea. Why don't you just go to the police or the FBI or get a lawyer or talk to OTT or tell the world or run away with me and change our names and live in New Guinea?

"But you're backed in a corner. I know it, I can see it. And you're one of the toughest people I've ever met. So, since I can't stop you and can't go with you, I'm stuck waiting."

Cooney shook his head and shrugged his shoulders. "I'll probably be goin' to the rodeo grounds about four. Rodeo doesn't start 'til 6:45 or so. But I want to hear from you as soon as you're out of . . . as soon as you're in the clear. Don't leave me hangin'. Please.

"It's noon," he said, looking at his watch. "I've got a meeting, sponsor lunch obligation. Just leave the DO NOT DISTURB sign on the door. Here's a key to the room."

Cooney rose. She got up and came around the table and stepped into his arms. They kissed tenderly. He put his hands on her arms and stood her in front of him. "You can do it. I know you can. I'll be your lifeline . . . you call, I'll come."

"You might be busy," she said, thinking of tonight's finals performance.

At that moment he could clearly see his future. It was a photograph: She was standing beside him in a driveway in front of their house. There were mountains in the background. She was smiling. "You call," he said, "I'll come," then kissed her again and walked out the door.

CHAPTER 64

December 10, Late Afternoon
Pica Gets Caught in Oui Oui's Room

AT 4:55 P.M. OUI OUI LEFT HER ROOM CARRYING TWO LARGE BAGS. PICA had been staking it out since 2:15. Pica called once about three o'clock posing as housekeeping and asked Oui Oui if she wanted her room cleaned. Oui Oui said she would be leaving about five or five-thirty. Anytime after that housekeeping could have admittance.

At 5:35 p.m. Pica called the hotel desk impersonating Oui Oui and announced that she was leaving the hotel and asked that her room be cleaned right away because she was coming back soon. Within fifteen minutes the hotel maid came pushing her cart down the hallway. Using her universal pass key she entered, then propped the door open and began to clean.

The hallway was empty and long. Pica made several passes waiting for the right moment.

There were two bathrooms in the suite: one in the big room, the other in the bedroom. With the timing of a NASA *Challenger* launch, Pica scooted around the cart, skirted the bedroom door, and hid in the guest closet.

Twenty minutes later the maid left the room shining. Pica stepped out of the closet and looked around. Her hunter's upbringing led her to sweep the surroundings, scanning for wild game or signs.

She was standing inside a large suite. The door through which she had entered was on a wall with no windows. The opposite wall had expansive glass windows and a sliding door that faced to the inside of the hotel.

Satisfied she was alone, she explored. Bedroom, guest closet, and bathroom doors were on the wall to her left, a single closed door to the adjoining hotel room was on her right. The two standing lamps, desk, lamp table, sofa, chairs, coffee table, large mirror, and entertainment center were tasteful and functional. It was so feng shui.

Pica walked to the window and drew the curtain part-way back. The sliding glass door opened onto a four-foot-wide ledge with protective railing. The twenty-eight-story hotel was designed as a large upright tube with an enormous convex, round ceiling that served as a movie screen. Video technology could project the appearance of the sky at any time or any weather condition the operator would choose.

For the most part the projection mimicked a sunny day with blue sky and fluffy clouds twenty-four–seven.

For special shows or presentations the hotel would re-create nighttime, complete with astronomically correct, brilliantly laid stars and the phasing moon. It was its own virtual planet.

The suite had given Pica no clues about Oui Oui and the feathers, but Pica had saved the best for last. She stepped into Oui Oui's bedroom. At least the bed was made. Pica walked to the sliding glass window in the bedroom and noted it had its own outside balcony. She stepped out onto it.

Looking down from her place on the twelfth floor, she could see the top of a jungle. The lush canopy reached up to the eighth floor. It was dense, very green, and warm. She was able to see the other balconies lining the inside circular wall from the canopy level clear to the top.

For those adventurous visitors a zipline from one side to the other began at the tenth floor and soon disappeared into the foliage. The zipline platform, which was two stories directly beneath Oui Oui's room, was reached by its own elevator from the lobby.

Back in the bedroom Pica began a methodical search for any clue. She was a good tracker, according to her father, and didn't miss much. What she saw confirmed that this was most certainly a woman's camp. It was apparent that the maids were instructed not to mess with the mess, just clean the bathroom and make the bed.

The opened closet doors were burgeoning with clothes. Shoes were scattered on the floor. The bathroom counter was heavy with lotions, potions, creams, utensils, applicators, pills, spills, and open kits.

What Pica was looking for was not perfectly clear to her, but she would know it when she saw it. Evidence. She was looking for evidence that in some way would connect Oui Oui to the smuggling frame-up. She started with the closet. It was lined hanger to hanger with a wide assortment of dresses, blouses, pants, jackets, robes, and lounge wear. Pulling out a flaming-red cocktail dress, Pica held it up to herself in front of a mirror. It was so big that the long shoulder straps and flouncy bodice made her look like she was wearing Shakespeare's shorts with no top.

In the back corner at the end of the pole was a foldable simulated-leather clothes bag. Unzipping it part-way she encountered a plastic dry cleaner wrap. Pica pulled the bag out by the hanger and laid it on the bed. It contained an absolutely beautiful garment. A jacket, she thought, then lifted up the plastic. It shone with almost fluorescent colors in the window's virtual sunlight. She lifted up the bag and had her first look at a halter top made from the Tetuchtan Pavo Real.

Her only point of reference was a photograph from the Internet she had seen portraying colors of the Glandular Y Cock. Although the feathers in the waist-length halter top were not the same type as had been found in Pica's bag, they were similar enough. *It's the proof I'm looking for,* she thought fiercely, *or at least close enough.* She replaced the halter top in the leatherine bag and zipped it up.

Pica straightened and looked around the room, then glanced at her watch: 5:41 p.m. Once again she returned to the closet, riffled through the remaining clothes, and looked on the upper shelf, which held the iron.

A search of the drawers revealed nothing useful. In the bathroom she looked through the drawers and three makeup cases. In the bottom of the third makeup case was a thin plastic envelope containing photographs.

Pica heard something clump. She became instantly alert. It sounded like a door . . . faraway, maybe in the next hotel room. She waited a full twenty seconds, not moving. Relaxing, she pulled the color photographs out of the envelope. Surprise, surprise. The top snapshot showed Oui Oui on a sleek boat deck, on turquoise water, posing against a horizon of palm trees and a resort waterfront.

The colors were tropical blues, greens, and tans. Oui Oui was modeling the very same garment that now lay on the hotel room bed. In the picture the feathers sparkled iridescent in the sun. The photo was full length. Oui Oui was tanned. Her streaked golden hair was flying loosely in the wind. An orchid was pinned in her tresses. Her left leg was straight, her right slightly bent against the breeze, heel cocked against left ankle. She had her back to the photographer, looking over her shoulder. Her chin lay against the feathers, and her lips were pursed seductively. The flower and the feathers were all she was wearing. Pica noted that she was tanned all over.

Flipping through the photos, she found one wherein the feathered halter top could be seen from the front. Oui Oui had modestly covered herself with what looked like a wine glass or diving goggles; it was hard to say. Pica kept this photo and the one from the top and replaced the others into the makeup kit. She then unzipped the garment bag enough to slip in the photos. Her watch now read 6.14 p.m.

Her agreement was to call Cooney every thirty minutes to check in. She was late. Folding the bag and swinging it over her shoulder, she looked down at her cell phone and punched in Cooney's code number. While it dialed she began gathering the two photos and turned to the bed to buckle the bag with the feathered halter top. Cooney answered.

"Cooney" she whispered, "sorry it's late. I'm here in the hotel room."

"Did you find anything?" he asked.

"Yes . . . I hit the ja . . ."

Cooney heard the phone drop, then a heavy clump. A voice growled, "Cochina!" Then the phone went dead.

Pica felt the heavy blow to the back of her head, then a fireworks display burst in her vision . . . followed by blackness.

CHAPTER 65

December 10, Saturday Afternoon
Oui Oui's Hotel Room, Feliz's Fashion Show

PICA, OUR HEROINE, BEGAN TO REGAIN CONSCIOUSNESS. THE FIRST SENSATION was pain. It made her squint her left eye and grimace, gritting her teeth. The throbbing felt like a railroad spike was jammed through the back of her skull and pressing against the inside of her forehead.

"Well, *buenos tardes*," said a man's voice.

Taking inventory of her position, Pica noted that she was sitting on the floor slumped between a dresser and the side of a bed up against a wall. Her hands were tied behind her back. She painfully worked her way into an upright sitting position.

"So, *ladrona*, you have sneek-ed this far to esteel deez *plumas de reinas, de realeza*. It wuss *como el jefe pronosticado*, tol' the future of. That you would be comin'," spoke the man. He was a slender, handsome Latino with a little mustache and a bump on his nose. You are the thief wot comes from the Canada. I haf seen the poster, *cuadrado*, of when you wuss bee-yoo-tee-fool! Iss too bad it is only deep skin!" He laughed at his own joke. He also had a tendency to malaprop, a habit he adopted working for Hurtado Herman Huachuca.

Pica lowered her head with some difficulty. It was as if the tendons on her neck had been nailed to the back of her head. It hurt, but she was able to see that her boots were gone. Her shirt was opened, her belt undone, and her fly unzipped.

She tried to gather her legs under her but found that her bound hands were also attached to the leg of the dresser behind her. She looked up at him with a mean glint in her eyes.

"Oh, iss nothin' to worry about," he said, grinning. "Don't flatten yourself. Iss jus' that I saw that big *pistola*, so wuss havin' to search you for hiding weapons. Nice knife," he said, lifting up the hunting knife that she had carried concealed against her right calf. "*Afilado,* berry esharp.

"Although, under more better conditions, like we wuss trap on a dessert eyelan', maybe, if you wuss clean up, I could think to buy you . . . una margarita," he raised his eyebrow in a leer. "What? Jew got nothin' to say?" he flared, then caught himself. "Don' misunderestimate me, I am, how you say, berry goot wit' the ladies, *las damas.*"

"So, now you just hold me 'til Oui Oui gets back?" Pica asked.

"Oh, she can talk. The Pajaro Pequinito can talk!" he said sarcastically. "Of course, but actually I haf a little business to conject . . ."

"Conduct," she corrected.

"It hass nothin' to do with a duck . . . oooh," he paused. "Yes, it possibly hass feathers like a duck. Like the ones you were to find in the betroom of La Oui Oui. You shouldn't haf come essnoopin'. But, that iss the water under the bucket . . ."

"The bridge," she corrected again.

With the speed of a striking snake Feliz lashed out and backhanded her on the side of the head!

Pica reeled back, the pain of the new concussion exploding behind her eyes!

"You think you are so essmart that you can make fun with the Latino estupido!" he threatened. "I got the news for you, I am the one with the upper arm, and you are the one caught with your hand in the bushes! So what do you think of that?"

Pica painfully turned her head his direction. "I . . . I don't . . ." She drew a shaky breath and said, "I'm wishing I could have an aspirin."

Feliz sat back on the bed and studied her. "You know Oui Oui, because you are trying to do her harm. If you were juss' a simple bugler I could leave it go, but you, she warn me to put an eye out for you, that you might come hunting her. She showed me your picher when you wass *mas joven,* more young. But now, I haf other business to deduct, and I am afraid to have you aloose. If I give you some aspirin and put you in the closet you would not make noise, would you? Otherwise I would juss haf to keep knocking you up *con este cachiporra.*" He showed her his nasty little blackjack, then slapped it into the palm of his hand. It made Pica jump.

"Eeeeejuela! Tha's hurtin'!"

Ten minutes later Pica was half-sitting, half-lying on the floor of Feliz's closet behind two closed mirrored doors. Her hands were still tied behind her back, but he had been good enough to give her four aspirin and one of his own personal prescription pain pills. She was asleep by the time the expected knock came at Feliz's door.

Feliz had his own business on the side smuggling endangered birds, rare body parts, hides, feathers, bones, seashells, and underground trinkets. He had made arrangements with Pilo Tatoon, pronounced "PI" as in "apple pie," who was a forty-eight-year-old self-made multimillionaire from San Francisco, to show him several exotic illegal Caribbean jujus. Pilo was not a collector. Well, he was a collector of beautiful women, who, themselves, collected expensive things. Pilo was accompanied by one of his collection. Her name was Streak.

Feliz led them into Oui Oui's suite. He offered them drinks and made them comfortable. After a short conversation, Feliz went back to his own room to begin the fashion show.

His first presentation was an anaconda waistcoat with a collar made of blue and gold feathers from the threatened blue and gold macaw. He carried it in on a hanger, displayed it like he was a peacock, then laid it on the glass coffee table in front of their sofa.

Feliz described in detail the materials as well as the story of the beasts and their habitat. The more protected, threatened, or endangered the beasts seemed to be, the more it impressed Streak. "Oh, it is so, like, awesome, ya know." She looked at Pilo. "What do you think, like, I, ya know, could try it on?"

"Model it for me, Baby," said Pilo.

Streak stood, took off her mink coat, and let Feliz help her get the anaconda coat on over her shoulders. Streak was very thin, very tall, and had pale hair with a black streak that started above her right eye and ran back over her head. She was twenty-one years old and had been modeling since she was fourteen.

She strode back and forth in front of Pilo, then over to the mirror. She was wearing tight pants that clung to her and stopped just above her knees. Just watching her move was a show in itself.

Pilo politely lifted a finger and signaled her to come to him. She sidled over, stood in front of him, and lifted her outside leg, placing a three-inch heel on the sofa arm where he was leaning. She bent over so he could feel the snakeskin and feathers.

"I could use a toke," she said in a friendly way. Pilo drew from his pocket a silver cigarette case and eased out a machine-rolled Guatemalan reefer. He lit her up.

282

"Senor Pilo," said Feliz, "maybe I will help la senorita off her *chaqueta* so the feathers, don't, you know, blow up in inflammation?"

"As you say, Feliz. As you say," agreed Pilo.

After trying on and showing crocodile full-length high boots with narwhal ivory buttons and a cape made from the down of one thousand American bald eaglets, Streak was loaded and giggling. Sitting, straddling, and lying in various positions on and off Pilo she kept up a silly commentary as the fashion show went on. Pilo had discovered a flask in his pocket and had downed half a pint of $64-a-bottle tequila. Feliz had the uneasy feeling his sale was going sideways.

"You want to try on some more?" asked Pilo.

"Oh, Pilo. You know how I love to hope, ya know. But . . . right now I'm, like, too mellow, too flexible to stand straight," she cooed somewhat incoherently. "I'm afraid I might fluctuate right here."

Pilo looked up at Feliz with a shrug.

Feliz could see his sale flickering out. "Uh, I haf an idea, Senor Pilo. Maybe if the senorita iss too relax to model, I could show you another one."

"Another what?" asked Pilo.

"Well, it is, see, my cousin's girlfriend iss comin' with me and she . . ." Feliz was thinking on his feet. "She has taken some pills to make her, uh, more happy, but she could model a couple more of the special jujus that I haf broughten for purchase by maybe you. You could find one that fits the senorita."

They both glanced at Streak, who was drawing circles on the end of the sofa with an upturned flower vase. Water dripped off her knee and into her tall boot top. She seemed transfixed by the repetitive motion.

"Is she very pretty?" asked Pilo, always interested in dysfunctional women.

"She iss more like, like the wildcat or, how you say, ocelot?"

"Fine, maybe she can liven up this party," said Pilo, taking a long draw on his flask.

"*Por favor, escusa me,* for a moment to get her preventable," said Feliz.

CHAPTER 66

December 10, Saturday, After Dark
Feliz Convinces Pica to Model

FELIZ WENT TO THE CLOSET IN HIS ROOM AND OPENED THE MIRRORED DOOR behind which Pica D'TroiT lay sleeping, her head thrown back, mouth open, snoring quietly.

He shook her. "*Gatita*," he said lowly.

"Huh?" she said, not opening her eyes.

He continued to rouse her. Finally she opened her eyes. She didn't seem to know where she was, but it didn't seem to concern her. "Who are you?" she said pleasantly.

"Feliz," he said. "Feliz is my name, and I need your help."

She slowly began to remember. "I was . . . I'm in . . . at the rodeo . . .?"

"No, you wass trying to essteel the beautiful feather *chamarra* from Oui Oui, and I wass catching you hot handed," he reminded her in a stern voice.

"Why do I feel so . . . good . . . if I was stealing?"

"Jew fell and hit your head, and I gave you some medicine. Now you are better, and I need you to model clothes for me to sell to this *rico* for his *novia* who can't model anymore because she is esstoned on the marijuana."

"What if I don't . . ."

"Jew don't have a choice," he said fiercely, grasping a hank of hair above her right ear.

Pica started to move, but her hands were still tied. She kicked up at him, and he sat on both her legs, pressing down hard. It hurt her, he could see.

He got in her face. "Lissen to me, jew crippled hyena. Jew do what I tell you. Things are no very bueno for you right now. I can make them a lot more worser, even before Oui Oui comes to find you esteelin' her clothin's."

Her grabbed her ear with his left hand and twisted. Her little gold earring cut into the flesh. She started to make a noise, and he clamped his other hand over her mouth. "Do jew understan' that I can hurt jew, and I will do it. I've got more of these pills that can knock you clear over and make jew a slobberin' *babosa* if jew don't do what I tell you.

"Right now I needs you to put this clothin' on your body for the rich man in the nex' room. Do you understand it?" He twisted her ear even more.

He could see the fear in her eyes above the hand that covered her mouth.

"*Do jew understan'?*" he growled in her ear.

She tried to nod her head, which he still held tightly.

"Okay," he said as he pushed back off her.

Pica lay still as he reached into the closet above her and brought down a shopping bag.

He roughly pulled her up and led her into the bathroom. She was disoriented. "Get in the shower there," he ordered, "and put this on." He held out a department store clothing box.

"Can I use the bathroom first?" she asked.

"I'm not leavin' you alone, jew unnerstan'. Jew can change behind *las cortinas*." He took her arm, turned her around, and unhooked the leather belt that had been her handcuffs.

She looked at him passively. He didn't move. She took a towel off the rack to cover herself, pushed down her jeans, and sat on the toilet seat.

Feliz had the decency to turn his back.

After the flush he turned to her and handed her the clothing box. She opened it and took out the item and held it up by the shoulders. It unfurled. It was an opaque nylon body stocking with what appeared to be tropical flowers made of feathers sewn in three strategic places. Each flower was about the size of a saucer. They were the same boring beautiful feathers that had become such a large part of her life.

Pica started to protest. Feliz dropped from his sleeve a seven-inch stainless-steel switchblade knife with a curving point and serrated blade. In less time than it took her to say, "I'm not . . ." the point of the knife was resting on her left cheekbone, one inch from her eye.

"Si, jew are," he threatened. "And jew better do everythin' in your womany powers to convince the rish man to buy it for his *novia* because your life iss hangin' on the balance . . . Jew see, I haf a lot of my own monies in this deal . . . an' I know jor secret of bein' wanted by the *policia*, so jew are screwed into the wall no matter whish jew are facin'."

"Do as you are tolen, and understand, one false move, and they will be fishin' your body out of the dumpster a finger at a time."

Pica stepped into the shower and pulled the curtain.

"Throw all your clothin's out on the floor," said Feliz. "And hurry up! I'm waitin'."

Four minutes later Pica pulled back the curtain. She had on no makeup, her hair was frizzed like a terrier, and the bruise on her face was turning blue.

The stretch fabric had short arms, a crew neck, was knee length and skin tight. It was opaque and what you would call flesh-colored. She had adjusted the three blossoms accordingly.

"Your hair iss messy," he said. "Put it in a *cinta* or something."

Without looking in the mirror or at him she reached back and tied her long hair in a ponytail.

"Okay," he said, then stopped. "On second thought, turn around." Feliz tied her wrists behind her back again with the belt he had previously used.

"Bueno," he said, pushing her. She slumped out of the bathroom door, head down, feet shuffling. He slapped the back of her head hard! "Jew better get a little springtime in your step. I mean it! Iff he don' buy this clothin' jew are goin' ofer the viranda."

He took her from behind, holding her shoulders, and squared her up in front of a mirror on the wall.

Feliz was about six inches taller than she. He pulled her head back by the hair.

"Look at jorself," he said. "Put on a happy face!"

In the mirror there was no doubt that the fits-all-sizes body stocking looked good on her, but her face looked like a battered woman poster.

CHAPTER 67

December 10, 8:00 p.m.
Pica Models, Cooney to Rescue!

PICA'S HEAD WAS STILL HURTING, BUT HER MIND WAS BEGINNING TO clear. A wave of shame, self-pity, and humiliation coursed through her. She felt a tear forming, then caught her resolve. *I will win*, she told herself. *Whatever I have to do, I will win.*

She stood up straight, threw her head back, and marched into Oui Oui's suite.

Pilo Tatoon was still sitting against the arm rest of the big, ornate sofa. Streak was flipping through a Las Vegas show magazine. The room was heavy with the aroma of marijuana.

"Here she iss," announced Feliz in feigned merriment. "Captured fresh today in the jungles of Venezuela, the wild kitten of the tropical ocelot!"

"Ummm," said Pilo, sitting up in his seat. "Handcuffs!"

"Esstrut jor body," directed Feliz.

A memory came back to Pica from what seemed years ago at the Greeley Stampede Rodeo Queen banquet and the presentation and poise lessons from that horrible Ms. LaNewt. *Lay it on*, she told herself. Long steps, turning on the balls of her feet. Every time she came down hard on her bare heels the feather flowers would bounce. Not good, Ms. LaNewt would have said. Swing, sail, rock and roll, or lift, but not bounce.

Pica did a couple of slow twirls and high kicks, but it was difficult to keep her balance with her hands tied behind her back.

"May I examine the kitty more closely?" inquired Pilo. "Perhaps sniff the flowers?"

Pica spun on him and made a feline growl.

"Ooooh, Kitty wants to play," said Pilo.

Feliz slid behind Pica, grasped her ponytail and the binding on her wrists. He pushed her to Pilo and bent her forward in front of him. "Jew may look more closer, but for to be touching we must discuss the expenses," offered Feliz.

Feliz ran the back of his fingers across the dangling feathers. Then, without warning, Streak fell across Pilo's lap, into his arms between him and Pica!

"Does Daddy want to play in the jungle?" asked Streak seductively, recapturing the low ground. She was looking up at both Pilo and Pica. "Maybe two kittens are better than one," she purred, reaching up for Pica.

Feliz twisted Pica's arm painfully. "Yes!"

"No..." groaned Pica, but it sounded sexy. "Only if you were wearing this . . . this three-piece suit," she blurted.

Oh," said Pilo, "two kittens in a three-piece suit . . . that could be interesting. I could do the flower arranging?"

"Si, Senor, berry interestin'," cooed Feliz, then pulled Pica back from the couch and spun her to his right out of their grasp. "But that would require the purchase of this beautiful gem, decorated with feathers from the endangered and protected Glandular Y Cock, which is priceless."

"Ah, but I'll bet you have a price that would make the priceless purchasable," said Pilo.

"Jew haf discovered me," conceded Feliz graciously. "This one is so espensive because it has been making the news."

"Yes," said Pilo thoughtfully. "I remember, it was that movie star caught smuggling . . . in Miami, yes, it was in the papers. And this is the very birds that were in question?"

"*Si*," answered Feliz. "That iss why it iss so espensive, *pero, para mi caballero estimado,* I can take fifteen thousan' *dolares,* not a peso more."

"Does it come with the girl?" asked Pilo.

Out of sight, out of mind momentarily, Pica was loosening her hands within the leather belt and listening to the banter. When Feliz mentioned the Glandular Y Cock she looked down at the gorgeous feathers festooning her *gran tetones.* So that's what they look like? She was hit with the irony that she was being taken advantage of again with the same bird feathers!

"I think," said Feliz, "that you would have to tame her first, but . . . I haf some taming pills *que hacele mancilla . . . aaaaag!*" He screamed, grabbing his throat!

Pica had the belt around Feliz's neck and her knees in his back! He was falling toward her trying not to go down. They crashed to the door! She was flattened, but he was turning blue!

She reached behind her, twisting the door handle just as it exploded inward, knocking her on top of the gasping Feliz! Cooney's momentum carried him through the door, by them both, and into the arms of Streak and Pilo!

Over his shoulder Cooney saw what he took to be a naked Pica stomping a man on the ground. In a matter of seconds Feliz rolled over and came out with an automatic pistol. He was cussing *un rayo azul!*

"Cooney, come on!" Pica jerked him out of Streak's arms and in six steps made Oui Oui's bedroom and slammed the door and locked it. "Push that chair under the door knob and grab that bag on the bed!" she shouted.

"What?" he said.

"Just do it!"

Cooney heard racket, yelling, and cursing from the other side of the door. He quickly pulled a desk chair out and propped it under the door handle. In the meantime Pica was kicking through the pile of shoes. Oui Oui wore a size 9. Pica wore a size 5½. She slid into some furry oversized bed slippers. The best she could do for clothing was a fur coat that hit her midthigh.

"That leather bag on the bed, get it!" she told Cooney again. The bag was a folded-over garment bag with a handle and a shoulder strap.

Feliz kicked at the door. Pounded it with the butt of his pistol. "I don' know where jew think jew are goin'," he said loudly through the door. "It iss a trap, your room and I am the only door out. Jew don' haf no shance."

"Call 9-1-1," whispered Cooney.

"They'll arrest me!" said Pica. "I'm the fugitive, remember!"

"Well, you're gonna be a dead fugitive if we don't do something," he said.

"What are you holding up?" Feliz demanded through the door.

Cooney looked at the bag in his hand. In his confusion he assumed that the man in the next room could see him. "It's just a bag," Cooney said to the voice. "I don't know what's in it."

"Evidence," said Pica. "He's a feather smuggler, and I've got the evidence! And we're gonna get him. Follow me."

She quietly slid the glass door open and stepped onto the balcony.

Chapter 68

December 10, Saturday, Final Performance of NPR Straight Turns Out His Horse

Straight was beside himself with worry. Earlier he and Cooney had been in the stretching room. They'd gotten the rigs out and adjusted them for the thousandth time. Cooney had gone to the bathroom. The Grand Entry horses were ready, so Straight joined his Canadian contingent of performers. He didn't really think about Cooney for a while. But Somewhere between the doggin' and the team roping Straight knew something was wrong. Cooney had not yet shown up at the riggin' chute to put his saddle on his bronc.

~

At the conclusion of last night's performance, the ninth, which Straight had won, a lot was up for grabs. Cooney, Straight, and Shelby Truax had ridden their broncs. They were the only three riders out of the fifteen who had ridden all nine. Cooney and Straight were tied in points, twenty-one ahead of Shelby. All three had an even chance, depending on the draw, to ride their tenth. If all three made good rides tonight, odds were that Straight or Cooney would win the average.

Cooney had already sewed up the PRCA world championship saddle bronc riding. No matter what happened in the average, it would not be enough for anyone to catch him for the world championship. But he was still in the race for the NFR average.

On the other side of the gold coin, due to a great week, Cooney was unexpectedly in the running to win the bull riding NFR average. And with it, maybe the PRCA bull riding world championship *and* the PRCA all-around cowboy world championship!

For Cooney to win the bull riding average tonight would require that the two next-highest-placed bull riders buck off, and he would have to score a eighty-seven or better on his bull. Stranger things have happened.

PRCA records show that a small number of rough stock riders have won three world titles in one year. Since 1950: Bill Linderman (AA, SW, BR) in 1950, Casey Tibbs (AA, BB, SB) in 1951, Harry Tomkins (AA, BB, BR) in 1952, and Jim Shoulders (AA, BB, BR) 1956–58.

Layer Pie and Skim Slayton, our Alabama XM Rodeo Radio commentators, were hyping the saddle bronc race as a close one.

"Yes suh," intoned the sonorous voice of Layer Pie, "we rodeo fans could not have asked fo' a bettuh climax, a higha pinnacle, an apogee mo' closer to the sun its ownself than this week's pufomance of the classic rodeo event, saddle bronc riding!"

"How do you see it tonight, Skim?"

"Trut be known, I'm not even seein' you too good, Pi Man. Maybe they could adjust our focus on that giant teleprompter in the sky. Least I'd know what was up," replied Skim Slayton, cowboy color commentator.

"What happened to yo' glasses?" asked Layer.

"'Member when dat big guy step on my face las' night?"

"You mean after you slosh yo' bevridge down his wife's shirt front?"

"Well, I didn't know it was his wife!"

"So, it's missing half of a lens, look to me like," observed Layer.

"Actually, it ain't missin'. I glued it back wit Crazy Glue, but it fell out jis' now, while I was concentrating on the nex' event, the two-man luge . . . Son!" he yelled off microphone, "bring me another beer and chaser!"

"Back to y'all, Layer," said Layer. "Thank ya! Thank ya! Lots of excitement tonight with three of rodeo's best saddle bronc riders wit' a chance to win the average . . ."

LAYER PIE LAID IT ON. HE TOLD THE AUDIENCE EVERYTHING WE ALREADY KNOW ABOUT WHAT'S AT STAKE. HE SET THE SCENE FOR THE BATTLE. ONLYEST THING HE DIDN'T KNOW THAT WE KNEW WAS THAT COONEY WASN'T THERE.

The first ten broncs were bucked out. Several good rides, no mistakes, no exceptionals.

The last five horses were standing in the chutes. Straight, in desperation, had gathered Cooney's gear and saddled his draw in addition to his own. In the stands and behind the microphone no one was the wiser, but behind the chutes Straight had spread the news that Cooney had not showed up yet. Several cowboys were looking for him under the stands.

Down to three. Shelby Truax climbed over his horse and set his rein. Straight was on the catwalk behind Cooney's horse, scanning the crowd.

Shelby nodded his head. Catclaw tensed. The gate swung wide, and the 1,100-pound spotted *caballo* made his entry. The book predicted that he would blow out of the box, but instead he hesitated, then shot out forward, catching Shelby off guard.

The cowboy's spurs stayed tight 'til Catclaw's front feet hit the ground, then the horse broke loose! He had a fantastic day! He stretched 'em out and laid 'em down! Shelby opened up and let 'er hang and rattle. It was fun to watch, and both horse and man received a grand ovation.

"A seventy-eight score!" boomed the announcer.

The crowd was happy. Then the announcer spoke as if he was going to announce the Ali-Foreman heavyweight championship. "Right now, at this moment that young man you just saw makin' a first-class ride on Catclaw is officially in first place in the NFR average!" A cheer went through the crowd. "Two riders remain! Should either ride their bronc and score more than fifty-seven points, Shelby will be reduced to second or possibly third place.

"Shelby, you're the king right now. Enjoy it, my young friend! We'll see how long it lasts!"

Boyd Nicodemus, rodeo announcer, said off-mike to the secretary, "Cooney's up first, I think, but . . . that looks like Straight behind the box. Can you see Cooney, is he up there?"

No one had an answer.

"We want to remind you of our awards presentation following the rodeo . . ." he talked on, filling dead air, waiting for a sign.

— ⁓ —

The chute boss was looking up over Cooney's horse at Straight, who was saying, "I don't know, Darrell. He was here at the start tonight, but I haven't seen him for an hour. I'm really worried. He doesn't answer his cell phone."

— ⁓ —

In fact, Cooney had shut off his smartphone. Not for a reason he would be able to give after the smoke cleared, but it had to do with Pica focus. He wanted no distractions.

One of the cowboys on the catwalk piped up and said he had seen Cooney walking out to the parking area before the grand entry.

The chute boss talked to the judges. Then he took out his cell phone and called the commissioner, who was sitting in the VIP section.

"What's the hold up?" asked the commissioner.

"Cooney Bedlam failed to show. Somebody saw him leave the building."

"That's crazy! That can't be . . . heck, he can win it all. He can't be gone!"

"Reckon I should turn his horse out?" asked Darrell.

"That's the rules, iddinit?" said the commish.

"Yeah, but . . . what if he's just on the pot, or his watch broke, or he . . . got in an accident?" asked Darrell.

"In that case we better call the police, but we can't hold up the show. Gimme a second to talk to the announcer's booth." The commissioner got the announcer's booth on the phone. "Let me talk to Nicodemus . . . Boyd. They can't find Cooney Bedlam anywhere. Make an announcement to the crowd . . . and shut off that music. Just explain briefly and . . . have him raise his hand, or let us know if he's here. Otherwise we gotta turn out his horse."

Boyd spoke, "Ladies and gentlemen, sorry for the delay, but something very unusual has occurred. One of the contestants, Cooney Bedlam, who is actually next up in the saddle bronc, cannot be located. Cooney, if you're here in the coliseum . . . better git yer butt down to the chutes."

A strong murmur ran through the crowd.

"No need to panic," said Boyd. "Probably some simple explanation, so relax and . . ."

The chute boss got up next to Straight. "Look, we can't wait much longer. And I don't think we'd be allowed to let him in if he walked in here after this event is over. What I could do, since I'm the chute boss, is let you go ahead and ride, then if Cooney hasn't showed when you finish we just disqualify him then."

Straight looked at the chute boss. "Uh . . . no. I . . . I won't ride out first, 'cause if I scored good, and he still isn't here, then he wouldn't have a chance to win. It wouldn't be fair."

Darrell had been a chute boss for many years at the NFR. He'd seen cowboys do a lot of things that didn't seem reasonable. "Well, if I turn his horse out first without a rider, he definitely won't have a chance to win. Either way, looks to me like he's a no-show."

Boyd was watching the confusion in front of the chutes.

"Ladies and gentlemen, looks like we've made a decision down at chute number 4. The chute boss is talking to the gateman, and he's . . . he's opening the chute gate! With no rider! This is Cooney Bedlam's last bronc in the final performance. Silver Slicker, a great draw, last year's saddle bronc of year! Turned out by the already confirmed current saddle bronc world champion!

"Well," said Boyd, "I guess that's that. We move now to chute 3, Straight Line, Buffalo, Alberta, comin' out on that great bronc Yukon King from the Calgary Stampede string. This horse bucked out in the fourth perf, and Tucker Houston marked an eighty on him. Straight has ridden this good bronc at least three times and made money . . ."

Down at chute 3 Straight had his seat in the saddle, working on his rein. He suddenly raised his head and looked back. Izzy Bosun was leaned over the chute helping. "He ain't here," said Izzy. "You just worry 'bout this horse here. You can win the whole shootin' match in the next 8 seconds. Whattya doin'?"

Straight nodded his head. The gate swung open, and Yukon King wheeled and rose into the air like a ricocheting waterfall! Straight released the rein, grabbed the rail, kicked his stirrups loose, and let Yukon King fly out from under him!

Straight swung back onto the catwalk, watched the horse buck off, then turned and retreated back behind the chutes.

The crowd was aghast. There was a long moment of "I don't believe it!" Boyd Nicodemus was speechless, and Layer Pie knocked over his spit cup.

IN THIS PREGNANT PAUSE THAT HELD EVERYONE DUMBFOUNDED, SEVERAL COWBOYS—SOME IN THE STANDS AND SOME ON THE CATWALK—UNDERSTOOD IMMEDIATELY. THEY COULD PUT THEMSELVES IN STRAIGHT'S VERY BOOTS.

IT'S THAT BOND BETWEEN TRAVELING BUDDIES. BUILT ON A HUNDRED DISAPPOINTMENTS, OCCASIONAL VOLCANIC EXHILARATIONS, AND MILES AND MILES OF SHARING THE SAME AIR, THE SAME FEAR, THE SAME HOPE, AND THE SAME PAIN.

THIS UNSPOKEN BOND IS NOT RATIONAL, BUT IT KNOWS WITHOUT THINKING THE RIGHT THING TO DO. STRAIGHT COULD NOT CONSIDER CLAIMING THE WIN BY DEFAULT.

"Ladies and gentlemen," said Boyd as two mounted riders raced around the arena following a cowgirl carrying a flag, "the winner of the tenth perf, Slake Downey, *and* our unofficial winner of the NFR saddle bronc average, Mr. Shelby Truax! Let's hear it for our two champion cowboys!"

"Duane?" asked Phyllis Bonite. "What happened? How come he didn't ride? I mean he coulda won it, right? I don't get it; he just gave it up."

Duane, who had gone down the rodeo road for fifteen years, ten of those with his best friend, Hi Oatman, understood exactly why Straight had turned out his good horse. "It's hard to explain," he said to his wife . . . and left it at that.

It is hard to explain. At a time in my life when I was "down to no keys," I met someone who changed my life for the better. At that first meeting he gave me something that was precious to him. I protested, "I can't take that from you. We're just, we're just friends." He handed it over and said, "You can't be more than friends."

CHAPTER 69

December 10, Saturday, Getting Late!
Pica and Cooney Escape
Down the Zipline

PICA WAS STANDING ON THE FOUR-BY-SIX-FOOT LEDGE THAT FLOORED THE balcony outside the bedroom door. Another ledge to the right, the one off the suite, was eight feet away. Beneath her she could see the jungle canopy in the broad fake daylight and the zipline platform beneath her.

She clambered over the four-foot rail wearing the mink coat and too-big bed slippers over her feather duster body suit. She handed the garment bag back to Cooney, who was standing on the ledge with his back against the door jamb. Holding the rail she turned, swapped her hand grips so her back was to him, and leaned out over the top of the jungle panorama twelve stories above the hotel-casino lobby.

Cooney almost swooned! "Stop" he yelled, "you can't . . .!"

Pica looked down at the platform below her. It was the highest one, on the tenth floor where tourist riders ascended to begin the zipline ride, back and forth, across, and through the jungle to the bottom. An attendant was daydreaming during a lull in riders.

The expanded metal floor of the platform was twelve feet down, a full story, and eight feet out from the inside wall. A level metal bridge extended from the inside wall to the platform floor. A vertical steel pole supporting the zipline cable rose eight feet up from the platform floor. Along the length of the pole were horizontal braces made of steel rods connecting the pole to the wall.

The closest horizontal rod to the balcony ledge was distant five feet horizontally and four feet vertically. It was still 138 feet above the ground!

Pica, an experienced rock climber herself, said, "Follow me!"

She pushed herself off the ledge, caught the upright pole, swung around the abaxial side all the way, and stood on one of the horizontal bracing rods. She was now facing Cooney from several feet below and looking up.

"Drop me the bag!" she said.

Cooney leaned out over the rail and dropped the bag. Pica caught it.

"Okay, you're next, hey. C'mon," she ordered.

"I don't think I can. I'm afraid of . . ."

A loud crash came from the room behind him! It was the bedroom door handle giving way to a .44-caliber hollow-point! The explosion was followed by a stream of Spanish profanity that was oddly musical and increasing in volume. Cooney slid the glass door behind him just as the rushing Feliz hit it with his shoulder!

Cooney scaled the rail and, without pause, leaped for the vertical post! Simultaneously Pica dropped to the platform, glancing off the surprised attendant! Cooney swung completely around the post with one hand and crashed into the steel rods, bloodying his nose, then fell to the platform. Thank goodness his fall was broken by the terrified attendant, who was skittering away like a scared crab.

Pica pulled the mink coat around her, slung the bag over her shoulder, grabbed a harness and without buckling it on, clipped it onto the zipline. Then she clipped another one right behind the first. "Get up!" she shouted at Cooney. The attendant immediately stood and raised his hands.

"Cooney," she repeated. "Grab this harness!"

He staggered up, ran an arm through the nylon strap.

"Hold on!" she said.

"Do jou want the safety instruckshunes?" ventured the OSHA-aware attendant.

Cooney screamed again and grabbed the harness with both hands as he tipped over the edge. Pica sailed off right behind him!

"*Pues,* maybe not now," said the attendant, straightening the collar on his uniform shirt.

From the Feliz-eye view, which was bleary, he saw Pica push Cooney into midair.

Feliz stuck his gun into his waistline and swung over the rail, descending to the platform. The attendant threw up his hands again when Feliz hit the deck.

But a memory straightened the dedicated employee's spine. His zipline platform superintendent had imbued in him a sense of duty, a responsibility for those people placed in his care. Each new trainee had sworn allegiance to the Ruken Brothers Zipline Exposition Ride Company upon completion of the four-hour course.

It was up to him to reestablish order.

"*Pongeme este!*" ordered Feliz, pointing to an empty harness hanging behind the attendant. Feliz looked down the zipline and saw his two fleeing enemies swinging wildly as they disappeared into the canopy of treetops.

"Yes, sir, but first I must giff you the safety *instrucciones.*"

"*Oyeme, pendejo . . .!*" Feliz began.

"It iss no juice trying to estop the *instrucciones* for it iss my duty . . ."

Feliz tried to grab the harness from the attendant. The attendant jerked back!

"Plees keep you han's and feets inside of the harness at all . . . Uunnn . . . times . . . ow . . . for jour own safeties pleeez do not . . ."

"*Dejalo!*"

"Do not tush the sipline or harness attashmen ass this may . . . Oww . . . may result in dis . . . dis . . . memberment . . . Stop it! . . . off jour body members."

"*Damelo, idiota!*"

"Ass jou descend pleez enchoy the magnifico foligment and . . . Ayyyiii . . . and do not feed the birts and . . . *Quita*, Senor . . . *espera* . . . and the wilelifes ass they are mate of plastico . . . hu, hu, hu . . . ess a choke, *una broma . . . sabes?*"

Feliz lost his cool. His switchblade flew open. "*Cuchillo,*" he said.

"*Piedra,*" said the attendant.

Feliz was puzzled for a second.

"Jou are spost to say '*papel,*'" reminded the attendant.

"*Pistola!*" said Feliz, pulling his gun.

"*Tijeras!*" said the attendant, smiling.

"*Muerto,*" said Feliz, pointing his pistol at the attendant's left eye. "*Dame el chaleco . . .* Pronto."

It took only twelve seconds to have Feliz on his way. A personal best, the attendant was thinking as Feliz left the platform swingin' like a smoked ham on a clothesline pole.

PUT YOURSELF IN THE ATTENDANT'S PLACE. WAS THIS A MOVIE BEING FILMED, AND HE HAD NOT BEEN INFORMED? WAS IT AN ELOPEMENT OF SOME KIND, MAYBE A REALITY SHOW? WOULD HE HAVE TO SHOW HIS GREEN CARD? HE MENTALLY FELT HIS WALLET IN HIS POCKET. HE WOULD BE SAFE IF THE BORDER PATROL ASKED FOR IT.

Ninety-six feet and twelve seconds away, at the level of the eighth floor, Cooney and Pica swung up onto the next platform. The attendant on duty nearly backed off the edge trying to get out of the way! Cooney had one arm through the harness and the other locked around the safety rail on the platform. Pica was on his back, clinging to his harness to prevent herself from sliding back. They were still four feet from the platform!

Cooney's feet were scrabbling wildly! "Help!"

This attendant, who was also a lifeguard in the summer, could tell a drowning man when he saw one! He locked one leg around a brace. Then he took Cooney's wrist and Pica's wrist and pulled them both onto the platform.

"Thank you," said Pica. "Now help me into this harness, please."

"Maybe you should . . ." started the attendant.

"Now!" she yelled in his face with red-haired fury.

"Okay, okay," he said, unhooking both clips from the incoming line. Then he strapped her into her harness and clipped her hook on to the outgoing cable. Cooney was still on one knee when she stepped to the edge.

"Now him," she instructed. As quickly as the attendant complied, Pica dove off the platform and flew down the line.

"You need to wait one minute 'til the light from the next platform turns green," advised the attendant.

Cooney, now strapped in his harness and slightly dazed, walked to the edge.

"Wait!" the attendant said. "Don't use the brake, don't touch the line, wait . . . let me hook you to the line!"

Cooney heard Feliz cursing from above and getting louder and louder. Cooney stepped off the edge and never looked back.

"Have a good zip," said the attendant.

Back and forth down three more ziplines our characters careened. Several times Feliz saw his prey flying through openings in the trees, but, like the compassionate criminal he was, he refrained from shooting. He didn't want to injure the pedestrians milling about on the lobby floor below.

At the level of the second floor the zipline ended in a bowl from which descended four spiraling Teflon slides. Each slide represented one of the four humors of man: Earth, Fire, Air, and Water. Which tank was connected to which slide was unknown to the rider.

"Unhook and slide down!" said a voice box attached to the bowl.

"Here," said Pica, steadying Cooney and unlatching him from the cable.

"Where do I . . ." Cooney started, then slipped on the moving floor and slid down the spiraling slide into Earth!

Pica looked up, saw Feliz. She unhooked her harness and turned to tell Cooney to jump ... but he was gone! She sat down in the next circling slide and headed for Fire.

Earth consisted of a large round tank filled with tan-colored plastic balls. Cooney managed to keep right side up when he hit the tank. It was five feet deep, and the balls kept him buoyant. He worked his way to the side, swimming and striding. He heard but couldn't see Pica hit the tank of Fire, which was filled with synthetic gummy worms!

Pica and Cooney climbed out of their respective tanks and headed for the big front door. Cooney stopped to look back. Feliz came off his slide and hit the tank filled with Air! Air was simulated by a large but tightly woven high-wire circus net. Feliz recoiled from his first crash back into Air!

Cooney was mesmerized for a moment. He watched Feliz through three jumps, each a minor revision of an orangutan walking through hot coals!

Cooney and Pica ran!

CHAPTER 70

December 10, Saturday, 8:30 p.m.
Cooney and Pica
Escape the Casino/Hotel

OUT ON THE STREET THEY WERE HIT BY A BLAST OF COLD AIR! PICA tugged her mink coat tightly around her. She felt for buttons, instead found a zipper. Before she could even look down Cooney pulled her by the arm into the crowded sidewalk.

Weaving and fast-walking they pressed their way through the chatter, clatter, gas fumes, and neon flash of Las Vegas at night on the Strip.

They crossed the street at a WALK/DON'T WALK sign. Pausing, Cooney looked back and saw Feliz trying to follow them in the crosswalk . . . except the light had turned to DON'T WALK. Cabs and limousines honked their displeasure as Feliz did the Caribbean jaywalk! Feliz finally hit the curb, realized he was attracting attention, and quickly affected a nonchalance, as if nothing had happened.

He patted the pistol in his pocket and the knife up his sleeve, then stretched to look over the heads of the sidewalk pedestrians. Just as he rose to his tiptoes, he saw Cooney look back. Their eyes met.

WHEW . . . MAYBE NOT THE BEST TIME TO INTERRUPT WITH AN INTERROGATORY, BUT WE HAVE THREE PROTAGONISTS WITH THREE DIFFERENT MOTIVES TO BE IN THIS PLACE AT THE SAME TIME: ONE TO CLEAR HER NAME, ONE TO CLAIM HER HEART, AND ONE TO SKIN HER HIDE!

COONEY IS THE ONLY ONE WITH AN UNSELFISH MOTIVE, ASSUMING LOVE IS AN UNSELFISH MOTIVE, WHICH I DO. IT IS A MOTIVE

STRONGER THAN EITHER OF THE OTHER TWO. THERE IS A PLACE
WHEREIN THEY CAN SAY, "YOU KNOW IT'S NOT WORTH IT." BUT NOT
WITH LOVE. YOU CAN'T WEIGH IT, MEASURE IT, SCORE IT, EARN IT,
DESERVE IT, STOP IT, BUY IT, OR SPEND IT. TRUE LOVE JUST IS, AND
ONLY THE HEART OF THE LOVER KNOWS IF IT IS TRUE.

Three blocks down the street in the B-Zhong Wedding Chapel and Notary
("*se habla Espanol*"), Bull Younumclaw and Trisket Thistle were in the prelimi-
naries of pledging their vows. Each was dressed in their sportiest "Hell's Angel"
formal wear. Bull was a big man, a beefy man, with big arms, a big belly, and the
obligatory corn maze of tattoos. He wore leather, torn denim, and chains. His
black hair was slicked back, and he had shaved . . . his cheeks, anyway.

His bride-to-be appeared to be a veteran of many a back-seat ride on
somebody's Harley. She was "chunky," I guess, but obviously tough enough
to handle any testy women's-wear clerk or passionate motorcycle-noise pro-
tester. Her occupation was listed as sign fluctuator. "You know," she would
say, "Slow. Stop. Slow. Stop." For the big ceremony she had chosen stretch
jeans, a low-necked turquoise tight T-shirt, her MoMMa membership black
leather jacket, and lace-up steel-toed boots.

She, too, was black-haired, but instead of a Fu Manchu mustache, she
wore bright red lipstick and a silver and onyx ring in her right eyebrow.

In addition to several curious spectators who had dropped in, a clutch of
club members stood around enjoying the excitement. The proprietor of the
place, presider, notary, and salesman Wally Okima, was fishing the crowd.
"You know that the price is very fair to be wedding two fine people for the
small sum of $349.12 . . . But if any of you in the party, like you, Sir," he
addressed an hombre whom Dog on the *Bounty Hunter* show must have used
for inspiration, "maybe you have been thinking it's time to settle down."

Bull interrupted, "That's Snag. He didn't bring nobody."

"Well," said Wally, "it's just cheaper is all. A double ceremony for only
$249.12 each."

"What if we got married twice?" asked Bull.

"That would be a double ceremony, okay, but I'd have to do it twice, so
it would cost . . ." Wally paused, calculating on his pad, "$498.24. And, think
about it, you'd only have to buy one ring!"

"Whattya mean one ring!" glared Trisket Thistle.

Wally charged on. "That way you'd save the money that he was gonna
spend on a second ring for that honeymoon in Hawaii!"

"You can't buy a honeymoon in Hawaii for $35," said Bull.

"You two are shrewd traders," said Wally. "Maybe if both you and Mister uh ... Snag, there both married Ms. Trinket in the same ceremony, using one ring, I could do it for $373.72."

"Can't do it. Snag and me are cousins," said Bull. "'Course, so is me and Trisket."

"Second cousins, idiot," responded Trisket testily. "It's my son that's married to your cousin who was my half-sister."

"Ah, shut it down, all you-all! Let's git on with it!" said Bull.

"Maybe ..." started Wally.

"No 'maybe'!" said Bull. "Git out your marryin' stuff and do your duty, or I'm gonna bend this chandelier around your neck and hang you in a basketball player's closet."

A little miffed, Wally slid on a formal suit coat over his Hilo Hattie shirt, put on a straw boater, gathered his papers, and walked to stand behind the small podium under the arbor decorated with ascending plastic vines.

He pointed to the Xs duct-taped on the floor that marked where the couple should stand.

"Dear brethern and sistern," began Wally.

A sudden racket of doors banging and furniture clattering stopped the program!

All eyes sought the source of the racket. A small woman with fly-away red hair and a fur coat came barreling through the door like a fullback goin' over the middle! Toppling in behind her was six foot of cowboy wearin' a black hat and carrying a garment bag over his shoulder.

"It's a raid!" cried Snag! "It's a raid!"

"I got my green card right here, officer," volunteered Wally.

It took a moment for the smoke to clear.

"Oh," said Pica, her chest heaving, "it's not a raid, don't call the police ... please, it's just ..."

"Sorry," said Cooney. "Pardon us. We ... what, did we interrupt something?"

"Just my wedding," said Bull aggressively.

"Oh, man. I'm sorry. Uh, don't mind us. We, uh," Cooney couldn't think of anything to say.

"Okay then," said Wally, "let's get on with it."

The door opened again; everyone looked. A handsome Latino man stepped inside. He looked around and immediately saw Cooney. Feliz evaluated the situation and nodded to everyone, then eased his way into the crowd.

Wally noticed the immediate fear in Pica's eyes and the tension in Cooney's. "Are you folks here to get married?"

"Married?" asked Cooney. "What would make you think that?" Cooney took a moment to look around, locating Feliz, who gave him the squint eye. Then Cooney's eyes fell on the sign, B-ZHONG WEDDING CHAPEL AND NOTARY. He nodded in understanding.

"Well," Cooney said, stalling, "we've thought about it. Given it some thought. Not a lot really but some . . ."

Wally responded. "You couldn't have picked a better time, better place. We are at this moment commencing to engage this lovely couple, Bull and Trinket."

"Trisket," said Trisket.

"Yes, Bull and Trisket, in the holy vows of matrimony, and it is just possible that you could join them in a double ceremony and save them a whopping $25 even."

"Sure," said Bull playfully. "We'd be glad to be your Siamese bride and groom, wouldn't we, Trisky?"

Cooney glanced back and noticed that Feliz had moved closer. "You know, that might be just the thing!" he said. "And it's something we've dreamed except for one thing . . ." Cooney looked back, staring at Feliz, who was now only ten feet away.

Everyone within earshot looked at Feliz. Feliz returned the attention with a sickly grin.

"Yeah, him," said Cooney. "He's stalking her."

A collective gasp rose from the crowd. Eyebrows furrowed, eyes slitted and shot daggers at Feliz, who raised a hand in protestation.

"Yeah," Cooney said, "he claimed he was her manager and she owes him seven more weeks working the street, but she claims he kidnapped her and forced her into dental servitude . . ." Cooney's impromptu oration took them all aback. "I was only trying to help her escape from his evil grasp . . . We want to marry, but he thinks he owns her and . . . that I should pay him for her!"

"Why, that scumbag!" said Trisket.

"That's what I felt," said Cooney. "He wants to take her back to Caracas and enslave her, but she is suffering from an incurable disease . . ."

"Where's Caracas?" asked Snag.

"Venezuela," answered Cooney, "but she can't get treatment there, and I've got insurance that will cover her organ transplant . . ."

A cooing sigh flowed from the crowd.

"Except . . . we have to be married for my insurance to apply. That's all we're trying to do, yet he wants to ruin our lives for a few pesos." Cooney shoulders dropped, and he sighed.

"Oh, you poor, poor sweethearts," said Trisket, stepping over to Pica and giving her a big hug.

"Oh, man," said Bull. "That's a terrible story. Listen, I'll even pay for your wedding. Snag, could I borrow a couple hundred?"

Feliz could take it no more! He shoved his way toward the betrothed waving his arms and shouting, "*Mentidoso! Mentidoso!*" His hand hit Cooney chest on! With an ingrained reaction learned in his high school wrestling days, Cooney grasped Feliz's right elbow just as it came around his neck, ducked, and, using Feliz's own momentum, flipped him against the wall!

Feliz caught Cooney's ankle as he went down and jerked him off his feet. They were fighting in close, most blows not landing effectively. In one burst they got to their knees, grappled, and took out one corner of the arbor! On the ground Cooney was wriggling, trying to get face to face. Feliz's hand came out of his pocket with a sleek black pistol.

Snag stepped in, twisted the pistol with the finger still in the trigger guard, and heard it snap! The finger, not the gun. By then Snag had Feliz's arm. There was another snap as the wrist broke. A howl came from Feliz! Then another snap as the radius and humerus bones disarticulated at the elbow. This was followed by a keening cry and collapse!

Cooney crawled from under the prostrate body of Hurtado Herman Huachuca's faithful bodyguard and black market feather smuggler.

The crowd exhaled in unison. Snag let the double-jointed arm drop. Feliz was making whimpering noises. Snag placed the hobnail heel of his heavy-duty black leather steel-toed motorcycle boot on the side of Feliz's face. He applied a little pressure. "If you can keep quiet for a minute or two, so's we can finish this here wedding, or weddings, I'll be glad to call the animal shelter to come pick you up."

Feliz remained docile.

"So . . ." asked Wally Okima, the presiding proprietor, "are we ready? We are gathered here together . . ."

CHAPTER 71

December 10, Saturday, 9:00 p.m.
The Wedding

AFTER THE "I DO"S WALLY ASKED, "DO YOU WISH TO EXCHANGE RINGS?"

Pica, who had remained in a bumfoozled trance during Cooney's lengthy oration and fisticuffs, said, "We don't have a ring."

"Honey," said Trisket, "you take mine. I'll get another."

"Oh, no! I couldn't!" said Pica, slowly rising from the misfiring synapses of confusion. "I couldn't."

BUMFOOZLED, PICA HAS HAD QUITE A DAY: BREAKING AND ENTER-
ING, THIEVERY, MODELING, BEING TIED UP, GAGGED, DRUGGED,
FOUGHT OVER, ZIPLINED, ESCAPED, AND NOW A NEW BRIDE. IT'S NO
WONDER HER SYNAPSES OVERLOADED. SHE'S LIKE A LOT OF US: WE
JUST NEED A LITTLE TIME TO LET THINGS SINK IN.

"Yes, you can," said Trisket, gently forcing the ring into Pica's hand. "You have so much to live for. And you've got a man who's willing to donate his organ to keep you alive. I insist. You never know how much time you have left."

Pica finally focused and was touched. "How about I trade you this mink coat for your ring, hey?"

Now it was Trinket's turn to be nonplussed. Pica assured her, "Those evil men in Caracas made me wear it. You can make it clean again." She turned so Bull could help her off with the fur coat.

"Okay," gushed Trinket with tears in her eyes. Then, like a magician whisking his cape away to expose the white tiger on the stage, Pica was suddenly revealed in her tropical feathered bodysuit finest!

"*Whoa!*" said everybody.

"I'd give two rings for that!" said an anonymous spectator.

Wally was caught in the headlights. It took a long four seconds for Bull to react and drape the coat back on Pica. Only it now opened in the back!

There was a moment of embarrassed self-consciousness in all the immediate parties, then Pica spoke: "Twister, Twissle . . .?"

Trisket said, "Trisket. Please call me 'Trisky' . . . like 'Risky as Whiskey' Trisky."

"Trisky, you've been so kind. We, my . . ." she looked at Cooney, "my man, this man and I are on a mission, so to speak, in a hurry, and I can't go dressed like this. Would you consider trading clothes with me? It's Spandex, ya know. Fits anybody. I could send you a check later."

A big smile spread across Bull's face.

"It could be like a trousseau for your wedding night . . ." Pica continued.

"What do you think?" said Trisket, looking up at Bull with a twinkle in her eye.

Bull was thinking how hard it would be to take it off—off Risky Trisky, not off Pica. But then he figgered they would have plenty of time tonight. "If that's what you want, little darlin', it would suit me fine."

"Do you have a dressing room?" Trisket asked Wally.

"Not really, but you can use my office. It has a private bathroom. I usually rent it out fo . . . Aggggg!"

Snag had stepped forth and clasped a large paw on Wally's clavicle. He clamped down, and Wally pee-peed in his pants. "I think it would be nice if you would let these fine ladies borrow the john for a few minutes at no charge," said Snag menacingly.

It took several minutes for Pica and Trisket to accomplish the switch. Pica didn't feel right taking Trisket's boots, but Trisket pointed out that the mink coat was worth several thousand, and she could buy new boots for $159.

They reappeared in the chapel to find that the grooms had already settled up with Wally and that all that was lacking were the signatures of the new brides. That accomplished, Trisket and Bull wanted to take their Siamese couple out on the town, but Cooney graciously declined. He had already asked for someone to hail a cab.

"You got the bag?" Pica asked Cooney, who had retrieved it from behind the arbor where it had fallen in the fight.

"Yes, Ma'am!" he said.

She started for the door.

"Stop, just a second," Cooney said to Pica, touching her shoulder.

"We've got to . . ." she protested.

"I know, just turn around for a second," he urged.

She did. They were standing in the lobby looking back into the chapel. A warm band of good-hearted people was watching them leave. They were smiling and holding up small plastic communion cups filled with grape juice that Wally had furnished, at no charge, in celebration for the newlyweds. "We love you!" shouted Trisket, who looked so fine in her new mink coat.

"Have a wonderful life!" they yelled.

"Take a deep breath," said Cooney. "Blow it out. Sometimes you gotta thank the bronc."

The cabbie honked his horn. Our two heroes climbed into the back and slammed the door.

"Thomas and Mack," ordered Pica.

The cab left the curb, and Cooney took out his cell phone and rang Straight. The conversation was short. Cooney said to Pica and the driver, "The rodeo's over. Take us to the Shazam!"

CHAPTER 72

December 10, Saturday Night
The Big OTT Party After
The Last Performance

OVER THE TOP ATHLETIC COSMETICS, MAKERS OF LIP LASTER, was throwing an invitation-only party in a small Shazam Casino and Hotel ballroom. More than one hundred cowboys, reporters, and at least three agents were seated at round tables or standing and visiting and enjoying drinks from the open bar and the hotel's hors d'oeuvres. Turk Manniquin, KroAsha LaTourre, and Nova Skosha mingled with their guests.

The big buzz on the crowd's collective lips was about Straight turning his horse out in honor of his friend Cooney who, the rumors now said, was in the hospital. It was a human-interest story that brought a tear to the eye of those who cherished the value of a friend.

Turk Manniquin had said to Straight: "I still don't get what you did. I understand that you turned your horse out so you wouldn't beat Cooney, but he was in the hospital. It wasn't anybody's fault. If you'd ridden your last bronco ..."

"Just 'bronc,'" corrected Straight. "'Bronco' is a football team."

"Okay," said Turk. "Your last bronc. You could have won the NFR average all to yourself. First in the average paid forty thousand! You could have won it all! As it is, you have to split the tie money for second and third, which left you with twenty-nine thousand! Can you afford to throw money away like that? I mean, it's like throwin' a game, not doin' your best. You'd never make it in basketball or the big sports. Seems like you could have at least faked it, fell off, maybe, make it look like you tried."

Straight knew that any explanation he gave to Turk would not help him understand. He said, "All I can say is there is more to the story than meets the eye. I don't know if it would ever make sense to you, but what I did . . . it was the right thing to do."

Turk smiled a big smile and shook his head. "You guys are different. I ought to know that by now. I hope Cooney is gonna be all right. I want you to know that the way it worked out, you being able to join us in the booth at the finals and all . . . your success after just making the cut . . . it was a good story, and I'm proud . . ." he started to say "you're on our team," but changed it to, "I got the chance to work with you."

PROFESSIONAL RODEO, MORE THAN ANY OTHER SPORT, IS AN INDIVIDUAL COMPETITION. THOSE WHO ARE PLAYING FOR A TEAM HAVE AN OBLIGATION TO THOSE PEOPLE PAYING THEIR SALARIES OR THEIR TUITION OR TO THEIR TEAM MEMBERS.

BOTH PROFESSIONAL GOLF AND TENNIS ARE ALSO INDIVIDUAL COMPETITIONS. BUT AT THE PRO LEVEL THE ENDORSEMENT FEES ARE SO ASTRONOMICAL IN THESE TWO SPORTS THAT IT WOULD BE HARD TO IMAGINE ONE OF THEIR STARS NOT PARTICIPATING IN A FINAL SET OR SKIPPING THREE HOLES TO AVOID BEATING ANOTHER PLAYER.

I HAVE NO EXAMPLE IN REAL LIFE OF THIS HAPPENING IN RODEO, BUT IF I WAS A BETTIN' MAN, I WOULDN'T BE SURPRISED IF IT HAPPENS NOW AND THEN.

COWBOYS ARE PRETTY INDEPENDENT. THEY'RE FUNNY THAT WAY.

ALLOW ME TO QUOTE OWEN ULPH, AUTHOR OF *FIDDLEBACK: LORE OF THE LINE CAMP:*

"THE COWBOY IS THE REBEL AGAINST THE GODS OF THE MULTITUDE. A CREATIVE, INTEGRATED, COMPULSIVELY SELF-RELIANT PERSONALITY TYPE WITH WHICH THE WEST, FACTUAL AND FICTIONAL, WAS AS SPECKLED AS A SPOTTED HOUND. DESPITE THE FREQUENT IRREVERENT AND APPARENTLY REPREHENSIBLE ASPECTS OF EXTERNAL CONDUCT, HE IS THE SEED BEARER AND ESSENTIAL CORE OF ALL ETHICAL CULTURES. INSIDE HIM BURNS THE CELESTIAL FIRE. HE RIDES THE POINT."

The voice of Nova Skosha carried over the crowd: "Ladies and gentlemen . . ."

Turk looked at his watch. He said to Straight, "Pardon me, Straight, it's time. You are welcome to sit at my table if you'd like."

"I'll join you in a few minutes, hey," said Straight. "I've got a couple things to attend to."

"Fine," Turk said and moved his six-foot-seven body through the tight crowd like he was turning into the key for a lay-up.

Nova was finishing her introduction.

"We at OVER THE TOP ATHLETIC COSMETICS, makers of LIP LASTER, welcome all of you rodeo fans to our little ta-do tonight. I hope you have enjoyed the hospitality. It gives me great pleasure to introduce to you a man many of you sports fans know, the president and founder of OTT, Mr. Turk Manniquin!" Nova gestured toward Turk, who strode upon the stage to enthusiastic applause.

Turk waited for the crowd to settle and spoke: "Thank y'all for coming. Some of you may wonder why a basketball player would involve himself in the sport of rodeo. I don't have a horse, had never been to a rodeo until this year. The only cowboys I know play football!" People laughed. "Also the only broncos I know are football players, too!"

"The spurs we know don't come from San Antonio!" someone shouted.

"Touché," said Turk. "We make cosmetics for athletes. Even the toughest athletes need good deodorant, hair cream, foot powder, skin-care products, shaving lotion, sunscreen . . . and lip balm! When we were planning our marketing strategy for LIP LASTER we saw the image of the cowboy wearing lip balm as striking and unusual. That was when we found Straight Line!"

Turk spoke for several more minutes about his company and how much he enjoyed being a part of rodeo, then slid into the next phase. "We don't intend to bore you with any more of our sales promotion. I'm just pleased y'all could come and join us. And now we have a surprise for you cowboys and cowgirls. As you know, two months ago the fantastic Oui Oui Reese became our latest LIP LASTER girl."

Several hoots and whistles came from the crowd. It made Turk smile.

"She has taken LIP LASTER to new heights, and we love her . . . put your hands together and welcome a star in its ascendancy . . . Miss Oui Oui Reese!"

A hearty welcome ensued.

Oui Oui took the stage like Sir Edmund Hilary taking Mount Everest.

File, backstage, controlled the sound system and began her canned music with "Hey, Big Spender, Spend a Little Time with Me."

She was wearing an outfit that made you think of the Dallas Cowboys cheerleaders. A plunging neckline, a waistband, and, to her credit, a real, genuine black western hat. The suit differed in that a skirt fell from her beltline clear to the floor but was split up the front.

311

Her hair was dark blonde with highlights and fell in waves over her bare shoulders. Dangling earrings and bracelets sparkled against her light tanned skin. She slithered up to the microphone and said, "Who wants to dance?" It sounded like a proposition.

The music changed to a bit of heavy bass, slow tempo jazz/blues. Oui Oui began to undulate and sway. Imperceptibly at first. But as the tempo picked up she began to rotate and swivel and writhe. It was then that the crowd noticed there was a bucking horse machine on the stage.

Like a mechanical bull, it was capable of simulating a ride. But instead of a bull rope to hold on to, it had a bareback rigging. A handhold like a suitcase handle was over the withers.

A mane as well as a tail had been added to the molded body.

Oui Oui flowed in the direction of the machine. There was a musical crescendo! She whirled like an ice skater and in one motion grasped her skirt and peeled it off! She was wearing chaps!

In one smooth motion she swung her right leg over the machine's body and scooted up against the riggin' and its handle. She scootched and snuggled and petted the hide-covered machine.

The CD player started to play a slow, rhythmic groaning. Like heavy breathing. The bucking horse machine began to tip forward, then back. Rocking slowly. With each movement Oui Oui's legs reached out around the horse machine's neck, then doubled back to rake the sides.

Her boots were spurless but came up to her knees, which one noticed when the chaps flew open as she rocked and fired to the beat of the moaning.

The crowd was mesmerized.

As the music grew more demanding her intensity increased. The bucking was growing faster and more jolting and perfectly coordinated with the sound track. Suddenly the lights went out, and a golden beam spotlighted the performance! She glowed. Her skin had been painted with some reflective substance so that her skin sparked electric blue!

The audience was coming to realize that it actually was a dance! The special effects, her graceful, powerful movements, her flying hair, reaching limbs, and painted face became surreal. Her performance continued to a climax and ended in a frenzy when she flipped backward off the horse and landed on her feet!

The lights came back up. Oui Oui moved to center stage, her chest heaving and her breath coming in gusts. One might have expected that she would have been wrung out, but her cheerleader halter top was still snug and tight, and you could now see that she was wearing net stockings under her chaps.

312

CHAPTER 73

December 10, Saturday Night
Still at the OTT Party

DURING THE STANDING OVATION FOR OUI OUI REESE, STRAIGHT stuck his head out the ballroom door and looked down the hall for the tenth time. There they were! Coming his direction were Pica and Cooney.

"Hey," said Straight, "you're right on time! Oui Oui is on stage."

Cooney showed him the photo of Oui Oui holding the feathered halter top up in front of her. It was obvious she was standing on a beach: bikini, sand, ocean. Certainly incriminating. Then he lifted the bag that held the halter top that was in the photo.

"That ought to nail it down, hey?" Straight said with a big grin.

Cooney looked unkempt, which was normal for him. It was also apparent that Pica had not had time to do much primping. She was wearing tight jeans, motorcycle boots, a turquoise T-shirt, and a leather jacket. She looked fairly good, but her hair had gone wild! It had the look of a lion's mane. And even though she wore no lipstick, her lips were plump, pink, full, and as succulent as a puckering tulip.

She had a look of determination on her face. "You ready?" she asked Cooney.

"After you, Ma'am," he said and handed her the photo and the sack.

~ ~

On stage Oui Oui was wearing a full-body net stocking, covered with leopard spots. She was mounted on a unicycle and carrying two bullwhips.

The music behind her was a light flowing melody with the occasional nervous brass riff. She was moving in a pattern around on the stage, smoothly laying out the whips like a fly fisherman laying the line.

313

Her long hair had been swept up on top of her head and tied in a knot She was wearing a cat's-eye mask.

Cooney and Pica followed Straight through the tables over to Turk and his crew seated with him.

All eyes were on Oui Oui, and the room was darkened except for the stage. Thus, when Straight came up behind the OTT table, the occupants were caught unawares. He approached between Turk and Nova Skosha. Straight squatted to his knees and laid the photo down on the table between them. They looked down. Their table was near the stage; thus, the photo was easily seen.

Turk looked at it, then back at Straight. He put on his half-glasses and picked it up. Nova saw immediately what it was and was aghast. "Oh, no," she said. "Oh, no, no, no . . ."

KroAsha, who was on the other side of Turk, was looking at the photo in his hand.

"Da feathers done hit da fan," she said.

Behind her Pica pulled the feathered halter top out of the sack and set it down in front of KroAsha.

KroAsha picked up one end of it and looked at the beautiful, unique natural design of the feathers of the endangered Tetuchton Pavo Real. She looked at Turk as the import of what they were seeing sunk in between them.

"What . . ." he began just as Pica picked up the halter top and started for the stage.

Oui Oui was in her own world. Under the spotlight she could not see past the first row of tables in front of her. She was working her unicycle-whip-dance routine and had the crowd in her hands. It like she was dancing with snakes.

Suddenly she was distracted by a person jumping up onto a table front and center. Oui Oui was circling in a pattern, lacing the air with her whip lashes, yet craning her neck to keep her eyes on the intruding specter.

The head she saw was all hair and mouth. Then the figure thrust her right arm up into the air, presenting a feathered trophy like Cochise displaying a mortal enemy's scalp! Oui Oui recognized it immediately.

"Where did you get that?" she roared. "That is mine!"

Pica D'TroiT tossed the feathered prize over her shoulder and leaped from the table to the stage! Oui Oui reared back with her right arm, cocking the whip. The snake end of the left whip lay quietly on the ground. Pica dove for it, picking it up on the roll and tumbling to Oui Oui's left side on the unicycle. The right whip flew around and cracked impotently where Pica had just been.

The unicycle was in constant motion as Oui Oui kept her balance. She swiveled to her left as Pica was coming out of her roll holding onto the tail of the left whip. Pica rolled to Oui Oui's left one more time, but the unicycle was too quick. Oui Oui's right arm snapped and followed through again. The popper cracked just above Pica's hip! It sounded like a gunshot!

Oui Oui cycled backward and ripped the left whip out of Pica's hand! Even though Pica's hands were tough from doing physical work, the friction caused her hand to bleed.

Pica rose and charged her. Oui Oui backpedaled, flailing her whips like she was doing the backstroke.

Pica dove under the lashing, tucked her head, and rolled forward in the direction of the unicycle. She slid across the stage, her head actually bumping into the tire. Oui Oui leaned out over Pica's prone body and drove her unicycle up over Pica's left shoulder, down her back, over her bottom, and down one leg, swerving off the right ankle!

A pain shot up Pica's right leg. She stood, wincing, and faced off against Oui Oui Reese, smuggler, attempted framer, and all-around self-promoter.

Oui Oui laid into her: "You common, white-trash, backwoods bimbo! You have no place in the glamorous world of glitz and style . . . and beauty and nice nails and plucked brows . . . of caviar, diamonds, or even a chauffeur! I knew that the first time I saw you, you were so, so scruffy.

"Trying to show you elegance and class was like teaching good grooming to a Woodstock groupie. You had no clue. Yeah, it was me in Caldwell! I set you up to dazzle them at the Rodeo Queen luncheon . . . you blew it! Couldn't even carry off a chance to stop the show.

"And these simpering wimps who are worried about that magnificent endangered feather halter top. Who do they think is qualified to wear it? And deserving of such a priceless wrap . . . Not them, not you. You don't even appreciate that beauty is made for beautiful things, precious things. You don't hang a diamond around a mongrel's neck!

"What those LIP LASTERS saw in you I can't imagine. When they had me! Right there! All along! Me! Look at me . . . I'm the perfect LIP LASTER girl! I'm gonna be in the movies, on magazine covers . . . Turk just said I'm an ascending star! You're not good enough to do my cuticles!"

Pica jumped so quickly that Oui Oui never had a chance to draw back a whip. Pica was in the air when she hit Oui Oui at the midline. Oui Oui was

315

backpedaling and into a spin as Pica climbed her back and wrapped her legs around her waist.

Oui Oui was tipping forward to catch her balance as Pica wrapped her arms around Oui Oui's head. The cat's-eye mask flew off! The unicycle careened around the stage, Oui Oui skillfully and desperately trying to keep it upright. At one point Oui Oui was at a 45-degree angle, the whips long since dropped, her tresses come loose, and Pica, with her left hand in Oui Oui's hair, her legs still wrapped around her waist, and her right hand thrown back like a saddle bronc rider at full throttle!

As you might guess, dear reader, this cannot go on much longer. As the author, I could add complications like crowd intervention, a banana peel, or someone calling 9-1-1, but this is the part where the good guy or gal—in this case our heroine—gets even.

But we did want to give Oui Oui her day, to make her a worthy foe. And she is. And now that the tablecloth has been pulled out from under her, she can be quickly dispensed with, but with this caveat: people like Oui Oui never give up. Pride and vanity will keep them egotistical until they are old and gray.

But maybe one good thing might come out of this disaster. Oui Oui's not going to have many friends after this, except her loyal, subservient File Blitzer. If she has any heart at all, any unselfish gene tucked away somewhere, she has a chance to make his dream come true. Let's wish him luck.

The double-barreled, overloaded, smoking, screaming unicycle flew off the stage and bounced onto the table front and center, which tipped forward under the weight and allowed the whole unit—wheel, operator, and passenger—to hit the carpet and crash into a photographer from *Western Horseman* magazine!

Cooney leaped into the fray. He was actually sitting on Oui Oui's legs, behind Pica, trying to hold her arms to stop her from pounding Oui Oui's head face down into the carpet. Pica was struggling to get free of his grasp. She couldn't. Finally she quit and sagged in his arms.

Oui Oui was having a minor fit. She slowly slid her hands up to cover her face. She was snuffling and cursing. A hand touched her head gently. She shook it off. Then two hands took her head between them and stayed there against some half-hearted resistance. Oui Oui quit shaking and moved one of her hands up to cover the hand that held her face.

"It's all right, Baby."

She recognized his voice. "Oh, Filey, oh, oh, oh. Was it okay?"

"It was okay, Baby. They'll remember it a long time."

CHAPTER 74

December 10, Saturday Night
Party Aftermath

THE POLICE HAD FINALLY EXITED WITH OUI OUI IN TOW AND FILE Blitzer close behind. The mayhem that occurred when Pica and Oui Oui took the fight into the crowd had simmered down. Nova Skosha and Turk Manniquin were in a deep discussion with security officers and the hotel night manager. Straight was surrounded by reporters, who were lauding him for his selfless sacrifice, loyalty, and uncommon grace for relinquishing his chance to win the NFR average.

Cooney stood with Pica off to the side, out of the spotlight, by the stage where a curtain hung down. No one had recognized her. Straight had outdrawn Cooney for attention. The police had questioned Pica. She didn't have much to say. Turk had smoothed everything over, diminishing Pica's culpability, so in the end she appeared to have been just an innocent bystander. No one was pressing charges; he didn't want any more bad publicity.

One of the officers saw Pica and went to her. "I just need to get your name," he said.

Pica froze momentarily. She was quite aware that she was still a fugitive, a suspected felon.

"Suzie Bedlam," said Cooney. "Buffalo, South Dakota."

She glanced up at Cooney just as KroAsha LaTourre arrived and spoke up: "Da real story here is dat woman on da stage that y'all done took away. There's been undercover federal agents that's been stakin' her out fo' smugglin' contraband. This little lady just happened to get in da middle of a fight 'tween the agents and dat woman."

"Nobody said anything about federal agents," said the officer.

318

"Dat man what walked out wit' her, you'd see'd him!" she charged on, "he's wit' the FBI-SA ..."

The officer flipped back a page in his notebook. "Blitzer? Mr. File Blitzer?"

"Yes, suh, dat be him," she said. "Federal Bureau Incorporated of Special Agents."

"And who are you, sir?" he asked Cooney.

"Her husband," Cooney said, pointing to "Suzie."

"Dey's innocent bystanders, basically, who got caught in the crossfire," intervened KroAsha.

"Well, thanks for your time. You okay?" the officer asked Pica. "That's a nasty scratch on your neck."

"I'm fine," said Pica. "I can take care of it."

The officer walked back toward the group where Turk was holding court, recounting his basketball career and signing autographs.

"My, oh, my," said KroAsha. "You come from outta nowhere, Honey. I seen what you throwed on our table. Dem feathers and dem pictures. It takes you off da hook, I bet. Well, I don't know how you did, o' if you 'sposed to be here o' wot. I think I don't wanna ax too many question, but when you get where you can call me, we'll work it out."

Pica stood unmoving and did not smile.

KroAsha backed off a little. "I guess you gotta right not to think too kindly of us, but we'll git to da bottom of dis, and if you in da clear, you come out all right. I'll personally make sure."

As soon as KroAsha turned her back, Cooney slipped his arm through Pica's and ducked behind the curtain. He worked their way through the kitchen and back ways until they came out into the parking lot in back of the hotel. It was 11:15 p.m. and cold. Pica stumbled. Cooney kept her from falling. She was spent.

"Look," he said, "we can't go 'round front for a cab. Too many people would recognize me ... or you ... I think we can catch one of these cabs before it pulls on around front ... like that one!"

A cab was coming around the parking area headed for the casino entrance. Cooney waved it down. "Take us to the Innercom Hotel. Around back, please, in the parking lot. My truck's back there."

It was midnight when they walked into a room at the Palms A-GO-GO on Maryland Avenue. It was a Best Western, $69 per night, one king-size bed.

Cooney sat Pica on the bed, clicked on the TV, and said he'd be right back. He was going to a Walgreens that they had passed on the way to the motel. "Anything you need?" he asked.

She shook her head wearily. He left.

CHAPTER 75

December 11, Sunday, 12:13 a.m.
Palms A GO-GO Motel

Pica was in a daze. It was hard for her to fathom what had happened since she had fallen asleep in Cooney's arms twenty-four hours ago: burglarizing Oui Oui's room, being made a prisoner by Feliz, modeling for Pilo Tatoon, escaping like Tarzan, witnessing the fight at the wedding chapel, physically assaulting Oui Oui, and proving herself innocent of the smuggling charges.

Cooney kept appearing in the kaleidoscopic memories, but where and when were not clear. Now she was lying back in a motel bed, waiting. Waiting for him but too tired to let her imagination go any further.

It took Cooney nearly an hour to pick up items he thought might be useful at the drugstore and supermarket. When he returned Pica was asleep on top of the bed, boots and all. The light was still on in the bathroom, and the TV hummed in the background. The room was quite warm.

Cooney looked down at this woman who had captured his heart in Tucson last February when he had been getting down onto a bronc in a match ride against Lionel Trane. Here she lay in deep slumber, no worry lines on her face, those gorgeous full lips parted slightly like she was blowing fluff off a dandelion.

The first time he actually had met her had been at that matched ride afterparty in Tucson. That night she had figuratively driven a stake into his brain! The dazzling smile, her gaze, her eye contact that felt like a physical connection, something wireless; maybe she sent out neural waves, like feelers on a jellyfish or whiskers on a star-nosed mole!

A STAR-NOSED MOLE? WHERE DID THAT COME FROM! CAN'T
EVERYONE SEE HE HAS BEEN ENCHANTED WITH HER SINCE THE DAY
HE MET HER? NOW SHE IS LYING ON HIS BED, COMPLETELY VUL-
NERABLE. A TWENTY-FOUR-YEAR-OLD STRAWBERRY BLONDE WITH
A SUMPTUOUS FIGURE, WHO MIGHT ACTUALLY FEEL BEHOLDEN TO
HIM. WHAT IS HE WAITING FOR?!

The black motorcycle jacket had fallen open. He could see her chest rising and falling slowly. The welt on her neck ran from behind her right ear and
down across her left breast and disappeared under the low-cut T-shirt that
Trisket Thistle had swapped her. He presumed it was a whip lash. She had
several other lesions, scrapes, and bruises from what he could see. Her hair
was pulled back but tangled, yet she looked peaceful.

Cooney slid a chair up beside the bed, sat down, and watched her. She
looked hurt, but he knew how tough she was. He'd never really seen a soft
side; she'd always been guarded around him. Of course, he admitted, he'd
given her good reason not to trust him.

The night before, he'd seen another side of her when she'd hit bottom:
exhausted, suffering, sobbing, depleted, and defenseless.

Tonight Cooney's heart is filling with compassion, affection, admiration,
empathy, lust, and shame. His chest is tight. He thinks about pulling off her
boots and jacket but . . . with too many thoughts circling inside his skull, he
finally dozes off in the chair.

Pica's mind is finally letting her dream. She is lying in a tent. The flaps are
closed. She is in a bedroll, Cooney on top of her. He is resting on his elbows with
her face in his hands. He lets a finger roll over the rim of her ear, then slide lightly
to her lower lip. He opens it slightly and runs his tongue under her upper lip.

She feels him swelling inside her. Her arms closed around his waist, her
fingers interlaced. She squeezes him. Her mouth engulfs his face; her lips
and her tongue press into him. She feels his hand slide off her face and trail
lightly down across her chin, linger in the Angle of Lewis, then across her
sternum, shushing this way and that like a skier sluicing left and right on the
glistening, snowy slopes on either side; then the fingers drop down into the
chute, lazily circling the curvature of her navel. She arches her neck and hears
the voice of Clint Eastwood in *High Plains Drifter:* "The man left the door
open, and the wrong dogs came home . . ."

Through habit of waking without movement or noise from countless
wildlife stakeouts, Pica slowly opened her eyes. Dreaming, she realized.

Scanning the scene, she saw Cooney sitting in a chair next to the bed. His head bent in slumber. The reflection of the television flickered across his upper body.

Taking inventory she realized she was still wearing the leather jacket and motorcycle boots Trisket had supplied her. She moved her eyes back to Cooney. Her focus widened until he became the center point of a motel room landscape: open bathroom door with light on, television playing, plastic shopping bags on the TV cabinet, Cooney's hat lying upside down by the shopping bags.

"Oh, my," she said in a breathy exhalation.

Cooney stirred, looked up, and blinked.

"Hi," she said, smiling pleasantly.

He took a deep breath and straightened in the chair. He hesitated. "About the marriage . . ."

She lifted her left hand. A gold band was on her ring finger.

He continued: "If you want to get an annulment . . . I mean, we were in the thick of it, and if . . . uh . . . does it fit?"

Pica realized that her answer would be taken as an answer to a much bigger question. No man had ever asked her to marry him. But that in itself was no reason to say yes. Did she love him? She didn't know how to describe her feelings. Her head started to swim.

Cooney watched as confusion clouded her brow. He raised his eyebrows and smiled quizzically.

She wished she could talk to her father right now. She envisioned his face. His words came back to her: "You've got good sense, Girl. Trust your intuition."

She felt the golden band and turned it around on her finger. "It fits just fine," she said.

CHAPTER 76

December 11, Sunday Morning, 3:44 a.m.

Consummation

COONEY ROSE, TURNED OFF THE TELEVISION, AND CLOSED THE BATHROOM door 'til just a sliver of light fell into the bedroom. He let his eyes adjust to the near-darkness, then sat down on the bed beside her. He leaned toward her, held her face in his hands, and kissed her lips. It was such a gentle movement that Pica wasn't sure he had really kissed her. She pursed her lips and felt the contact. He was just that close, a pucker away.

He delicately traced a line completely around her lips with his tongue, moistening them. He backed off enough to see that her eyes were closed. He kissed her again but with increasing firmness. Pica responded. Slowly they became engaged in a silky, slinky, slow, deliberate, delovely, connubial confection that was candy sweet, marshmallow soft, and seductively sensuous . . . and it was only a kiss!

He backed off. She opened her eyes. He slid the sleeves of the motorcycle jacket over her arms and, placing his palm in the small of her back, slid the jacket off the field of love.

Between kisses and touches he slipped off her shirt, pants, and boots as tenderly as a geisha would peel a peach. Then he pulled the sheets up over her, turned and disrobed himself. She watched. She could see only his silhouette against the backlight. He had muscular arms and shoulders and a narrow waist. Her heart flipped. As if an air bubble in her veins had popped inside her chest. Her skin began to tingle; she felt flush. He lifted the covers and crawled in next to her. They were touching the length of her body. Her lips were on his, his hands were on her, and then . . . as easily as Zorro holstering his *pistola,* they became one.

They came together like blueberries stirred into vanilla yogurt. She was as sleek as velvet. Smooth as a baby bunny. He glided along her skin, held tight by some bodily Bernoulli force.

He was as tender as he could be, letting her come to him, not pushing, just catching. He was so aware of her physical injuries. Once his hand ran across a rough abrasion on the back of her leg. He expected her to wince, but if she felt it, she was somewhere else.

She was indeed somewhere else! She was on new ground in a place that she had imagined so many times yet had never experienced. It was like the first time she had tasted a dark chocolate truffle or heard Ian Tyson sing or flown over the mountains she loved!

Pica could feel herself rising to meet him, up and up, then the breath-taking sensation of falling over a brilliant, silvery waterfall!

They could have been locked together in a paint-shaker! They could have been rising off Cape Canaveral at daybreak! Two electrons colliding at the speed of light, spiraling off into that indefinable galaxy of exquisite pleasure! Suddenly she was floating, featherlight, dreamy, and diaphanous on a trans-lucent blanket of butterfly wings. She closed her eyes, laid her head back, and escaped the tenuous bonds of Earth.

IT WAS AS GOOD AS IT COULD GET!

They relaxed in their honeymoon embrace, letting the tension flow out with each exhalation. Neither spoke. Neither was sure what the other was thinking. They settled and fell asleep in each other's arms.

CHAPTER 77

December 11, Sunday, 7:30 a.m.
In the Hotel Room with the Bedlams

COONEY WOKE AT 7:30 A.M., SLIPPED OUT OF THE BED, AND SHOWERED. There was a complimentary continental breakfast in the lobby. He put together a selection of edibles plus two Styrofoam cups of coffee and walked back to their room.

He found Pica lying in bed, still disheveled and watching a replay of Saturday's final rodeo performance. The team roping was on.

"Bronc riding is next," she said.

Cooney handed her the coffee. "It seemed like you liked it black?" he said.

"I do," she said, remembering the last time she had said those words.

He set two paper plates with victuals on the nightstand, then sat down beside her up against the headboard.

The professional sports broadcaster and the cowboy color commentator gave the play-by-play. To the credit of the camera crew and the producers of the NFR, the coverage and replays were equal to those of most pro sports.

Cooney was glued to the screen, watching his peers show off their stuff. There wasn't a bad ride. *These cowboys are so good,* he thought to himself. Anyone was capable of winning it all. When Shelby Truax rode his bronc and scored a seventy-five, the announcer proclaimed that, for the moment, Truax was leading in the race for the NFR average championship.

The announcer went on to embellish and incite excitement with the news that only two riders were left who could beat Truax out of the buckle. Both, he said, were at the top of their game. He talked on and on 'til he finally said there seemed to be some delay.

On the television replay some of the confusion had been edited out. The broadcaster announced that Cooney Bedlam had been injured and was not

326

there to ride, so they turned out his draw, thus disqualifying him for this performance and eliminating any chance that he could win the average.

The camera followed a big paint horse packing Cooney's saddle, with no flank strap, as it came out of the chute, made a short circle into the arena, then pranced out the exit gate. There was no applause from the fans, who were somewhat bumfoozled. Then the announcer introduced the final bronc rider of the season: Straight Line, Buffalo, Alberta. The announcer repeated the story of how the two-time world champion had come to this year's finals in fifteenth place and now was one ride away from winning the NFR average. Straight needed a solid ride of fifty points or better.

The camera remained focused on Straight as he stood on the catwalk overlooking a short-coupled black horse with a white blaze named "Whizzer." On close-up Straight seemed to be vexed and looking around, even though Cooney's ride had already left the dock. He was in a tight discussion with the chute boss, who was down in the arena by the chute gate.

Then Straight climbed over, sat on the saddle, stirruped his feet, took the hack rein, then raised his head again to look around once more. He looked back down and nodded his head, and the gate swung open.

The long camera view that Cooney and Pica were watching on the television showed Whizzer rainbow out of the chute . . . with no rider! The horse continued to buck for five jumps, then broke into a run. The pickup men raced after him.

The close camera picked up Straight standing on the inside rails of the chute, looking back over his shoulder at his buckin' horse. He waited until the 8-second buzzer sounded, then climbed back onto the catwalk and disappeared.

"Ladies and gentlemen," Cooney and Pica heard the announcer say, "we have no explanation for this unexpected conclusion to the saddle bronc riding event, but we can say with a great deal of certainty that the winner of the NFR average in the saddle bronc riding is Shelby Truax! And here he comes right now!"

Shelby rode a big, lanky black and white horse around the arena at a gallop following one of the flag ladies. The crowd applauded, but the vocal buzz sounded like a beehive.

Pica punched the remote. The television clicked, and the picture faded out.

"I guess I assumed he'd won," said Cooney, puzzled, "or maybe lost. We didn't have any time to even say anything last night. And it wasn't on the top of my mind to ask him how it went while you were scattering feathers and fighting Goliath. So . . ." he paused and thought a moment, "last night when we talked, he'd already . . . he'd already turned out his horse."

The weight of the act, the offering, the profound sacrifice, sank heavily in Cooney's heart.

Pica watched Cooney's face as the realization of Straight's gift soaked in. Cooney turned to her but seemed to be looking through her. His eyes were glistening. His lips moved as if he was going to say something, but nothing came out. A full five seconds passed.

"I need to go to the washroom," she said.

He snapped back to reality. His brain freeze had thawed.

CHAPTER 78

December 11, Sunday, Midmorning
Waking Up to a New Day

IN THE MORNING-AFTER LIGHT, THIS MOMENT BETWEEN COONEY AND Pica was awkward for them both. They were married, of course, but for only about twelve hours! They had made love . . . in the dark. Should he leave the room while she got up? Or avert his eyes? Should she ask him to hand her clothes to her? Or should she rise as naked as Venus on the half-shell and march into the bathroom?

"Let me go run the tub so you can soak. Would that be good?" he asked.

"Yes," she said, "that would be good . . . nice."

While he was filling the motel bathtub-shower combination she peeled off the bed spread and wrapped it around herself. He stepped out of the bathroom, and she went in.

She was in there for a full thirty minutes. He heard the hot water being replenished several times, then the shower running. The reality of Pica in the *shower* pushed thoughts of calling Straight to his back burner. Cooney paced around the confining motel room, nervous, peeking through the curtains to the parking lot below. It was 10:10 a.m. He was unable to maintain any train of thought for more than a few seconds. Her proximity vexed him.

Checking his cell phone, he saw that Straight had called and left several messages this morning already. His mother, his cousin Sherba, and Pica's brother had also left messages. Cooney planned to return all the calls; he knew the callers were worried, but right now he didn't want to get distracted. She, yes, *she* was in the *shower*! He was able to shed this kind of anxiety before getting down onto a bull. He had perfected customized Zen. But right now he couldn't even get his being to stay calm for five seconds!

He heard the shower turn off, the tub drain, heard the sound of her moving around. He heard her brushing her teeth. My gosh, he'd actually bought her a toothbrush, but it was still in the shopping bag. She must have borrowed his from his dop kit!

The door opened, and Pica stepped through the bathroom door wearing a towel on her head and another around her body. Cooney's heart jumped in his throat. He had never seen a more beautiful picture. He quickly recovered and took charge of himself.

"I bought some triple antibiotic salve and some Ben-Gay, alcohol, Band-Aids, gauze . . ." he offered.

"You didn't happen to buy a big comb or hair brush, did you?" she asked.

"No, dang it!" he said. "I wish I'd uve thought it out." He dug a six-inch black plastic comb out of his back pocket. "You could use this."

She smiled and shook her head.

"I was thinkin'," he said. "If you'd lay back on the bed, maybe I could, uh, take a look at your wounds. Check 'em out, doctor them if they needed it."

"That shower sure helped," she said, "but they sting a little."

She crawled under the sheet and let the towels fall to the floor. She turned onto her stomach.

Cooney dumped his "doctor bag" onto the bed. He gently pulled the sheet down to her waist. Her skin was light pink. Freckles sprinkled across her shoulders. Three whip lash-bruised contusions ran horizontally across her back. The leather jacket she had worn last night had kept the skin from breaking. He touched the contusions. They were warm, reddish, and swollen.

Cooney applied the antibiotic salve carefully. There were several abrasions on her shoulders. He secured the little bottle of motel lotion from the bathroom and tenderly massaged her shoulders and neck.

Pica had closed her mind. Gone somewhere else to avoid feeling any pain from the healing hands. He heard her steady, sonorous breathing, noting she was in her own Zen. With only the tiniest trepidation he pulled the sheet down another six inches. Coursing vertically across her left cheek was a second black and blue streak an inch wide! In places the skin was broken. He lifted the sheet to follow the wound. It ran down her left leg, leaving a large scrape just above the ankle. *No wonder she was limping last night*, he told himself. Maybe it was the bicycle or that unicycle.

Using a dry rag, alcohol, salve, cream, and massage he completed treating what he could reach. Even when he covered her and then rolled her over onto her back she did not show any sign of consciousness.

When he prepared to examine and treat the long purple-red welt that ran from the right of her neck down diagonally across her chest, he stopped to steady his hands. Cooney pulled the sheet down to see the extent of the wound. His heart leaped again!

C'mon! he said to himself disgustedly, *you lecherous pig. She's hurt, she needs . . . I can do this! She needs me right now to help her . . . to get well. Just play like it's Straight. He's hurt! Doctor him!* Cooney's heart was beating so hard that he could feel it in his neck as he reached to apply the antibiotic ointment to her wound. His fingers traced it as if they were needles on a lie detector!

A left hand came out from under the sheet and put itself over Cooney's shaking right hand and held it in place. He jumped slightly, then looked down to see what she was doing. He looked up at her face. Pica looked pleasantly relaxed: easy smile, half-closed lids.

She reached up from under the sheet with her right hand and ran her fingers across his cheek. Her fingers pulled him slowly down toward those heart-shaped, luscious, inviting fleshy folds that pursed in anticipation. Their lips touched.

OH, MAN! THEY DID IT AGAIN! IT HELPED THAT THEY WERE BOTH AWAKE THIS TIME. BUT THIS TIME IT WAS WITH THE EXHILARA-TION OF WATER ON THE STOVE BOILING OVER! THE TOP COMIN' OFF THE DOM PERIGNON! THE $100,000 JACKPOT LIGHTING UP THE NIGHT SKY IN NO-LIMIT NEVADA!

Both felt like Columbus when he first saw land. They explored like Lewis and Clark, they panned for gold, drilled for oil, dived for pearls, read each other like a treasure map. They intertwined like DNA climbing a ladder to the stars. Reaching, stretching, ascending, defying gravity until they hung in the balance between madness and euphoria! That special place where amnesia protects the brain from catching on fire!

She clung to him, her self-control in tatters. They were a jet engine, and when the afterburners kicked in she screamed! "Love! Oh, love! In love! All love! I love! . . ." He held her in ecstasy, on the tip of a Vesuvian fountain, as she moaned and cooed, but when he finally picked the penny off the bottom of the pool, they both collapsed!

WELL . . .

IT WOULD BE IMPOLITE TO BOTHER THEM IN THE AFTER-MATH. THEY DESERVE THEIR PRIVACY. SUFFICE IT TO SAY THEY

COMMUNICATED IN A DIFFERENT WAY. LIKE ANIMALS DO. HE GRUNTED LIKE A BEAR, AND SHE PURRED LIKE A LION. SATIATED, THEY RESTED UNTIL THE RESPONSIBILITY GENE THAT BOTH HAD INHERITED STIRRED THEM TO ACTION.

"Mrs. Bedlam, I am pleased to have made your acquaintance," said Cooney. "But we have calls to make. Many are worried about us."

Pica climbed over on top of him and kissed him full upon the lips. It was a hard, firm, fierce kiss full of passion and possession that penetrated to the bone! She raised her head and looked directly into his eyes. Tears were running down her cheeks beside her tight smile. Words would not come.

She held his gaze a few moments more, trying to say something, then finally stood up, shed her sheets, turned her head, and walked as naked as Venus into the bathroom.

CHAPTER 79

December 11, Sunday Afternoon
The Bedlams Leave Town

COONEY AND PICA SPENT THE AFTERNOON BACK IN HIS HOTEL ROOM while Cooney made the calls to their families. They deemed it best to continue to keep Pica under wraps until they got her back where she belonged in Canada. Cooney, without giving away any details that would incriminate Pica, told the vague story that he had had an emergency illness and had been unable to contact anyone. He was sorry for the worry. He told Pica's brother that she was safe and asked the brother to tell the family, but Cooney couldn't go into details. He asked the family to trust him on this.

Straight was one of the few people who knew where Pica was and could be trusted. He had picked up his earnings for the NFR. He split second and third in the saddle bronc average with Cooney: $29,000 each. Cooney never asked why Straight had turned out his horse. He knew why. They talked around it. Someday Cooney would be able to put into words what it meant between them. Maybe fellow soldiers who had saved each other's lives would have a similar bond. Pica let them work it out.

Straight confided to them that OTT had already made him a nice endorsement offer but that since last night he had been approached by two different agencies to represent him. His story was a wonderful, salable item, they said. A book deal, maybe a movie. Cross-country tour. His value for endorsements could be worth millions!

Cooney asked who they could talk to at OTT to extricate Pica from her situation. Straight gave him Nova Skosha's cell phone number.

Cooney called the contestant rep for saddle broncs and explained that he had a health emergency and had been unconscious and in medical care during the final performance. He apologized and asked the rep to let the rodeo brass know that he would be making a public statement later in the week when he was able. For the time being he was not available for interviews or interrogations. They could send his checks and his buckles to his address in South Dakota.

He and Pica discussed a plan at length. Her greatest concern was to avoid being caught here in the States. OTT should use the evidence to clear her name and lay the rightful blame on Oui Oui. But that might take a while. They both agreed that the fewer who knew what was going on, the better. They decided not to involve Teddie Arizona.

By dark they had packed their bags, loaded his pickup, and headed up Interstate Highway 15 going north.

February 27, 6:00 p.m., Sunday Night, Two Months after the NFR At La Fiesta de los Vaqueros in Tucson

TUCSON'S BIG SPRING RODEO WAS OFFICIALLY OVER. THE LA FIESTA DE LOS Vaqueros rodeo committee had produced another spectacular show. Rain held off all week and the weather stayed cool. The majority of the crowd had departed this last performance, but three hundred to four hundred faithful fans stayed to watch the vaunted Post-Ride Party activity. Thus the arena lights were turned on and attention was focused on a group of committee members in front of the bucking chutes.

Cleon List, exuberant fan and wealthy committee member, was now holding court at his eleventh annual Post-Ride Party.

The highlight of the party was the matched saddle bronc riding, pitting the just-crowned champion of the Tucson Rodeo against the reigning world champion. Tonight's contest, a match-up that had been ordained by the "Angels on the Heavenly Rodeo Committee," pitted Cooney Bedlam, reigning saddle bronc world champion, and Straight Line, who earlier today had been crowned winner of the Tucson Rodeo saddle bronc riding.

Our two heroes had become the two most-talked-about rodeo personalities in the world. The two had been the subjects of endless articles, interviews, speculations, and psychoanalyses. Rumors flew around the sports world that the two would be the first duo to be named "Best Athlete of the Year." They were on the cover of *Sports Illustrated* and sought out by all sorts of promoters who promised they could make the two famous and negotiate their book deals, endorsements, commentator opportunities, and movie offers.

It had been a tumultuous seventy-five days for our heroes between the finals and the Tucson Rodeo. Cooney had taken fewer than three days to get Pica back across the border, where they lay low through Christmas holidays at the ranch in Pincher Creek and stayed in touch with Straight.

Straight had come back to Canada a hero! Canada is known for its social liberalism, tolerance, and acceptance of diversity. Canadians are admired by many for their acquiescence to seemingly anybody else's infringement on their culture, belief, or values. Straight was idolized in Ottawa because he had done the Canadian thing and sacrificed his chance at winning a "virtually guaranteed championship," as the *Globe and Mail* put it, so his American friend would not be offended. Canadians are nice.

The eastern Canadian press never quite understood the difference between winning the NFR average championship and the PRCA world championship. It was lost in the details, as was the real reason Cooney had missed his last ride.

Of course, that such a story about Canada didn't involve mad cow disease, harboring of baby seal killers, or a flitty prime minister's wife was a welcome blessing!

While Straight was drawing the lion's share of celebrity, Pica had found a friend to help her with her legal problems—none other than Nova Skosha! Through the holiday season, Nova had stuck like flypaper to the OTT lawyers on Pica's behalf. The lawyers complained to Turk that she didn't understand that it would take time. Three governments were involved, federal crimes were committed; the authorities couldn't just drop the charges. Besides, Christmas and New Year's vacations were involved! Turk climbed onto their backs as well, but the lawyers just added to his bill with every phone call.

Nova Skosha was frustrated. She made two trips to Canada to visit with Straight on behalf of OTT seeking his endorsement for another year. And then something unexpected happened: She and Straight found out they had more in common than a contract! Suddenly she had a conflict of interest. To be fair she called Turk and explained the problem.

"How big a problem is it?" asked Turk.

"You see," she said, "I think we are not offering him enough money. If he ever gets smart enough to hire another agent, we're going to have to pay him what he is worth."

"Well, it's your job not to let that happen," said Turk.

"I'm not sure I can do that," she said.

"Well, that certainly is a conflict. How do you expect to do your job if you're personally involved with a client? he asked.

"Ya know," she said, "there are other factors working here that . . . listen, could I take a month off to think this over? Who knows what's going to happen?"

"Sorry, Babe," he said "It's us, the OTT team, your $60,000 salary, $30,000 expense account, and a future in sports marketing, or . . . what? Am I getting the drift that your sentimentality is poking holes in your ruthless marketing brain?"

"I'll get back to you," she said and hung up.

Two days later, in mid-January, Nova booked a flight to Calgary, called Straight from the airport, and said she was on her way out to the ranch with a proposal. Within one week she had convinced Straight that she could be his agent, manager, and wife! They were a perfect match, she said. She would work on a percentage. Two days later they had also signed up Pica D'TroiT (Bedlam) as a client. Then she called Turk and resigned.

Who better than Nova Skosha to negotiate with OTT for Straight's services? He was "hot property"!

She would eventually work his rodeo success and "grand gesture," as it would come to be called, into motivational speaking, self-help books, inspirational CDs, instructional DVDs, personal appearances, reality shows, commercial endorsements, guest lectures, and a line of tack, gear, and clothing. She made him into an industry . . . and a husband!

Right away they used Straight's visibility and integrity to publicly bring Pica's case to the public on talk shows, interviews, Twitter, Facebook, YouTube, exploitive magazines, and the Internet. Bloggers were demanding that the Canadian, United States, and British governments right this egregious wrong. Within two weeks Nova had convinced them to lift Pica's travel restrictions to the United States. By the time the charges were dropped, Nova Skosha had negotiated with Powder River Projectiles, makers of fine firearms, for Pica to be its Pistol-Packin' Powder River Pawnshop Pinup Girl for a tidy six-figure contract.

～～

Back at the Post-Ride Party in Tucson, Cooney stood to the side of the pre-ride cocktail and Calcutta party, watching Straight and Pica D'TroiT (her stage name) visit with Tucson's upper-crust cowboy crowd.

"When are you gonna let me help you with *your* career, Cowboy?" asked Nova Skosha. She had walked up beside him and was alluding to her two celebrity clients, whom he had been watching.

"Ha!" he laughed. "I'm not in their league, but I shore appreciate what you've done. Pica's very thankful. If it wasn't for your relentless efforts she might still be a convict! And Straight! You've made his dream come true! I can see your fine hand in so many of his achievements.

"I've got a lot to be thankful for, but I'm just happy for him," said Cooney sincerely.

"I love him," she said, smiling.

"I know," said Cooney. "It shows."

"But back to my offer," she persisted. "I think I could do you a lot a good, make some money on the side, get some benefits, maybe future opportunities."

"Truth is, Nova," he said, "I never had it so good. I'm not a talker, inspirational like Straight. I'm not that ambitious, and I'm not pretty or organized like Pica. I just ride broncs. Long as I can do that and keep from gettin' killed, that's as far down the road as I can see. But Pica's already gonna be there down the road, and so is Straight, and whether I'm punchin' his cows, guiding her dudes, or driving their limo, whatever makes their rooster crow will be just fine with me."

AND NOW, DEAR READER, I OFFER YOU ONE LAST RIDE.

The Calcutta finished, and Cleon List took the podium: "My many friends in this great community and rodeo committee, we invite you to walk over to the grandstand and watch the premier event of the night: our matched saddle bronc riding."

As the crowd worked its way over, our heroes, Straight and Cooney, made their way to behind the buckin' chutes. The rodeo producer had left one of his chute hands to bring the broncs home after the matched ride. He had already saddled the boys' horses. Straight and Cooney put on their chaps and spur boots and stood on the catwalk when their broncs came in.

To reduce favoritism, accidental calls, or criticism in determining the winner, Cleon had hired four judges. Each would award points to the horse and to the rider. The four would be collected after the ride, then the top and bottom scores would be eliminated and the remaining two averaged. It was a method used in the Olympics when it was more than just a timed event.

Pica was up on the catwalk to help get them down onto their horses. They flipped to see who went first. Straight was chosen.

Cleon had paid Benny, the stock contractor, to save him back five saddle bronc horses that were good draws. Cleon paid well enough that all five selected had been to the national finals in the last three years.

Straight's draw was Ace's High, a huge black-brown Morgan-Slidesdale cross. *Sweet*, thought Straight, high on pride. It was not vanity or conceit, that was not in his makeup. But the self-inflicted bruises to his ego had healed since the finals, and he allowed himself to admit that he had done okay.

At the nod and swing of the gate these two professionals, Ace's High and Straight Line, rose to the air as one. They cleared the fog of the riding slump: the disappointment of not making the finals, the animosity of his brother, the fallout with Cooncy, and the mountain of self-doubt. Straight ascended on Ace's High, who had grown Pegasus wings, up through the smoke hole in the sweatlodge, where good broncs and good bronc riders could appreciate each other.

From the view in the stands he made a classic ride: spine straight in the saddle, right arm thrown back, in rhythm, toes pointed, and the look of an eagle with his eye on the prize.

"Picture perfect," said a fan with admiration. She said it all.

Cooney had drawn a white horse named "Virgil," the most unpredictable lot of the five—the kind of draw Cooney liked. Being an all-or-nothing kind of guy, he'd either get bucked off or make an over-the-top ride. It was his kind of game.

Straight had dismounted, accepted the accolades of the crowd. To heighten the excitement, his score would not be announced until both men had ridden. He returned back behind the chutes and climbed onto the catwalk. Cooney had three people helping him get down onto Virgil, so Straight stayed back.

Just as Cooney nodded, Virgil reared up in the chute! The horse was about 10 degrees off due north vertically! The cantle kept Cooney's butt from sliding back, and his spurs were locked into the neck. It was as if he had leaned back in a kitchen chair and had fallen over.

Two of the cowboys reached out to keep him from banging his head on the rail! Cooney's free hand actually clasped the vertical upright post behind him. In the photograph taken at this moment the horse appeared to be going over backward into the chute a fraction of a second before the rider became a pancake!

The subconscious mind and finely tuned body of both horse and rider work together on autopilot in moments like these. Time goes by in nanoseconds. Horse and rider sit on the razor's edge.

In this microsecond Cooney saw Pica's face on the back of Virgil's head, right between his ears! She was the redtailed hawk with the head of a fox. Her smile widened until her lips covered her face just like the Cheshire cat! "I know who you are," she said. "You are both."

The rest of the ride was as haywire and chaotic as the proverbial "shot out of the box"! Virgil managed to sidestep and fall sideways until he caught his balance. In the last six seconds he tied himself in a knot, tried to roll, sunfished, bounced off the gate, swung his head, did a quarter-circle to the left, and at one point reared up like Trigger! Cooney sat there like a fly on a buzzard's nose as Virgil kept trying to swat him off!

When the whistle blew Virgil stopped and dropped down to one knee, and Cooney stepped off just like they had it planned.

Oh, man, the crowd loved it! It was Cooney Bedlam at his finest. People were laughing so hard that they bent over holding their sides. How, they wondered, would a judge ever score something like that?

Straight jumped into the arena and ran over to Cooney, who was dusting off his hat.

"What a ride!" said Straight. "You'll do anything to win! Unbelievable!"

"Unfortunately," said Cooney, catching his breath, "unorthodox never trumps classic. Congratulations, amigo. Yer the best."

Over the microphone Cleon List invited the two men to join him at a small table set up in front of the reserved bleachers. The two walked over that way, arms around each other's shoulders. Camera flashes caught the friends, rodeo buddies. As close as two fingers in the cookie jar, *compadres*.

"Just a minute," said Cleon. "Ladies and gentlemen, we have seen two of the best, at their best, right here in front of you tonight, but, and that is a big 'but,' there has always been some suspicion, some controversy regarding the, how shall I say, the fairness of the competition."

Cooney looked at Straight and did an "I don't know" shrug.

"To clear the air once and for all," said Cleon, "I have arranged to put the matter before you tonight. In chute number 4 let me introduce that renowned Canadian bronc rider Miss Pica D'TroiT!"

All eyes went to chute 4.

Pica stood on the catwalk above a blue roan bronc. She looked at these two men, so important in her life, these brothers in the band of good rodeo hands, standing over in front of the bleachers. Pica was not the same person that she had been a year ago, at this same rodeo. She had become an adult with all her inherent skills still intact, but a stronger sense of self. Her heart was bigger and braver. Her self-confidence in worldly matters had grown. Cooney's ability to accept and enjoy life was rubbing off on her. Straight's organized ambition inspired her.

The scariest part of the whole preceding year had not been her hair-raising escape from Feliz. Instead, it had been the fear of being entangled in the bottomless red tape of the criminal charges she had faced. She realized how frighteningly possible it was that she could have spent years lost in the system trying to prove her innocence.

She still suffered the occasional bad dream, but the cure was easy: just reach under the covers and touch her man, her white knight. The magnitude of his sacrifice to save her was still too big for her heart to encompass. It surrounded her like a protective cloud. She was letting it absorb slowly. It allowed her to grow closer to him with every passing day. If they were separated, he was as close as the phone. He always answered . . . always.

Two weeks ago Nova had negotiated for Pica a three-year endorsement contract with Powder River Projectiles or, as Cooney and Powder River called her, "the Pistol-Packin' Pawnshop Pinup Girl." She had already made two appearances at gun shows on the way from Pincher Creek to Tucson, one in Billings and another in Salt Lake City. Her posters were circulating around the country and were wildly popular. The Elk Foundation had lined her up, as had the Federation of North American Wild Sheep and Cabela's.

On a personal note, Pica's family loved Cooney! Uncle Firmy thought he was an intellectual, especially when they'd been drinking! And her dad approved. In the last several weeks she had begun to realize that Cooney and her dad were alike in many ways. Not a surprise to most, knowing how much she loved her dad.

The voice of Cleon List brought Pica back to the present: "This year we decided to abridge the rules and include probably the most well-known woman bronc rider of our time . . ."

As Pica lifted one spurred boot onto the rail to climb over, she glanced back at "her boys." Straight was looking at her studiously. Cooney had a surprised grin on his face and made a "why not?" gesture with his arms.

She blew them one big kiss from her famous lips and climbed on over. She sat in the seat, stirruped her feet, pulled back her chap legs, straightened her spine, and lifted the rein. The big horse snorted. As she nodded her head she imagined they were launching into space.

Pinochle, she thought, *isn't the only game where you can shoot the moon!*

Pistol-Packin' Pawnshop Pinup Girl

She stood out from the guns and knives and other pawnshop treats
Like a head of iceberg lettuce in a sea of sugar beets.
It was then I pledged allegiance to what set my heart a-whirl,
'Twas a pistol-packin' poster of a pawnshop pinup girl.

I don't know what piqued my interest, but perhaps it was that pose
In her gunbelt bandoliers, breathing gun smoke up her nose.
A blonde bombast of bullets with a heart of gold beneath
Like Hemingway or Roosevelt, a rose between her teeth.

Calm ye down! I bade my urgings, Wonder Woman was not real.
She was just the dream of some poor fool's imaginary zeal.
Yet before me blazing brightly with her hands upon her hips
She stared down from an eagle's nest, a feather on her lips.

She had a little smile with a quizzical appeal
That either said, "Come closer" or "Cut the cards and deal."
It's a look that men have pondered since Eve came out of her shell.
Lancelot got lost in Guinevere's, Pancho Villa knew it well.

Poor fools down through the ages, be they kings or pimply teens,
Have spent their lives and fortune in pursuit of what it means.
Thus, she held me with those eagle eyes, as sure as with a sword
That pierced my heart and pinned me to her bug collection board.

Where I sit today, a captive of her Mona Lisa guile
With her hammer cocked and ready and her lever-action smile.
'Cause I've hocked my last resistance to temptation in this world
For a pistol-packin' poster of a pawnshop pinup girl.

Acknowledgments

EDITING FICTION ABOUT COWBOYS, WRITTEN IN COWBOY LINGO CAN BE frustrating for those who revere spell check and the Oxford Dictionary Punctuation Guide. It can be especially difficult if the author makes up words. So it is with souflacious gracissitude that I praise Erin Turner, my editor, and Linda Konner, the agent-in-charge, for turning my meandering story into a book.

I also am beholden to the PRCA and the cowboys who have befriended me and let me be a part of the great sport of rodeo. A special thanks to Wally Badgett for saddle bronc riding quality control and a final plaudit for Carolyn Nolting, who trod the creative path of Straight, Cooney, and Pica with me as their tale unfolded. She has that special quality of being able to set aside reality where cowboys are concerned.

It is a genetic defect. Her dad was a cowboy.

About the Author

Cowboy poet and large-animal veterinarian Baxter Black says, "I was raised with the coyotes. No, this is serious. I was raised in New Mexico, did three years at New Mexico State University in Las Cruces, then four more years at Colorado State University to earn a doctor of veterinary medicine degree.

"Throughout the summers of my college years I worked at different livestock operations as 'cowboy labor.' To help support myself, among other things, I had a band and rode a few bulls. Upon graduation I practiced for thirteen years in the livestock business and would still be there if cowboy poetry had not hijacked my life.

"Since poetry is virtually illegal in the United States, I have had to work around the edges of the mainstream to make a living—outside the box, as it were. For thirty years I have been successful performing cowboy poetry (think of Shakespeare rather than Robert Frost) at venues across the country and in Canada. It has all been word-of-mouth.

"To augment my performances, over the years I have expanded into books, CD and DVD publishing, a regular column, a commercial radio program, National Public Radio and Television appearances, satellite television, and production of commercials.

"Our entertainment business, my wife's and mine, began in Colorado. Several years ago we moved to Arizona. I still have a heavy travel schedule, and we have five employees in our operation. Cindylou and I have a daughter and a son.

"We live on a small ranch close to the Mexican border, and I punch cows when I'm not on the road. It ain't a bad life.

"This is my third novel. Rodeo has been a running theme. I have always been a fan and follow the action. The National Finals in Las Vegas is my favorite extravaganza! My thanks to the PRCA, who have always included me as one of their 'characters.'"